Gilead's Blood

As HE FELT the hilt of his sword come into contact with his assailant's sternum, Gilead turned and swiftly scanned the area again. Time was short on any battlefield, even for a warrior of his consummate skill and shadowfast abilities. Yes, Fithvael was still with him, a hundred yards to his right, fighting strong.

The foe were all around them. Tall, darkly noble, yet twisted and corrupt. Elves, kin and yet not kin. Blasphemous parodies of their race, death-pale, dressed in reeking black armour, eyes rotting in skulls, breaths foul from black-lipped mouths. Their rusting armour was decorated in flaking gilt, fading silks, worm-eaten brocades.

Elves. Ruined elves. Broken, twisted, decayed echoes of noble warriors.

Gilead's Blood

Dan Abnett & Nik Vincent

A BLACK LIBRARY PUBLICATION

Games Workshop Publishing
Willow Road, Lenton,
Nottingham, NG7 2WS, UK

First US edition, April 2001

10 9 8 7 6 5 4 3 2 1

Distributed by Simon & Schuster
1230 Avenue of the Americas
New York, NY 10020

Cover illustration by Paul Dainton

ISBN 0-7434-1163-3

Set in ITC Giovanni

Printed and bound in Great Britain by
Omnia Books Ltd, Glasgow, UK

See the Black Library on the Internet at
www.blacklibrary.co.uk

Find out more about Games Workshop
and the world of Warhammer at
www.games-workshop.com

For Jon and Nik, who never grew
out of it either.

I
Gilead's Wake

I was anything and everything.
I was a myth.

I AM A poor nobody, so please you, who has crooked his back against the plough for fifty years, and done nothing more heroic than raise five daughters and a son. My whole world is this unremarkable village, in this undistinguished corner on the edge of the Empire. There is nothing in me worth a bent copper.

Except, perhaps, the stories. At hours such as this, when dusk falls and the winter moon rises, you all come to my hearth: the young, the old, the scornful, the curious. And you ask for my stories again.

You call them myths, and the land is full of those. But my stories are not myths. They are something altogether rarer. How many fireside myth-spinners do you know who can vouch for the truth in their tales? I may be a poor nobody, but I have known great men.

The oldest story that is mine to tell begins close to its end, with a lone warrior sitting with his back against the trunk of a tree, trying to sleep. His name, in the old tongue, was Gilead te tuin Lothain, ut Tor Anrok. Call him Gilead, if you please.

Ten bitter years had brought him to that spot.

He tried to sleep, but sleep did not come easy. For ten winters and ten summers in between, his slumber had been troubled and disturbed, haunted by the memory of hoarse cries and the scent of blood.

He sat back against the tree bole in the darkness, at the edge of a campfire's glow, and looked down a long alpine valley. Down there in the night, the fires of a fortified stockade glimmered. It looked so small and insignificant a place to be the goal of a decade-long quest.

Gilead sighed.

This wild place was lonely and remote. It had been several days since Gilead had last passed a settlement – a human village, whose name he had not bothered to learn as he rode around it. There had been a tavern there, where humans gathered and drank and told each other stories. Gilead wondered what stories they were telling this night.

Perhaps even now, some drunken wretch was slurring out a tale of the House of Lothain, of the deathless warrior and his decade of blood-enmity with the Darkling One. Of course, others at the fireside would mock and scoff and claim this was only a myth, for myths are just myths and the land is full of them. They would sneer that no vengeance was ever so pure, and no pain so bright, not even the particular curse of pain that was Gilead Lothain's.

And they would be wrong.

Gilead's mind filled with darkness, burning darkness that rushed in and ignited the papery memories in his head. He remembered, ten years before, on a night far blacker and deader, flamelight that flickered outside a rusty cage door.

TORCHES RAISED IN their fists, two figures shambled back along the stinking passageway towards the cage.

Is this my death? wondered Gilead. If it was, it would be a relief perhaps. Three days, without even water, chained from an iron rung, suspended like a broken puppet in a cold and airless cave deep in the neglected reaches of the Warrens. His pale skin – for his captors had all but stripped him – was blue with bruises from the regular, gleeful beatings. There was a ghostly, hollow ache of pain where the fourth finger of his right hand had been.

The captors were at the cage door, grinning up at him, their brutish human faces split with feral glee and slack with wine.

They had looked that way the first night, when they had come to take his finger.

'A sweetener,' one had called it.

'To jog the memory and open the purses of your kin,' the other had added. Then they had laughed and spat in his face and opened the jaws of the rusty shears.

'They're goin' to pay, elf scum!' one now snarled through the bars of the cage. 'We just had us word. They're goin' to pay handsome for your miserable hide!'

'Your brother himself is bringing the blood money tonight!' chuckled the other.

For the first time in three days, Gilead smiled, even though it hurt to smile. He knew that his brother was doing no such thing. These vermin may have been told a ransom was coming, but a rather different surprise was on its way.

For when they kidnapped Gilead Lothain, this band of carrion had made the last mistake of their lives.

Galeth was coming. Galeth, and five other warriors, the cream of the remaining warriors that the old fastness of Tor Anrok could muster. Even now, they were rappelling down the vent of the brick flues west of the Warrens' main entrance, sooty shafts that had once been the outlet for an old mill forge that some said the rat-kind had built under the earth, ages past. Gilead could smell the air that Galeth and the others breathed, feel the course burn of the rope as they played it out and dropped vertically into the blue dimness.

Galeth Lothain: his brother, his twin. Born a minute after the midnight chime that had marked the first moments of Gilead's life. Born under a pair of crescent moons, within a week of a falling star; born to new snows marked only by a fox's print and the kick of a hare. Good signs, all of them. Good augurs for long, proud, brave lives. Gilead and Galeth, the left and right sides of the mirror, the left and right hands of Cothor Lothain, master of the Tower of Tor Anrok.

Twin siblings are always close; they share so much, not the least being the same face. But Galeth and Gilead were closer still, a fact first noticed by their wet-nurse, and then by the ancient sage summoned by Cothor Lothain to school them in physic and the lore. Their minds worked as one, as if there was a bridge of thought between them. In one room, Gilead could cut his thumb on a flensing knife – and in another part of the Tower,

Galeth would cry out. Abroad riding, Galeth would fall and soak himself to his bones in a frozen stream – and home by the fire, Gilead would shiver. Their spirits were bound, said Cothor's counsellor, Taladryel. They were one son in two bodies.

So it was, twenty seven winters after the midnight that welcomed them to life, that Gilead knew of his brother's approach.

He could smell the mildew stink in the dark, half-flooded cisterns where Galeth and his men now waded, charcoal-darkened blades drawn ready. He could hear the slosh of the thick, stagnant water, the scratchings of the vermin, the gentle rustle of the wick crisping in the hooded lantern.

And in turn, he knew that Galeth was sharing his experience. Galeth could feel the bite of the chains, the ache of bruises, the throb of his finger's stump. It was that sharp beacon of weary pain that led him on.

THE WALLED TOWN of Munzig lies in the patchwork of Border Princes south of the Empire. You may know of it, perhaps. Surrounded by deep forest and shadowed by the jagged profile of the Black Mountains, it is a market town on the River Durich, and a stop-over for travellers climbing the forest ways to Black Fire Pass. For over a century, it had prospered. But at the time of my story, Munzig had become a place of fear.

In the town, the citizenry spoke anxiously of the Carrion Band. No one knew their faces or their strength, or quite what villainy spurred them on except for a craving for gold and pain in equal portions. Tavern rumour said they made their fastness in the Warrens, a crumbling maze of tunnels and subterranean vaults in the foothills of the Black Mountains, a few leagues from the town.

No one knew who had built those tunnels, or how far they ran. Old myths said they were the work of the skaven rat-kin, but myths are just myths, and the land is full of them. There was, for example, a fine fireside tale of how the settlers who founded Munzig had been protected by elves from the forest, elves who had summoned up their war forces to drive the skaven out and make the land safe. Children liked this story especially, squealing with glee as adults imitated the shrill voices of the rat-kin bogeymen. Another story said there were still elves in the forests, living in a beautiful tower that only appeared by full moonlight and could never be found by humans. Yet another declared that these elves would reappear to protect the land if the rat-kin ever returned. Unless told to wide-eyed children at bedtime, such a tale would usually be greeted by a hearty laughter and a demand for more drinks.

Then the Carrion Band had come, striking for the first time the summer before. Ambushing a wagon on the forest road, they seized the daughter of a local merchant. A ransom was sent and desperately paid. The daughter was returned, dead, by the Durich's autumn flood and the money lost forever. Eight more such crimes followed, gripping the Munzig in a tightening band of fear. Loved ones were taken, monies demanded and blood cruelly spilled. In every case, the families had never dared not pay, even though they knew the odds were slim they would ever see their kin again. In the taverns, estimates had been ventured as to the fortune so far lost.

Thirty thousand gold, said some.

And the rest, said others.

Prince Horgan, Elector of Munzig, called town meetings and a state of emergency. Trade, the life-blood of the town, had all but dried up. Plans were drawn up by the frightened gentry. Guards were doubled, patrol circuits were widened, gratings were made to block the river sluices under the city wall. By now, the old Warrens seemed the likeliest hideout for the Carrion Band, and popular myth spoke of underground passages riddling the town's drains. No one was safe.

Balthezor Hergmund, a merchant whose wife had been the reavers' third victim, had put up a reward and urged the town council to undertake a purge of the Warrens to drive out and exterminate the killers. But even the most willing had to admit the futility of such an act: the Warrens was vast, unmapped and unknown, and the City Militia numbered only four score of irregular infantry and Horgan's own cavalry, a dress unit more used to displays than combat.

What about the elves, the forest elves, someone would surely have suggested? *What about the old pact, the old myth? Wouldn't they help?*

Laughter – nervous but damning – and another round of drinks.

So the fear grew, the cost in life and gold mounted, and the bloody career of the Carrion Band continued unchecked.

* * *

STRANGELY, IRONICALLY as far as any of the human inhabitants of Munzig were concerned, there certainly was a tower out in the forests beyond the town walls, a beautiful tower never glimpsed by human eyes, magically secreted deep in the wilds of the woods.

Called the Tower of Tor Anrok, in memory of the sunken city, it had for the longest time been home to the House of Lothain, a dwindling familial line who traced their blood back to the ancient, distant kingdom of Tiranoc.

There were only a few inhabitants of the hidden tower now: old Cothor, too weak to stand; a handful of loyal warriors, household staff and womenfolk; and Cothor's twin sons, Galeth and Gilead. Their ancestors had indeed driven out the skaven from the catacombs now known as the Warrens. But that had been in older, stronger days.

When word of the Carrion Band's molestation of Munzig reached the tower, it had been Galeth who had wanted to send word to the prince and covertly offer aid. He yearned to begin his warriorhood with a worthy victory, but old Cothor had been unwilling. The patriarch had decreed that there were too few of them left, their blood too rare, to waste it on what was clearly a human dispute. Human raiders, human prey. Elfkind shunned the company of humans, knowing that men regarded them with fear and suspicion. Whatever had happened in the past, the House of Lothain would not rouse itself now.

Galeth had been disappointed but Gilead, sensing his father's anguish, had taken up the argument and eventually dissuaded Galeth from taking it further. As the eldest, Gilead took his responsibilities to the House and the bloodline with solemn gravity.

It had been a crisp, winter afternoon, three days after this debate, that Gilead had ridden out into the forest with just one companion, Nelthion, the tower's elderly horsemaster, who had trained both youths in the art of riding. Gilead had said they were to exercise the horses, but in truth he had wanted to blow the cobwebs from his mind with a hard gallop through the frosty woodland.

Gilead never knew if it was opportunity or plan; whether the Carrion Band had chanced to hear them riding close and fallen into cover, or if they had deliberately stalked the tower and watched its comings and goings. A dozen of them pounced, dropping from trees or sweeping up from under snow-cloaks, humans and a couple of ugly mixed-blood blasphemies.

A billhook took Nelthion out of the saddle and they fell on him with flails. There was crimson blood in the snow. Gilead turned, his golden-hilted sword loose and scything, but they were many and they were ready. A cudgel smacked him sideways but he stayed up, spurring his mount to bolt clear. Then another of the reavers killed his horse out from under him with a pike and they closed on him with coshes and sacking.

So Gilead Lothain came to be the prisoner of the Carrion Band, chained deep in the Warrens. So, too, did he become their first error, for they had not reckoned with the fact that he, unlike all the others – the humans – they had preyed upon, could lead the wrath of his kinsmen right to their hidden lair.

GALETH AND HIS men skirted the lip of a dirty pool and stepped lightly, like cats, up a buttress twisted by the slow and ancient passage of roots. Gilead smelled the wet soil, felt the weight of Galeth's sword in his hand.

The Carrion Band had not posted sentries. They had every reason to suspect this damp corner of the Warrens would never be located by search parties. Their only concession to chance discovery was a series of tripwires strung out along the slim, natural caves adjoining the vaults they used as a smoke hall and dormitory.

Old Fithvael, Tor Anrok's veteran swordmaster, knelt and cut the trips one by one with his bodkin, slowly releasing the tensions on the severed cords so the bells sagged without ringing.

Seeing this through sibling eyes, Gilead smiled.

Five red-fletched arrows were nocked against five tight strings, the men looking to Galeth for the command. Galeth nodded them in, under a mossy, decorated arch where the features of a bas-relief titan had been all but worn away by seeping surface water. They smelled cook-fires, sweat, blood and swill from where a hog had been butchered, urine from a latrine. They heard laughter and rowdy voices, and a rasping viol heaving out the rough tune of a drinking song.

Galeth stepped into the firelight. Gilead's breath caught in his mouth. They both saw the sweaty, puzzled faces that turned to look. The viol stopped, mid-note.

The killing began.

Like a brief drum roll, five hollow beats in quick series marked the five impacts of elven arrows. Three reavers died on their benches, one toppling into the fire pit. Another was spun round across the table by a shaft in the shoulder, and passed out across the spilled, smashed pitchers of stolen beer. A fifth was pinned to his chair back by an arrow through the gut and began to scream as the pumping blood covered his lap. His screams rose until they and their unnerving echoes filled the vault and the chambers, like a hideous hell-music to accompany the killing.

Across the table in a leap, Galeth met the first two reavers to find their weapons, his scarlet cloak flying. All told there were twelve left alive in the smoke-hall, each scrambling for sidearms and bellowing like stuck pigs. Gilead knew of at least another half-dozen asleep in the cellars behind the hall – and so Galeth knew that too.

The elves put up their bows and surged into close combat behind their young master, who had already sheared one neck with his longsword and was splintering the flail of his second target. Some of the elves had longswords and bucklers, with a knife brandished in the shield-arm's fist. The others swung long-hafted axes. All wore scarlet cloaks and hauberks of glinting, blue-black ithilmar mail. Their hair and their skins were as white as ice. Their eyes were dark with fury. Smoke, and a mist of spittle and blood hung in the damp air. The roar of fighting shook the buried vault.

Fithvael, his axe sweeping, cut through the belly of a visored swordsman and was first into the tunnel to Gilead's cell. As the fighting raged behind him, he pulled the key-ring off a nail and slammed open the cage door. Noble Taladryel, Cothor's counsellor, soaked in the blood of others, was at his side a moment later, and together they eased Gilead down from the chains and swaddled a cloak about him.

'We have him! He lives!' Taladryel bellowed, but Galeth already knew this. He and the other three warriors from Tor Anrok cut down the last of the routed Carrion Band. A few survivors, no more than four or five, had fled into the Warrens.

Fithvael and Taladryel carried Gilead out into the vault to a cheer from the bloodied elf raiders. Galeth knelt by his twin and embraced him, tears streaming from both brothers' eyes.

Gilead noticed the red weal that circled the fourth finger of Galeth's right hand.

Fithvael put the place to the torch, then they formed up to move out the way they had come, wary of any harrying from the reavers who had fled.

No one had noticed that the wretch brought down across the table by the first flight of arrows was still breathing. No one saw him stir in the billowing smoke and flames behind them as they moved out beyond the titan arch.

The crossbow made just a tiny snap as it fired.

Gilead froze the souls of his kin as he screamed.

And Galeth fell, a steel bolt transfixing his heart.

GILEAD WOKE.

The moon gazed down at him, full and ghost pale. Somewhere in the forest a wolf howled and was answered. The tree bole against his back was hard and cold like iron. In the valley below, the stockade lights had been put out.

Gilead shivered. Even after ten years, the dreams came down at night and fell on him like robbers, murdering his sleep.

He got to his feet and stooped to poke at the thin fire. Pine cones had been the main source of fuel, and a thick pungent scent filled his nostrils as he raked at the embers.

Pine, astringent and cleansing, always made him remember the infirmary at the tower where the veteran Fithvael had nursed him back to health. Fithvael had prepared pine water and hagleaf to clean Gilead's wounds and to soothe his weals and bruises, using the old skills of Ulthuan. His skill at healing was exceeded only by his talents as a soldier and ranger. But he had had nothing to nurse the wound in Gilead's mind.

Gilead had shared his brother's death, a pain that defied sanity. And after it, he had survived the lingering emptiness left in his mind. Some said he was dying too, that the bridge of thought that he had shared with Galeth was allowing the slow, cold stain of death to seep through into his body from the other side.

If that was true, Gilead Lothain had been a long time dying – a decade of slow pain since Galeth had fallen to treachery and spite in the Warrens. Ten years of wandering and blood.

There had been mourning when Gilead left the Tower of Tor Anrok. Ageing Cothor bewailed the loss of both sons to one crossbow quarrel. Was he to be left with no heir? Was the old house of Lothain, which had existed ever since his kind had come to the Old World from Tiranoc, to fall at last?

Gilead had not replied. He had set out. He would return, he told himself, one day when his work was done. But he hadn't returned after five years, when news that his father was stricken with a wasting illness had reached him. Neither had he after nine when a messenger brought word of Cothor's death. His inheritance awaited. Still now he did not turn back.

Fithvael came out of his tent and found Gilead by the fire. The five warriors who had formed Galeth's raiding party had all voluntarily followed Gilead on his mission. Now only the veteran Fithvael was left. Gilead thought of the lonely, god-less places where they had buried the others, each one in turn.

Fithvael looked at the sky. 'Dawn in two hours,' he said. 'Tomorrow... that will be the day, at last. Will it not?'

Gilead breathed deeply before answering. 'If the spirits will it.'

Fithvael crouched beside Gilead. Even now, after ten years, it pained him to see his lord's face, pale and cold as alabaster, his dead eyes sunk like glittering chips of anthracite in deep, hollow orbits, his hair silver like frost. Gilead the Dead, they called him, those that met him on the way and spoke of him in taverns. They said it with a shudder. Gilead the Haunted, the walking dead whose mind was tied into the hereafter.

'Can I ask you a question?' Fithvael murmured. Gilead nodded. 'I have never spoken this before, and only now do I feel it. Ten years we've been, ten years hunting the stinking Foe. Ten years, and every second of it your poor brother deserves. But will it be enough?'

Gilead looked round sharply. 'What?'

'When tomorrow comes and your slice your blade through that rat-kin's fur... will it be enough?'

Gilead smiled, but it was not a smile that Fithvael liked. 'It will have to be, old friend.'

THE FOE. They didn't know his face. And he had many names – Gibbetath, or the Darkling One, or Skitternister. He had first come to Gilead's attention a month or so after Galeth had been laid to rest in the sacred grove, when Taladryel and

Fithvael had captured one of the fugitives of the Carrion Band hiding out in the woods. The human had been questioned, and it was he who told them of the Darkling One and his secret empire.

Gibbetath was a skaven. The rat-kin, his mind as sharp a dagger, was never seen, but his money, his ideas and his schemes orchestrated dozens of clandestine operations that riddled the southern parts of the Empire. Black market spices ran through his networks and the skimmed revenues filled his coffers. He arranged mercenaries and spies, and dealt in intelligence to the highest bidder. It was said he had started two wars and stopped another three. His bawdy houses in the border towns ran the finest women, and took the fattest cuts. An entire guild of thieves answered to him and his assassins, shadows all, were the finest gold could purchase. It was an empire of filth, a vermin's enterprise, a hidden fraternity of thieves and killers and sinners running scams and turning tricks in a dozen Old World cities to line the pockets of the Darkling One, the mind behind it all.

The Carrion Band and their ruthless cycle of crime had been one of Gibbetath's profitable schemes. He had outfitted the men, furnished them with supplies, presented them with information on likely targets, and took ninety percent of the ransoms. It was his decision that no hostage be returned alive. It made the band vulnerable.

It was said that the Darkling One was most annoyed when Galeth's raiders exterminated his Carrion Band.

So just think, Gilead had told himself more than once, how annoyed he would be when scything elf steel split his head in two.

The Darkling One was his target, his prey. For ten years the elf had stalked him. The rat-kin was ultimately responsible for Galeth's death and Gilead swore he would not rest until the skaven bastard was dead too. He was – and his regret over this was beyond words – fulfilling belatedly the very quest that Galeth had wanted, to drive the evil out of the Warrens and destroy its source. If he had but listened back then, if he had only agreed…

In ten years he had followed every clue to the Darkling One's whereabouts, destroying every one of the skaven's operations he uncovered as he slowly closed the noose on his quarry.

In the last three years the Foe had fought back, sending assassins and war bands to halt the relentless elf avenger. To no avail.

After ten long, bloody years, Gilead was at his door.

DAWN CAME. Gilead struck.

He had not really been sure of what to expect, but the wooden stockade in the forest was not quite the stronghold he had pictured for the Darkling One. He mused that a surface stronghold seemed unlikely for a creature that dwelt beneath the earth. But the Darkling One had ever been just such a mystery, just such a contradiction... no one had seen him, or knew him, no one even knew what infernal lusts drove his relentless power-building enterprises.

A tub of dwarf black powder took out a ten yard stretch of the timber wall, and Fithvael picked off the sentries from cover with his bow.

Pikemen with mail charged Gilead as he strode in through the smoking gap, but his longsword was a blur. He fought as Galeth had fought. At Galeth's death, his skills with bow and blade had flowed across that cold bridge in Gilead's mind to merge with Gilead's prowess.

One son in two bodies, Taladryel had said. Now, for certain, two sons were in one body.

Blood flecked the avenger's corselet of ithilmar mail. He was shadowfast, a killing wraith that sliced through the defenders without mercy or pause.

The human guards – those that weren't cut to tatters – began to break and flee. Pushing through them, two ogres came at Gilead. Nine feet high, the ogres' great bulk rose like a buttress wall to block him, foam snorting from their flaring nostrils. One had an axe, the other a vicious morning star.

The axe-ogre moved, swinging his huge, flat blade at Gilead. The son of Cothor leapt sideways and, before he could swing again, the hulking beast stumbled back, squealing, a red-flighted arrow embedded in its left eye. From cover by the breach in the stockade, Fithvael loosed two more arrows that dropped the brutish thing dead. The other roared and spun his star at Gilead, but the elf pressed his attack, closing with the huge foe rather than retreating. He let the enemy's charging weight do the work and impaled him on his sword.

Silence. Smoke drifted across the smashed stockade and the twisted bodies. Somewhere, a wounded man moaned. Bow ready, Fithvael joined Gilead and they looked around, their scarlet cloaks fluttering in the wind. The defence was shattered. The doors of the blockhouse beckoned.

Fithvael made to move forward but Gilead stopped him. 'This is the last act,' he said. 'I will face it alone, Fithvael te tuin. If I fall here, someone must take word back to my father's house.'

His companion swallowed hard, but he nodded.

Gilead stepped forward alone.

THE BLOCKHOUSE was a long hall and woodsmoke clung to the rafters. The interior was dark, deep and full of dancing shadows thrown by the torches in the wall brackets.

Gilead paused for a heartbeat then entered, his blade ready.

His eyes grew accustomed to the gloom. He saw the empty sacks and coffers that littered the floor of the hall. Was this really the heart of the Darkling One's empire?

As if it had heard his thoughts, a voice said, 'Not much, is it?'

Gilead moved into the gloom, and saw at last the thin, miserable human who sat hunched on a high-backed seat at the far end of the hall.

'You are Gilead, the elf?'

Gilead made no answer.

'My guard said there were only two of you. You and a bowman. You took my stockade alone, the pair of you?'

'Yes,' Gilead said after a long pause, answering in the clumsy human language with which he had been addressed. 'Who are you?'

'You really don't know?' the ragged, sick-looking man looked round at him. 'I am…whatever you call me. The Darkling One. Skitternister. Gibbetath…'

'But–' began Gilead.

'I'm not the rat-kin monster you think you've been hunting? Of course not! Rumours… myths… they help to keep me, and the truth, safer. Or they did.'

The man looked around himself pensively. 'In some towns I was a rat-thing, in others a beast of Chaos, in others still a sorcerer. Whatever suited the local superstitions. I was anything and everything. I was a myth.'

'A myth…'

'The land is full of them.' The man smiled.

Gilead wanted the blood to race in his head, the anger to come so he would surge forward and–

But there was nothing. He felt the emptiness, the dismal finality of this wretched blood debt. Was this what Fithvael had tried to speak of the night before around the fire?

The puny man got to his feet. Gilead could see how the wretch shook, with a palsy or an ague. He was frail and thin, and his limp hair was greying. There were bald patches on his scalp and sores on his skin. He shambled forward and fixed Gilead with rheumy eyes.

'I was richer than kings, Gilead Lothain. My name was just a whisper in the back streets, but for three decades I was more powerful than monarchs. I had palaces, mansions, coffers of gold, an army at my beck and call…'

He paused. 'Then I made the mistake of killing your brother.'

Gilead's hand tightened on his sword hilt.

The man sat down on a stool, his brittle joints cracking. 'We meet for the first time, but you have destroyed me already. When I first heard you were coming for me, years ago, I thought nothing of it. What did I have to fear from a band of elf revengers? You would be dead or tired of the quest long before you came close to me.'

'But you did not give up. I began to spend money and effort hiring men to dispose of you, setting traps, laying false scents. You avoided them. Still you came. My health began to suffer… nightmares… nerves…'

'Do not expect me to feel sympathy,' Gilead said icily.

The man held up his thin hands in dismay. 'I do not. I merely thought you would appreciate knowing how fully you have broken me. One by one, you've burned my palaces and houses, looted my reserves, put my minions to the sword. My empire has crumbled. I have run from fastness to fastness, pouring away my wealth to keep my deserting warriors loyal. And behind me, always, you have come, leaving destruction in your wake.'

He gestured around them at the grim blockhouse. 'This is all that's left, Gilead Lothain. This last humble outpost, those last few soldiers you have killed. I spend half my life scheming my fortune, and then I spend every coin I have trying to protect myself from you.'

He straightened his head to expose his saggy, wizened throat. 'You bastard elf. Take your shot. End my misery.'

Gilead trembled, his blue-steel sword heavy suddenly.

'Do it!' rasped the Foe, leaning closer. 'Finish your revenge and a plague on you! Give me peace!'

Gilead wiped his brow with the back of his hand.

'Do it!' screamed the frantic, wretched ruin of a man, sliding off the stool to his knees.

Gilead stared down at him. 'You want me to end your misery? Cutting your throat won't end mine. Ten years ago, I thought it might.'

He turned and stepped towards the door. Behind him, the Foe wailed. 'Finish me! I have nothing left!'

'Neither have I,' Gilead said simply. 'And living with that is the true price.'

OUTSIDE, THE COLD mountain sun burned down through the stands of pine. Gilead spiked his sword in the soil outside the stockade and sat down on a slanted log.

'Is it over?' asked Fithvael.

Gilead nodded.

'The Foe is dead?'

Gilead shook his head. Fithvael frowned, but knew better than to ask any more.

A meadowlark sang. Somewhere deep in Gilead's mind, a lingering pain refused to ebb away.

I KNOW FOR a fact that the Tower of Tor Anrok stands yet, hidden amidst the forests beyond the town of Munzig, though no one may ever find it. Its grounds are rambling and overgrown, and its windows are empty, like the eyes of a skull. It is just another pile of dead stones in the wilderness.

Some say there is one last Lothain alive, the lost son of Cothor, who will return from the wilds one day and unlock the old doors of the hall. They say he roams the furthest edges of the Old World, a deathless daemon with a sleepless blade, howling out his pain to the moon and warring with the tribes who follow the dark ways of Chaos. Some say that death is in his eyes.

Perhaps it is just a myth. The land is full of them.

II
Gilead's Fate

*I will not stir from here
until Death comes for me.*

So you would hear more of my tales?

Well, this land is full of stories, but to be sure most of them are foolish prattle. In Munzig, away in the forests, they'll tell you of a magic songbird that haunts the woodland glades and sings your future in sad trills as it flies from clearing to clearing. If the hour is late, too, they'll speak of a dark shape that hunkers in the graveyard and eats the marrow from bones living and dead. Nurses and watch-mothers, old guard captains and innkeepers, they are all alike. They keep a store of tales to entertain the children, amaze the passing travellers and intoxicate the locals after hours.

Lilanna was wet-nurse to the Ziegler family, wealthy merchants from Munzig. A dumpy woman with silver hair in a bun and starchy black clothes, she would tell her stories to the Ziegler children at bathtime and before bed. Gleefully, they would wriggle down and beg for 'just one more'. The best were of the elf-folk, the pale watchers of the forests, haunters of the glades and waterfalls.

Lilanna had two good stories about such folk. The first was of a tower, the tower of Tor Anrok, which was older than time and lay deep in the forests beyond the town, out of reach of man. It only appeared when the moons' light fell upon it, she insisted. She wasn't sure why, to be honest, but it gave the story some charm.

The other was of a pool. Its exact position was not fixed, and that made the details of her yarn easier. The pool was called Eilonthay, she swore, and its waters were still and translucent like glass. In time of need, according to the old woman, the people of Munzig could go down to this pool and beg a wish from the elf-folk of Tor Anrok. They were bound to help, she said. The dwellers in the moonlit tower had watched over the people of Munzig for centuries. They would answer any call, honestly asked. It was their way.

The children laughed. There were four children in that house: Russ, the eldest, strong and firm; Roder, the joker; Emilon, the golden-haired girl; and little Betsen. Lilanna was full of myths and they loved every one.

As STORIES GO, the fate of these children was better than any innkeeper or wet-nurse could dream up, even in their most salacious moments. Russ was found nailed to the oak-beam ceiling with the other adults of his family. Roder roasted on the hearth. All they ever found of Emilon were some bloody scraps of her golden hair. Lilanna the nurse was cut into five pieces, as were the other servants of the house, and strewn indiscriminately with them upon the midden. Only Betsen survived. Thirteen years old, she had been away at court in Middenheim, preparing for life as a lady-in-waiting to the Graf's wife.

She returned for the burials. A pale, silent ghost, she was looked after by Prince Horgan at his palace. She spoke to no one.

It was a summer night when she found the pool at last. Two years had passed and, despite her guardian's repeated urgings, she had ridden out most evening and afternoons, into the emerald glades of the forest. She had always believed the tales her old nurse had told her. Now they were all she had left.

The pool was deep and clear. Translucent. It stood in a glade far off the regular paths, surrounded by twenty solemn larches. She knew it was Eilonthay the moment she came upon it.

Betsen dismounted, pulling her velvet gown close around her. She went to the water's edge and knelt down.

'Folk of Tor Anrok, help me now. I seek vengeance for my family, cruelly slaughtered as sport. Do not turn away from me.'

She knew it was just a myth. But that did not stop her coming, night after night.

HE PUT DOWN his wood axe and knelt. His heart was heavy in his chest. There was the human girl again, kneeling by the clear water pool, sobbing out her wishes. How many times had it been? Twenty? Thirty? How many times before he noticed her?

He coiled himself into the tree so he would not be seen, and bit his lip so he would not answer her as honour demanded.

Finally, she stood again and moved back to her waiting horse. A moment later, she was gone into the moonlight.

Fithvael, last warrior of the tower of Tor Anrok, sighed. It was not right. If he had only been younger, stronger. But he was old and he was tired. Years and years ago, before that decade-long quest and the miserable years since, he might have acted differently. But he was just an ageing woodsman now, haunting the glades, tending the trees, cutting logs to feed his hearth, waiting for a quiet death.

THE TOWER OF Tor Anrok was as silent and secretive as ever. Daylight, stained green by the canopy of leaves, fell upon its high, peerless walls. From a distance, its beauty remained. But close to, its decay was evident.

Since the passing of Lord Cothor, it had fallen into ruin. Briars overgrew the outer walls and lichen discoloured the pale stone. Casements had rotted and fallen in, and birds nested in holes amongst the roof slates. Sections of wall had slumped and spilled exquisite hand-carved sections of translucent stone onto the loam.

Fithvael approached it apprehensively. The many tricks, traps and magical wards that protected the tower glades were still active though the place was dead, but they held no threat to Fithvael. He had lived in this place for most of his life, and as swordmaster had maintained those very defences. His feet knew where to step, what stones and paths to avoid; his hands knew the glyphs he had to make to cancel charms.

His apprehension came from what he might find here. He remembered too well the day when he and Gilead had returned to the Tower of Lothain after their long vengeance mission, and found it derelict. The misery of that day had never left him. Lord Cothor had died – they found his grave in the sacred grove – and it seemed all other life in the tower had vanished over night. The household staff, the guards, the ostlers, the very life itself had simply gone. He and Gilead had searched miserably for a while, but they had found no trace. The Tower of Tor Anrok was overgrown and empty.

He had not returned there in a long while.

Fithvael set a red-feathered arrow against the string of his black yew bow and crept into the dismal courtyard. He was almost invisible. Long before he had packed away his scarlet cloak in favour of a dull green huntsman's cape. His corselet of ithilmar mail was covered by a moleskin tunic. He gazed sadly around the unkempt yard, where brambles and thorny roots had split the flagstones. He remembered the long ago days when the warriors had trained there; great men like Taladryel, Nithrom, Lord Cothor himself. And the boys, the twin heirs.

'Gilead?' he called softly. 'My lord?' he added cautiously.

Silence, but he did not expect an answer.

He found Gilead in the throne room, slumbering in the great gilded chair that had been Cothor Lothain's. The elf warrior, slim and powerful, lolled in the seat, his longsword dangling from his slack hands. The blue-white steel had mottled and the golden dragon hilt had dulled. Plates of spoiling fruit and meat stood nearby, and empty flasks of wine.

'Gilead?'

Gilead Lothain awoke, shaking off some dreadful dream. 'Fithvael? Old friend?'

'Lord.'

'It's been a long time,' Gilead murmured. He reached for a nearby bottle, realised it was empty, and sank back into his seat.

'Twelve moons since I last called upon you,' Fithvael admitted.

'And how goes your life?' Gilead asked absently. 'In your little hut out there in the forest? You know there is always room for you here in the tower.'

'I would not wish to live here anymore,' Fithvael said bitterly, looking about the ruined shell, seeing the grey daylight falling through spaces in the tiles and walls. Broken glass lay under each window. There was a smell of rot and mildew.

'Yet you're here? Why?'

'True to our old pact, the pact with the humans of the town hereabouts, someone has come to the pool and asked for our help. A human girl. Her plight is great.'

Gilead shook his head. 'Those days are gone…'

'So it seems,' Fithvael said sourly.

Catching his tone, Gilead looked up, fierce. 'What do you mean?'

'We should help her, lord. It was our way, the way of the old pact that was in place before your late father's time–'

Gilead swore softly and waved Fithvael away. 'I have done my work. Ten years, avenging my brother. I will not stir from here until death comes for me.'

'Your brother would have helped. Galeth would have helped.'

Even before the words were out of his mouth, Fithvael knew he had opened the old wound. He froze, ready for the onslaught.

Gilead got to his feet, unsteadily. The dulled blade dropped from his hand with a clatter.

'You dare to speak to me of that?' he hissed. The hiss turned into a cough. It took a moment for Gilead to recover his voice. 'Galeth was one with me, my brother, my twin! We were one soul in two bodies! Do you not remember?'

Fithvael bowed his head. 'I do, lord. That is what they said of you…'

'And when he died, I was cut in two! Death entered my soul! Ten years! Ten years I hunted for the murderer! Hunted for vengeance! And when I found it, even that pleasure did not slake the pain in my heart!'

Fithvael turned. He would leave now. He could not face this.

Then he paused. His heart was pounding in his chest. It surprised him, but there was anger in his blood. He turned back again sharply, fearing what he would see. Gilead still stood, glowering at him, dark sunken eyes glaring balefully from his thin, wasted face.

'I was there too!' Fithvael growled at his lord. 'Ten years I stood with you, till the end of the matter! I was the only one of your followers who survived the quest! Did I not suffer too? Did I not give you my all? Did the others die for nothing?'

'I meant–' Gilead stammered.

'And look what became of this proud house in your absence! All dead! All gone to dust! The pride of Tor Anrok withered because the son and heir was lost in nowhere, hunting his own pain! The line of Lothain, thrown away for your solace!'

Fithvael was quite sure Gilead would strike him, but he cared not. His lord shook, anger blazing in his eyes, but Fithvael strode towards him, snarling out his words.

'I pity you, lord! I have always pitied you and mourned your loss! But now… now you wallow in that pity, waiting for a death that may not come! A warrior of your mettle, indolent and wasting away when others may benefit from your skills? You may crave death, but why not use what life you have to aid others? That was always our way! Always!'

'Get out!' Gilead screamed, shaking with anger. He kicked wretchedly at the plates and bottles that littered the floor around his throne. 'Get out!' He stooped and snatched up a bottle from the ground and flung it at his oldest friend.

It missed by a yard and shattered. Fithvael did not duck or flinch as he stalked back out of the hall.

FOUR DAYS PASSED. Gilead Lothain knew little of them. He slept, or drank, hurling the empty flasks out through the broken windows of the hall, watching them smash and glitter on the yard outside. Pain thumped in his skull, pain that could be neither unloosed or fettered. Now and then, he would howl at the night sky.

Dawn came, waking him. He was lying at the foot of his father's gilt throne, dirty and cold. The pain in his mind was so great, it took a few moments for him to realise that it was not the pale light that had woken him. It was the frenzied croak of ravens.

Unsteadily, he walked out into the tower yard. Ravens lined the walls, dark, fluttering, rasping. Many others circled overhead. Occasionally, one would drop down and peck at the huddled form on the flagstones of the gatehouse.

'By the Phoenix Kings!' Gilead stammered, as he realised what the shape was.

Fithvael was almost dead cold. Terrible wounds had sliced into his ancient armour, and blood caked his body and arms. Gilead drove off the carrion birds and cradled him. The veteran swordmaster's eyes winced open.

'Who has done this?' Gilead murmured. 'What have you done, old friend?'

Fithvael seemed unable to talk.

'Have you… have you shamed me, Fithvael? Did you go to help this human girl?'

Fithvael nodded weakly.

'You stubborn old fool!' Gilead cursed.

'M-me, lord? S-stubborn?' Fithvael managed.

Gilead lifted him up and carried him into the tower.

THE WALLED TOWN of Munzig, as I may have said, lies in the patchwork of Border Principalities south of the Empire in the forests below the Black Mountains. It is a steep, gabled, timbered place surrounded by high curtain walls. Lofty and proud, the Prince of Munzig's palace stands on a promontory of rock above the market town, commanding good views of the River Durich and the forest tracks rising beyond to Black Fire Pass.

Betsen Ziegler had lived at the palace for two whole years since her return, since the funerals. She had rooms in the west wing, where for months she had done nothing but slumber uneasily and weep. The palace staff worried about her. Fifteen years of age and yet far older in her bearing and mind. Pain does that to a person. Pain and grief.

After a year at the palace, she started to request books to be brought to her, and she would go out into the town and renew acquaintances with those that had known her lost family. In the evenings, she liked to sit in the palace's herb garden and read.

That particular evening, the scents of the garden were thick and heady around her, and her book lay unopened on the bench at her hip. The ancient one, the strange elf woodsman with his kind eyes and soft voice who had appeared to her by the pool, had promised her so much, yet she had heard nothing. She was beginning to believe she had dreamt it all. Another night, then she would slip away from the palace after nones and ride to the pool again.

A breeze swayed the thick lavender and marjoram around her. An evening chill was settling. She was about to rise and go in when she realised there was a figure behind her. A tall, slender form, just a shadow, was watching her.

She gasped and started up. 'Who–'

The figure stepped into the light. At first she thought the ancient elf had returned. But it was not him. Where her mysterious guardian had been kind and unthreatening, this one was lean and powerful, and his noble, pale face was almost cruel. His alien gaze burned into her. He was cloaked in scarlet, and beneath she saw intricate armour. He was truly like a creature from a dream.

He spoke, in a musical language she did not understand. Then he spoke again, tutting softly to himself. 'Of course. I must be employing the leaden human tongue. Are you Betsen Ziegler?'

Despite herself, she nodded. 'Who are you?'

'I am Gilead Lothain, last of my line. I was told you came to Eilonthay and asked for my kind to help you.'

Again, she nodded. 'Another warrior answered me and told me he would render aid,' she began. 'I do not understand why–'

He hushed her. 'Fithvael is a brave soul, but his fighting years are passed. He has asked me to take on your errand and complete it.'

'I– I thank you for it,' she said, still nervous.

'Collect your things, a mount, and slip out of the palace at darkfall. I will meet you outside the city gate.'

'Why? Can't you just–'

'Your quest is one of vengeance, as I have been told it. I know all about vengeance. You must come with me.'

She blinked, struggling to form another question, but he had gone.

IN THE DARK trees a hundred yards from the gate, he was waiting, sat astride a slender warhorse. Betsen rode up to him until they met under the limbs of an old elm that sighed in the night breeze.

'Am I dreaming this?' she asked.

'Humans often dream of my kind because they don't believe we exist. But I do exist. I live. Of that much, at least, I am sure. Let us begin.'

The girl was bright and sharp-witted, and that surprised Gilead, who had never been much impressed with the mental dexterity of humans. Not that he had had much truck with them over the years. When she told him of the crime against her family, of the dreadful murder done, he felt an ache of sympathy that also surprised him. Once she had told of the killings, she was silent for a long while. Gilead found himself watching her. She was fifteen, young even by the miserably short human timescale, but pretty, in that vulgar, human way.

Then she began to tell him what she had found out in the two years since the crime. For the third time he was impressed. It must have taken a great deal of wit and ingenuity, not to mention courage, to tease out this intelligence. These were the facts as she knew them, and as she had told Fithvael, the facts that had sent him off to his wretched defeat. She repeated them now to Gilead.

There was a merchant lord called Lugos, who dwelt in an old fortified mansion maybe ten miles beyond Munzig. He was old and very rich – as rich as the prince himself, some said; richer still, said others. In fact, no one could account for the way a merchant, even a prosperous, successful man like Lugos, could have amassed quite such a fortune. He had ambitions too, courtly ones. The Border Princes could always stand another count, another duke.

The most whispered rumours said that Lugos had crossed into the Darkness. That he had dabbled in forces he did not understand and should not have unlocked. Even that he was a sorcerer, married to evil. No one had proof. No one, except perhaps Betsen herself, had even dared to find any. Lugos was a respectable man, a powerful man. He had a personal militia that rivalled the standing garrisons of some small towns. His mansion was a fortress. He had the ear of powerful men at Court.

Betsen knew that her father, who had been an up and coming merchant, had entered into business with Lugos in an attempt to increase his trade. Lugos had nurtured him, as all good merchant lords do when they find an eager trade partner. Betsen believed that in the course of this business dealing, her father had learned a little too much about Lugos – and Lugos had decided to silence him. And he had done it in the bestial manner his unholy masters had determined.

The mansion was a stronghold indeed; a great blackstone building with good walls and picket towers along the perimeter.

Gilead watched the place from the cover of the tree line. He did not need solid proof of the evil within, not in the way humans seemed to need. He could feel the vile filth of the place oozing out at him. If he had found this place under other circumstances, he would not have needed the girl's urgings to feel the need to destroy it. It was an affront to the nature of the world.

'Stay here,' he told the human girl, handing her a light cross-bow. 'I will send for you when the time comes. This device is loaded. Aim carefully and squeeze this if you need to. But I think you will not be so troubled. I will keep them busy.'

'Alone?' she asked.

'Alone,' the elf agreed, eyes dark in the shadows. 'I will deal with them alone.'

'I meant me,' she returned fiercely.

'You'll be safe,' he repeated, catching her tone in surprise. She was sharp, sharper than he expected of a mere human.

He made to ride on, but she stopped him. 'Your... the other, Fithvael? He told me about you. About your pain and loss and... what you have been through.'

'He shouldn't have done that,' Gilead said, his slanting eyes dark and unfathomable. 'It was not a human concern.'

'He told me so I would understand why he was undertaking my quest and not his master, the great warrior.'

Gilead was silent.

'I understand,' she said hurriedly. 'I understand your pain was so great you had no desire to become involved in another's pain. What... what changed your mind?'

'I was reminded of the old duty my kind chose to take up. That changed my mind.'

'He said you wanted only to die.'

'I do.'

'But he also said he thought you should be using your life to help others until death came.'

'He said a great deal.'

She smiled. 'I suppose he did. Are you embarrassed?'

'No,' he lied, hiding his feelings in the lumpen human language.

'I think he was right, anyway. Even a life of pain is not worth wasting. Don't you think?'

'Perhaps... I am here, am I not?' Gilead added after a pause.

'So what will you do with your life after this is ended?'

Gilead spurred his horse on. 'First,' he answered, 'I will see if there is to be a life after this has ended.'

THE BLADE OF his knife was dulled with ash so that the moon-light would not catch it. It went through four throats and slid in between the back-plates of three cuirasses as his left hand tightly stifled cries. By midnight, he was over the main wall, a shadow running the length of the ditch towards the mansion itself.

There was a high window above the inner dyke. Pausing to hide as another guard went past, Gilead unslung a silken rope and with a deft throw looped its end over a waterchute. The stone of the wall was black and sheer, wet with slime and moss. His feet found every toe-hold as his arms pulled him upwards.

On the ledge of the window, he coiled his rope again and drew his longsword. Below him, in the hall, he could hear singing and merrymaking, the croon of viols and pipes, the clink of glasses.

'Now,' he breathed, and dropped inside. He landed in the middle of the main table. The light thump was enough to bring the merrymaking to a sudden halt. There were thirty in the hall: nobles, women, servants, warriors and musicians. They all stared in dismay at the armed warrior in their midst.

At the head of the table sat Lugos, a withered old human in yellow robes. He smiled.

'Another elf?' he chuckled. 'Two in one week. I am hon-oured.' He nodded to his men, who were already scrambling up and drawing weapons. The servants and woman backed away in fear. 'Let's see if we can't kill this one outright. I'd hate for him to get away and bleed to death in the woods like the last one.'

Gilead was transfixed by the cruel glee in Lugos's face.

They rushed him. But you cannot rush one who is suddenly shadowfast. Gilead was abruptly in a dozen places, his sword whispering as it scythed. Two dropped, then four more. There were screams and cries, the clatter of falling weapons, the pat-ter of blood.

Lugos frowned, observing the slaughter before him. He turned to his aide, who stood quaking at his side. 'Wake Siddroc.'

'But master–'

'Wake him, I say! This one is a devil, much more than the last fool! Wake Siddroc or we are all finished!'

Gilead cut left, thrust right. He severed a sword arm and decapitated another fighter to his rear. Blades flurried around him like grouse beaten from cover. Some broke against his flashing longsword like shattered mirrors. Others rebounded, blocked, before the ancient longsword stabbed in under loosened guards.

Gilead rejoiced. It had been so long, so long since he had felt fire, felt purpose. His sword arm, his warrior soul, had slept. He spun again, cut, thrust, sliced. And they were all done.

Gilead turned, eyes bright and sword red, and faced Lugos down the length of the long table. The only sounds were the spitting of the logs in the fireplace, the moans of the not-quite dead and the drip of a spilled wine flagon as it drained.

'You are Lugos?' Gilead said.

'I do hope so,' the human said calmly, 'or else you've made a terrible mess in someone else's hall… elf.' He pronounced the word as if it were a curse.

Gilead stepped forward. 'Speak before you die. Confess the nature of your crimes.'

'Crimes? What proof do you have? Believe me, elf, the very best of the Empire will hound you out for this affront to my estate. The White Wolves, the Knights Panther… you will be hunted and torn apart as a murderer.'

'Such things do not scare me. I can smell the evil here. I know you are a dabbler in the black ways. I know your crimes. Will you confess them before I make you pay?'

Lugos raised his glass and sipped. To Gilead he seemed almost supernaturally calm for one of his short-lived, frantic race. 'Hmmm, let's see… as a young merchant, I travelled far and dealt with many traders, dealing in many fine objects. One day, a necklace came into my possession. It was finely wrought and very old, the crafting of some ancient place. Liking the look of it, I placed it around my neck!'

Lugos's face grew dark. 'It was cursed. Cursed by the Dark Gods of Chaos. At once, I was in their thrall.' He pulled open his tunic and showed Gilead the metal traceries buried within scar tissue around his throat.

Gilead remained silent.

'You see, I have no choice. I deserve some sympathy, don't you think?'

Still Gilead said nothing.

'There's more. Since I was cursed I have ordained countless human sacrifices, murdered dozens of innocents, arranged the foul deaths of any who stood in my way–'

'You are a monster!' Gilead said plainly.

'Indeed I am!' Lugos agreed with a hearty laugh. 'What's more, I am a monster who has been keeping you talk–'

The doors at the end of the hall behind the merchant burst open. A snuffling giant shambled in: a huge, inhuman thing clad from head to foot in barbed green armour the colour of a stagnant pool.

Gilead froze. Raw evil emanated from the creature. Its visor was pushed back and it appeared to be eating, its great jaws chewing on bloody gobs of flesh. A rank smell filled the room.

'This is Siddroc,' Lugos said. 'He's my friend. My guardian. My dark masters provided him to keep me safe.' He looked round at the vast creature and tutted melodramatically. 'Oh, Siddroc! Have you eaten another of my aides? I've told you about that!' The creature turned its huge head and snarled. 'Very well... this intruder has caused me a great deal of trouble. Dispose of him and I'll give you all the flesh you can eat.'

With a reverberating growl, the creature shambled forward, casting aside the last scraps of the unfortunate aide. In his right hand he whirled a chain attached to a spiked ball the size of Gilead's head. In his left, he held a curved cutter-blade that surrounded his meaty knuckles with spikes.

Gilead leapt clear as the first blow came down and demolished the table. The elf landed and rolled aside hastily as another shattered the flagstones where he had sprawled. For all its immense size, the abomination was fast. The elf sidestepped another huge blow and cut in with his own, but the longsword rebounded from the creature's armoured shoulder with a ringing chime.

The thing called Siddroc knocked Gilead off-balance with a sideways chop and the flat of the cutter blade sent him flying, blood spraying from a slice to his jawline. He landed hard in the hearth, crushing two viols that the musicians had left there in their haste to leave. He barely had time to get up and clear before the spiked ball destroyed a bench and the iron fireguard.

Gilead flung himself forward again, trying to find some opening. This time, his beloved blue-steel sword caught against the cutter blade and broke, leaving him with about a foot of jagged blade. The creature started baying – laughing perhaps, it was impossible to tell – and charged the elf.

Gilead thought fast. He faced certain death unless he tried to evade. But death… death was what he wanted! At this moment he could do anything. Even if he failed, he would still be rewarded with the thing he most craved. Calm swept through him.

Gilead did what Siddroc least expected. He met the charge head on. The jagged end of the longsword stabbed into the visor slit of Siddroc's vast helm. There was a pneumatic pop and a crack of bone, and stinking black ichor spurted out of the neck seals. With a monstrous scream, the great creature toppled.

Gilead rose unsteadily from the great, twitching corpse. Once again, he noted darkly, death had chosen to take his side. He looked around. Lugos was gone.

Gilead caught up with him in the main yard of the mansion. The gates were open and the servants were fleeing, taking whatever they could with them in their panic. Gilead ignored the humans as easily as if they were sheep.

Lugos was face down in the dirt, impaled by a crossbow bolt. Betsen stood over him.

'That's him, isn't it?' she asked the elf, her whole body shaking.

'Yes,' he replied simply. 'And that is your vengeance served.'

She looked up at him, tears in her eyes. 'Thank you… but it doesn't feel anything like enough.'

'It never does,' said Gilead Lothain.

And for Gilead, it truly never would. But for a while, the determination of the human girl, Betsen, had shaken him out of his dark despair. The cold touch of death in his veins had faded a little, driven back by the heat of purpose.

He stood in the ruined main hall of Tor Anrok, alone. It was dawn and the light was watery and thin. He fixed his eyes for the last time on his father's golden throne. A few minutes before, he had lain a twist of thorn-roses, as scarlet as the ancient livery of House Lothain, on Cothor's grave.

He took little from the tower: a few trinkets and keepsakes, three or four of the oldest texts from Taladryel's decaying library, a few last flasks of the rare elven vintage from the cellar. His own possessions were few.

His father's longsword was a regal piece, its platinum guard encrusted with rubies. But it was not for him. He left it, locked in its casket, in Cothor's chamber – where it still lies, so I believe. Gilead chose a more suitable weapon to replace the precious blade he had left shattered in Lugos's hall: Galeth's sword. It was the twin of his own: a long, slim blade of blue-steel with dragon beaks flaring from a hilt set with a single scarlet ruby.

Gilead nodded a last, silent farewell to Tor Anrok, strode out into the tower yard and reached his horse.

On his own steed, to one side, Fithvael watched him, leaning low in the saddle to ease the ache of his healing wounds.

'I never thought…' he began.

Gilead swung up into his own saddle and took the ancient elf's hand. 'The past is dead, Fithvael. It is gone. You showed me that much. I do not know what I have in my future, but I will continue with it… until I find death at last.'

'Then let me ride with you until that day dawns,' Fithvael said quietly.

They spurred away into the morning mist. Behind them, Tor Anrok stood forlorn. Protected by its ancient charms and wards, shrouded by the mysterious forest that only elven skill could penetrate, it would never be seen by mortal eyes again.

III
Gilead's Chosen

*There is too much magic
in this place!*

WHAT? WHERE DID they go after that?

I've whetted your appetite, I see. Pass me that wineskin and let me think now. The stories have been in my head for fifty years, and they were old before that. They flutter around in the dry attic of my skull, waiting to be let out again. I remember only scraps. Forgive me.

Leaving Tor Anrok for the last time, Gilead and Fithvael set out upon an almost aimless voyage into the world. There was some business with a great, horned beast in the savage wilds to be found to the east of Marienburg, but the details I have forgotten. And raiders too, I recall, practising banditry on the high passes this side of Parravon. They did not live to regret their mistake in stopping two lonely horsemen.

What else? Damn my memory for a musty thing! Wait... wait... two whole seasons below ground? Yes, in lightless catacombs, at war with the rat-kin! Such deeds there, such a tale! But I have sworn never to tell it in full. Some stories carry a curse and that is one of them.

As the tales were told to me, this was a better time for Gilead Lothain, despite the dangers. Consider this much – he owned a wounded life: the death of his twin, the desolation of his ten year quest for vengeance, the misery and gloom that followed. But his companion, Fithvael, had brought him salvation of a kind. First, by spurring him to hunt the damned merchant-lord, Lugos, and then by persuading him to abandon his ruined birthplace where nothing remained save ghosts. Their wanderings gave Gilead purpose, be it bandits, beasts or the foul skaven-things. There was valour and combat and justice enough to stave off the clammy hand of doom that reached for him, across the abyss, that old rapport with Galeth which persisted now and touched his soul with death.

The companions shared a degree of happiness, comradeship, endeavour. A worthy time. But Gilead's heart was still tainted and darkened, and the misery that dogged his life would not remain at bay forever. Ah yes, a good and worthy time. It would not last, and once it was gone, it would never return. Merciful gods, I knew I had it. Now I recall what transpired next. Fill up your cup, sit back, and I'll tell you the story of what followed. But there's no happy ending, I warn you.

First, I must tell you about the voice.

THE VOICE HAD begun to call soon after Gilead had first turned his back on Tor Anrok. Gossamer-faint to begin with, he would hear it fleetingly, just the once, and then not again for months at a time; a very infrequent chiding whisper in the dead of night. Over the months and years, however, it grew, becoming stronger and more frequent. First it seemed to be the voice of his father, then his brother. Then it became a single, crystal-light, intonation in his mind, the voice of an elven woman. Eventually it was a voice Gilead felt he had always known, a voice of the past, and of the future.

Gilead had by then resolved to seek out any remnants of his kind. Veteran Fithvael, at his side day and night, privately believed this to be a fool's quest. The old kind had gone from these shores, its spaces usurped by the crude, short-lived humankind or the loathsome subhuman races. But he humoured his companion. The notion of the quest calmed Gilead, made him eager, curious, determined. It made him alive, and for that little comfort Fithvael was deeply grateful. As I believe I said, this was a good time for them both.

As it started to come to him more frequently, Gilead found himself beginning to follow in the direction of the voice, taking Fithvael with him, until they reached a tangled region deep in the Drakwald where none lived for fear of beastmen. Only now Fithvael faltered, but Gilead was resolved. There was one of their kind here somewhere, one with the power to enter his mind and lead him. He would follow it, to his death if need be.

Now, each long, dark night, her voice filled Gilead's dreams. When she came to his mind he welcomed her gladly. Ever since the promise of his young life had been taken from him, he had seen nothing in his future. It seemed like a lifetime since he had dreamed like a young man; dreamed of desire, dreamed of a lover, a wife, an heir even. The voice in his mind made him feel such things were possible again.

Pressing on through the tangled forest by day, he concentrated now only on following the voice and finding its owner. He thought nothing of what might happen beyond meeting the elf-woman who called in his mind.

'Do we continue eastward again today?' Fithvael dared to ask one morning as they broke camp and made ready to move on.

'Eastward until I learn otherwise,' Gilead answered.

'And what do we seek in the east?'

'A life,' replied Gilead, mounting his steed and turning her head toward his chosen route.

Fithvael did not pursue this conversation, just as he had not pursued so many like it in the preceding weeks. He had begun to mistrust the eager purpose that infused his friend. For so long they had simply wandered idly, sometimes making a little progress, sometimes casting huge circles in one remote area. Gilead seemed now to know precisely where he was going, but he had shared no information with Fithvael. The old warrior well knew the vagaries of Gilead's mind when it was disturbed. Yet now, Gilead had a kind of calm about him, coupled with a channelled energy so different from the murderous frenzy that Fithvael had so often feared to see in his companion.

So Fithvael followed Gilead's lead and waited for a better time to question him.

TWO DAYS LATER, at that time of day when the forest colours became one uniform dull grey hue in the fading light, Gilead turned to his companion. They could not see each other's faces as they sat side by side in the gloom, but Fithvael could sense the thrill surging through Gilead's body.

'We're very close now,' said Gilead, as if this explained everything.

'Close to what?' Fithvael asked.

'Not to what,' his friend said, 'to whom! The voice that calls to us!'

With that, he spurred on through the deep grey shadows of the primeval woodland. Fithvael smelled the churned up loam, the moss, the bark-rot in the trees. He heard the rheumatic creak of ancient timbers, the snuffling of wild boar some hundred paces away, the whirr of glossy beetles in the mulch beneath their boots. Yet he heard no voice, except the one in his own head that told him: *Turn back now and leave the young fool to his insane quest.*

Fithvael stroked his steed's mane, loosened his blade in its sheath and, knowing he was liable to regret it, urged it to trot on after Gilead.

HER NAME WAS Niobe. She made herself as small as possible in the filthy, stinking place into which she had been thrown.

She dared not open her eyes for fear of what she might see around her. She concentrated hard, trying to cut out the cries of her fellow captives, the inhuman wails and screams that filled her ears and echoed in her head. She tried to block out the deep grunts and growls of the bestial guards. She closed her mind to all that she had seen and done.

It was to no avail. The hypnotic, charismatic charms of Lord Ire ran through her soul like poison in blood. She knew what he was doing and why he had brought her here... her and the others.

There was nothing she could do except make herself small, shut her eyes, block out the sounds – and call.

When Lord Ire and his foul beastman brood had first dragged her to this grotesque place, with its sense-churning architecture and its hideous stench, she had set a part of her mind aside. She had locked it shut and poured all the energy she could muster into its solitude.

She knew that Lord Ire was using her magic, harvesting it and putting it to some dark use. And she knew that if he drained away all of her arcane powers, she would have nothing left to fight him with, and nothing left with which to reach out into the world.

Her mind-magic had always been strong, even as a babe in arms. It had made her blessed and special in her father's tower. Now she portioned off a tiny part of that magic and used it to send out a plea for help. If there was any of her kind within a thousand leagues of her, any of the ancient race prepared to listen, then that plea would reach them and perhaps bring them to her rescue. It had been so long now. Months, years even, alone in the darkness, her magic forever ebbing as it was drained away. Yet she called again, knowing it would not be long before she could call no more.

THE VOICE RANG in Gilead's mind once more.

The trees of the Drakwald grew more choked with each passing day. They were in the oldest part of the vast tangle of ancient trees now, a dark, forbidding land that had been this way since the earliest times. An eternal forest, its prehistoric glades undisturbed for a hundred thousand generations, dark and misshapen, with a rank smell and black, twisted trunks and branches that felt spongy and decayed to the touch. Densely overgrown, the pathless depths of the forest might render the most gifted ranger lost and bewildered, and there was a constant scent of subhuman fear on the air.

Yet still Gilead felt energised, invigorated, and ready for anything, the beautiful voice of the elven woman luring him on.

The sky had long since been hidden beyond the tree canopies that formed a heavy, claustrophobic blanket high above. The branches made a vault above their heads, sealing in the dank, moist atmosphere. The air was heavy with dank vegetable smells and the creaking, flexing sounds of the forest. The two riders came to a halt, listening for the familiar sounds of birds and undergrowth creatures. But this part of the Drakwald was dead, and nothing but the most primordial life could survive here.

Fithvael started. Their steeds were suddenly nervous, pricking their ears and flaring their nostrils. The sweet smell of horse sweat rose from their twitching flanks and they pawed the ground, eager to move on.

The riders had reached a dense, high wall of foliage, a heavy hedge of twisted black branches with shiny, dark green leaves that smelled of rotting corpses. They dismounted and approached the barrier. It shivered in the breeze like a living thing and seemed to lean and reach out towards them, almost as if trying to surround them. The rustle of leaves and twigs became a cracking cacophony as the hedge strained to grow thicker and taller around them.

'There is too much magic here,' Fithvael said, trying to dispel his unease.

'And there is elf magic in my mind. We have nothing to fear,' Gilead replied, arming himself with the pair of blades that were always ready at his side.

Gilead struck out at the hedge, both blades whirring through the air, tearing into the leaves and branches before him. As they died, the leaves soared into the air, floating there, drying and browning, shrivelling to dead veins before disappearing into dust. Dismembered boughs screamed and twisted in death throes, spitting sticky brown sap that burned in the throats of the two companions.

Fithvael coughed and gasped, tearing a strip of cloth from his shirt and wrapping it around his mouth. But Gilead fought on, oblivious to the hot rasp of breath in his throat, and to the smouldering places on his attire where the acidic sap had begun to corrode his clothing.

Fithvael breathed easier through his makeshift mask and, arming himself, he ducked under Gilead's scything sword-arm to join the fray. As the pair of them cut away at the dark wall, it twisted and grew around them, until the pair could feel new growth brushing against the backs of their legs.

'Faster!' Gilead cried, slicing and chopping in the confined space.

As the two warriors worked in concert, they began to destroy the barrier faster than it could re-grow. Fithvael struck hard and fast beside his friend, trying to slash away the new growth that burst from the ruptured stems.

They hacked away at the foliage as if it were an army of green-skins, merciless with their elven blades. Small shoots of new growth showed black against the older, dark green leaves, but there were many places now where the sliced and torn twigs remained bare.

'It's working!' Gilead bellowed in triumph and, redoubling his efforts, he forced his blades deeper into the thorny barrier.

He strode forward into the breach in the hedge, slicing and chopping and powering his way through. Standing close against Gilead's back, Fithvael kept the new growth at bay as best he could. They were cocooned now in the densely growing wall of vegetation, with barely room to move, but they were still making headway.

Fithvael fought back the thought that they would be suffocated by the noxious plant, walled in by the dark magic that had somehow created this barrier. Then tiny threads and chinks of light began to penetrate the dense greenery before them. At first, pinpoints of light showed through and then stronger bars of sunlight dappled the scarlet of Gilead's sap-bedraggled cloak.

'We are here,' breathed Gilead. He repeated the words over and over to the rhythm of his sword and dagger as he cut away the last of the hedge. It crumbled and broke behind them, defeated, dry and dead. Moments after breaking through, while they were still breathing hard from their exertions, Fithvael and Gilead turned back to the wall. They saw nothing but their own faded path leading back through the dim glades of the forest, their horses nearby.

'It wasn't real!' said Fithvael. 'That hideous barrier... it was just an illusion.'

'Our sweat and fear was real enough!' Gilead answered, turning from the space where the hedge had so recently been. There was nothing now but the sour-sweet corpse smell that had followed them from the moment they had entered the Drakwald, more pungent than ever.

Gilead took a step – then stumbled to his knees. Fithvael hurried to him.

'What? What is it?'

'We are very close, Fithvael tuin. Our guide awaits us... she just told me her name.'

'Her name?'

'She calls herself Niobe,' said Gilead, drawing his cloak around him and rising unsteadily. 'She is so very beautiful...'

'Of course she is, but–'

Gilead hushed him abruptly with a raised finger. 'We are very close. She is showing me visions. A path.'

IN THE PARTITIONED chamber of her mind, Niobe had stored up a host of images of her prison. Some had collected there unbidden, others she had gathered deliberately, hoping they might be of use to her in freeing herself and her comrades.

She could feel him close to her now, the one whose mind she had reached with her voice. He had followed her calling, he had come for her, and now she could begin to feel his mind and judge his strengths. She probed his psyche, finding many avenues barred and many doors closed. It was as if he was wounded inside, damaged, shut off to the outside. What pain had haunted his life to make him so?

She saw him in her mind. He was fair, tall and graceful, and his sword hand was strong and fast. She encountered both defeat and triumph in the brooding depths of his soul and was satisfied. Despite his pain, despite the soul-deep wounds that laced him, he would be the one.

Her mind burned suddenly with the bright new image of the monstrous living thicket, bursting out its thorny new growth. Niobe knew at once that Lord Ire had also detected the existence of her interloper, of the unwanted intruder into the land he had annexed with his dark Chaos sorcery.

She knew she had to warn her rescuer.

'BE ON YOUR guard, Fithvael. She is penned in by beasts, and a great magic force that is not her own surrounds her. She is warning me this place is evil.'

'Is that so?' Fithvael said sardonically. He had known that for days. Biting back his cynicism, he paused abruptly. 'Do you hear that?' he asked.

'I hear the growl and snort of beasts,' replied Gilead.

Fithvael drew his sword and slung the edge of his moss-coloured cloak over one shoulder, freeing his sword arm from its confining folds. He braced himself.

'Aye, the growl and snort of beasts, where once we heard only the creak and groan of vile, twisted branches,' Fithvael said.

But Gilead did not acknowledge him. He had drawn his own sword the instant he saw Fithvael reach for his. They turned their backs to each other and Gilead shut out the images that were now flashing in his head – images of a huge, shimmering, faceless man in black and grey noble's garb, with pewter and silver ornament; images of a vast, ethereal fortress; images of magic war machines that spewed ball lightning out over the forest. Images surely planted in his mind by Niobe to warn him of his fate.

'On my word,' Gilead breathed to Fithvael as their cloaks brushed close and they moved together. Wary, they stared out into the twilit forest, watching for movement.

When it came, it came without stealth or ceremony. A deep, bellowing howl and a tide of frothing, jeering man-beasts washed down upon them.

They were distorted, mangled beast-things with flattened craniums and dislocated, distended jaws. Many had horns and tusks crowding in amongst crooked teeth and flaring nostrils. Their flanks were naked and hairless, and their leathery hides were the colour of pumice, which lent their skins the sheen of death. Fithvael saw spine pelts and crowns of coarse hair. He saw the grey-white, seemingly sightless eyes of the beast nearest to him and he charged, a war cry on his lips.

Gilead thrust his sword at the grey, hump-backed creature that loomed before him. It was half as tall again as the elf and three times as wide, with massively bulging joints in its stocky limbs, and huge, broad-knuckled hands that wielded a short-handled, double-headed axe. The blue metal of Gilead's sword was met by the crudely hooked blade of the beast's axe. Gilead swung his blade down in a sudden arc, sliding along the curve of the monster's axe and taking advantage of the weakness. He rested his blade momentarily in the curve and then thrust upward. The beast was turning, and took a deep wound to the top of an upper limb that was less an arm, more a living cudgel.

The beast cried out through its clenched mouth, the mandible too distorted to open wide. Gilead saw flecks of spittle hovering in the air for what seemed like minutes. Time stood still for him as, shadowfast, he dived forward, cleaving the beast's face in two across its jaw, severing the monster's jowls. Its exposed teeth flashed through the filthy ichor that gouted from the wound. Gilead made a second thrust through the neck while the beast was in mid-howl, and it fell to earth, dead.

Fithvael drove hard at his assailant, avoiding its blank-eyed stare and slicing with his sword. The abomination parried with the iron-capped club that it wielded one-handed, but Fithvael ducked and swung, side-stepping the heavy blow. Still the beastman stood solid; its weapon whirred through the air, passing Fithvael's head as he bent his knees and drove his blade upward. He connected with the monster's bullish neck, gouging a wad of flesh and tearing through arteries, but still the creature stood its ground. Fithvael looked once into its eyes and saw his target. Swinging his blade high, he drove it down into the eye socket of his wailing adversary.

'Left!' cried Gilead as a spiked mace sought contact with the back of Fithvael's skull. The veteran warrior did as he was bidden, curving his body to avoid the weapon. Gilead drove his sword through a ribcage and another beast fell.

Gilead and Fithvael fought together in practised unison with little need for words and signs. They swung and sliced, ducked and feinted, taking one beast out at the knees, another through the chest, a third in the gut.

As the day darkened, and the canopy blackened above them, the warriors fought and killed three dozen grey skinned, white-eyed beastmen.

GILEAD WOULD HAVE continued on that same night, but they were both tiring and Fithvael persuaded his friend to rest and take up the quest again the following day. Gilead was unsettled, almost frenzied. He knew that he was close to Niobe now. He could feel her mind probing his and see the pictures she was sending out to him. But he respected Fithvael's counsel. He would rest if he must.

LORD IRE, CHAMPION of Chaos, stood at the top of a steep, sweeping staircase made of sparkling, black obsidian lapped to a mirror finish. Gilead looked up at the man, who appeared far taller than the elf; a statuesque figure of preternaturally perfect proportions. He was dressed from crown top to toe tip in a million shades of black and grey. His cuirass and coulter looked like polished slate and his cloak clasp, buckles and ornaments were pewter and silver. He stood in profile, his head turned away. Gilead concentrated on that profile, marvelling at the perfect tail of blue-black hair that hung in a swathe down the man's shoulder.

Gilead looked on, eyes unblinking, at the giant of a man before and above him, waiting. Waiting for the man to turn and face him. Waiting to look into his eyes and see what horrors lurked there.

It was only as Gilead made to draw his sword that the man finally turned his body toward the elf. The turn was slow. Lord Ire's head seemed to remain in profile for minutes. Gilead watched the man turn, knowing from Niobe's pictures and from her voice in his mind that this was the fell beast-master who held her captive. Lord Ire finally turned to face his would-be assailant and took his first step down the long stairway.

Gilead used every ounce of his will to rest his hand on the hilt of his sword and draw it, but he could not do it. He stared up at the figure, and into that face as it came closer, trying to quell the terror in his mind.

In profile, Lord Ire's face was pale and elegant with a long straight nose and narrow upper lip over a strong jaw line, appearing more elf than human, though human he was. He was clean-shaven and the perfect arch of his half brow was a work of art in its own right.

But full face there was no symmetry. The left hand side of Lord Ire's face was a very different kind of art. Hair that grew low over this forehead was held back in a silver brace that bisected his head top to bottom and left to right. The upper quadrant was all hair, black and slick and oily. Where a single eye might have shone out between blinking fringed lids there were a series of slots in the beaten silver mask, the spaces between showing a single lidless orb, hard and white like a marble, staring out, unblinking and blind. The lower part of the face was covered in another swathe of the same black hair, straight and glossy, slashed across by a slack purple mouth, slick with bloody spit.

As the elf stared, Lord Ire's sighted eye looked down on Gilead, and the perfect half of his mouth twitched in a wry smile.

Gilead tore his eyes away from the hideous visage and bent to examine his sword hilt. He concentrated for a moment, grasped it and at last managed tofree it from its scabbard. As he did so, he looked up again to where the Chaos lord was descending the steps. He saw one footfall and then no more. Lord Ire seemed to disappear before his eyes.

Then Gilead heard the steady, long stride of a huge man above his head but looking up he saw no ceiling. He saw nothing except mist.

Startled, Gilead looked down to see that his beautiful blue steel sword, Galeth's sword, with its ornate gold hilt and elven rune engravings, had disappeared. He was left holding what appeared to be a rough wooden thing made of two laths, the kind he had learned to swing before he had taken his first infant steps. The kind he and Galeth had play-fought with in the main yard of Tor Anrok, under the tutelage of Taladryal and Nithrom, all those years ago. But it could not be.

Gilead ran for the staircase, throwing the toy weapon away. As he reached the first step, he saw that the staircase descended rather than ascended… yet Lord Ire had been above him, coming down these very steps.

Turning about sharply, his stance low and defensive, Gilead found himself by a second staircase. It was straight and the ascending slate steps had no visible means of support. They simply hung in the air. Gilead took the first step tentatively, but finding it firm and strong, he took the next three at ordinary walking pace, then broke into a run, taking two and three steps at a time until he reached the top.

Suddenly there was a wall before him that he had not seen as he ascended. And then the stairs sloped into a new position and locked together in a steep, unforgiving slope. He slid backwards frantically until he found himself at the bottom of the drop and fell over the lip.

Gilead landed on his feet at the opening of a long, arched tunnel.

This place was not real. It could not be real.

He paced forward and found himself in a huge arsenal. Coming through the great portal in the north end of the store, the warrior-son of Cothor Lothain could not see the south, east or west walls, although he knew they must be there. Above him, some half a mile up, he could see that the ceiling was vaulted in a series of gigantic, interlocking domes.

Gilead gasped a horrified breath as his eyes focussed on what was laid out before him. Massed in the otherworldly building were more war machines than he had ever thought to see in a lifetime. Elaborate, multi-armed trebuchets were ranked beside rows of massive war cannons with iridescent barrels that stretched high into the vaulted ceiling. Giant crossbows with ornate winching handles, armed with bolts shaved from entire tree trunks, stood alongside giant catapults which looked strangely fragile and ethereal, like mere shadows.

As Gilead stood in horrified wonder, the machines began to throb and jostle as though wakened from some deep sleep. Gilead closed his eyes and breathed deeply into his chest. A second breath cleared the elf's mind and a third calmed the adrenalin rush to his body at the sight of so great an armoury.

He opened his eyes and for a brief moment he was surrounded again by the sights and sounds of the Drakwald. He sighed his relief.

Then the arsenal grew up around him once more, as vast and seemingly real as when he had first crossed the threshold. Gilead fled, turning and running desperate miles to reach the door that had been right behind him only moments before.

Stone and wood, metal and mortar had no meaning here. In this place, space was a malleable commodity. The rules of architecture, the rules of reality held no meaning. The rules had been bent until they were so broken and twisted that they no longer existed at all.

FITHVAEL ROUSED AS dawn broke over the forest, to find Gilead already awake and standing beside the remains of the campfire. His friend was fully clothed and armed, but he looked pale and drawn.

'We must leave,' said Gilead. 'We must get the Lady Niobe out of there and we must do it now.'

'There is time, old friend,' Fithvael said in the soothing tone he used when Gilead became moody and obsessive.

'No!' Gilead said in a tone that brooked no compromise. 'My mind is so full of her, so full of the images she places there, I know not what is real and what an illusion. I know only that I must fight for her.'

'I have fought beside you before, te tuin,' said Fithvael, 'and I will no doubt fight beside you again. But if I'm going to follow you, you must tell me what you know.'

'Only that Niobe needs our help. She is in mortal danger.'

'The voice, the pictures in your head come from her? But who is she?'

'My future and my past,' said Gilead, drawing a trembling hand across his furrowed brow.

'You know this woman?'

'I have always known her,' answered Gilead.

'From Tor Anrok?' Fithvael asked, excited.

Gilead dropped his head. 'I don't know. Gods of Ulthuan, Fithvael! I don't know! I only know I have to fight for her!'

Fithvael threw his cloak about himself in resignation. 'I guess that is good enough for me,' he said.

GILEAD STOPPED IN his tracks and took a deep breath as he parted the undergrowth in front of him. What stood in the barren space before them was vast. He could see only the facade of the building, and looking to the left and right gave him no idea of its width, since he could not see as far as its corners. He dropped his neck back and the building curved up and away before him, reaching into the sky so far above that he could not see its roof structures, only great granite and flint walls cut off in the distance by black clouds.

Fithvael pulled up abruptly behind Gilead and looked over his friend's shoulder to see why they had stopped so suddenly. He took two steps back in astonishment, almost falling over a bulging tree root on the ground behind him.

'How... how did we not see this from a hundred leagues away?' Fithvael asked.

Gilead did not answer. He stepped through the undergrowth. The massive, grim structure before them was only a hundred yards from where they stood, but the forest halted its growth abruptly at their feet and nothing grew in the shadow of the edifice. They stepped onto a no-man's land that looked unnaturally hard, black and level. Gilead lifted one foot suddenly from the liquid surface and Fithvael let out a yelp as his own foot sank into a hot, black swamp.

A dark geyser a thousand feet high suddenly gushed a few hundred yards from them to their right, spraying the elves with hot, murky filth, and the entire wasteland became a bubbling, gurgling quagmire.

Gilead drew his sword and began to wade across the swamp until he was buried in it to his hips, his red cloak wrapped slantwise across his shoulder, clear of the stinking heat and filth of the mire. Fithvael pulled up his boots, tightened his belt, rolled his cloak into the pack on his back and followed Gilead.

'Arm yourself!' Gilead warned, turning to his friend. 'Hurry!' he screamed, surging his way back toward Fithvael.

Behind Fithvael, rising from the mud as though awakened from deep slumber, rose a monstrous being. Huge horns curled downward on either side of a flat, pitted head, and red eyes blinked open as swamp mud trickled away in runnels down a scarred, green face covered in suppurating sores. The monster flexed its jaws and threw its half-submerged body forward, screaming as its paddle-like upper limbs ripped free of the swamp.

Fithvael turned as Gilead threw his dagger by its tip. It whirred through the air, end over end in a graceful arc, and came to rest in the exposed throat of the great swamp beast.

The creature brought one long, webbed hand up to the dagger hilt, but Fithvael was quicker, though still unarmed. He thrust his entire weight against the dagger, driving it deeper and lower into the monster's upper chest. Then the elf heaved on the gore-covered hilt, first pulling it free and then embedding it in the monstrous throat again, lower this time.

The huge, slimy paddles of the beast came around Fithvael's shoulders, embracing him and dragging his feet from the swamp bed. Losing his balance, Fithvael could feel the hilt of Gilead's dagger digging into his own chest. The monster lifted Fithvael with ease out of the sticky mud on the swamp floor. Fithvael pulled up his feet as quickly as the sucking action of the mud would allow and, drawing his knees into his body, he planted his soggy boots firmly in the beast's belly and thrust hard.

Fithvael fell heavily onto his back, creating a slow, broken ripple of mud. The vast thing rose up above him.

Gilead had only been able to stand and watch the action as Fithvael blocked his target, but as soon as the animal's huge bulk emerged, he attacked.

Gilead tore into the lumpy, calloused surface of the beast's back with his sword, hacking through the thick greenish skin until he exposed a cage of heavily gnarled, brown bones. The creature began to convulse and one of its paddle-limbs came floating slowly to the surface. Gilead reached his left hand down into the swamp, found a handhold on Fithvael's jerkin and dragged his friend out. Fithvael coughed and spluttered and took long urgent breaths, as he watched the thing they had killed slide back into the waters that would now become its grave.

As FITHVAEL REGAINED his composure, Gilead sought out Niobe in his mind, latching on to the persistent urge of her call. She had brought them this far and he trusted her to bring them safely to her.

Setting off again in a half-walk, half-swim, their hands paddling the surface of the swamp as it undulated around them, the two warriors made good progress, and soon found themselves within arms reach of the towering, slick walls of the castle.

'Do you see?' Fithvael asked, searching the immediate surface of the wall.

'There are no joins,' answered Gilead. 'The walls are solid.'

Gilead splashed back some way and focussed higher up the wall, looking for patterns that might give him some clues about the structure of the impenetrable wall. He could see reflections on the surface of the ooze around him, forming slanting, rectangular shards of light. He looked up the towering wall again and saw that the reflections fell from windows. They were very high up, but huge. The glass in the windows had a heavy gloss like black mirrors, and they were set flush with the stonework; no frames or sills were visible. Gilead was reminded of the impossible building in his dream and closed his eyes to concentrate again on Niobe's voice.

Fithvael and Gilead sloshed their way along the base of the wall, which seemed to curve gently along its length. Gilead was looking for something, but it was Fithvael who saw it first.

'There!' exclaimed Fithvael. 'Could that be the place?'

Gilead could see nothing ahead of him, though he examined the wall thoroughly.

'Two feet to your right, a hand's-breadth above your shoulder,' Fithvael instructed.

'I see nothing,' answered Gilead and backed away toward Fithvael. Gilead took up Fithvael's old position, and now he too could see the opening in the wall: a kind of grilled storm drain, arched and menacing. The oozing mud of the swamp seemed to lap up to the open slate work of the grille, but did not penetrate it.

This whole thing is an illusion. Remember that! Gilead told himself and then he made his way back to where the storm drain should have been, but again it eluded him. Fithvael was right beside his friend now, but the opening was invisible to him too.

Fithvael turned back and retraced his steps to the position he had been wading in when he had first spotted the drain. It took him several minutes to get the view just right, but he managed it. Following Fithvael's explicit directions, Gilead pulled himself up by the bars of a grille that was invisible to him.

He tried to look beyond it. There was nothing to see. A rush of cold air around Gilead caught the last son of Tor Anrok off-guard. He shielded his face for a moment and when he opened his eyes again he was back on solid ground. The mud and filth of the swamp had disappeared from his clothes.

'Fithvael, we're in!' Gilead said and turned to look out of the grille, but behind him was only a solid wall.

In his mind, Niobe reached out to him, covering his eyes with her hands in a dream tableau that she planted in his waking mind.

Gilead closed his eyes and felt the wall in front of him. It had been hard and shiny to look at, but felt sandy and crumbly to the touch. There was no opening.

Gilead took his cloak from around his body and tore off a narrow length of dense cloth from the hem. He placed this around his face, shielding his eyes in several tightly wrapped layers of cloth. Although effectively blindfold, Gilead closed his eyes once more and reached out his hands.

He could feel the grille before him and passed his hands through it.

Fithvael was sure he had not blinked and yet his friend had disappeared through the grille without him seeing it happen. He knew he must make his own way to it now.

He carefully measured the distance along the wall by eye and slowly made his way toward the opening. As soon as he moved it became invisible to him again, but he trusted his mental measuring and carefully walked his hands along the wall, end to end, counting out as he went. Having reached his apparent destination, Fithvael passed his hands tentatively over the solid surface of the wall. He could feel no grille or opening of any kind and he began to despair.

At a distance of only a few yards, the storm drain had seemed overlarge, yet he could not find it even with a hand-search.

Fithvael moved a step to his left and lifted his hand higher on the wall, sweeping across another large area of stone with his open palms.

Nothing.

Fithvael dropped his head for a moment in concentration and then looked hard at the wall, as though he were trying to look into it, or through it.

Fithvael felt the hands on his shoulders before he saw them and tensed in an instant, ready to fight off another foe. Then he caught sight of Gilead's long slender hands, recognising his companion by the missing finger on the left hand. Gilead's arms were protruding through a solid rock wall.

In another instant Fithvael was standing next to his friend, clean of swamp filth, but more than a little confused. He sought Gilead's gaze.

'You must get used to it,' said Gilead. 'I have seen too much of this place already and it is all the same. We are no longer in our world, Fithvael tuin.'

'I can feel it,' said Fithvael. 'I can smell it and taste it. It crawls across my flesh and penetrates my body. Corruption!'

'Fight it then,' answered Gilead, 'as we have always fought evil… but fight it only for yourself. The evil and the magic of this place are too great for us to fight alone. Our purpose is to release Niobe and then to get out of this vile otherworld.'

Gilead stared hard at his friend, that he might remember the warning, and then strode off down a long, curving corridor, deeper into the alien realm of this huge stone fortress.

NIOBE GUIDED THEM well, yet they were still confused by the architectural deceptions and optical illusions of their surroundings.

Spaces that looked huge at a distance were claustrophobic once they were inside them. Floors and ceilings sloped out and away from each other, lengthening perspective, or simply bulged and flattened, changing shape and dimensions before their eyes. They hit walls they could not see, walked apparently on ceilings, and climbed stairways that seemed flat.

Fithvael peered out from one of the black glass windows that was crystal clear from within. He only did it once. He glimpsed a huge panorama of seething desert with volcanic black sand dunes driven by some abominable sirocco against the horizon. Nothing grew there, but the land was ever-changing. The veteran elf saw a huge sandstorm loom in the distance, turn into a tornado five miles high, and then burn out again in an instant. He had no explanation for what he saw – save that this was truly a realm in which the Ruinous Powers held dominion.

NIOBE COULD FEEL Gilead and see through his eyes. She saw the smaller, older warrior following in his master's wake and she saw the confusion on Fithvael's face when confronted with the trials of the unnatural surroundings. Fithvael, his name was Fithvael. She pitied him.

They were so close now that she could almost reach out and touch them. She had touched no other being for so long. She did not know if it was days or years. Time, like the fabric of this place, was twisted and distorted to suit the tastes of Lord Ire, who dwelt in Chaos.

Niobe knelt on her block, for she was too tall to stand and her hands were tethered by a narrow, near-invisible strand of perfect silver chain, light and fragile looking, but with the strength of links wrought by dwarfs. The block was a narrow column no more than a yard across and perfectly round. It floated less than a third of the way up the steep cathedral-like room that housed all the sorcerous slaves that Lord Ire had collected with such relish.

With every day, sometimes with every hour that passed, the configuration of the columns altered. She dreaded those moves. The way her column floated through the great cavity of the endless cathedral made her sick and dizzy... or was it the knowledge that the higher she rose, the nearer she came to her ultimate destiny?

If she reached the top, what would she feel there? How would she die? She had stopped looking at the skeletal forms that still adhered to the uppermost columns. Those columns had ascended bearing living creatures: humans, dwarfs, elves. All races and species were represented and all were alive during the ascent. Not all the columns descended with their cargoes intact. Many simply tumbled back through the other columns, spilling their desiccated bodies from them. The bodies evaporated into dust and then into nothing before they ever reached the bottom again.

Those columns that descended slowly, bearing skeletons and sometimes rotting corpses, did so only because there was some mote of magic left in the bodies after the life breath had been extinguished. These columns hovered and languished, seeming not to move as often as the others, nor as far.

Niobe could not bear the thought that she might soon be one of them. If she was to die here, then let it be a clean and quick end. For her, there could be no magic without consciousness and no consciousness without life.

Niobe had stopped looking at the other magical beings around her, the living and the dead. She had tried to count them when she had first been chained to her block, but they were countless, numbering tens of thousands that she could see, and she knew not how many lay beyond in the upper reaches of the cathedral. She had stopped watching the new arrivals as they were bound to the blocks vacated by the dead, or to new, white marble columns, fresh hewn, that would be as dark and aged as the others in time.

But more than anything else, Niobe had stopped looking at the altar. It had a mesmerising effect on all that cast their eyes upon it.

The altar was a massive block of solid rock covered in shifting black and grey runes, which would fizzle with light periodically and, occasionally, bleed blue-black viscous liquid. It took up the central position in the elliptical space where a floor would have been – had there been any visible floor. Niobe could see nothing below the altar, yet it seemed to hang in the air, as though hovering, much as the columns did.

Between the writhing Chaos runes that swept across the altar, every inch of space was taken up by tiny pinprick sockets into which silver tether strands were located, tens of hundreds of thousands of them. Many of the threads were silver; some few shone out with the shifting colours of an unlikely rainbow; others were copper-coloured or black and eroded with decay.

Upon the altar lived the Cipher, a being that took no sustenance save what it absorbed from the altar itself. It had no features; no limbs, no eyes or ears, and no voice. It was vast and still, pulsing slowly from time to time, or throbbing a fast spasmodic rhythm of its own. It was changeless and ageless and formless, yet Niobe knew it to be the most powerful element of them all. It was the altar that drained the slaves of their magic while sustaining their physical forms. The threadlike tethers that connected the slaves to the altar were like umbilical chords, binding them all to the will of this place and of this dark thing.

FITHVAEL AND GILEAD wove their way through the structure that had no structure, aware only that they followed Niobe's mind patterns. They looked constantly for an enemy: a beastman, a Chaos monster, even the hideously beautiful lord who Gilead had seen in his dream.

They longed to feel a weapon in their hands, something solid, real, unalterable in this nightmare place. They longed to concentrate their minds in the only truly fulfilling way they knew how; they longed to fight, to shed blood and ichor, to slash and tear and rend flesh, any flesh.

'Where are they?' asked Fithvael. 'Where are the enemy hordes?'

'My sword hand itches too,' answered Gilead, sharply, his fingers flexing less than an inch from the hilt of his sword.

Every inch of this place reeked of evil corruption, and even taking a breath made the elves tense to screaming point.

'Where are we?' Fithvael asked.

'Just follow,' retorted Gilead, flexing his sword hand again and glaring at his companion.

WITH EVERY STEP that Gilead took, Niobe's heart responded with a beat. And as he came closer, his feet beat faster and harder on the floors and steps and ceilings he traversed. She almost filled his mind now. He had forgotten the absent foe that Fithvael still expected at every step, and felt only Niobe. He was moving so fast that Fithvael could hardly keep pace with him without breaking into an aching run.

Niobe's pounding heart beat ever faster and she gasped for breath, trying to pull her hands up to her chest, but having to drop lower on her knees and let her head fall to her shackled hands. In her desperation to maintain the link to him, she had tied her being to his too closely, and now there was a price to pay. Frantic to find her, Gilead was verging on a state of shadowfast. She was weak, at the limits of her endurance. Her body, her mind and her soul were racing helplessly to the rhythm he set, unable to slow down, unable even to break off the link. The mind-magic she had worked to effect her escape was killing her.

Her heart fluttered, failed. She fell.

THE VOICE FELL silent. Gilead winced at the sudden emptiness. He took a last few steps and entered a room vaster than any cathedral.

He stopped, his feet resting on the rock lip overlooking the abyssal vault of the immense chamber. Above, below and around him, the numberless blocks drifted in the cold, crisp darkness. He saw the miserable figures chained to each one, the living, the dead. He heard the moans and distant wails of the captives. Far away, through the litter of drifting blocks, he saw the pale flicker of the altar.

'Niobe!' he screamed. There was no echo. The space was dead air.

The smell had gone. The filthy stench of corruption was completely missing in this vast space. There was no smell at all. Every ounce of power was extracted from the magic slaves; nothing escaped the tethers, no smell, no energy, nothing at all.

Gilead stood hopelessly at the edge of the gulf. Fithvael came up behind him.

'By all the gods of Ulthuan…' stammered Fithvael. His voice was deadened too.

'She's here somewhere,' Gilead stammered.

'Where?'

'I don't know. I can't hear her any more.'

Gilead feared the worst. He strained to catch some trace of her. Nothing. Niobe's voice and heartbeat had fallen silent five full minutes earlier.

'We have to find her…' he began.

Fithvael looked out into the space beyond them. It had no colour, no tone and no shade. There seemed to be no light sources and no shadows. He could see no walls, only sensing that they must be there beyond the thousands stacks of floating plinths that surrounded him on all sides. He looked down.

There was no floor.

'Then we find her!' he snarled, and leaped from the lip of the threshold onto the nearest block. It wobbled slightly as he landed. The wasted, emaciated human-thing chained to it groaned.

Fithvael bounded across to the next, casting his gaze around at the floating plinths and the beings shackled upon them. There were species and races here that he had never seen or heard of, even in legends. Each stood or knelt or crouched or lay dead on a perfect disk of floating rock. Castaways, imprisoned on tiny islands in the darkness. He had never seen so many varied sentient beings in one place, nor had he ever been in one place that was so vast, and yet so claustrophobic – and so cruel.

Filled with a sudden, consuming rage, Fithvael began to move again, leaping from one block to the next, oblivious to the drop below. He started tugging and tearing at the beings, trying to wake them. None stirred, or even seemed aware of him. When he couldn't wake them, the old elf tried to free them. He drew his sword in a grasp that whitened his gnarled but slender knuckles and bared his teeth as he went into a frenzy of hacking and slashing at the delicate threads. He could not break a single one of them.

The sight of his friend moving from block to block galvanised Gilead Lothain. He leaped out too, over to the nearest platform, where a tethered dwarf lay curled in a foetal ball. He tried to shut out the thought in his mind.

She was already lost.

In a bound, he moved on, then again and again. Fithvael was far below him now, almost out of sight.

'Niobe!'

Something made him look over at the body on the block below him, to the right. It was slumped and curled up tight. Long hair draped over the side of the plinth and a hand rested down one side of it. The face was grey, but he recognised it from the images in his mind.

Gilead jumped into space. He almost missed his target, but clawed at the lip and pulled himself up onto the block next to her.

Niobe took two short, gasping breaths, several seconds apart, and stirred slightly. He could hear her inner voice, distant and frail, right at the back of his mind.

Gilead bent to lift the elf maiden. She was light, almost insubstantial. He could raise her only three feet above the plinth before the tethers tightened and would not give. Gilead looked at the tiny silver threads that tied Niobe's slender wrists together then disappeared into the plinth she had been placed upon. He took them in both of his hands in order to tear them. They felt like nothing in his hands and he looked at his open palm to reassure himself that they were there. He made a snapping motion between his hands, but the threads did not break.

'You won't do it,' said Fithvael's voice. He was perched on a block that floated above and to the left of Niobe's. He was sharing the block with the tethered form of a young human male who sat silent and unresponsive. 'Nothing can free these poor creatures,' he said, gesturing around the vast space. 'Nothing will cut those cursed tethers.'

'No! That cannot be true!' Gilead declared. 'She's alive! Very weak but alive!'

He drew his sword and wrapped the slender chords around it twice. He then flicked his weapon hard into the air, but it stopped abruptly before it had formed the elegant arc he had expected. The threads did not break.

'I said–' Fithvael said, his voice dulled by the deadened space.

'Hush!' Gilead tried to think. There had to be a way to break the physical thread that held her mind and siphoned her magic away.

Niobe's voice, broken and fragile, spoke in his mind. 'Do not… cut the threads,' it said. 'Destroy the block.'

Gilead planted his feet squarely, shoulder width apart, and taking his sword in a two handed hold he plunged it down into the rock.

'What are you doing?' Fithvael called.

The blue steel of the blade bit into the block in a flurry of cold, white sparks. Gilead thrust it again. The blade began to take on the same colourless darkness as everything else in the space, and he looked down at himself for a moment. His cloak bore no red colour and the hilt of his sword was no longer gold and gleaming. The vault was draining them too.

Gilead drew a deep, sustaining breath, and Niobe's chest rose and fell in sympathy. He struck again, and a fissure cracked across the face of the block. Shards fell away into the void.

'In the name of Ulthuan, Gilead! You'll fall to your death!'

'If that's all you can say, keep it to yourself.'

With a despairing curse, Fithvael stood up and unwound the long skein of eleven cord that he carried around his waist. His practised hands lashed it twice around his own block, moving around the motionless boy. Then he called out to Gilead and threw the loose end across to him.

Gilead caught it, nodded a curt thanks, and tied it around Niobe's body, under her arms. Then he resumed his rock-shattering blows.

In his hands, Galeth's blade began to take on a hint of its old colour. Gilead was weakening the power. Just here, just in this tiny place, he was cutting through the leeching cold and sparking life and colour back.

His blows became more rapid. As he became shadowfast, the blue steel of his blade shone out and the gold of its hilt became bright and iridescent.

Fithvael watched in mounting alarm, his hands around the lashed cord ready to take up the strain. Even from his vantage point, he could see Niobe's chest fluttering and heaving like the wings of a butterfly. She convulsed in agonising spasms as her heart palpitated at a rate beyond anything Fithvael had ever witnessed. Much more and the strain would kill her.

Scraps of rock began detaching from Niobe's splintering block and became skeins of mist, which floated away into the dead atmosphere of the chamber.

The block shattered. Niobe's limp form pitched off the breaking rock and dropped sharply, her tethers freed from the anchor point. With a guttural cry of effort, Fithvael dug his heels in and dragged at the rope, arresting her fall in an abrupt jerk so that she swung like a pendulum beneath the block that supported him. Teeth gritted, he nearly slithered off the rock himself.

Gilead fell. He spread his arms and tumbled in the cold air, turning like a leaping salmon. He half-landed on a block forty feet below, but the impact twisted it around like an ice floe in fast moving water and he fell again.

Darkness rushed up. Then he landed, square and hard, on a blackened platform, crushing the mouldering bones tethered there.

Fithvael hauled Niobe up and onto his own block and then peered down.

'Gilead! Gilead!'

A moment's silence, then Gilead's voice floated up.

'I'm alive. Take the maiden. Make for the doorway.'

Sparks of light flickered in the icy darkness of the vault. In freeing Niobe, they had broken a link in the magical chain, disrupting the workings of the vast arcane mechanism Lord Ire had constructed.

There was a low rumbling. Screams shuddered across the vastness as some of the enslaved beings woke up and realised their nightmares were real.

With Niobe over his shoulder, Fithvael crossed back from rocking plinth to rocking plinth, towards the doorway. He could almost smell magic now, torn, broken magic. He was breathing hard. Each leap was an effort.

He reached the solidity of the threshold and set Niobe down. She moaned softly in her sickly slumber. Fithvael looked back across the chamber. There was no sign of Gilead. The lights were still sparking in the darkness, and incandescent vapours were pouring from the altar far away.

'Gilead?'

'Your hand!'

Fithvael looked down and saw Gilead scaling the bruised rock face below the threshold, clinging to every scrap of purchase. He reached down and hauled Gilead up over the lip.

SWORDS DRAWN, THE old comrades made their way back through the impossible halls of the fortress. Gilead carried Niobe. Hearts in their mouths, they expected discovery at any moment, but the place seemed empty. No one barred their way.

OUTSIDE, A STORM raged, lashing the ancient forest. The elves could not deduce whether it was day or night, but the sky was mirrored black, seething with curls and blooms of cloud. Spears of lighting jabbed down at the high walls of Lord Ire's bastion. The rain was like a veil. They staggered through it, boots mired in the filthy mud, until they found their terrified horses, tied up in the glade beyond the limits of the stronghold.

Gilead cradled the slender form of Niobe against his chest while Fithvael prepared a bed for her in the shelter of the trees. When it was done, he sought fresh herbs with which to treat her. He could find none; plants of health and healing could not grow in this place, and so he had to make do with the dried provisions he had packed some months before.

After some hours, the rain began to ease off. A pale greyness filled the sky. Fithvael lit a fire and revived the dried herbs in a little of the elven wine they kept in the single wineskin that remained from the stocks they had packed at Tor Anrok.

'You may have killed her,' said Fithvael.

'Not I,' retorted Gilead. 'That terrible place maybe.' He spat in disgust, the taste and smell of Lord Ire's residence returning sharply to his mouth

'Indeed, Gilead te tuin,' Fithvael placated. 'She surely would have perished if she had stayed in that place, but I fear I should warn you that we might have... have hastened her end anyway.'

'How so?' asked Gilead, watching Fithvael prepare his potions in the pestle and mortar that he always kept with him.

'The Lady Niobe sought you out and drew you to her. Her voice, you said. Like a hook in a fish's mouth. She pulled you in, first through this miserable forest and then through the insane architecture of that palace.'

Fithvael rinsed clean rags in a little more wine and wrapped his herbal potion in them to form a poultice for Niobe's chest before setting water to boil for a reviving infusion. He looked up at his companion. 'You and she have become one in a profound way. Because of the link she wrought with you, your hearts beat in time, your souls overlap. What she feels you feel, and vice versa. Your actions affect her life force.'

'And that would kill her?' Gilead asked.

'She's weak, and yet her body had no choice but to mirror yours when you were shadowfast,' answered Fithvael. 'It may have been too much for her. I don't know if she can survive so fierce an assault on her body.'

Gilead slumped to the ground, heedless of where he sat, and dropped his head into his hands. 'Am I so cursed,' he said, 'that I lose one twin and then kill another who twins herself to me?'

Then he looked up sharply. Fithvael was amazed to see a smile on his rain-streaked face. 'No,' Gilead answered himself, 'if my bond with her is so great that my strength injures her... then she has that strength to heal her too!'

Fithvael nodded at the logic. 'Maybe–'

'Damn your "maybe", Fithvael! You know I have it right! If I am calm, restful, if I gather my strength, then by our bond she has no choice but to recover too.'

'No choice?' Fithvael smiled. 'You're going to order her back to health?'

Gilead told Fithvael what he thought of that in no uncertain terms. He rose and walked slowly and surely through the forest, making circles around the camp that Fithvael had built. He breathed steadily, made no sharp moves, and focussed upon the heart of himself. He felt strong. He was strong. He held on to that feeling and watched the day grow dim as he cast his thoughts on Niobe and tried to walk her back to health.

FITHVAEL TENDED THE limp form of the elf maiden for three days, watching over her. Gilead amazed him with his determination to play his part in the healing process. Fithvael found his old friend more eager to take sustenance regularly and exercise gently, although he could not convince the elf warrior to sleep.

By the end of the three days Gilead had almost walked himself into a trance. He tried not to think about the place they had been in or what had been done there lest it affect Niobe.

He tried to think only of Tor Anrok when it was alive with his family, when Galeth had been by his side, and his father had ruled their estate. When Fithvael had been a youthful and faithful guard. When the chamberlain Taladryel had advised and coached the twin heirs of Lothain. When Nithrom, that great elven warrior, had played at sparring with him in the courtyard. He retold the old family stories in his head, letting Niobe into the best parts of his past. He could feel her deep in some recess of his mind, listening.

As they ate by the fire at the end of the third day, Gilead suddenly heard a soft voice in his head again. He pushed away his plate and went across to where Niobe lay on a bed of bracken under his red cloak.

When she awoke, Gilead was standing guard over her. She looked up at him and smiled.

'I know you, Gilead te tuin Lothain, last lord of Tor Anrok,' she said and closed her eyes again.

Gilead slept that night as he had not slept in years. He slept as he had once done after a long day playing and fighting with his brother. He slept like a tired, happy boy.

It was five full days after the rescue before Niobe woke for any length of time. She ate a little, said less, and slumbered a lot, accepting the ministrations of Fithvael with grace and gratitude while watching Gilead's every move with tired, delighted eyes.

TEN DAYS AND ten bleak nights passed without incident. Fithvael became concerned; their good fortune could not last much longer. They were in the dark heart of the Drakwald, the most dangerous and unpredictable region of the lands the humans called their Empire. Why had there been no beastmen? Why had there been no vengeful attack from the Chaos lord? The veteran elf was eager to move on and began to break camp on the morning of the eleventh day.

'She is well enough to travel with us,' Fithvael explained to Gilead. 'And in this place, to travel is safer than to rest in one place for too long.'

'Of what do you speak?' They both glanced around in surprise at the lilting, feminine tones. Niobe was sitting up, regarding them.

'Of leaving this place for another,' said Fithvael. 'It is no longer safe here for us. We have stayed as long as we should.'

'Then it is done,' she said, smiling and lying back. 'Lord Ire is destroyed.'

Fithvael looked to Gilead, and Gilead shook his head and walked away. The older elf made Niobe comfortable and then followed his friend a little distance into the forest. Gilead would not say what he needed to say in front of the elf maiden.

'Niobe called me, and I answered her call. She is released from that disgusting place and we will not return.'

'Then you will deceive her,' answered Fithvael. 'But she knows you, Gilead te tuin. She's in there,' he added, tapping Gilead's brow. 'If she knows you then she will find this deception out.'

Gilead shook his head. 'If her purpose was to destroy this Lord Ire then she will be disappointed.'

'Where are your wits, friend?' Fithvael scoffed. 'I thought you said you knew this maid, knew her by that intimate bond she fashioned. She did not call you for her own selfish reasons, nor would have put our lives in danger simply for the sake of her own.'

'Meaning?'

'She thinks you are a great hero, fool. She called you to put an end to Lord Ire for the good of all those he has enslaved! It's as plain as a rune on a white stone! Rescuing her – only her – was not the point of this.'

THEY RODE THROUGH the morning and stopped by the shores of a dank woodland mere where bottle-green dragonflies shivered between the bone-white reeds. Niobe sat on the salt-grass, twisting old twigs into a bare garland wreath, and told her story to them at last.

Gilead barely needed to listen. The images she shared with his mind had already told the tale so vividly. Gilead felt her revulsion of Lord Ire as though it were his own; he felt her pain as she exposed the fell lord's dark design.

'Lord Ire, who rose to power in some unnameable domain lost to Chaos, where he rules as a demi-god over the subhuman spawn that lurk there, has long looked on this warm, lit world with envy. I think he may have been human once, many ages ago before he meddled with sorcery and forbidden necromantic lore and was cast out into the pitiless wastes of Chaos far north of here. Some vestige of that humanity remains, and it makes him yearn to possess this he left behind. He has but one purpose.'

As she spoke, pictures of the tall man with the mane of glossy hair and the grey garb came clearly into focus in Gilead's mind. He shuddered.

'Ire means to invade this warm world. He has marshalled great forces of destruction in his forsaken domain, raised up engines of war. He has made pacts, I believe, with the true lords of ruin, the foul daemons who fill the outer voids with their insane howling. He is their instrument. His plan pleases them and they have given him power to fashion a gateway, a gateway between this mortal world and his own diseased kingdom. But to keep the gateway open takes power, vast resources of magic.'

'Hence the slaves,' muttered Fithvael.

'Exactly, Fithvael te tuin.' Niobe smiled softly, though her slender face was still pale and drawn. 'Creatures with magic in them, whether they knew it or not. Beings of every race, breed and kind. Creatures like me. He stole us from our lives, often in bloody raids mounted by his bestial warriors, and harnessed us to the gateway. Through the tethers, our magic was milked away to feed the Cipher.'

'What is that?' asked Gilead sharply, but he knew. The monstrous thing on the altar was vivid in his mind.

'His pet, his servant? I don't know, except that, bloated with stolen magic, it keeps the gate open for him. And through that gateway, his invading army will come.'

'None of it is truly real though, is it?' Fithvael asked uncertainly. 'His bastion, all the rest? It was like a dream place. An illusion.'

'It's real enough – in his benighted realm. What you saw, what you fought your way into, was… like a ghost of it, an echo of his fortress projected here into this world through the gateway. It grows more real with each passing day. Soon it will be more here than there, solid, physical, impregnable. Then its doors will open.'

Gilead cleared his throat. What he was about to propose flew in the face of his entire being. 'We… we could warn the humans. Take word to the leaders of this… this Empire of men that claims the land here.'

'And they would believe the words of an elf? A thing stepped from the shadows of their folk-tales?' Fithvael almost chuckled at Niobe's words.

'They have fought off invasions before!' Gilead snapped. 'Their armies are not without strength…'

Niobe nodded. 'Many invasions, indeed. But every one of them assaulted the human territories from outside, from the fringes and borders. This comes from within. Imagine how long proud Tor Anrok would have stood if Chaos had welled up within the throne room itself.'

Fithvael sighed. 'So you are saying that we must go back – and close the gate?'

'Yes, Master Fithvael. That is so. Go back and close the gate.'

Gilead rose, shaking his head. He remembered how hard he had fought to destroy but one plinth out of the hundreds of thousands in that place. He knew that he could not liberate so many beings, even if he had ten lifetimes in which to do it.

'We could not free them all,' said Gilead tersely.

'No indeed,' said Niobe, 'but we could close the gate.'

The emphasis she placed on the word 'could' chilled both the warriors.

She brushed out the creases in her dirty gown. 'In Talthos Elios, my father raised me to honour the old pledge. The pledge our kind made in the last years, as our numbers dwindled and we retreated from the world that had been ours. We may regard them as a crude, ignorant child race, but the humans are our heirs to this land. My father taught me to honour mankind, with my life if needs be. Our time has gone, my friends. The world is newer and sparer than we in the days of our forebears.

'There is a term the lords of Bretonnia use: "noblesse oblige". I see from your faces you know what it means. We owe our heirs. My magic was stolen and used to further the foul strategies of the Ruinous Powers. I would gladly give my life to destroy that gateway.'

'Suicide,' muttered Gilead.

'No, my lord – *honour*. We must honour our legacy. And to honour that, we do not free one slave, but allow a thousand to die if it means that Lord Ire's twisted gateway dies with them.'

Fithvael looked at Gilead, but the elf warrior said nothing.

'You want us to kill them all? All the slaves?' asked Fithvael.

'I do not know,' answered Niobe, looking around at them both. 'But I know that Lord Ire has only one weakness.'

'Then tell us,' Gilead said in a flat tone.

'I saw something in Lord Ire's mind, but I dared not dwell there, lest the Chaos filth infect me. I have no answer except that he knew there was a weakness, and that weakness was his son.'

'His son?'

'He has a son. It is his only vulnerability.'

A long, desolate silence hung over them all.

'Will you help me? Will you do it?' asked Niobe after a while.

Gilead dropped his chin, not wanting to meet her gaze. 'I think not,' he said.

GILEAD ROSE FROM beside his friend and the woman he now believed he loved, and walked away from them. Fithvael stumbled to his feet and followed him, calling out to him as he strode away.

'Gilead! Lord! Will you deny your duty?' he called, but the elf did not turn back.

Fithvael quickened his pace until he was right behind Gilead and, reaching out a hand, he turned him roughly by the shoulder.

'Tell me to my face! Tell me that you are going to walk away from this. Do you not remember Galeth and the ten year quest that brought you to his killer? Do you not remember the years you drank away in the ruins of Tor Anrok, miserable to your marrow? It was your sense of duty that saved you from ruin, your duty to a human. The Ziegler child! Remember her? Oh, I had to punch it into your dulled brain to make you realise… gods, I had to come near losing my own life! But you saw it by and by. Our time has come and gone, Gilead Lothain. It hurts, but it is so. We have nothing left but what we leave behind now. This is your destiny, my friend, our destiny. Don't deny it now.'

'And if I were to lose Niobe?' asked Gilead.

'My friend, if you do not do this thing, then she will surely be lost to you anyway! And if you cannot bear to destroy Lord Ire for the good of humankind, then do it for Niobe and for yourself.'

'And you?' asked Gilead.

'I'll be going anyway. But I'd do better with you at my side. You, Gilead were bred to fight. That's how Cothor raised you, that's why Nithrom trained you. A warrior, of Tor Anrok, of the old kind that is passing away. It is your life's blood. If you deny all else, you cannot deny that.'

Gilead stared at him. For a long moment, Fithvael expected to be struck. Furious pride pinched Gilead's face. The last lord of Tor Anrok glanced away at Niobe, watching them from the water's edge, and then looked back at Fithvael.

'Let us go and do this thing,' he said at last. 'But milady stays here.'

'But we need her, Gilead. Only she can guide us in, only she can trace this son of Ire. If we go… when we go, she surely comes with us.'

NIGHT FELL, COLD and dank beneath the lowering trees. Fithvael checked his weapons and the field pack that he always carried, replenishing what stocks he could and ensuring everything was clean and dry. He also packed restorative herbs for Niobe, whom he recognised was still fragile.

Gilead checked his weapons, ensuring his quiver was full and his bow strung to tension. Most importantly, he spent some time with his sword and dagger, cleaning them and honing their blades to bright, hard cutting edges. He laid his fingers, for a moment, on the elven runes that decorated the steel and thought of Tor Anrok and the ideals his family had always lived by. He wiped mud from his long, narrow warshield. Then he buckled himself into his leather armour and slung the quiver and shield in a cross against his back.

It was time.

Niobe had prepared herself. She had tied back her long hair, and cut off the hem of her gown above the knee so she could run and move without hindrance.

She was so beautiful, Gilead's throat caught.

'Why so sad, tuin?' she asked, handing Gilead back the long leaf-bladed knife he had lent her to cut away her dress.

'Not sad, just… ready. You keep that.'

'I was raised with many skills, Gilead, but warfare was not one of them. Take back your dagger.'

'No, Niobe. Tuck it in your belt. You may have need of it tonight. Thrust with it, don't slash. And don't hesitate.'

She slid the blade under her leather girdle. 'As you wish, tuin. Teaching me now, are you?'

'If it keeps you alive, I will thank myself at least.' He paused. A stale moon had risen, and the trees cast long, mournful shadows across them.

'What?' she asked.

'What happens to us… afterwards?' he breathed.

'Afterwards?' Her vivacious smile lit up her face. She pushed at him playfully. 'Let us pray there is an afterwards.'

'There will be.'

'Such optimism, Gilead.'

'One of my better qualities,' he lied. Nearby, Fithvael snorted.

Niobe laughed. 'Cothor Lothain sired a beautiful son… even when he is lying.'

'You didn't answer my question,' he persisted.

She reached out and touched his temple gently. 'I have been in here a long while now. We are bound together,

Gilead. Whatever happens tonight, that bond will remain. I swear to you.'

Shaking, he took her in his arms and as long as their precious kiss lasted, the danger seemed far away.

Fithvael looked away and busied himself settling the horses. They were loaded and ready for the ride out of the forest. He would leave them loose-tethered, anticipating a hurried getaway.

THE THREE OF them clasped hands in the moonlit glade. A silent pact, done in the old manner. Then, side by side, the elves strode away into the whispering forest, towards the great, ghostly bastion of their foe.

An hour passed, and they met nothing. For most of that hour, the three had been able to walk abreast. Once or twice they had to proceed single file and when they did so, Gilead drew his sword and took the lead, with Fithvael bringing up the rear. But even on these narrow tracks all was calm and quiet.

'We must stop,' Fithvael said suddenly. 'Something is amiss.'

Gilead turned to him. 'I hear no threat. All is calm and well. Fithvael, you jump at shadows.'

'No,' replied Fithvael, unslinging his crossbow and winding up its tension. 'Does it not concern you that there are no shadows to jump at? This is the Drakwald, a place of terror, of beasts, and yet we walk through it as though it were the playground of our youth.'

Gilead looked around and into the night sky, through the canopy above them, tensing as he realised that Fithvael was right.

'Do you sense anything?' he asked Niobe.

'The forest is full of menace, but a little mind magic can drive off a legion of ignorant creatures,' Niobe replied with a knowing smile.

Gilead and Fithvael stared at her. It was obvious now: their safe passage had been secured by Niobe, using all the power of her magic to seek out the beasts and monsters of the forest, and to plant images in their feeble minds, distracting them from the trio's scent.

'We are safe because of you?' Fithvael asked.

'For now,' Niobe answered softly. 'When we reach the portal

my powers will be exhausted and confused by the corruption there.'

'Lock away your magic,' Gilead told Niobe gently. 'Don't let Lord Ire get a hint of it. What we meet here, we will deal with.'

He took out his blue-steel sword.

'As you wish,' she nodded.

STARLESS NIGHT ENCLOSED them now, cold and murky. They started at every crack and rustle in the thickets around them. They'd gone perhaps a half mile when she suddenly froze.

'To the left! It's... it's...'

As she stammered, Gilead unsheathed his sword in one fluid movement, the rotten stench of Chaos suddenly heavy on the air.

A huge beast charged into the narrow clearing, sheering off lengths of cracking wood from the trees and shrubs as it broke cover. The creature was the size and stature of a stag, with a pattern of mottled grey and black in its coarse fur. Its cloven hooves grew from thick powerful ankles and were a foot across, dividing into dull, horny toes. The back legs of the animal were shorter than the forelegs and the tail was vestigial, like that of a goat. The monster pawed the ground, scoring a deep groove in the rotting ground, while it raised a pair of powerful humanoid arms that grew on either side of a barrelled chest.

Gilead saw in a moment that the beast's arms ended in muscular hands, each equipped with two, single-jointed fingers, echoing its cloven hooves. A black, calloused thumb completed the hand that was grasping a crude but massive crossbow, with a bolt almost the size of Gilead's forearm already fixed in position.

The stag's neck was as broad as a man's chest and above it rose a half-human head, perched there incongruously, narrower than the throat and peaked with a single wide, curved horn.

The beast-thing growled as it made to loose the bolt straight at Gilead, who dived in a feinting pattern first right, then left. The huge bolt whistled a high-pitched scream as it cut the air. It missed Gilead by inches as he rolled and defended his body with his shield.

The bearded head of the Chaos beast seemed to chuckle, making a throaty braying sound as it slid another bolt into the housing on the crossbow.

Gilead's view of the beast was head on and at close range. He saw nothing above its flexed, upright neck and head, concentrating only on the immediate threat.

Fithvael, a few yards to Gilead's right, had a different view, and for a split second he was mesmerised by what he saw.

Upon the back of the stag-thing sat a second monstrosity. The beastman sat astride the creature on a bulky saddle made from pitted green leather. Huge, flat stirrups cut from the same material hung right up against the lip of the saddle, cupping the rider's paw-like club feet. Its legs were short and malformed, the thigh bones twisting into the swollen knees.

The rider's body also seemed too short and too wide, consisting only of a torso without waist or abdomen. By contrast, its arms were long and powerful, and its shoulders high and strong. The monster's head was human in form, but ugly and bulbous, covered in warts and almost toothless and it rested between the bulky shoulders without a neck. The rider held a cleaver in one huge hand and a flail in the other, and its face broke into a toothless grin as it swung the pair of weapons in small, interlocking circles across its body, preparing to bludgeon and tear them all limb from limb.

Gilead ducked the second bolt, which landed squarely in a tree trunk behind him. Two-thirds of the bolt's length protruded from the far side of the trunk. The elf drove forward, low to the ground, and brought his sword up under the stag's chest, using the momentum of his short charge to drive his blade at the creature's heart. The sword penetrated half a dozen inches and then hit bone with a force of impact that made it stop dead. The warrior elf tried to wrench the sword out of the bloodless wound, but the blade was stuck fast.

The stag-thing dropped its crossbow. It reached out for the elf's neck with its huge deformed hands.

Still holding onto his sword hilt with one hand, Gilead grabbed for his long dagger. But the scabbard was empty. He had given it to Niobe. He threw himself down, rolling to avoid the stamping hooves.

'Gilead!' Niobe cried, already knowing what he needed, and threw the dagger across the glade.

He caught it and slashed up into the arm that reached for him. He ripped into muscle and tendons, exposing bone and sinew. There was no blood, no ichor, no body fluids at all.

Drawing two weapons himself, Fithvael drove forward to attack the godless creature that straddled its bestial steed. He struck first with the tip of his sword, swiping it along the creature's thigh and tearing a jagged wound there, which quickly filled with yellowish black, oozing liquid. The downward sweep of the stroke allowed him to drop his head and shoulders, ducking the creature's studded flail as it swept towards his face.

Fithvael took heart that the beast was undisciplined in its use of the flail and kept his position, rising again to drive his sword at the monster's chest. The flail came once more, wrapping its coarse black chain around the blade of Fithvael's sword. With a whipping action of his wrist, the veteran elf freed his blade and sent the flail swinging back toward its master. It thudded heavily against the beast's chest, but the thing seemed not to notice as it brought the weapon over its shoulder in another ragged swing.

Fithvael sliced another chunk from the monster's leg, carving into the knee and almost separating the foot completely. The beast responded by turning its body in the saddle and bringing a heavy cleaver down in a strong, accurate swing that took Fithvael by surprise. The elf fell to his knees to avoid the blade, regaining his feet quickly before the beast could bring his weapon back into play.

Gilead freed his sword and rolled onto his back on the ground, beneath the stomping hooves of the stag-thing. From his new position, he swung his sword again, slicing into the join where the beast's foreleg met its body. The dry wound gaped down at the elf, but the rhythm of the monster's hoof beat did not change.

This time Gilead drove his long blade up towards its chest at an angle, aiming for the throat with his dagger. He found a space between the great, barrelling ribs and thrust his sword home to the hilt, and then he twisted left and right and withdrew the weapon. At the same time, he drove his dagger into the beast's throat, disabling its braying voice and opening a ragged hole in its airway.

His work done, Gilead stepped back and watched the stag-thing trying to breathe through the hole in its throat. The tissue around the tear flapped in and then out again. The monstrosity tried to bring its crossbow up once more, but the hand on the end of the torn arm shook and could not find a place for the bolt.

Fithvael rose to his full height and lunged his sword at the mounted creature's torso. The blade of the cleaver parried Fithvael's lunge and the elf's arms received a heavy jolt before he could bring his sword around. Fithvael cursed, span back and impaled the rider on his sword in a single, fluid motion.

The bloodless stag dropped to its knees slowly and keeled over, still clutching its crossbow in its one good hand. As it tipped forward, its rider was thrown against its neck and Fithvael was able to withdraw his sword and plunge it in again. The rider toppled from its mount and dropped its weapons, lifting itself upright on its fists and using them like feet to make its escape.

Gilead nocked an arrow at a distance of fifteen or twenty yards from his target and finished the beastman off with one well-aimed shot through the head.

Fithvael dusted himself off and sheathed his sword with a sigh of relief. The two elves made their way back to Niobe, leaving the carcasses in the forest behind them.

THE TRIO HAD continued their journey only a few hundred yards further when Niobe brought them to a halt.

'We have arrived,' she said, turning to face Gilead and Fithvael. 'How do you wish to proceed?'

Fithvael looked over her shoulder as she faced them.

'I see nothing,' the veteran elf said. 'Where is Lord Ire's castle?'

Niobe turned slowly until she was facing the same direction as her companions, and in the haze before her Fithvael and Gilead saw the vast outline of the Chaos champion's castle take shape, shimmering into vision from amidst the forest nightmists. 'You see it only through my eyes,' explained Niobe, 'but do not doubt that it is here.'

THIRTY PACES FROM the monumental facade of the castle, a long, low ramp began to rise out of the swampy ground, leading to a portcullis in the centre of the great wall before them.

'A welcome,' Gilead said coldly. 'More then we were granted last time.'

'It's simply an entrance hidden from all but those who have the magic to see it,' answered Niobe. Her light, confident manner belied her fear. The rank stench of Chaos permeated the air they breathed and the earth on which they stood, and she felt it more acutely than her companions. But she had Gilead's strength to draw upon, and in return he had at least a taste of her magic powers.

As they approached the portcullis, Niobe found her way to the head of the group, stopping only yards from the heavy, grilled entrance. The square spaces in the otherwise solid structure began to throb and warp, until a narrow gap opened wide enough for the three elves to step through.

'How do you shift reality so?' Fithvael asked in wonder.

'Because it isn't reality,' answered Niobe, simply. 'Not yet, anyway. It's growing ever more solid, but it's still illusion, an afterimage of the real bastion in Ire's domain, projected here. I can expose it, show it to you. All the while it is insubstantial, neither truly here nor there, I can work upon the illusions and shape them to our own purposes.'

'But this place is evil,' said Fithvael, struggling to understand her skills and how they might be used.

'Evil, yes,' said Niobe. 'This place is thoroughly corrupt because the magic is manipulated by darkest evil, but believe me when I say that magic power by itself is not evil.'

They stepped into a long, wide space that might have been called a great hall. Bolted doors ran along the walls, at a variety of heights, leading, Gilead supposed, into rooms beyond. Passageways led off in other directions, and staircases, ascending and descending at impossible vectors, seemed to add another, unwholesome dimension to the three that were naturally invested in the space.

Niobe made only the briefest examination of the topography before leading Fithvael and Gilead on through the draughty hallway and up a staircase that had seemed a moment before to be plunging into the bowels of the castle.

Another moment or two, and they stepped through into a huge, cuboid area, which appeared to have been wrought from some metal, pewter perhaps. Where walls, floor and ceiling met each other, the joints were invisible. The walls had a beaten, matt finish, without windows or doors, or any other visible entrances or exits. The light that fell across them was even and cast no shadows. Worryingly, there was no obvious light source.

Gilead and Fithvael raised their swords as a foul smell began to leak into the room out of nowhere.

'Ire–' Niobe gasped.

A figure stepped out of shadows and it seemed to grow in stature as it strode toward them. It filled the space, and the space expanded to suit the growing stature of the man. The cube-shaped metal chamber had been perhaps ten paces in all directions, but was now a hundred feet across every measurement.

'More space for me to work in,' said Gilead aloud, staring into the unknowable divided face of Lord Ire.

Gilead and Fithvael lowered their stances in an aggressive posture.

As if mocking the very sight of them, Lord Ire threw back his head and let out a sound that might have been a laugh, but that seemed to echo round his huge body before escaping through his divided mouth.

'Now!' shouted Gilead, his voice sounding like music after Lord Ire's extraordinary bellow.

Gilead and Fithvael circled and lunged around Lord Ire, but as they did so the room began to move on some invisible axis, tipping the floor and turning the walls. The elves were disorientated, and their feet faltered as they looked about them for a solid flat surface.

There was none.

Gilead could no longer see Niobe, but he could hear her sweet tones in his mind. 'Shake off the illusion! It's in your mind. He owns this place and he will use it, but it is as nothing if you deny it!' she instructed him.

He watched Fithvael drop to one knee as the room rocked and turned about them.

'It's mere illusion, Fithvael!' he yelled. 'Block it out!'

The warriors lunged at Lord Ire again. Again the room rolled and twisted, but this time Gilead and Fithvael kept their feet.

Lord Ire drew his sword. It was long and broad, but the Chaos lord held it in one hand, flicking casual figure-eights around his body.

Fithvael stepped in to parry the first lunge of the fearsome weapon, but he was swatted off his feet as if he had been made of paper. Lord Ire swung again at Fithvael, and the elf dropped and rolled. The huge blade struck the pewter surface, sending blue-white sparks flying.

Gilead lunged at Lord Ire, slashing back and forth, but the monster's slate armour denied all his blows with ease.

As the three fought on faster and harder, the room spun more violently, pivoting and wheeling on a set of invisible axes. Gilead and Fithvael kept their feet throughout, both now fighting head on with Lord Ire. The Chaos lord slipped around their attack and brought his sword down towards Fithvael, slicing into his right shoulder before Gilead could block it.

Slumping to his knees, Fithvael lost his concentration and rolled helplessly around the revolving cube. Gilead watched his faithful friend fall and saw him tossed heedlessly around the metal box.

'Illusion! It's all illusion' Gilead yelled, but Fithvael still slammed remorselessly around the turning pewter box of the room.

'Fithvael!'

Fithvael disappeared.

'Where is he? What did you do to him, corrupt scum?' Gilead cried, throwing himself at the chuckling nightmare. Lord Ire threw him aside.

But Gilead was not be denied. Suddenly shadowfast, he became a twisting blur, thrusting and lunging, chopping and slashing with his blade. The room spun and bucked but Gilead unconsciously did as Niobe was instructing him: he ignored the illusion and focussed only on Ire.

NIOBE WAITED IN the small dark space with Fithvael.

It was an antechamber, though beyond that small fact, she had no idea where she was. By force of will, she had taken Fithvael and herself out of the rocking metal cube.

'Hold still,' she hissed.

'It hurts!' Fithvael protested as she bound up his wound.

'Of course it does! Hold still!'

'Where is Gilead?'

LORD IRE GATHERED an echoing bellow in his gut and let it out in a long, rolling sound that filled the space around Gilead. The last son of Tor Anrok had just slashed his blade through the metal guard covering the dead eye on the subhuman side of Ire's twisted face.

Gilead seized the advantage and danced in again, moving so fast now that the room seemed to have come to a lightly vibrating standstill. Whether it was the speed that Gilead had generated or the savage wound that Lord Ire had sustained, the elf warrior began to see something very different before him. The dark champion began to lose his shape and form, blurring at the edges. His form flowed for a split second into an amorphous pulsing mass, before returning unsteadily to his former, humanoid shape.

NIOBE STARTED. She had seen Ire as Gilead had seen him, and the truth made her cry out.

'What is it?' asked Fithvael, his voice dulled by pain.

'The son... I have seen the son...'

NIOBE LED FITHVAEL back through a nightmarish maze of passages, until at last they arrived once more at the vast chamber where the slaves were tethered.

'Why have you brought me here?' Fithvael asked as Niobe looked around.

Her voice was assured. 'Do not mourn them, Fithvael te tuin. They will welcome death if it brings relief from this existence. Whether they live or die, you will have saved them. And live or die you will have saved humankind from a far worse fate than this.' She believed what she said and the elf warrior believed it too, but a tear still found its way down the perfect contour of her cheek.

'So which of these poor souls is the son of Ire?' Fithvael asked, readying himself for the most distasteful kill of his career. He had slain many in battle, but to destroy a poor soul tethered lifelessly to a yoke solely to provide magical energy, that was murder and it held only disgust for him.

'None of them,' answered Niobe.

'Then I ask again,' Fithvael said sternly, 'why have you brought me here?'

Niobe turned and looked down at the altar below them, at the innumerable strands plugged into the vast square rock and at the shifting patterns of Chaos runes squirming on its surface. She pointed, for she could barely speak.

'The altar. The thing on the altar,' she breathed.

'What thing?' asked Fithvael, whipping his head around to get another look at the abomination far below.

And he saw it. For the first time, he realised that there was something on top of the altar. The sight of the mesmerising runes and the thousands of glistening tethers had drawn his attention away from the dull shapeless top of the altar, but he truly saw it now. A lifeless mass, amorphous and colourless, entirely without form. He saw it because Niobe had seen it.

'That is… the son of Ire?' asked Fithvael, incredulous.

'The Cipher,' said Niobe weakly. 'It collects and controls the magic.' Her voice was broken and her mouth dry. She tried to speak again, Fithvael bent to listen to her.

'It looks like Ire…' she whispered.

'That is what Ire looks like without his illusions in place?' Fithvael said, already raising his sword.

IRE'S GREAT BLADE cut the air and Gilead darted back. The metal box that contained them continued to spin and roll. Gilead swung again, but the monster's blade tip found his cheek and gave him a bloody gash. Gilead fell, and began to tumble as the box rolled.

It was real now, everything was too real.

LEAPING FROM BLOCK to block, Fithvael made his way towards the altar, He knew he had little time.

He leapt down onto the wide ledge of rock that surrounded the monstrosity and the first of the slave guard appeared. There were four of them, variously armoured. They had stone for skin, cracked along the joints and covered in nicks and scratches made by a thousand blades and missiles. When the creatures flexed their bodies their stone skins moved with them, like the hardening crust of a lava flow.

The mutated hellspawn stood four abreast in front of the altar, holding only batons and whips for weapons. They were the slave guard, and had never needed more than those light arms to control their prisoners.

Fithvael did not hesitate. He flew at them, blade swinging.

It merely sparked and spanged off the impenetrable skins of the Chaos beasts.

* * *

IN THE TUMBLING pewter box, Gilead slid down a turning wall and flinched away just in time as Ire's massive blade scored the metal that had supported him.

He tried to gather his wits. Plaintive and far away, Niobe's musical voice still called to him.

'It's all illusion, Gilead… all illusion…'

He rose, his blade clashing with Ire's in a sparking shower of purple light. Again, again a deflection, a parry. Lord Ire's skill with a sword was masterful.

But Gilead had been trained by Nithrom, and the sword he swung had been his brother's. He would not lose this fight.

FITHVAEL SMASHED OPEN the stony hide of the guard nearest him and fell back in revulsion. Underneath the slate armouring the monster's legs was one huge, putrescent wound. There was neither skin nor bone, merely black, decaying flesh and an army of maggots and parasites feasting on the rotting body.

Fithvael drove himself forward, attacking the weakness. He sprayed stinking grubs and ichor all over himself and his blade. The guard toppled and burst at the seams, spewing out a host of foul writing things along with the decayed matter that had once been its guts.

Fithvael leapt past the disgusting remains, dancing between the slashing weapons of the other guards. Above him, at the summit of the alter, the Cipher shifted slightly, as though uncomfortable.

GILEAD SWUNG IN again, and his blade made a gouge in Ire's shoulder guard. 'Hurting yet?' Gilead goaded.

Ire made no answer.

'No matter… I believe I have kept you occupied long enough.'

Lord Ire suddenly froze, and glanced around at something Gilead couldn't see.

'Yes, I think I have…' Gilead smiled.

FITHVAEL RAISED HIS sword and thrust it down into the disgusting amorphous sack that the Cipher. Rank viscous fluid ruptured out all over him and drizzled down the sides of the alter. The corpse-stench was overwhelming.

'Lord Ire!' Fithvael shouted defiantly, his hands still clutching his victorious weapon. 'Your son is dead!'

THE PEWTER ROOM had gone. Lost in a fortress built solely upon dark magic, Gilead murmured Niobe's name and tried to hold on to the last traces of her voice.

REALITY SPLIT APART. They fled amidst the decaying illusion as towers collapsed and a nightmarish storm erupted in the ravaged sky over the bastion. Spurs of magical energy vented into the sky, blowing out sections of wall that were only half-real.

Heading for the gatehouse, Fithvael almost fell into Gilead.

'Niobe? Where is she?' Gilead bellowed. The abused and frustrated forces of Chaos were stripping the place apart around them.

'Did she not return to you?' Fithvael rasped.

Then, amidst the maelstrom, they saw her slight shape, running and dodging towards them through a storm of exploding magical energy.

But the storm had gathered and fashioned itself into a hideous form sixty feet long with a comet-like tail extruding from it into infinity. It was Lord Ire, part angelic human masterpiece, part gelatinous, seething mass, part wind, part grotesque noise; all writhing, clawing, vengeful Chaos.

Gilead reached out to grab her and drag her with them. He took her hand and pulled at her with all his failing strength.

Niobe shivered and convulsed under the force of the sorcerous hurricane – then found herself lifted cleanly out of Gilead's arms. She rose and whirled in the current of air that grasped her firmly in a deadly embrace.

Fithvael looked on, only yards away, yet still out of reach. He watched the great raging force sweep Niobe from Gilead's desperate grip and, embracing her, whirl itself up in an energy tornado that whipped out into endless black space and was gone.

Then night itself came down and combusted the ruins of Lord Ire's bastion into a vast explosion of shockwaves and smoke.

FITHVAEL CAME TO his senses opened his eyes. He stood in their last campsite amidst the midnight trees of the deepest

Drakwald. Two horses stood nearby, heads bent, feeding on what little fresh vegetation they could find.

Fithvael lowered Gilead gently to the ground and, all his energy spent and his will used up, the loyal elf lay down beside his friend.

THERE IT IS, for all its worth. My bitterest tale. I warned you. No happy ending. But still, I have more heroic stories up my sleeve, more triumphant ones.

But this is the story that matters. He lost her. Gilead lost her. She had bound himself to his mind and he let her slip away.

Few get over the death of a twin, but this...

Words fail me. Yes, that's it. Fill my damn glass to the brim. I'm tired of these stories. They take it out of me.

What's that you say? Did he ever find her?

I'm afraid I do not know. I hope so. All I know is what happened next.

IV
Gilead's Path

I fear your dreams. I fear we are too old.

So, you'd know the rest then, would you? The dark times that followed their defeat of Lord Ire and the loss that brought? Gods! Well, then, perhaps another one. I can manage that. Listen well…

From the smoking mere that was all that remained of Ire's illusory bastion, they rode for days, months.

Every morning, they rose to the yellow glow of dawn and directed their course according to the fall of their shortening shadows. At noon, the light was white and clear, and the shadows warm and dappled, and with the light Fithvael's hopes would rise. Then he would see the drop of his friend's head and the white-knuckled grip of his hands on the wear-polished reins of his steed, and he would know that the light would soon fade and the shadows would grow long once more, until there was nothing but darkness again.

Each evening, the diminishing light turned every colour, tone and hue to a dull, uniform grey. That grey was echoed in the pallor of Gilead's face. There was no expression there, save the dark, closed sadness that Fithvael had become accustomed to before, long ago, when Galeth's memory was what drove

Gilead. But his friend's blank eyes held a new pain now, a new yearning.

Fithvael kept pace with Gilead, watching him as the heavy blanket of evening sky turned quickly to become a purple night that drove them to a new campsite and the torture of another sleepless, dreamless nightmare.

Weeks passed and, beneath the worn and weary hooves of their steeds, many miles of thinning black forest and tracts of lush green pastureland were crossed. They brushed the hem of the human world. Gilead loathed the crass man-made patterns he detected in the felling of trees, the cultivation of fields and the construction of their despised towns. He hated the humans for their heavy faces and their dull minds. He hated them for their short lives and their hard hearts. He hated them all.

Above everything, he hated himself for coming near them and among them. He had saved them, though they little knew it. He had saved them and it had cost him everything.

Still they continued, daily, southward.

AT FIRST THEY had buried themselves in the deep of the forests, avoiding the humans, keeping to themselves and looking only to the landscape.

'Tor Anrok survived...'

Fithvael had heard Gilead murmur it a hundred times a day.

'Tor Anrok survived, all those years. How many other fastnesses and refuges of our kind might be out there? Niobe spoke of her home... Talthos Elios. We will find it if it still stands.'

Fithvael's brow would furrow with the pain of watching Gilead on his hopeless quest in this human desert. There were no elves here. There had been no elves here for centuries past. This place was human, so human that the elf was almost a myth, a story told by old men to wandering bards, and by bards to taverns full of wide-eyed, incredulous men and women.

In those first weeks after Niobe was lost, Gilead spoke of looking for her himself. Fithvael had barely the heart to point out the futility. Instead, they looked for any and all signs of elven life. Gilead would see breaks in the landscape that reminded him somehow of the trace of Ulthuan. A low, flickering fire would burn in his eyes and he would dismount, leaving his horse for Fithvael to secure, bent only on what he had seen, or on what he thought he had seen. He would trample through thick undergrowth, scarring his boots and gloves on the spikes and thorns that grew there. He would wade to his thighs in heavy, brackish water with its foul smelling blue and green scum. He would study every stone and rock that stood out from the landscape, looking for signs of their kind. Looking for signs that were not there. That, perhaps, had never been there.

Then Fithvael would watch as the light died and the blank, hollow expression returned to Gilead's face.

Gilead ate only when Fithvael prepared food and forced it upon him. He drank only when his friend offered a full flask. He slept not at all. And if Fithvael slept, he would wake to find Gilead staring into the purple night, living his waking nightmare, wishing only for death or for love. Wishing only for an end. It was as if they were right back at the ruin of Tor Anrok, before Betsen Ziegler's cause had roused Gilead from his wasted misery.

They found nothing.

With every day that passed, with every new landscape they searched, Gilead's desperation increased. He no longer simply examined the streams and rocks and changes in the patterns of the land. He tore and rampaged and desecrated and plundered the land for every clue. He ripped his hands and his clothes, covered himself in filth and stench, and time and again he fell to his knees, his lank, matted, sweat-streaked hair falling across his face, his body wracked with fatigue.

'Galeth!'

Fithvael heard him cry the name and a cold fist would clench in his gut. Gilead cried out in his delirium. Only on the best of these worst of days would he cry Niobe's name.

Fithvael watched and waited as Gilead became more distant, more desperate, thinner and increasingly delirious. He watched and he waited for the time when Gilead would open his eyes and his mind and see that there was nothing here for them. There were no elven relics, no elven homes and there were no elves. This was no place for them to find a home with people of their own kind. This was no place for them at all.

Fithvael had seen the decline before. After Galeth, after the decade-long quest, Gilead had returned home to find that he was the last of his people. He had not only lost his brother and ten long years of his life, he had lost a little of himself, a little of his sanity, and the rest he had buried in a thousand indolent, self-absorbed days and many hundred flasks of liquor. Tor Anrok had crumbled around him, crumbled with him, and been lost.

But with the loss, a tide had turned. Gilead had found a new fight and then another, and with every new cause he fought came the possibility of his death and an end to the pain. Gilead had left Tor Anrok and Gilead was the last of his line. Everything was gone.

Fithvael saw now that Gilead's quest was a vain attempt to restore what he refused to see was lost forever. But as he watched Gilead weaken into madness, destroying his mind and body both in his futile struggle, Fithvael knew that there was no turning from this path.

THE TWENTIETH DAY passed, and the thirtieth, and the lush greens and golds of the days changed to the deep, burdensome hues of the dying season. Gilead saw nothing, but Fithvael recognised the pattern as surely as he recognised the lines coming to his own face. The nights fell faster and lasted longer, but it mattered not to Gilead, whose personal darkness enveloped him more with every passing day.

Fithvael reckoned they were fast approaching the fortieth day since leaving Ire's fastness when, riding again, as they had every day, Gilead abruptly wheeled his steed around in the shaded clearing they had reached. Fithvael thought they were to stop, that for once Gilead might ask for food or drink or some other sustenance. Gilead wheeled again… and again. Fithvael watched his friend make small circles, skinning the clearing of its low grey carpet of fragrant sage and camomile. The circles became smaller until Gilead demanded his steed turn on its hind legs, like a show horse in a parade square.

'GALETH!'

The ground shook with the confused horse's heavy hoof-falls. The air shook with the anguished bellow. Foaming at the mouth, the horse began to ooze long threads and patches of sweat along its flanks and down its neck.

Fithvael drew closer, his own horse pawing the earth and tossing its head with a frightened whinny.

That veteran warrior and faithful friend dismounted and, leaving his horse to trot to a safe distance among the trees, he hunkered his body down into itself, making himself small and unthreatening, and took slow steps towards the unified, terrified, obsessed creature that was Gilead astride his steed.

Drawing low beneath the horse's neck, Fithvael reached out a tentative, ungloved hand and began to make soft, reassuring noises. Not to Gilead, but to the horse.

'Hsssst there. Gentle down, gentle down.'

Sliding his feet slowly forward, Fithvael tentatively rested his hand on the damp, cold neck of the animal as it twisted away from him in its ceaseless quest to tighten the circle it was stamping in the earth.

Fithvael ducked as the horse travelled, bringing his hand up again and again to touch the animal. His breath came soft and even, like no breath at all compared to the snorting, flaring hot nostrils of the troubled beast.

Finally, after a dozen or more passes, time began to slow for Fithvael as he focussed on his task. With every pass he rested his hand for longer on the horse's shoulder or flank, until his hand held contact there, travelling over the beast's trembling, flinching muscles. With every turn the tossing of the horse's head lessened, the tension in its neck fell away, and finally Fithvael was able to take the slackening rein and bring the weary animal to a slow, rocking pace, and then to rest.

Gilead sat in the saddle, completely upright, the stains of his own sweat seeping through his heavy clothes and smearing a darkening V down the back of his scarlet cloak. Sweat ran in long runnels down his cheeks and fell in heavy droplets from the lobes of his pointed ears. Everything that made Gilead himself was lost to Fithvael in that moment. He stepped in front of the bow-headed animal that Gilead still straddled and looked up into a face that he no longer knew, into eyes that he no longer understood. Gilead failed to meet the test. Failed to meet his friend's gaze. Failed.

Still holding the reins firmly in one hand, lest Gilead repeat his madness, or find some new horror to perpetrate on his loyal steed, Fithvael moved to the side of the horse. He took a firm grasp on Gilead's boot. He shoved hard, releasing it from the heavy leather stirrup. Then, lowering his centre of gravity, he slid his feet shoulder-width apart, and braced himself.

Fithvael took a deep breath. Holding it, he cupped Gilead's boot in both hands. Gilead did not move. Freeing his breath in a great, resounding gasp, Fithvael launched Gilead clean out of his saddle and onto the ground with a heavy thud and a heavier winding. Standing and brushing off his hands on the sides of his tunic, Fithvael caught his breath.

'That was for the horse,' he said.

FITHVAEL TORE HANDFULS of long feathery grass from around the bases of the trees across the clearing. When he had a generous fistful he folded the grasses over in his hand to form a firm, but gentle brush. He stroked the long, slender nose of Gilead's steed with one hand, while grooming the neck and shoulders of the beast with his makeshift tool. The horse whinnied lightly and thrust his nose into Fithvael's armpit, breathing regularly now after its ordeal. After working his way thoroughly down both sides of its neck and shoulders, the elf cast aside the used grass, now moist and brown, and began the process again. With fresh grasses, the veteran swordmaster worked his way down the steed's slender forelegs, moving slowly, resting one reassuring hand on the beast all the time, whispering soft noises as he worked.

The animal was exhausted and made no protest as Fithvael began to remove the saddle, working straps and the reins, buckles and fastenings. He could smell the sweet elven sweat of his companion mingled with the sour aroma of the horse's fear. As he lifted the saddle, Fithvael sighed. Around thick, whitening sweat-marks he saw deeper, red abrasions. The smell of freshly stripped, raw flesh filled the air and fat, black flies began to swarm toward the bloody, bruised areas on the horse's back.

With two short clicks of his tongue, Fithvael summoned his own horse from the shade of the trees. It trotted toward the elf and beast, ignoring the heap of flesh, armour and rags that still lay, catatonic and foetally curled in the middle of the clearing.

From the saddlebags on his own horse, Fithvael took boxes and flasks of pungent waxes and oils. He sat on the spongy, moss-covered earth beneath the spreading canopy of a tree and set to work, grinding and pounding using his dagger hilt and a large flat stone he had found in the undergrowth. The two horses stood nearby, nuzzling each other and finding solace in the new-found tranquillity. Fithvael gathered leaves from the ground and scraped the papery red bark from a young tree with his dagger. The air was filled with a sappy fresh smell, mixed with the aromatic musk of well-prepared oils. As Fithvael carried his preparation across the clearing to Gilead's steed, flies buzzed and flitted away from the little wooden bowl cupped in his hands.

Fithvael spread the ointment on the saddle sores, thanking his old gods far away in Tiranoc that his healing extended to elf and beast alike.

The thought made him hesitate and he cast a frown towards the figure that had once been his friend and master, still and broken on the earth.

FITHVAEL SPENT THE rest of the afternoon tending to both of the horses, finding clean water for them and to refill his flasks, and putting them out to pasture among the trees. Relieved of their tack and riders, both horses by turns grazed the undergrowth and paced quietly together. For weeks they had rested only after dark and they felt the relief of a break from the daily monotony. Yet they seemed solemn to Fithvael, watching them at a distance.

The elf warrior made camp, foraged for food and the herbs he would need, roughly cleaned his garments with some of the water he had collected, and as the purple evening spread above him, he built a small fire.

Gilead still did not move. The only sounds were those of the forest all around and the horses resting nearby. Fithvael savoured the solitude all the more, knowing that he must break it soon.

Hours passed and the daylight moved slowly on as Fithvael ate and pondered his next move. He could not go on with Gilead's madness. He needed a plan of his own. The veteran swordmaster doubted, still, that Niobe's home, Talthos Elios, might be found in the south, where for so long humans had lived and reigned. Yet he could not refute that Gilead had sufficient cause, in the first instance at least, to make this journey deep into human territory. If it was so, then south they would proceed, but they must find new ways to trace the old ancestors. The landscape had given them nothing but grief and despair. The landscape had brought on Gilead's madness; a blight consumed his sanity and was never deep beneath the surface of the cheerless, austere elf-lord.

Earlier, in the mauve twilight, Fithvael had thought to leave his master, who no longer deserved his love and trust and obedience. He put the thought from his mind. Their history was too long, too entwined, and Gilead could not survive alone here, not now.

By the last indigo shadows of the evening Fithvael was minded to waken his companion, but the peace was too complete, too sweet without him.

The night came, turning the clearing black, save for the yellow, opaque light around the fire. Fithvael rose and strode over to look down on Gilead, still curled, not moving, but with wide, open, depthless eyes. Old habits and deep-seated loyalty caused the old swordmaster to throw a horse blanket over his semi-conscious friend, but with all that had passed, no amount of fellow feeling could take away the pleasure of his relaxed solitude, and Fithvael left his companion a while longer.

The elf sat through the dark of the long night, watching the fire, glancing occasionally at his friend. By dawn he was preparing the potions and poultices that would bring Gilead out of his strange non-sleep and restore a consciousness that Fithvael could only pray might be undisturbed by the obsessed, delirious behaviour that had grown and matured in the weeks since Niobe had been lost.

WITH THE FIRST strands of daylight marking the horizon with an ochre haze, Fithvael rose and crossed to where Gilead lay. He touched the deep, smooth brow of his friend and tilted his head. He drew his bowl of restorative before Gilead's sightless eyes and then tipped it to his lips. Much of the thick, herbal infusion ran away along Gilead's vice-tight jaw, and Fithvael tilted the elf's head further; if the potion was to work, it must first be imbibed. Two or three spoonfuls made it past Gilead's drying lips, but bubbled back, warm and clear and brown. There was no swallow reflex.

Fithvael began again, tilting Gilead's head on its rigid neck and massaging his exposed throat to promote the swallowing action. Perhaps he had left it too long.

After several minutes, just as Fithvael feared he would have to make more of his potion, Gilead finally gasped a choking gulp. His closed throat gurgled and his neck stretched in a reflexive spasm that showed suddenly in his eyes. Tears came to the corners of those languid, rolling orbs.

His coughing fit at an end, Gilead jumped wordlessly to his feet and cast about him, eyes staring at his unremembered surroundings.

'You are safe, old friend,' Fithvael said softly. 'A minor episode, nothing that a few herbs could not treat.'

Gilead said nothing, but lunged his head and body around in circles, his feet spread apart in an aggressive, attacking posture. His hands searched for the hilt of his blue-steel longsword, which, thank Ulthuan, lay safely in his saddle's scabbard.

Fithvael rose, approaching his over-wrought friend. 'Calm yourself, Gilead. You only need a little rest. Sit with me a while.'

Gilead flailed at him, waving his arms and thrusting one leg out in an uncoordinated kick that all but swung him off his feet.

'Have no fear! It is I, Fithvael, your faithful friend and companion. I would do you no harm.' He stood tall, walking slowly closer, knowing he had nothing to fear from Gilead's exhausted body, wary only of his master's deranged mind. The potion had done its work on the form of the elf, but perhaps not so much on his spirit.

'Galeth!'

With the return of the doleful cry Fithvael's face became stony hard and steel came to his eyes. Enough was enough.

Fithvael drew the short dagger from his belt, the one he had used to collect leaves and scrape bark, and with both hands drawn up and away from his body he made a charge at his erstwhile friend.

'Galeth is dead!'

'Galeth is dead?'

'You are dead!'

'Gilead is dead?'

Fithvael lunged at Gilead with his open, empty hand, more to ward off his friend than attack him. Gilead went wild.

He kicked at Fithvael's open hand, turning his body close to the old elf's. His four-fingered hand struck out to grasp

Fithvael's wrist, but his reach was too short, or too clumsy, and he took the blade of the paring knife firmly in his grip. Fithvael looked down as ribbons of blood, seeming black in the dawn light, streamed from Gilead's hand. But Gilead felt nothing.

Fithvael let go his grip of the knife's turned bone handle, brought his arm back in a short but powerful swing, and connected his bulging knuckles with Gilead's jaw. There was a screech of teeth sliding too tight against each other and the harsh sound of bone on bone. Fithvael shook his hand out with the pain of the blow, but Gilead remained standing, whirling rather, dervish-like and manic.

'Don't make me hit you again, Gilead,' Fithvael spoke, almost to himself. 'For I will, if needs be.'

Fithvael had no need to approach Gilead again, for this time it was Gilead that charged, in a bolting, uncontrolled lurch, head down, feet almost losing their hold of the dew sodden ground. Fithvael turned just before Gilead's crown would connect with the veteran's gut. The veteran swordmaster took Gilead's neck in the crook of his elbow instead, wrenching and turning, pulling the elf off his feet and dropping him on his back in the sappy grass. The scent of bruised camomile filled Fithvael's nostrils. Gilead reached out for the older elf's legs.

Finding himself suddenly on his back, Fithvael hollered, 'Enough!'

But Gilead was nowhere close to having enough. He fought as if for his very soul, in a savage, daemonic way that made Fithvael cringe back. Relieved that Gilead was weak and ill-coordinated, he merely blocked and defended himself against the flailing arms and legs. But only seconds into the brawl he knew that Gilead would go on until exhaustion overtook him – or until Fithvael broke him. Gilead had a long way to go to be sound of mind and body again, and exhaustion now might kill him. Yet Fithvael feared that, with just one more blow, he might kill the elf himself.

As Gilead grappled and pawed at Fithvael's cloak, attempting a stranglehold, his companion curled on his side, bringing his knees up to his chest. He pressed his feet lightly against Gilead's sternum, sensing the thrumming, birdlike heartbeat there, and having found his target, he thrust his legs out to their full extent, grunting a deep exhalation as he heaved.

Gilead's body curled as all the breath was taken from him. Winded, he gasped for air, his eyes bulging, his jaw finally slackening. Fithvael waited as several empty seconds hung in the air. Then it was over. Gilead rolled onto his side, his arms folding tight around his knees, and Fithvael heard the first sob, saw the hitch in the hunched shoulders as the elf warrior's body was wracked with the agony of realisation.

Gilead was awake. For the first time in days, perhaps weeks, Gilead was back.

'Now my work really begins,' Fithvael muttered to the whitening light.

GILEAD SHOOK AND rocked as his friend looked on, preparing further infusions and gently warming the poultices he had made the day before. Finally, Gilead was still, and, for the first time since Niobe had been lost, Gilead actually slept rather than lost consciousness. He slept on as Fithvael ensured his comfort, placing a warm poultice on the back of his neck and a cooling balm on his forehead and wrists.

As Gilead slept on, Fithvael prepared a simple meal – a salad of curative herbs, several patties of unleavened bread, and for himself a pair of small but fat perch lifted in quick hands from a dark stream nearby. When the repast was made and laid out in the small clean dishes that Fithvael carried in his pack, the elf revived Gilead once more, knowing that this time his old master would awaken bewildered but meek and receptive.

FOR ALMOST A week the pair remained in the clearing. They ate and talked and rested, as their steeds relaxed and recovered too. Gilead's horse healed quickly, much faster than his master. On the third day, Fithvael related the incident in the clearing, for Gilead had never lived that day to remember it.

'You did your duty to me and to the horse,' Gilead said sadly. 'I could ask no more of you.'

Gilead's first, faltering words. An apology, perhaps a form of thanks, it mattered little to Fithvael, who had come to expect nothing at all.

'I threw you from your horse for what you did to the beast. And I would do it again,' he answered gruffly.

On the fourth day Gilead was able to walk unaided around the clearing. Reaching full circle he ran a second lap and then a third, exhilarated.

'Sit, Gilead,' Fithvael commanded and the younger elf folded himself back onto the warm ground without question.

'This search. This quest for Niobe, for the old kin, for your salvation – call it what you will. This search: it must end.'

Gilead stared at the veteran elf.

'Or… if we continue, then you must listen to reason. You must begin again, and be led by me.'

SO FITHVAEL VOICED his plan, firmly, without any intention of giving way to the now subdued Gilead. They would continue, but they would find a real trail. They would skirt the human villages and towns, and listen in the darkest corners of ale-houses and taverns to the stories of the local people. They would take their lead from the myths and legends that were told or sung in these alien places. And if they found nothing, their quest must end.

Gilead, now both stronger of mind and sounder of limb, did as he was bidden. The two of them spent the next few days eating, sleeping and exercising by turns. Fithvael talked long into the night of reason and rightness and of the possibility of a futile quest. He did what was in his power to prepare Gilead, knowing that this might be his last chance to save his master from the madness of his tortured mind, perhaps even from death by some senseless suicidal yearning to set things right, to turn back the wheels of time, to restore the noble elves to this land.

ON THE EIGHTH day, Fithvael and Gilead cleared the traces of their camp, saddled their steeds and left the clearing. They were searching now for signs of human habitation and they found them easily, within an hour of their departure.

They exercised great caution at first, entering the outskirts of tiny villages only after nightfall. They sat in the darkest recesses of tiny backrooms where one tapped barrel of ale served all for a week or more and where the food was meagre or non-existent. They covered or bowed their heads and listened to the humans, attuning their ear to the hard, clipped accents of the south, learning as much from tone and cadence as from the words themselves. They listened without talking, drinking a single glass of ale each and leaving, remarked on only as strangers. None had seen an elf in these parts for a hundred years, and none expected to see an elf, so no elf was seen.

Little by little, as the companions moved from village to village and on to larger towns, they began to pick up a trail. The humans loved to hear stories, often pleased with the same legend repeated over and over. Fithvael and Gilead began to see the patterns in the weaving of the human tales. They moved onward as their ears became attuned to the human sounds and their minds became adept at translating the harsh, quick language. Tales of elf towers and great warriors and noble elves, who had helped avert human tragedies, wove together to create an ever-richer landscape of elf habitation of this land. And Gilead had been right: the further south they travelled, the clearer and more regularly came the stories.

BARELY A FORTNIGHT later, Gilead and Fithvael entered what might have been their twentieth tavern. A little larger than the last, they had become increasingly confident of their invisibility to these dull human folk. Fithvael strode to the barrel and plank structure that served as the bar, as Gilead, behind him, turned about looking for a safe, dark corner in which to be seated.

As he turned, he almost struck his head on a broad, dark beam that traversed the ceiling of the low, ochre-washed room, and he instinctively took a half-pace back, stepping right into the path of a serving girl. He lowered his head by instinct as she turned to him to apologise, fearing she had been the clumsy one. Only inches from her, Gilead's eyes fell deep into the swollen cleavage, spilling from the girl's too tight bodice. He thought to look away from her vulgar bulk, the very antithesis of elven beauty, but he could not.

Two or three inches of the cleft between bold human breasts fell sharply into focus as Gilead watch a bead of sweat ripen and run down the sweep of creamy flesh, before becoming entangled in the perfect twist links of a beautifully wrought heavy gold chain. The thin line of sweat caught up with itself and formed a bead again, plump and glistening on the link of the chain before falling to the next, clinging and growing and tumbling again. Time froze in that instant as Gilead's gaze followed the fall of sweat down the chain until it reached the half-buried disc that nestled between the swell of the girl's body and the tight ribbons that traversed the gap where her bodice would no longer meet.

'Ex... excuse me, sir,' she said, trying to turn in the narrow space between stools and tables.

The spell was broken and suddenly Fithvael was at Gilead's side.

'A table, wench?' Fithvael asked, flattening and lowering the timbre of his voice, and using as few of the strange human words as he could.

'Certainly, sir,' she said. Resting her hand on Gilead's flinching arm, she added, 'My apologies, I should had been looking where I was going.' Gilead mumbled something incoherent to her in a singsong tone that made her frown. She removed her hand, looked at him once more as he turned, and then went about her business gesturing at a nearby table as she went.

'Did you see that?' asked Gilead, speaking before he was even seated. 'Did you see?'

'Only that you broke her path and spoke to her. A human. We must be circumspect. We must go unremarked in these places.'

'Fortune favours us now, Fithvael! Did you not see it?'

Fithvael was agitated by the encounter, hoping it had not lasted too long, and that Gilead had not exposed them to recognition. He was eager, now, to leave the tavern at the first opportunity. This was his plan. A plan adopted under duress. A plan that must be followed to the letter, and that meant as little contact with these humans as possible. He looked around him as he sipped at the bitter tasting ale, but very few minutes of surveillance reassured the old warrior that no harm had been done. Cautiously, he turned back to Gilead.

'What was it you saw, old friend,' he asked.

'Around the serving girl's neck. It was the chain at first that drew me, such craftsmanship. But I saw it, I know I saw it.'

'You make no sense. Tell me slowly what it was you saw.'

Gilead took a deep breath and looked solemnly into Fithvael's face, leaning forward across the narrow bench-table, as though telling a secret, or intimating the ghostlier parts of some torrid tale, as the travelling storytellers did.

'I did break the path of the serving girl. And when she turned to me she was standing very close. I cast down my eyes, lest she recognise my race, or question me in any way. And that was when I saw it. I have not seen such a thing these many years. Many times I have thought never to see such a thing again.'

Gilead was in earnest, Fithvael could see it, and there appeared to be no madness in his eyes, only purpose.

'The chain was such as my mother or sister would wear, fine twisted gold links in ranks with gold thread and beads woven between them, intricate as a puzzle. Only one of our own kind would wear so beautiful a jewel. No human would make such a thing, could make such a thing.'

'Such jewels were common among us, but all held a purpose or a promise,' Fithvael said. 'This chain could be a copy of some old design. It has no significance without its seal or talisman.'

'And there it is!' cried Gilead, bringing his fist down, remembering, only at the very last, not to punch the table in his rapture.

Fithvael looked around sharply for the girl, but he could not see her in the now smoky tavern, that throbbed with local life.

'She has a talisman?'

'She wears it against her stinking bosom, tarnishing its significance, as though it were nothing... but that matters not,' Gilead went on, calming himself. 'She surely knows something of us, of our kind. She can help us in our quest.'

Not wanting attention to fall upon himself and his eager friend, Fithvael led Gilead out of the tavern. In the alleyway alongside the rough old building, they talked softly of what they might do to learn where the maid's talisman had originated, but there was no time to decide. Only moments passed before a slight figure, head bowed and covered in a light shawl, entered the alleyway, almost knocking into the elf warriors, then jumping back in alarm. The shawl dropped to plump shoulders and Fithvael caught a glimpse of the chain that circled the girl's short, white neck.

'*Sigmar!*' she exclaimed. 'You quite frightened me.'

'We will not hurt you,' Fithvael said, forgetting to lower his voice, and once again the serving girl frowned and looked harder at the figures before her.

'Who are you?' she asked, taking a pace backwards, pulling the shawl tighter about her neck and hiding again the talisman that lay there.

'We are not what we seem,' Gilead said, stepping forward and making no attempt to hide the cadence of his voice or his alien accent as it rolled over the unfamiliar human words.

'We quest for our own people and we desire your help in our purpose.'

The startled girl tried to back out of the alley, but Gilead was too quick for her, holding her gently but firmly by the arms. The shawl fell away again. Fithvael picked it up from the dusty floor of the alley and wrapped it around her trembling shoulders, taking the chain lightly in his slender hand once it was settled there.

'Where did you find this, child?' Fithvael asked, caressing the delicate chain in his hands.

The girl twisted her fingers into her cleavage and lifted out the thick flat disc that had lain beneath her bodice, brandishing it before her until her knuckles turned blue-white.

'I didn't find it. It protects me from the likes of you. It'll ward off any evils!'

'I know, child,' said Fithvael, losing his hold on the chain and stepping back a little. 'Once, a long time ago, it belonged to one of my kind. It was made for and worn by my kin. A powerful talisman and a great protector, as you say...'

'Yet if you didn't find it, where did it come from?' Gilead stared into the girl's eyes and put a little more pressure into the grip his narrow hands held her in.

'Ouch! You're hurting me,' she cried and tried to turn in what felt to her like a vice.

'Let her go free, Gilead,' Fithvael said in the only language he knew that would ensure his friend did his bidding. Gilead dropped his hands to his side. The girl stood, staring at them both, before looking down at the disc she still held in her hand.

White-faced and trembling, the servant girl hesitated only for a moment before lifting the back of her hair with her short, plump hands, then unclasped the chain and amulet from its place around her neck.

'Th-this m-must belong t-to you,' she stammered, head held

low. She held the talisman out, at arm's length, for Fithvael to accept from her shaking fingers.

Fithvael looked long and hard at the disc on the end of its beautiful chain, turning it in his hands and committing its multiple inscriptions, in the ancient script, to memory. Then he placed the talisman back in the girl's hand again and closed her fist gently around it, his long narrow hand with its elegant fingers engulfing hers in one simple movement.

'No. It belongs to you now,' he said, thrusting one hand back at Gilead for him to keep his silence. 'Tell us only where it came from and what you know of it.'

'And never speak of us,' added Gilead.

'None would believe me,' answered the servant girl, looking into Fithvael's eyes. It seemed she had made her decision. 'Follow me, lords. I know a quiet place where I can tell you all I know.'

IT WAS LATE into the night when Gilead and Fithvael returned to their horses and their camp. The grey-black embers of their banked fire reddened as Fithvael stirred life back into it and by its pale light wrote down the inscriptions he had seen on the talisman.

It was the first solid piece of evidence that could lead them on the right track. With the inscriptions and the story the servant girl had gladly told them, albeit embroidered a little and crudely embellished here and there in the human way of telling and retelling, the elves knew all they needed to know to continue their quest with renewed vigour and determination.

IN THAT PART of the Empire, all roads led to Nuln. From your nod, I see Nuln is known to you.

Keeping to the woodland paths to the north of the trade route from Averheim to that old city, Fithvael and Gilead made good time and were unseen by the human traffic that swelled as it approached Nuln. As the city came into view on the horizon, the companions turned to the west, following the course of the River Reik until they discovered what they were seeking.

From the first, the elves were surrounded by reminders of home. There was no need to forage for the smallest sign, no desperate search for a single stone or plant that might signify an elven presence. The landscape was waist-deep in elf design and culture. The plants were right, the ebb and flow of the land was right, and when they came upon the buildings of Ottryke Manor it was clear to them that every foundation stone had been hewn by elves and placed by elves. Fithvael dismounted and led his horse away to a safe distance amongst the trees. All Gilead could do was stare.

Watching Gilead from cover, Fithvael clicked his tongue twice. Gilead's horse lifted its nose, whinnied gently and turned to look at the veteran elf warrior. Moments later Gilead turned his head and responded to the gesture that Fithvael made to beckon him back into cover.

'We have arrived,' Gilead said, dismounting, 'Do you not see? Elves have been here before us. This was once a great elf dwelling.'

'It surely was,' Fithvael replied, and there was an eager look in his eyes. 'The human maid spoke true.'

I INHERITED THE *talisman. It was a gift to my grandmother, you see. My family worked on the estate of Ottryke, cousin to the Elector of Nuln. My grandmother was a very beautiful woman and a favourite of his Lordship. He gave her the talisman as a forget-me-not, she said, when she married and left his service. In return she sent my mother to work for him in his great house. And she works there still.*

'WE MUST FIND the servant girl's dame,' said Gilead, eyes glistening with anticipation.

'Less haste, lord. Let us first reconnoitre the area. It may be that these humans have no sympathy for our kind after so long a time.'

Gilead demurred, the guilt and shame of his mental lapse still fresh in his mind.

They spent two uneventful nights scouting every inch of the estate, but everything they saw only served to convince them of what they already believed to be true. The humans had built their own great manor on what had once been a large elven estate. The house was oriented in the traditional fashion and even the livestock pens and crop fields followed the classic elven pattern, not to mention some of the architecture – the foundations of most of the larger buildings, external walls, and even some ancient fencing were all elven in design and construction. The signs, hidden in plain view beneath and behind cruder, more recent human constructions, were there to be discovered by any eyes that could see them for what they were.

THE MANOR WAS *built on an elven ruin generations ago. All the family jewels were said to be elf-made, discovered in the grounds years before. My grandmother always wore this talisman for protection against evil. I did not know if the stories were true.*

'HOW ARE OUR visitors?' the lord asked the man who stood before him, his cloth hat being steadily wrung out in his hands.

'The fire has been warm two days now, sire. I haven't seen them yet. They're not there after dark or before dawn, and I dare not seek them in the daylight.'

The audience took place in the lower hall of Ottryke Manor. Lord Ottryke was generally very hard on trespassers and intruders, but the gamekeeper had piqued his interest. These were no poachers – they had killed nothing. And their campsite was too well organised to be run by vagabonds. There was evidence of well tended horses and of thorough meals with elegant cooking utensils. 'Strange and wonderful,' the gamekeeper had described them.

'Very well. You may leave,' said Lord Ottryke. 'Say nothing to anyone.' And with a wave of his bejewelled hand, he dismissed his gamekeeper.

'SOMEONE HAS BEEN here again. A human, no doubt,' said Fithvael, stirring the fire back to life a little after dawn on the third day. 'We must decamp. We place ourselves in danger here.'

'No, Fithvael, we will remain. Some human has seen this place, but none has hunted us or attacked us. They think nothing of our being here.'

'Perhaps they survey us as we survey them.'

'And if they do, perhaps we can help each other. I wish only to find Niobe or traces of any others of our own kind. We have a duty, you and I, Fithvael. It is too long since we knew what it was to be part of something greater, to have a family and our own people around us. What would you not give to have such a thing again?'

'I fear your dreams. I fear we are too old, and have been too solitary for too long to do justice to women and offspring now,' Fithvael said, so low his companion did not hear.

Gilead slept now, even by daylight, when for months he could not sleep during the darkest of nights. Now it was Fithvael's turn to be wakeful. They were being watched, and he had seen signs that they had been visited; yet Gilead seemed to have no fear of these humans. A character of extremes, the elf felt fear of everything or of nothing, love of life or a passion for death, was shadowfast or comatose.

Fithvael sat beside the campfire, keeping it low lest it give off tell-tale smoke, and kept watch. He spent the day preparing for the next night, without knowing what more there was to find on this estate. He kept watch over his friend and their few belongings. He laid his short sword within reach if he was seated and at his belt when moving around. He lived the day in fear, not of what the humans might do, for they must do something, nor of when the humans might come, for come they would. In his heart he lived in fear of Gilead and of what he might cause to happen to them both.

Dusk drew on, turquoise and amber. Gilead would wake soon, so Fithvael prepared a meal, stirred the fire into fresh life and leaned back against the welcoming nest of roots and bark afforded by the largest tree in the tiny clearing. Gazing into the darkening sky, Fithvael watched blue-grey wisps of cloud crossing the gaps in the leaves high above.

WHEN THEY CAME, as Fithvael had known they would, it was at twilight, that time when a black thread and a white, held equally against the light, both look grey.

Fithvael lay half upright against the tree, his eyelids fluttering and his feet twitching in unquiet sleep. Gilead lay in shelter on his side, well rested, close to waking.

When they came, they did not pour into the tiny clearing on horseback, stamping the ground, rearing their steeds and banging swords against shields.

Fithvael reclined, dozing, nostrils flaring with a new smell, unfamiliar at his time of sleeping. Gilead rolled instinctively onto his back, so that his semi-comatose senses might better hear the new sounds approaching the clearing.

When they came, they came by stealth, parting the leaves and branches of the trees, creeping on near-silent feet into the clearing. They came unarmoured for silence, sporting only the insignia of their lord embroidered on the front panels of their jerkins.

Fithvael took his weight back into his body, breathed one long, slow breath to clear his head and half opened an eye. Gilead gained his feet, hunkered down to keep his shelter; eyes snapped open, one hand, hesitating in mid-air, inches from the haft of his dagger.

They had thought to take the strangers by stealth. But the human scent is strong in the nostrils of an elf, and their footfalls sound loudly in the ears of the ancient folk. Even as an elf sleeps, he hears and smells and feels, and Gilead and Fithvael were no longer asleep.

In the half-blink of a single eye, Fithvael had seen the five men stalking around the clearing, skirting the fire, examining the food cooking there, and looking for the shelter which echoed the shapes of the low canopies of immature trees, and was invisible in the twilight. He knew that Gilead was with him; he could feel his presence, crystal sharp like the edge of an elven sword. Fithvael himself could take out the two men at the west side of the clearing. Gilead would do the rest.

In a matter of two heartbeats, Gilead registered five heavy pairs of feet in his hearing. Two off to the west of the clearing, two more central and one coming closer, to the east of the clearing. Gilead could easily defeat the three humans nearest to him; he knew that Fithvael would be on hand to tackle the remainder.

None of the men spotted the shape of the elf warrior, leaning against the tree, nor could they see the shelter where Gilead lay. The five men thought to wait for their quarry as they skirted the patch of open ground, marvelling at the construction of so neat a fire and the elegant preparation of such a meal. They assumed from this that the men in this campsite would be sophisticated, urbane people; they would be reserved, slow if it came to a fight – and so the nercomers expected nothing more.

Gilead took the first, emerging from the unseen shelter, lunging forward, attacking low. Galeth's sword rested heavy in its scabbard at his side and his dagger was still in his belt. The warrior elf tackled the short, squat man at the hips, below his centre of gravity, and swung him onto the ground on his back, winding him badly. A well-aimed blow to the jaw laid him out unconscious. To his right, Gilead could hear Fithvael emerge into the clearing.

'Do not kill them!' he ordered, and Fithvael automatically put up his sword, always used to taking orders from his faster friend on the field of battle.

As Fithvael floored his first opponent with a flat-handed but powerful blow to the sternum, Gilead was attacking his second, a bewildered young man who instantly dropped the staff he was carrying and waved his arms in alarm in front of him.

'No! No!' he cried, his voice high and wavering.

Gilead squatted, swiftly, and took the end of the staff in one hand, swinging it lightly against the back of the boy's knees and landing him unceremoniously on his rump.

Fithvael grappled with the biggest of the men, but for all the human's bulk he was also fast, and after seeing the fate of his comrades, was now ready for the elf's charge. The guard lifted his axe and swung, but Fithvael was still lithe for an old warrior and, ducking, he caught the haft of the long handled axe, below the head, and set himself into a spin. The force threw the big man off his heavy feet and into the trunk of the tree that Fithvael had, only moments before, been sleeping against.

As he looked up the last assailant was going down. He was the tallest of them, standing almost height for height with Gilead as they circled each other. Gilead made his move, grabbing his opponent's hand, raising and turning it, taking with it the tall man's entire body. Lifting him almost off his feet, Gilead ducked under their conjoined hands and threw the human over his shoulder. The man landed on his back; his head whiplashed back and he, too, was unconscious before he even knew what had hit him.

'How... how did you do that... sire?' a small voice asked from the middle of the body-strewn glade.

Fithvael and Gilead stood over the only conscious human left in the clearing.

'How? They are all fighting men with weapons. I'm only beginning... but they...'

The frightened boy stammered and chattered, as the elves stood over him, silent.

Gilead pointed at the insignia.

The elven rune, *senthoi*, signifying unity, was newly sewn, on the front of the boy's fresh, starched tunic.

MY GRANDMOTHER *told me that the lord still uses one of these old symbols on his crest, although none now remembers what it means or signifies. It's beautiful, I think.*

STILL STANDING OVER the jabbering boy, Fithvael and Gilead uncovered their faces.

'By Ulthuan…' Fithvael uttered in his native tongue.

The boy heard nothing more. The two faces and the single, alien voice had taken any remaining sense clean out of his head and he fell backward in a dead faint.

THEY DISMOUNTED IN the courtyard of the manor house and, since the usual watchman for this hour had rode in on the rump of Fithvael's steed, none dared stop their entry. The boy, Lyonen, was white with shock and he seemed in a daze as Fithvael helped him gently down from the horse they had shared.

Lyonen skittered and skipped ahead of Fithvael and Gilead into the lower hall of the manor, as he felt the toes of Gilead's striding boots on his heels. The elf companions made no attempt to hide their identities, and as a dozen faces turned upon them silence fell faster and more completely than it had ever fallen in that room before.

'Guards!' cried a squat, hawk-faced man, his dark hair streaked with silver. 'The rest of you leave, now!'

'You wanted to speak with us?' Gilead asked the lord, who in his confusion and disbelief had risen, although it was his right as lord of the manor to sit in the presence of any but the highest ranking stranger. After a few moments of bustle, the room was empty save for the guards, who looked on, some pale, others openly gaping at the mythical strangers.

'I…' the lord began, glancing behind him to ascertain precisely where his chair was situated, that he might fall into it with at least some assurance. 'I merely wanted to know who was trespassing on my land.'

'You sent five armed guards on a stealth mission,' Gilead observed, a wry smile almost crooking his lips, but kept out of his straight-talking eyes.

'And you return with only one, and the weakling at that,' said the lord, with increasing composure. 'Am I to believe you have killed the others?'

'Since they had no chance of taking myself and my companion, dead or alive, it seemed a little indiscriminate to slay them on the spot. No doubt they will return when they have nursed their sore heads and regained their sense of direction,' Gilead returned, enjoying the sparring.

Usually an elf, when he met with a human, came upon someone in need and in awe of the 'fairyfolk', or someone intimidated and unbelieving, as the lord's guards appeared to be. This human, however, after taking a moment to compose himself, seemed neither afraid nor awe-struck.

'I see what you are, elf. But what brings you to my estate?' the lord came to the point. But Gilead had need of a little more sparring.

'If you know the history of your homestead, then you know why we are here,' Gilead answered, gesturing slightly at Lyonen's tunic.

'Then it seems we both know the legends that surround this land,' the lord countered. 'Perhaps your reason for being here coincides with my reason for sending a stealth party to recover you, rather than killers to finish you.

'Please, put up your weapons and be seated.'

Gilead nodded to Fithvael and they both passed their weapons to the boy, assuring his continued stay in the room, as they took their seats. And thus the meeting commenced.

AS MY GRANDMOTHER *told it to me, the last of the elves that had lived at Ottryke, when they knew their time was ended, took most of their treasures to their family tombs and buried them. But that's just an old woman's story.*

FITHVAEL AND GILEAD were not invited to stay in the manor that night, but their weapons were returned to them and Lyonen returned to the campsite with them. It was he, after all, who had brought the elves to his lord, and his lord had need of their skills.

When they returned to their camp, it was empty of humans and nothing had been touched. Fithvael and Gilead talked long into the night – their youthful guardian watching them solemnly, understanding nothing at all that they said – as the two elf warriors debated the rightness of what they were to do.

Fithvael was aghast that Gilead would dare sanction the plunder of an ancient elven tomb. On Gilead's part though, he argued that the ends most assuredly justified the means. If he could possess the documentary treasures of this branch of an elf family, then the price was reasonable enough.

ANOTHER DAY PASSED as Fithvael gathered herbs, replenished their water skins and tended the horses. Lyonen followed everywhere in his wake, watching each task with wonder and curiosity, asking a hundred questions. Fithvael began to warm to the innocent eagerness of the boy, and his terse answers soon became a commentary on what he was doing, and then a dialogue like that between a mentor and his pupil. Even in such simple domestic matters, the ways of the elf were completely at odds with the crude toil that typified a human's daily labours.

The boy observed the other, Gilead, only at a distance – afraid, not because the warrior was an elf, but because that one kept all and everyone at a distance, even his elf companion. The boy's loyalties were already conflicted between the master he had grown up to laud and observe, and these wonderful elf-folk who knew so much and seemed so complete.

On the second day following their visit to the manor, Fithvael and Gilead received the lord and his entourage in the camp that they had made on these estates less than a week before. Fithvael heard hooves before dawn, as Lyonen helped him to load the horses and check their tack. Gilead stood firm in the centre of the clearing as he was surrounded by the lord, dressed in a kind of hunting outfit, and five of his guardsmen, clad in drab clothes and cloaks, bearing none of the lord's insignia. The armed men fooled no one; both elves recognised them instantly as soldiers of the lord, here to protect his interests against all-comers, including Fithvael and Gilead.

'Welcome, lord,' Gilead said formally, yet without showing signs of obeisance to this dull, avaricious human. 'Do we all understand our purpose?' He did not wait for an answer. 'That I lead you to the ancient tombs of my ancestors in return for any documents we discover there, all other property belonging to you as the current master of Ottryke.'

'We are in full agreement,' Lord Ottryke replied. 'All artefacts of material worth found during this mission belong solely to myself and my family.'

'Then we are agreed. Let us depart,' Gilead said, mounting his horse, Fithvael in concert with his every move.

Moments later, Lyonen, with a gasping clumsy effort, also managed to gain his saddle, accompanied by a glare from Gilead, and a tut or two from the lord's followers.

THE FIRST DAY'S ride was uneventful. The terrain was flat and easy, the steeds sure-footed and confident. If Ottryke's guards were a little nervous it was only because they were in the company of elves, creatures they knew might have existed in the deepest reaches of the world's history, but none that they could believe in here and now. As Gilead and Fithvael rode a little in advance of the rest of the party, six pairs of sneaking, wary eyes watched them constantly.

Lyonen, not quite knowing his place, rode sometimes at the back of the guard, unable to converse with men, who days before had thought him worthless and now only feared his connection to the elf-lords. When he forgot himself and his loyalties he chose to ride alongside Fithvael, causing head-shakes of disapproval, even consternation amongst his own people.

After an uneventful night under the stars, the second day brought them to the low slopes that signalled the foothills of their mountain destination and the first expectations of danger. The head of the guard squad spoke to the feared elves through Lyonen, who translated nothing and interpreted nothing, but merely repeated his sergeant's words of caution.

And danger there was.

Gilead came to a dead stop, Fithvael following suit mere paces behind him. Gilead raised his hand to halt the party, but they were only human and the best they could do was shuffle and hesitate and shuffle a little more, coming to a silent stop far too late. Their control of their steeds was clumsy, and it cost them.

The great beast came from nowhere, carried by the scent of human flesh and animal sweat into the rearguard of the group. As Gilead started to turn to admonish the coarse humans he saw it come, shambling, swollen legs bent; huge, hairless paws low to the ground. Ottryke's men grappled with the hilts and hafts of their various weapons as Gilead wheeled and galloped from his turn straight past them. His sword already in his hand, leaving a trail through the air that the humans could almost see, Gilead howled a cry of anger and attack. Those guards who had managed to arm themselves started to raise their weapons to face the elf.

Behind them, the last man was already half out of his saddle, kicking furiously with his single stirruped foot at the broad, scarred, naked body of the monster. The bestial chest was the size of a barrel and as hard as rock, and the guard made no impression on his attacker. A bone-clawed fist reached up at him and snapped at his neck, encircling it easily and wrenching him from his terrified mount.

Gilead wheeled his own horse around and his slender elf sword came down hard, slicing into the beast's back just as he heard the startled cry of a soldier behind him, biting off the barked orders of the sergeant that hung in the air, unheeded. His first blow clove a deep cleft in the brute's unnaturally curved spine, causing the great beastman to turn, screeching at Gilead and spraying yellow spittle out from between its scabby grey lips and rows of broken and pointed teeth. Throwing its head forward, the beast aimed its jaw at Gilead's exposed left leg, but before the teeth could connect with the finely muscled tissue there, the elf had plunged his dagger into the hollow of the beast's broad throat, which spread wider than its narrow, flattened cranium. Black blood spurted from the fatal wound and gushed into the beast's lowered maw, making it wretch in its asphyxiated death throes.

In the stunned silence that followed, the lord and his guard gathered around the fallen, twitching monstrosity. Fithvael alone made to tend the shaken, but only slightly injured target of the beast's ravening hunger. Lyonen's mouth hung open for several moments, and when he finally collected himself he automatically made to applaud the elf warrior, preventing himself just in time.

Gilead dismounted and adjusted his reins. Lord Ottryke remained mounted, looking loftily above him. When Gilead looked up their eyes locked. The guards inhaled a deep breath, as one man, and held it. Brief seconds passed in a slow age.

'You owe me nothing,' Gilead said eventually.

'Indeed,' answered the nobleman, raising his chin as he turned his horse away.

'THAT... COULD HAVE been me!' Lyonen whispered conspiratorially to Fithvael when they had re-formed and were back on their trail. 'If I hadn't been riding alongside you just then...'

'Then continue to ride with me,' Fithvael said kindly. 'I do not anticipate that things will become any easier.'

GILEAD LED FROM the front as the landscape climbed up into rocky lowlands, with the shrubby growth of orange and mauve heathers marking the route. Coming to a stop again by the side of a spring that trickled from between glinting grey rocks, riddled with coppery bright veins, Gilead motioned for the party to gather.

'This is where it begins,' he said, looking down at the narrow stream.

One jump should carry them across the burbling, splashing, clean white water. The gathered group dismounted and stood by the stream, looking bewildered. The boulder above the stream had a barely visible, time-worn engraving on it. Only their lord remained mounted, sneering down at Gilead.

'Is this some kind of elven joke?' he asked lightly, looking around at his men as if expecting them to applaud.

'Cross this stream on that horse and you will no doubt find out.'

'Sergeant!' Lord Ottryke started. 'Your opinion?'

Before the sergeant could answer, Gilead stepped in front of the nobleman's horse and took a firm hold of its bridle.

'You pay me to be your scout and the sergeant to protect you from me,' the elf said darkly. 'Will you allow me to do as you bade me, or shall I leave you here for the next beastman to feast upon?'

The lord dismounted, Gilead still holding the reins of his horse.

While the last of the party tethered their horses, a large young man from the centre of the group – Fithvael thought he must perhaps be their corporal, and knew his name to be Groulle – danced on the spot for a moment and then launched himself at the stream before either of the elves could stop him. He could have cleared a small river eight feet wide or more from his position. He was a popular man, making any number of jokes and observations along the way, mostly at the expense of the elves. His laugh was a loud, echoing bray that had startled Lyonen out of his saddle more than once and had caused Gilead to grimace at the human's lack of subtlety.

'No!' Fithvael cried, simultaneously throwing himself after the huge corporal, but it was too late.

Groulle's left foot hit the bank of the stream.

Groulle followed through, hitting the air and paddling his legs in a running motion intended to carry him yards. The rest could only watch, stunned, as the springhead became a boiling, bursting geyser of hot yellow fire. The bank of the stream shook as the others looked down at the footprint Groulle had left in the soft earth. The ground tore apart and collapsed, swallowing the footprint into black fissures that spread fast around them. There was a deep rumbling in the earth, as the rest of the party retreated, still staring at Groulle, who seemed to hang in the air for many minutes.

As he hung there, he could see the bank of the stream push its way outward and the water below him turn bright and luminous as the geyser spat hot droplets of stinging fluid at him. However hard and far he travelled through the air, the opposite bank of the stream moved faster and further from him, until even he did not believe he would make it across.

Groulle leaned forward, thrusting his arms and shoulders as far ahead of him as he could, foolish and frightened and praying aloud to his god in a screeching voice that the others heard only as terrified screams. Finally, his arms made contact with the now steep and cracked far bank. The earth felt hot and dry, but he heaved against it, trying to drag legs he could no longer feel out of the bubbling water. Then there was nothing. As Groulle's feet left the thundering viscous liquid behind, the corporal blacked out.

When Groulle awoke, apparently only moments later, the spring was once again a pretty, narrow, babbling white strand of water that trickled harmlessly away between the rocks.

Gilead nodded at Fithvael and then took in the rest of the group with one glance. He saw faces ashen with fright – and noticed that Lord Ottryke had retreated to the rear of the group and was again sitting astride his horse.

A wry smile passed across the elf's lips as he asked, 'Who will go next?'

Six men and two elves spent the rest of the day negotiating the rocky outcrop and crossing it above the source of the spring and its dim engraving of the elven rune, *sariour*.

It was nightfall by the time they rejoined Groulle. He was unconscious again. His long boots and leather breeches were entirely burnt away, along with the bottom quarter of his leather scabbard. The end of his sword was blackened with tarnish. Groulle's legs up to the knees were a mass of black blisters and red ulcers, the pus already forming beneath the skin and bloating the sores. Lyonen turned away from the sight, as an older guardsman stepped forward. He wore a neat, grey beard and long sideburns, and carried only a crossbow for protection, while the rest of the guard carried at least two weapons, and possibly a plethora of others concealed about their persons. A strap around the veteran's shoulder harnessed a pack to his body; it ran down his left side, tied around his waist and again to his thigh. The pack contained a series of pouches and pockets of various sizes and shapes. Freuden, for that was his name, unstrung the pack from his side and began to arrange bandages and medical instruments on a clean cloth on the ground.

'Human medicines will not work here,' said Fithvael, placing a hand on the stooping man's shoulder. Freuden flinched.

'Then what do you suggest?' he asked.

'Have you a spare pair of boots and some clean breeches amongst you?' asked Fithvael, not looking up from examining Groulle's legs.

Freuden nodded dubiously.

'Then fetch them.'

* * *

GILEAD JOINED Fithvael beside Groulle, as the veteran began to lance the blisters and boils, releasing a strong and sweet stench along with blood-stained, black pus. Gilead picked up a small, soft wineskin from the ground beside Fithvael, weighing it in his hands.

'You plan to anoint a human with this?' Gilead asked, a hard edge to his low voice.

'It is the only way, Gilead. You know it. The rune showed that our people controlled nature in this place.'

'I also know this man is a foolish, worthless hu–'

'And we may yet need him,' interrupted Fithvael. 'You end life if you have to. I will preserve it if I can. And this is the only decent alcohol we have. It will clean his wounds and begin the healing.' And with that Fithvael took one of the last flask of rare Tor Anrok wine from Gilead's hands and began to pour it, a few drops at a time, into Groulle's wounds.

'It is the last of that vintage,' Gilead said harshly.

'Then it should be used to do good.'

ON THE FOLLOWING day, Groulle's wounds were a little better, and he elected to continue with the rest. Progress was slow as they made their way up the side of the mountain in search of an entrance. Gilead and Fithvael had to stop over and over again to wait for the slower, clumsier humans. The guards surrounded their noble master, guiding and helping him, the slowest of them all, up the ever-steeper incline.

In the middle of the afternoon, having travelled only a few hundred yards, Gilead was growing impatient. He would have been faster and safer alone, but there was a price to pay for everything and today the price was a tomb full of ancient elven treasure – and knowledge.

He shook the thought free of his mind and resolved to concentrate on the job in hand. Reaching a jutting, coppery rock, sticking out at shoulder height to his crouched body, Gilead vaulted lightly on to it and, able to stand, he surveyed the mountain face. A little below him and to his right he found what he was looking for. The rock appeared, on closer inspection, to be a little too smooth and Gilead could see a light, reddish haze around it – and the faintest trace of another elven rune, *arhain*, for secrets. This was his entrance.

He waited for the rest of the motley party to assemble below him.

'This is where we go in,' Gilead said, pointing to the flat, copper-grey boulders below.

'Where?' asked the sergeant, 'I see nothing but rock.'

'Then follow me and you will see all,' answered Gilead, dismounting his boulder with easy grace and stepping lightly down a shallow crease, toward his target.

'Wait!' Lord Ottryke commanded. 'If you go in first, how will we know that we can follow? We do not see your entrance.'

'Then you must trust,' Gilead answered, meeting the lord's gaze squarely.

'No!' argued the lord. 'If there is an entrance then we shall send one of my own men in first.'

'L-lord?' stammered the sergeant.

'What is it, man?' the nobleman spat back, exasperated.

'Two of my men have been injured already... and we do not know what lies behind the rocks. It might be more... prudent if the elf did take the lead.'

'The stakes are high, sergeant,' Lord Ottryke snarled. 'Men will be lost. But if you prefer, we will send in the boy. He has little value as a warrior and I question his allegiance. Yes,' he continued, maliciously, 'let us test the boy.'

LYONEN TOOK ONE last, wide-eyed look at Fithvael, who nodded his head gravely, and then he put his hand out to meet a rock face that did not exist. The boy's eyes grew even wider and he felt the sweat drip down the inside of his shirt, down his sides and back. He shuffled his feet out onto the tiny, solid lip before the illusion – and found that the first few inches of his boot were invisible. In another moment both of his arms had disappeared and then his head and torso. Another heartbeat and the guards looked on in horror and amazement as Lyonen's trailing foot, the last they could see of him, disappeared behind the rock face.

Several silent moments passed.

'He's in,' their lord pronounced. 'Proceed!'

But they all stopped in their tracks as they heard a high-pitched, ethereal scream, muffled in the mountainside. They gasped as one skinny, disembodied hand clawed at the air in front of them.

Fithvael was the first to lunge into the rock, disappearing almost before they had seen him move. Then half of his body re-entered daylight, shouting for help. Then he disappeared inside the mountain once more.

FITHVAEL KNELT IN the dark, surrounded by a hazy red light and a rough-hewn tunnel dripping with dark slime. He could see the boy only as shades of grey on grey in the almost total darkness. He let his hands pass over the writhing body on the floor in front of him, until a shattering cry of pain echoed around the tunnel and the boy became still. His breath was coming in short, flat rasps.

Fithvael found the thick haft of a bolt protruding from Lyonen's sternum. Only an inch remained outside his body. It had penetrated too deeply. Fithvael felt the polished, silken texture of the end of the bolt. It spoke to him like only an elf-made missile could speak to an elf warrior. Fithvael's hand covered the eyes of the human boy, while the heel of the other pressed hard and suddenly against the end of the beautifully-wrought elven bolt. The boy had already met his fate at the hand of an elven weapon. All that Fithvael could do for him now was end his suffering.

Fithvael stepped to the edge of the entrance, thrusting his head and hands out through the penetrable rock, so that the rest could see only the irate expression on his face, and the blood staining his hands.

'He is dead!' he said. 'The first of your men is lost, lord, and there was none more loyal in your guard, if you did but know it.'

'But is it *safe*, elf?' Lord Ottryke called.

Fithvael dropped his hands and they disappeared back behind the rock, a look of disgust on his face.

'Who knows how many ancient traps there may yet be in this tomb? Not I,' he said and vanished.

Slowly and with great caution, Ottryke's men followed Fithvael through the hidden entrance into the elf tomb. They lit small lamps and stood around Lyonen's body. In the light they could see the wire he had tripped and the crossbow that had loosed the bolt that killed the boy. It was crude, by elven standards, and any good human scout would have seen it, but it had been too much for the brave initiate.

The medic, Freuden, examined the body. 'What a waste,' he muttered.

'The boy died in the line of duty,' the lord said pompously.

'His name was Lyonen,' Fithvael said coldly, staring into the noble's eyes.

TENSION MOUNTED AS they continued into the mountain. Fithvael was silent, grieving the death of Lyonen, an innocent lad who should not have been there at all.

The guards had begun to mutter amongst themselves. It was becoming obvious to them that their lord was no leader and they must take direction from Gilead, the elf-warrior, if they were to survive. There were no more traps in the tunnel, but the guards stayed close behind Gilead and watched his every move. When the tunnel opened out into a wider, vaulted chamber, they turned to the elf and none dared move into the open before him.

Gilead took a lamp, adjusted the wick to produce more light and then threaded it onto the barbed end of a halberd borrowed from the sergeant. He swung the light out over the cavern floor, which showed up as a series of worn, interlocking tiles, and then around the walls where he could see five dark openings in the rock. The tiles came in two distinct shapes, larger octagons interspersed at intervals by tiny squares. Although worn, the floor was lustrous and fresh in places, and just as the tiles interlocked, so did the intricate pattern of runes engraved upon them too.

'Do you see the pattern?' Gilead asked Fithvael.

'It is simple enough,' Fithvael returned. 'I will go first.' He had read Gilead's mind.

Gilead made his way to the back of the group, passing instructions along the waiting line of guards. When he came to Lord Ottryke, he said simply, 'Follow in the footsteps of the man in front, unless I instruct you to the contrary.' Then he fell in behind the nobleman.

Fithvael began to make his way across the floor, the toes of his boots falling precisely and lightly, two short steps to the right and then a half-stride backward. He kept his eyes on the floor around him, looking for every trap. Groulle came next, working hard to keep himself from staggering on his seared limbs as Fithvael wove his path. Then came Freuden, the apothecary. When he had led the first two men perhaps a third of the way across the floor, Fithvael turned and called to the sergeant, who was just stepping out onto the floor.

'You can no longer follow my path,' Fithvael instructed. 'Listen,' and he gave the sergeant a whole new set of instructions that seemed to lead him to the left of the cavern and away from the first group.

Suddenly the sergeant stopped, two toes perched, almost overlapping on one of the tiny squares of stone tile. He wanted to wipe his sweating hands on his breeches, but dare not, lest he overbalance in the process.

'Where are you sending me,' he called into near darkness, as he felt himself moving further from the lead group.

'You must trust,' Fithvael replied in a low, soothing tone. The sergeant turned his head slightly, he saw the remaining two of his men following in his footsteps and determined that he would not let them down. Taking a deep, slow breath and steadying his mind, the sergeant called again to Fithvael.

'Lead on,' he said.

For the next hour Fithvael led his party across the void, and guided the sergeant. Only Gilead and the lord remained.

'Why do you lead us like children playing at monsters? The floor looks solid enough to me,' Lord Ottryke sniffed disdainfully.

Gilead looked at him and then into the smouldering grey of the light ahead of him. He took a quarrel from the quiver slung across his back, broke it twice over his knee and wrapped it tightly in a scrap of cloth.

'Sergeant,' called Gilead, 'catch this for me.'

He threw the tight little parcel out over the floor. The sergeant's hand, reaching out to grab at the cloth, was suddenly lit with a deep orange fluorescence. The broken arrow had fallen short and now a patch of floor was lit up and pulsing around it. In a moment the quarrel was smouldering with green light and sending off shooting white sparks in all directions. Then the floor became fluid, like oozing, bubbling-hot treacle and the parcel was swallowed into the viscous liquid. Next to the first tile that had dissolved, a second started to melt away, and then a third.

'You go first,' Gilead told the startled-looking nobleman. 'And step only where I instruct you.'

Only Fithvael and Gilead knew that with every group that crossed the floor, the elven magic became less forgiving. It took an hour for Fithvael and his party to cross, more than two for the sergeant and his two men. Ottryke and Gilead only reached the opposite side of the cavern after five gruelling hours. The journey was longer and more treacherous, and all around him tiles were melting away into the treacle ooze that bubbled and belched in disgust. When he finally reached solid ground again, Ottryke looked pale and was shaking violently. The apothecary came to tend him, but was sent away with an exhausted wave of the hand.

'Give me some of your liquor,' he said to Gilead.

'Elven wine is not for human consumption,' the elf lord answered flatly.

Lord Ottryke insisted on resting in the dark, cramped exit of the cavern. Fithvael changed Groulle's dressings and the sergeant went from one guard to the next, clapping each on the back. When he had spoken a few words of encouragement to Groulle, the man laid his hand on Fithvael's shoulder and held his gaze for a moment. No words passed between them.

FITHVAEL JOINED GILEAD in the dark recess of the cavern, farthest away from the grumbling humans.

'Is this wise, Gilead?' he asked. But he got no reply. 'The men are wasted by a lord who does not lead them, confused as to their duty. Where will this end?'

'All the humans are worthless and treacherous,' was all Gilead's reply.

'Lyonen was a worthy lad and the sergeant seems a thoughtful sort, for a human. I believe he is resolved to follow your direction.'

'It matters not,' Gilead said. 'The end will be the same.' And he turned away from his old friend, deep in his own thoughts, a dark look on his face.

THE LIGHT DID not change in the cavern, although outside the dawn was fast breaking. Gilead and Fithvael were preparing to continue their underground journey, and after watching them for a few moments, the sergeant began to round up his men. They had slept little and eaten less; only the encouragement of their superior brought them to their feet. The lord still slept, slumped in an undignified posture, his drool making clean tracks across his filthy cheek.

Despite some respectful shaking, the sergeant could not rouse him and turned to Gilead for instruction. Gilead sighed and unsheathed his sword, sending it ringing against the rock-face beside the man's head. Spluttering and crying out, Lord Ottryke came round with a start, but said nothing when he saw it was Gilead who had awoken him.

FITHVAEL LED THE party down through one of the recesses in the cavern wall and into a narrow, lightless corridor, Gilead again taking his place to the rear, just behind his lordship. The passage was steep and tall, but only wide enough to accommodate the narrow shoulders of an elf. Soon realising that Groulle was struggling, Fithvael advised he remove first his weapons and drag them behind him, and then, only yards later, his heavy outer clothing. Despite the tight squeeze, Groulle complied without question. But when it came to his lord's turn, Ottryke complained vociferously to Gilead, who could still walk easily in the space.

'Find us another route!' Ottryke demanded. 'This was not the only tunnel.'

'Then take another,' came Gilead's reply. 'But be warned: the elven inscriptions weave intricate spells, and only by studying them for hours was Fithvael able to lead us safely.' Gilead spoke calmly, but when Lord Ottryke became red in the face and began blustering in protest, the elf drew his sword in the narrow tunnel, blocking the lord's retreat. In this space, at this range, the human lord was completely unable to defend himself, or call on his guard to defend him. He had no choice. Struggling to turn his back on the elf and continue up the narrow passageway, Lord Ottryke cursed the filthy inhuman beast under his breath. He had never before been humiliated by a man, let alone by an elf such as Gilead.

As the tunnel continued deeper into the mountain, its narrow walls became smoother and were covered in crisp carvings that looked just as they had on the day they were carved. Progress was very slow; all the humans were reduced to travelling sideways, their backs and elbows against one wall.

Groulle continued without complaint, even though his knees and elbows were scraped with every step, leaving trails of fresh blood, which were wiped away by the shirts of the men behind him. The pain was nothing, but he hated to be in contact with those awful elven runes, the same runes that had almost spelt his doom.

Fithvael, a step or two in front of him, ran his hands casually across the carvings as they passed, marvelling at their beauty and smiling at the welcome they spelled out.

In the rearguard of the company, Gilead's hopes began to rise – but with them, his impatience with the party's patron. Ottryke seemed to stop and inspect every last graze and scratch that came his way, huffing his breath and sucking his teeth, lest he say anything that might cause Gilead to turn on him again. He refused to remove even his outer clothing and kept hold of his weapon, for all the good it would do him, long after his guards had shed theirs. It was plain from his face that only his greed was keeping him going.

Ottryke forgot every complaint in the blink of an eye when the tunnel came to an abrupt end. Below him, as he gazed down from the top of a deeply terraced slope, he could see it all – his new-found wealth was spread below him in a gleaming, glistening mountain of beautiful, elven objects. His men were spread along the top terrace, in various stages of tattered undress, looking down in awe and wonder at the sight they beheld. Groulle's face was pale and grey in the strange internal twilight of the cavern, his eyes bulging, unblinking. Freuden stared wearily, his face a picture of disbelief. Their sergeant stood next to Fithvael, grinning.

'May you find your own riches here too,' he said quietly to the elf.

Then Gilead, the last, stepped out onto the terrace. He watched in disgust as Lord Ottryke stumbled, incoherently down the terraces, taking huge, rambling strides, stripping off his heavy leather jerkin and helm as he went, cackling and screeching. To Gilead the nobleman looked like nothing better than a drunken street brawler floundering after some voluptuous, but disinterested whore.

'The documents are mine. The history is mine.' Gilead reminded him in a firm tone. 'Take the gold – but leave me my people.'

Lord Ottryke turned in bewilderment. 'What care I for you or your precious dead?' he said rhetorically, and turning back to his prize, threw himself down the last of the terraces until he was waist deep in cold, heavy gold.

Fithvael and Gilead carefully picked their way through the ancient treasures. The air was dry and sweet smelling, and everything looked perfect. It took some time, but the two elves, searching methodically, finally found a series of leather cases, boxes and cylinders, standing together in a three-sided, stone repository, kept separate from the rest of the artefacts.

All around them they could hear the commands of Lord Ottryke and the bustle of his men as they hurried to obey his frantic commands. They all wandered around, trying to assess the bulk and weight of the relics in order to work out a way of removing them to the lord's manor.

Ottryke himself had given up counting his wealth and had already begun to spend it in his mind, perhaps to oust his cousin, the Elector of Altdorf, from his seat. Wealth and power, power and wealth; inextricably tied in Ottryke's mind they meant only one thing – greed.

GILEAD LOOKED longingly at the real treasures he had found. He sat on the polished stone floor for what seemed like an age, examining the heavily embossed leather, strewn with golden runes that seemed to flicker and change shape before his eyes. He looked at the great, scrolling gold clasps and hinges. He breathed in the beauty of the craftsmanship and the perfection of the proportions of each piece.

Fithvael stood behind him, not quite knowing what to say, but hoping, perhaps for the first time, that their long quest might finally bear fruit. He crushed the hope before it grew too great for his mind to contain, and closed a mental door on it, for now at least. Between them, he knew that he and Gilead could carry the entire burden of the history held in these sacred books and scrolls. His only other concern was how to safely leave the tomb. They could not return the way they had come. The elves who had built and booby-trapped this place had been far too clever for that. He began to look about him for answers and quickly found them high above them in the soaring, vaulted ceilings. He and Gilead could surely escape, but what of the humans? Would they have the skills or the stamina required?

As Fithvael pondered this dilemma, his eyes were drawn down again by a low, fearful gasp. As he looked down at his friend, he saw Gilead snatch back his hand as if burnt in a furnace, then a tiny cloud of dust settled in a yellowish smudge on the perfectly white floor.

'Too late!' Gilead whispered in terror. 'We come too late!' With these words he rose on his knees, threw his head back and let out a vicious scream of pain and despair.

'What... what is it?' Fithvael asked, after the cry had subsided. 'What is it, old friend?' he asked, his hand hovering inches above Gilead's shoulder, which, as much as he longed to, he could not bring himself to touch.

When he got no answer, Fithvael leaned over Gilead's slumped body to rest his hand on a beautifully tooled leather scroll within his reach. His fingertips had barely rested upon it before it was gone, crumbling into the air. Gilead's second anguished howl did all the rest. All around them, whether because of some charm triggered by their presence or even the new air they had let in to this ancient place, everything was crumbling to nought. Whatever precious knowledge might have been preserved here was now lost.

When the echoes of the horrible sound died, they were followed by another bellow. A deep-seated belly laugh, almost as raucous as the cry had been terrifying, filled the chamber. Lord Ottryke pointed one stubby finger at Gilead, rolled back his head and roared with laughter.

'Your race is dead!' he said maliciously, his mouth wide with laughter. 'I have it all! And you – you have nothing!'

'NOTHING!' he screamed, the laughter over. All that remained in the noble's face was triumph and hatred.

Lord Ottryke raised his arms and turned full circle, inviting his guard to hail him the victor. Slowly they too began to laugh and point. Groulle looked ashamed and embarrassed for a moment, but caught the infection soon enough and he too laughed along with the others. Freuden took one sympathetic look at Fithvael's blank, bleak expression and he too began to snigger, almost in spite of himself. At the back of the group, the sergeant sat down heavily. His drooping head shook slightly and he covered his face in his hands. But the gesture alone was not enough to save him when weighed against the scorn and derision of his company.

THE JOURNEY INTO the mountain had taken days. The journey out, undertaken by two lone elves, took merely hours.

They walked away from the mountain, ignoring the faint, distant cries that turned to screams behind them, and retraced their steps to their waiting steeds. Gilead had brought nothing out of the mountain with him. Tucked inside Fithvael's outer garment was a scrap of bloody cloth embroidered with an elven rune, the last remains of a new tabard, once worn by the youngest member of Lord Ottryke's household guard. If Lyonen had survived perhaps Fithvael could have found some way to save all the humans.

When they reached their steeds, Fithvael pulled the scrap of cloth from its place against his heart and stowed it in his saddlebag. Gilead watched for a moment and then caught Fithvael's gaze.

'I have broken no bond,' he said.

'Let me grieve for the boy, at least,' answered Fithvael.

'You must grieve as your heart instructs you,' said Gilead. 'I made a contract with the scum lord to lead him into the tomb, a one way journey. He neither requested, nor paid, for a return trip.'

And with that Gilead mounted his horse and started to ride back down the mountain, away from his people's crumbling past and away from Ottryke Manor.

V
Gilead's Test

Promise me only this: look into my eyes and see what I see.

ENOUGH NOW. You've had your share of tales from me this night. I'm tired, and the cold gets to my old bones. Sit up, if you will. Drink my wine, enjoy the heat of my fire. My bedroll calls for me and my throat is hoarse from too many stories.

Well, of course there are more. More of Gilead, of loyal Fithvael. More sad and bloody stories of their twilight world.

So they are just myths, are they? Think what you will. I know better. Myths are ten a penny and the land is full of them. The stories in my head are made of better stuff. Truth, for a start...

You doubt me? Well then, hear this one before I retire.

Time had gone by since their dealings at Ottryke Manor. Perhaps a year, maybe two, maybe less. And there was a battle. Bloody, devastating, furious. The hills and woods rang with the sound. Such deeds were done, but what matters for my story happened afterwards.

The battle was at an end. There was nothing more to be known except the dirge of the wind, sighing through the blackened elms that marked that deep tract of the Drakwald.

Fithvael began to rouse. It was cold and lightless as he lay on the dank earth of the battlefield. Yet it was neither the chill nor damp that had woken him. His unconsciousness had been broken by the singular strangeness of a warm, pulsing body lying against his. It was a sensation he did not particularly relish.

Fithvael drew his body carefully away from the warmth. He could sense his own fragility, though he could locate no definite pain. He could feel with every fibre of his warrior instinct the devastation that surrounded him.

But he had no memory of where or how or why.

He cleared his nose of ash and blood and the first invasion of scents brought back stark reminders of the ten-year quest he had undertaken with Gilead, and their continued fight against the darknesses of the world. It was the stench of unnatural flesh. Dead, unnatural flesh. It was the putrefying, astringent odour of Chaos, a stench that could be mistaken for nothing else.

Slowly, the veteran warrior elf allowed his other senses to return. Now he could feel the pitted earth beneath his body and the places where puddles of gore and stale water had formed, soaking into his outer garments and making his joints feel rigid and useless. He wanted nothing more than to move, to release his stiff, locked body and relax the muscles that were tightening with revulsion against his surroundings.

But first he would listen, tune his hearing to this place and discover if his life was at any immediate risk.

The silence was nearly entire save for the pulse and breath of the body that remained utterly still beside him. There was a reassuring taste in his mouth. The sweet-sour taste of sleep and his last long-forgotten meal. The feared metallic tang of his own blood and bile was entirely, blissfully absent. At least he had suffered no grievous injury.

Regaining his confidence, Fithvael gradually opened his eyes. He had hoped against reason that the body beside his own would be Gilead's, broken perhaps, but alive and stable, needful of the elf's ministrations. It was not to be, and the veteran warrior smothered his disappointment.

Fithvael and Gilead could never be as close as the twin siblings, Gilead and Galeth, had been. But the swordmaster had devoted his life to Gilead and to the quest when Galeth had died, and their relationship had become intensely close. On the battlefield, they fought as one and could communicate any amount of information with a glance or the nod of a head.

They had one goal, represented one force. Their relationship had long since ceased to be that of master and servant, man and boy, or even companions. They were as much at one as two such singular, disparate individuals could ever be.

Fithvael's elven eyes adjusted instantaneously to the last of the night's darkness. He smiled to himself and moved freely for the first time in hours. His mare turned her head to him, whinnied and then stood up from her resting-place beside her master. Her vigil was over.

AS HE FELT the hilt of his sword come into contact with his assailant's sternum, Gilead turned and swiftly scanned the area again. Time was short on any battlefield, even for a warrior of his consummate skill and shadowfast abilities. Yes, Fithvael was still with him, a hundred paces to his right, fighting strong.

The foe were all around them. Tall, darkly noble, yet twisted and corrupt. Elves, kin and yet not kin. Blasphemous parodies of their race, death pale, dressed in reeking black armour, eyes rotting in skulls, breaths foul from black-lipped mouths. Their rusting armour was decorated in flaking gilt, fading silks, worm-eaten brocades.

The last son of Tor Anrok and his swordmaster had penetrated the darkest depths of the southern Drakwald in search of the Tower of Talthos Elios, the birthplace of lost Niobe. They had uncovered recently coined tales that said Talthos Elios stood watch over a foul barrow, an ancient crypt that legend said descended into hell itself. Wars had been fought there, skirmishes of light against dark, until the line of Elios had sundered the spawn of darkness and driven it underground. From that day, their tower had stood, guarding the breach against further incursions.

So the myths said, and the land is full of them. But it was a start, the faint hope of a clue, and Gilead had seized at it eagerly.

Rumours came to them thick and fast as they trekked into the great forest. Rumours of darkness reawakened, of a custodianship long fallen away. And then, all at once, the enemy had been on them. Not beastmen, not bulky warrior clans of Chaos.

Elves. Ruined elves. Broken, twisted, decayed echoes of noble warriors.

Gilead wrenched his blade from a weeping chest. He swung the sword again, in a singing arc, drawing the weight of his body around with it and sinking it so deep into the neck of the assailant behind him that it just stood, expressionless and quite literally dead on its feet.

The stench of the bubbling, tarry fluids that gouted from the fatal, gaping wound would have been more than enough to fell a weaker constitution. It gave Gilead the merest moment to breathe and regroup. The body shielded Gilead from the onslaught of another, which had to tear its own comrade down to lunge at Gilead head on. Its jagged rows of black teeth were bared, and its lean arms, each ending in a mass of bloodied spikes, flailed wildly at the warrior elf.

Gilead took advantage of the fact that he was holding his longsword low, two-handed, in front of him. He simply raised the blade as this latest horror surged forward. It was an easy kill. The tip of the long sword entered the enemy's gut low, the hilt crashing home against a grotesquely misshapen codpiece. Gilead began to pull the blade free, but his adversary grabbed at it with its spike-armoured fists. The warrior sliced upwards, cutting both bestial hands in half, and his sword finally came to rest against the neck seal of the dying enemy's body armour.

Gilead's eyes swept in another arcing scan, once, twice... Fithvael was gone. But the fighting was not over yet.

Gilead had quested for ten long years to avenge his brother's death. The ghost of Galeth had remained with him throughout, but the living twin seemed neither of this world nor the next. Ten years of his life had been spent fighting the forces of evil to bring down one pathetic man. He questioned, often, the value of his task. There was no satisfaction.

Yet his struggle had continued and chiefly because of Fithvael. At first, Gilead had been compromised into fighting on the side of right. Now it had become his life, he would use whatever force was at his disposal to war against the darkness until the day of his death came and released him from this violent existence.

He had no brother now, and precious few kin in this fading age of the world. But he would fight. Fight on. Against the darkness.

And so he fought now, plunging hard steel into misshapen bodies, severing limbs, scything through torsos and necks, disgorging the foul-smelling ichor and mortal fluids of the things. Gilead abhorred his enemies, bodies corrupted and twisted, infested with evil. From their stench and their symbols he knew them. Bestial, lasciviously decorated devotees of the abomination, Slaanesh.

Gilead fought on as the earth beneath his feet turned to gore-soaked clay. Dark water gathered in the prints left by the heavy footfalls of the enemy. Bodies fell in all directions as the screams and battle cries of the foe became fewer. With every fresh onslaught, with every breath taken after the kill, Gilead's eyes swept the field. Fithvael was still nowhere to be seen.

Then it came. His concentration must have waned momentarily, his thoughts with Fithvael or perhaps with Galeth, instead of with the foe. He was felled. Felled by the last surviving enemy on the field. A foe, fatally wounded, but not yet dead. Gilead's body reeled, parodying his own gymnastic battle-swings, and his startled face watched as his assailant collapsed to his knees. The foe's cadaverous, drawn visage slapped into the cloying mud just before Gilead's head came to rest on its dead back.

As THE SUN began to rise, Fithvael led his horse out of the carnage to a green place with fresh water. He tethered her there and she contentedly began a hearty breakfast. She had earned it. But Fithvael needed more. He needed to find Gilead.

Fithvael did not remember the battle, nor did he recall the last time he had seen his partner. His intention was to follow the course of the battle, mapping its action as he went. He picked his way across the field, no more than a hundred yards or so wide and about the same long. He counted some three dozen bodies, but Gilead's, thankfully, was not among them. The pair of elf warriors had taken on and utterly destroyed an entire band of the foul wights. There were no mounts, so wherever Gilead had gone, his trusted horse had gone with him. A second good omen.

Fithvael began to distinguish his own kills from Gilead's. It wasn't difficult. His own were neat and accurate enough, but Gilead's were a sight to behold. With each group of bodies, Fithvael was able to track every move the elf warrior had made. His mind's eye noted every pirouette, every firm stance. Each lunge, parry and faint came clearly to him. He felt nothing but

immense respect for Gilead's fighting skills. Every kill was
clean. There were no false starts, no unnecessary swings, no
butchery. One stroke, one swing, one plunging blade had
destroyed each monster in its turn. Fithvael took in the wide
variety of strokes that Gilead had brought to bear in the battle.
He could almost hear the whistle of the blade through the air
and could even detect where and when the elf had changed
hands. His three-finger grip was as effective as the conventional four-finger grip of Gilead's whole hand. Gilead had lost
his finger, but Galeth had been there to save him on that occasion, so long ago.

The exercise of dissecting the battlefield began to clear and
concentrate Fithvael's mind. He remembered events from the
day before and of the week, month and year, but nothing
seemed important since Gilead was missing. The veteran warrior spent the rest of that day crossing and re-crossing the
battlefield, breaking it down into a grid and searching each
sector for clues of his friend. There were no footprints to be
found, the earth was a mess of gore and tarry puddles and the
enemies' decaying bodies covered most of it in any case. So
Fithvael began to look a little deeper.

He found his eyes continually drawn to the corpses of the
foe. So like his own kind, so unlike. Elven forms corrupted
from within, their ancient armour and weapons tarnished and
overlaid with the dank remnants of satin swathes and gold-
leaf. What had befallen these... these things? What misery had
overtaken their lives, overcome them with rancorous passions
and destroyed them?

He set it from his mind.

He could find no shreds or fragments torn from Gilead's garments, no shards of armour, no hair. The elf had left nothing
of himself behind in the carnage. Fithvael counted this the
third good omen. Even his scent was absent. It would have
been hard to detect over the heavy backdrop of malodorous
Chaos, but if Gilead's blood had been spilled, his old friend
would have found the traces.

With the fall of his second night on the battlefield, Fithvael
retired to the green haven where he had left his mare, content
in the knowledge that Gilead was alive somewhere. All day he
had used physical evidence to work out what had happened.
All night he exercised his mind with suppositions and

possibilities. He could only conjecture, but the one thing he could be sure of was that something had caused Gilead either to leave his old friend or to forget him. If Gilead had searched the battlefield, as Fithvael had done, he would have quickly found the veteran, in spite of the dark, cold and carnage. He would not have passed the old warrior off for dead. He would have rescued him and ministered to his needs. Of course, the old elf had suffered some amnesia, but his mind had never lost sight of Gilead. Evil was as thick in the atmosphere as the smell of the Chaos spawn, but surely the elf warrior's mind was too strong to succumb to the dark influences?

So, Gilead was alive, unscathed, physically at least. Yet Fithvael knew that he must find his old friend, for something was sorely amiss.

GILEAD'S HEAD nodded in the light slumber of semi-consciousness. He knew that he was mounted and could sense the reins in his hands, but he was unaware that a rope attached to the bridle was leading his horse. If he had realised, he would simply have assumed that he was being led by Fithvael, for there was no one else. He could not awake, he could not summon the energy to rouse himself. Yet neither could he quite comprehend his own complacency.

He slumbered on, unaware of time and space and unconscious of any needs, desires or appetites. He questioned nothing.

DAWN AGAIN. Fithvael had slept little. His mind would not still.

He rose to his elbows on the cold ground and resolved he would begin a new quest. A quest for Gilead, and if it took ten years, as the quest to the memory of Galeth had taken, then so be it. Pray that Gilead was lost to some other fate than death.

THE ROOM WAS softly lit with candle lamps, whose steady flames illuminated wall hangings, depicting epic battles between noble elf White Lions and Chaos beastmen. The rugs that covered the stone flags of the floor were deep and warm-looking in the muted colours of autumn and the heavy, rough-hewn items of furniture were rendered majestic by the gold and silver shawls and cloths that covered them and made them inviting. On a little table by his bed stood a pitcher of water

and a bowl of sweet-smelling petals. Soft clothes for bathing
his wounds half obscured an ornate little hand mirror in its
gilt frame. The soft light of the candles flickered and reflected
in the bright surface of the mirror, casting light on Gilead's
face.

Gilead rolled lightly over in the warmth of a clean, sweet-
smelling bed, and awoke. He suddenly knew the kind of
comfort that he had long denied himself. Fully alert for only a
moment, he sighed and spread his limbs in the luxurious
space.

'Awake, warrior. Your slumber was both long and deep.' He
heard the low, soft cadences of his own people, spoken in the
lilting, breathy tones of a young woman. Familiar, somehow.
'Awake now and take a little sustenance, sir.' Her voice was so
beautiful, and so familiar, that he dared not open his eyes lest
he be dreaming.

'Let him sleep a little, daughter. There is time enough.' The
same voice, but male and lower, with the slight creak of age,
but familiar, and elven – wonderful to Gilead's ear.

He opened his eyes, not knowing how long he had slept, nor
how he had come to this place. Comfort dulled his instinct to
enquire. He felt clean and could sense the ointment on his
bruises. He smelled, not of the battlefield, but of fragrant
soaps and unguents and of sweet sleep. Someone had tended
him gently and well.

'Father, he wakes!' That familiar voice rose slightly with
delight, and a smile showed the neatest row of small, white
teeth in a frame of perfect lips. Gilead smiled back and
adjusted the sheet around his torso.

'Leave us, child.' Her father dismissed her and she left the
room, casting one last gaze down at Gilead. A gaze that
showed him her entire face in all its elven glory. The wide-set
eyes and lean, straight nose of his kind; the deep, intelligent
brow and narrow jaw. Niobe! It was Niobe!

Her father smiled down at him. 'Welcome, warrior. Welcome
to the Tower of Talthos Elios.'

'Then… I have found it?'

'You were searching for us? We are… perhaps hard to find.
We have secreted ourselves in the darkness of the forest for
many years. These are lean, dangerous times.'

Gilead look up. 'Who am I to thank for salvation?'

'I am Gadrol Elios. I welcome you here.'

'Your daughter–'

'She told me how you rescued her, son of Tor Anrok. I am in your debt. I am happy to have rescued you in return.'

'But how did she escape… escape the Chaos scum, Ire?'

'Niobe was never less than inventive. She slipped his bonds after you weakened him, and found her way home.'

Gilead remained in bed for several days, receiving visits from Lord Gadrol, and meals and other necessities from elf servants of the court. On the second day, Niobe reappeared and with her came the reassuring scent of the woods and herbs that she had gathered to tend him with. The same plants administered to his cuts and bruises when he would skirmish with Galeth as a child. The same he had used to restore Fithvael to health after the fool had come to the aid of a the human girl Betsen Ziegler, without Gilead's help…

Fithvael?

Gilead became agitated.

'Your friend fell on the field…'

'I saw him. No, that's not correct: I lost sight of him. I don't truly know what happened,' Gilead interrupted his nurse.

Niobe soothed the warrior's mind with her gentle words and calm, lullaby tones. 'The rescue party found only you alive on the battlefield amongst so many monsters. The carrion beasts had been at work. There was little left of any corpse. It must be your dear friend met a heroic death. To take on so many and to triumph. You two, alone, fought and killed three dozen of the dark ones.'

'And what are they?'

'The old curse. Half-formed ghouls from the barrow it is our duty to guard. Chaos once more raises its head in these gloomy forests.'

Gilead fell silent, not really hearing her as she spoke further. Fithvael was dead. Fithvael was dead.

Throughout the third day and the fourth, the Lord of the Court came to listen to Gilead's story. Gadrol spoke too, in turn, of the rise of the dead things from beneath the barrow, rotting things that came stinking their way out of the earth to haunt the living. Dark beings from a vale beyond. Once more his tower's garrison had armed to guard the land. The barrow-kind held a sway of fear across this region. Raids, murders and the like were common. One of Gadrol's patrols had found Gilead. The warrior had countered a raiding pack from the barrow single-handedly.

He... and his fallen friend, of course.

Gilead was sad, but strong and resolute before the older elf. When he spoke to Niobe as she nursed him, his voice often broke and he openly mourned the loyal Fithvael, the last of his questing warriors. On the evening of the fourth day, Niobe took the little mirror from the table beside Gilead's bed. 'Look into the mirror,' said Niobe, 'see who you are and all that means for the future.'

Gilead looked into the mirror, and was surprised at what he saw there. His skin was clear and bright and he was clean-shaven. He looked like the carefree young warrior, who had sparred with his twin and laughed and played and enjoyed life. He thought that time, his quest and the battlefield had aged him and made him cynical, but he did not see life's scars in his face. It gave him hope, brought him calm.

As DAWN BROKE, Fithvael awoke with a start. His dreams had brought him nothing but anguish. He was exhausted, fatigued by tortured sleep and restless nightmares; wracked with the aches and pains of an agile but ageing body punished on the field of battle; troubled by the ever-present stench of Chaos in the air and by Gilead's absence. All of his faculties were compromised, but he hadn't enough sense left to realise it. His body and spirit were broken and his tired mind increasingly obsessed.

Fithvael contented himself with a handful of clean water for his breakfast. He didn't remember when he had last eaten a meal. He untethered the mare and began to lead her in a wide sweep around the battlefield. She whinnied and snorted and kept her muzzle upwind of the foul arena.

Only hours later did Fithvael find what he was looking for. He had been circling, resolutely, since dawn and must have passed the hoof prints several times already. He and Gilead had ridden into battle and Gilead had ridden out, but these were the only tracks the veteran had found and he would follow them, blind now to reason and probability.

Fithvael sat astride his horse hour upon hour, following whatever hoof-print trail he happened upon, regardless of direction or number. He did not feel useless now. He was on a quest.

GILEAD'S GRIEF WAS sharp and weighed heavy upon him. Heavier because he was surrounded by his own kind. He would see Fithvael's wisdom in the old lord's face, or recognise the old warrior's tone in the words of a servant at the court. His pain dulled only with the kindnesses of Niobe. Her soft words were as effective a sedative as her sweet-tasting tonics. To find her again… it was a victory, a blessing.

A week passed, two, a month. He roused himself, first from his bed and then from his chamber, and soon he began to take his meals with the family and their courtly retinue. They made him welcome and celebrated his recovery, and also talked about the constant threat of the barrow. In turn he recounted for them stories of his quest and of his warriors' unerring bravery. He told how, one by one, he had lost them all and he recounted for them the heroic death of each of his questing comrades.

For Niobe, Gilead saved the stories of his home, the tower he had abandoned before taking up his life-quest. He told her of his dead twin, Galeth, and of how he believed he had taken on his sibling's life force to conquer evil. He talked of Fithvael, of the dead elf's loyalty to the old traditions and ideals of Gilead's ancient family. A family that would become extinct with his own death.

Niobe sat for many hours, head bowed over some piece of woman's work, while she listened intently to Gilead's epic tales. At these times, Gilead's feelings would sometimes catch him unawares and he would find himself searching her face for signs of her response to him.

When he was alone Gilead would lift the mirror to his face and see there something new and positive, at last, for the future. He began to forget Fithvael and Galeth and the hard fight and pain of his past.

THE AIR WAS cold and moist and the dusk a dirty brown. Fithvael could not distinguish the dense, grey cloud from the murky, tumultuous sky. Night was falling, sluggish, heavy and moonless. There were no stars to navigate by, even if the old elf had known where he was or which way he needed to go.

Fithvael was so tired that he had long since dropped the mare's reins and was allowing her to meander through thickening woodland. Everything fell into a flat sepia-grey landscape, and he could no longer see colour or judge distance.

Days without food and with little water had taken its toll on Fithvael and his mount, and the mare slowed to an exhausted stop, bent her head and slowly grazed the woodland clearing. Fithvael slumped across her warm neck, then slowly rolled off her back, landing heavily on his empty, aching side. Sleep, he must sleep. Pulling his cloak around his head, Fithvael gave in to his fatigue, trusting that his horse would stand guard for him once more.

Who knows how long he slept? Dull, dark days wove seamlessly into cold, dark nights. There was no sun to wake him. The mare lay beside her master as the old elf sweated and twitched and cried out. Delirious dreams tortured his sleep. Awake, his mind had been full of Gilead, of tracking him, finding him, fighting for him. He'd thought of nothing else since waking on the battlefield, but nothing of his rational mind was left in his slumber, and the nightmares raged.

Gilead was dead. Gilead was dying. Gilead was being torn apart by a horde of cannibal beastmen. Gilead was walking towards him, body slashed open, oozing decaying gore, trying to say something through broken, seeping lips. Gilead was coming back from the dead. Gilead was a monster.

Even Fithvael's dreams did not wake him. He fought his way through them, killing Chaos beasts, reaching Gilead too late. Over and over again the dream circled round in his head and each time the veteran warrior fought harder and dirtier. He needed to get to Gilead faster. Each time he was too late.

Yet again the stench of Chaos was in the air and abruptly he was awake. Fithvael sprang to his feet, knees bent, arms wide. His staring eyes flicked around the clearing, penetrating the foliage, searching out the enemy. A shadow moved and the warrior plunged towards it, a weapon in each thrashing hand, arms flailing, a howl screaming from his dry throat. He threw himself on the adversary's back, plunging twin blades into its collarbone, shoulders, arms, indiscriminately stabbing and scratching at the thing that had taken Gilead. At last the enemy, a corrupted echo of an elf warrior, sloughed off the berserk Fithvael, dropping him unceremoniously on his back and staggered away, trying to staunch a bursting gash in its neck.

Fithvael lay on his back in the failing brown sunlight, awake, breathing hard. The enemy had been real, and, fuelled by his dreams, the old warrior had injured it and sent it on its way. Tired and starved, though he was, Fithvael found new purpose. He felt weak and winded and knew he must eat, but he also now had a beast to track. A direct lead back to Gilead. He had a chance. He had hope.

The mare had a full belly and was well rested. The old warrior gathered together some supplies and ate some of the fruits and nuts he had found. He shook out his dirty, crumpled cloak and washed away the ichor that had splashed from the foe's random wounds. He took a little time, knowing that the beast would be moving slowly. He didn't want to catch up with it. He didn't want to have to kill it before he had found his friend. The pleasure of the kill would come later when he was fitter, when he had tracked it to its lair and to Gilead.

THE TOWER OF Talthos Elios was built inside the four sides of a large, open courtyard. It rose into the grey sky, above the drab walls and black-leafed trees, like a finger of ice. A glassy, perfect structure, the work of the gifted and blessed of Tiranoc's dispossessed offspring centuries before. The curtain walls that faced the outside world were thick and solid, without windows. This was a fortress from the outside, but a haven within. The walls that overlooked the courtyard had many windows and doors and even balconies and internal verandas. Gilead began regularly to take up a position on one of the tower's first floor balconies and watch the business of the day unfold below him.

This was where the lord's warriors would practice their combat skills, exercising and sparring with blunted weapons. Gilead began to long for their company and to share his skills with them.

Late one afternoon, Lord Gadrol joined Gilead and they began to talk of the world outside the tower, and the endless duty of the Elios line. The barrow lay in the dark combe beyond the walls and the warriors of the tower patrolled the woodlands. They alone guarded the barrow-breach, an ancient wound in the order of the world and one now recently reopened. It was a hard and unforgiving duty. Gadrol welcomed any help he could get.

Three or four months after being brought to the castle, Gilead was in the courtyard with the other warriors, revelling in the staged battles and the camaraderie. His body had become soft with recovery and with lack of exercise, but his mind was as sharp as ever.

By the half year, he was spending fewer nights carousing with the household and longer days honing his body to its former levels of combat-fitness. He often laughed, in the early days, as he failed to parry a shot from his sparring partner, or lunged too late and fell over his own feet. But as time passed the value of his war-craft came back to him, and with it his old fighting skills. Once more he could wield a sword in either hand, he could move with the kind of dancer's grace that had always characterised his defensive strategy and, finally, late one afternoon, he became shadowfast.

He had spent all day sparring in the courtyard with the Elios warriors who had become his friends and allies. Suddenly Gilead sensed an attack from behind, then another to his left. It was a regular habit of the warriors to ambush each other in this manner, for battle awareness or, at the end of a long day, for fun.

Gilead's adrenalin began to pump hard. He disarmed the elf before him, spinning his opponent's wooden stick high into the air before catching it deftly and boxing the elf on the ears in a resounding double blow. While the practice pole was still in mid-air, he had spun round, dropping the warrior behind him with a swing to the legs. A second blow to the back of the knees sent Gilead's unsuspecting assailant sprawling across the cobbled courtyard, landing him face down with a severe crack to the head. The third elf had no time to fight off the advance of two twirling, spinning staffs. He did not see them coming. One cracked his sword arm at the shoulder and the second beat, point first, hard into his sternum, winding him. Then the first staff came back, wrapping itself around his neck. Gilead had almost strangled the bewildered, broken wretch before he relaxed and let the elf drop, gratefully, to the cobbles.

One moment Gilead had been struggling furiously against one sparring partner. The next he was in three places at once; defending himself simultaneously on three fronts; disarming and felling three fine warriors in no time, with no apparent linear progress. Shadowfast, as of old.

On the ground lay three spent warriors, breathing hard and reaching for the wooden weapon-substitutes that had been broken or confiscated in Gilead's onslaught. He looked at them for a moment, aghast, then began to laugh, throwing his head back in a hearty roar.

He was close to his old pitch of ability. He longed now for more than practise. To face the ever-present incursions of darkness from the barrow, with these brave warriors at his side.

In the meantime he, somewhat sheepishly, helped two of his combatants to their feet. The third was carried away, unconscious. They all took several days to recover sufficiently to rejoin Gilead and their fellows in the exercise yard.

THE SKIES NEVER cleared and the foliage grew ever more dense around Fithvael, but the trail was hot with gore and ichor, and the tracking was easy.

The wounded foe had but one purpose: to return whence it had come. It made no attempts to cover its tracks or move with any stealth. Camouflage was unnecessary for both the pursued and its pursuer, since nothing was visible in the depths of the densely wooded landscape. Fithvael was careful, though, not to be heard and at regular intervals he ate and rested, building his strength.

Fithvael came upon the broken body of the foe less than an hour's gentle ride from his last halt. Cautiously, he dismounted and stood beside the body. He could feel its warmth and sensed that it was still pulsing. If it was not dead, then it could still lead Fithvael to his quarry.

The old elf remounted and the mare took a step or two backwards, then Fithvael reared her, letting out a fierce war cry of his own as the mare whinnied and snorted in surprise and stamped her front feet hard. The noise seemed massive in the still and quiet of the forest, but the wight was not roused. Fithvael reared the mare again, dancing her in a circle around the fallen thing, crashing amongst the undergrowth and clanging his long sword and dagger together over his head. The single-minded elf did not perceive the risk of raising hell in an area rife with Chaos. His only thought was to drag this sorry half-corpse back to consciousness.

The dark one whimpered, then screamed, convulsing in the filth of torn undergrowth and damp, peaty earth around him. Fithvael dismounted, still crashing his weapons together and letting out his ancient war cry. It could feel neither fear nor motivation. It couldn't, wouldn't stand. Then it ceased to writhe. It glared up at Fithvael, ichor still finding an oozing path through the thick, crusting scabs around its dozen or more wounds. He saw it wanting nothing, except to kill him.

It couldn't even do that.

Fithvael turned his back on the beast, bitter and angry that his plan had failed. Then rage crept into his eyes and overtook him. His long sword entered the fallen thing's chest a split second before the dagger reopened the fatal wound in its neck. Death was instant now, but Fithvael took no pleasure in it.

The old warrior had no choice but to continue his quest in any way possible. He assessed, as best he could, the direction the beast had been taking and decided to follow its course. He moved faster now, more urgently. His dream kept flashing in his mind, images of the forest-wights intercut with the knowledge that, in his nightmares he had been too late. Too late to save his friend. Too late to rescue Gilead and renew their partnership.

Fithvael fought his feverish mind… and lost. He began to crash through the forest, heedless of the noise he made and the trail he left. Forgetting that woodland was his natural home, his natural ally, the elf tore a path through the forest, destroying as he went. The ground was churned up beneath the now frantic hooves of the frightened mare, and all but the largest of the trees were hacked aside out of his path.

His mind would not see an end to the struggle, so when the elf suddenly found himself in a steep, sheer pass of black conifers it was a moment before his sword arm rested and he reined in and calmed his mount.

His paranoia turned to glee. In the distance before him, Fithvael could see the tall, glinting sides of a structure. Taking refuge in the lea of the trees, he stopped and looked again. A fortress, a tower, a dank place of evil, this was the monstrous place where he would find his friend. This was where the foe had been making for.

THE TOWER OF Talthos Elios glowed with magnificence. Pennants and banners were raised in the great hall. Gold and silver cloth adorned the benches and grander courtly chairs around the long table, which groaned under the weight of the food that covered it. Meat, fowl and game of all kinds were arranged amongst wide dishes, standing on tall feet, which were heaped with mountains of spices, fruit and bread.

There was to be a grand feast day on the morrow and the Lord Gadrol and his fair daughter Niobe were arranging everything. It was a special occasion and Gilead was to be the guest of honour. He had resided at the castle for a year, so tomorrow was to be his anniversary and his formal inauguration into the court. He was to become one of them and to have so illustrious a warrior join their cause delighted all at the castle. They had every reason to celebrate.

Gilead, too, was ready to celebrate and eager to become a full member of this society. They had so much to offer: companionship, a good cause... and then there was Niobe. The reason he was here. The beautiful elf maiden had restored Gilead's health, ministered to his needs when he was mourning Fithvael, been constant companion and confidante. She had even made a radiant new suit of gold and blue for Gilead to wear on his feast day.

As Fithvael advanced up the pass, coming ever closer to the tower, the last remnant of caution left the veteran warrior. The tower was derelict, dilapidated. Its walls stood tall and square to the outside world, but as he cast his eyes towards the top of the walls, the stone seemed insubstantial. He couldn't focus on individual stones; they seemed to move around each other and he could see the sky through them. The lower walls of the edifice were covered in a brackish black slime of moss and lichens. Fithvael placed his hands on the stone, but felt only the softness of the moss. There was nothing solid there. Working his way around the outside walls, Fithvael found the space where a doorway had once been. One huge, black-studded rotten door still hung from one hinge, the other had fallen inward towards what must once had been a courtyard, but was now a wilderness of rock and dead and dying plant-life.

The warrior elf was confused and disappointed. He had been convinced that this was the place. This was surely where

Gilead was being held. Yet there was no sign of him or anyone – until a swift, unseen blow felled him from behind.

GILEAD WAS SPARRING in the courtyard, as usual, when the slumped body was carried in. Patrols left from the castle at regular intervals, but since Gilead had been brought here there had been no new arrivals. He was excited to see that the elf guards' latest expedition had been more successful.

Dropping his wooden weapons and nodding his thanks to his sparring partner, Gilead bounded towards the two warriors who carried another, ragged elf between them. Fithvael was unconscious, one arm around each of the warriors' shoulders, feet dragging across the courtyard and his head down. Gilead did not recognise his old friend at first. He simply wanted to help this newcomer, this stranger like himself. He threw the body over his shoulder and took him up to his own room, the room where Niobe had nursed him back to health.

Only when Gilead had gently laid his burden on the clean bed, did the elf realise that it was his dearest friend who had been rescued.

'Fithvael! Fithvael, my old friend… I thought you were dead…'

Gilead called Niobe and Gadrol and the three kept a bedside vigil for the old elf, while he slowly regained consciousness. Gilead could think of nothing more perfect than to have Fithvael join him tomorrow on his feast day in his new home.

As Fithvael's eyes began to open, Gilead leant over his old friend.

Fithvael sat bolt upright, staring past Gilead's gently smiling face at the room he found himself in. The walls crawled with putrid vegetation and lice. The furniture was black with decay and the food by his bed was rotten and riddled with squirming parasites. The stench of Chaos was all around him, yet this was indisputably Gilead before him.

'Fithvael. It is me, truly. You are alive. You are saved. I want you to meet my great friends and rescuers, Lord Gadrol and his daughter, the Lady Niobe. Gods, you must remember Niobe!'

Two hideous… things stepped out of the gloom behind Gilead, leering at Fithvael and malevolently baring their blackened teeth. Startled and cowering, Fithvael blinked terrified eyes – and saw, in that blink, a majestically magnificent room, decorated in elven style. He saw the beautiful young elf woman, Niobe, and her doting father. He saw fresh fruit and herbs and smelt sweet medicinal potions.

But it was a mere blink and when he opened his eyes again the room had resumed its rotten, filthy demeanour. Fithvael embraced Gilead, closing his eyes for a moment, concentrating only on his friend.

Eyes clamped tight shut, Fithvael felt the syrupy ooze of magic around him. He had seen for an instant what Gilead believed to be the truth. But Fithvael would not succumb. He saw Chaos and realised that they meant not to kill Gilead, but to recruit him, to corrupt him as they themselves had been corrupted. To turn to evil one such as Gilead would delight their perverse minds. The wights wanted to harness Gilead's skill, his knowledge, his tenacity, his bravery. They were elves corrupted by the foul allure of Chaos. To recruit one of their own kind, the best of their kind, was a goal worth pursuing.

Fithvael lay back on the bed, concentrating hard on his quest. He had sworn that he would save his friend, but now he was no longer sure he could. Gilead didn't see what was truly around him and Fithvael could not defeat so many of the dark things without his old friend's help.

He took a deep breath. If he couldn't fight his way out of this situation, he would have to think his way out. He would have to show Gilead the truth.

Fithvael lay in bed, refusing potions and food and talking little. He let Gilead talk. And Gilead could speak of nothing but his feast day on the morrow. His inauguration into the community of Talthos Elios. His new life.

'How long have you been here, my old friend?' asked Fithvael.

'A year tomorrow, Fithvael. I am happy that you will sit by my side at the feast. I have been content here, these are good people…'

Gilead talked on as Fithvael lay, deep in thought. Even time was false here. Fithvael had left the battlefield, where he had last seen Gilead, only a single lunar month ago. And now the old elf had only one short day before Gilead would be lost to him forever, bound to Chaos by whatever disgusting ceremony they had prepared for him.

* * *

AT DAWN, THE tower was glorious in the sunlight. Banners streamed in the blue, windy air. Horns sounded clarion notes from the battlements. Gilead woke at their sound and smiled.

The day was full of tournaments, displays of skill, friendly contests. Then, as dusk settled, thousands of lamps and candles were lit in the great hall.

Gilead dressed in the beautifully crafted suit that Niobe had made for him, but Fithvael saw only the old, worn and dirtied battle garments that were his friend's usual attire. He saw only the filth on his friend's hands and face, smelt only that the elf warrior had missed as many baths as he had himself.

The population of the tower gathered in the great hall, to the strains of musicians in the gallery and took their places at the long tables.

The feast began. Fithvael felt a mounting sense of doom.

He had tidied himself and sat at Gilead's right hand at the head table. He kept his face against his sleeve. The piles of rotten, maggot-ridden food were enough to make him nauseous, but the stench of the gathered host was worse. Fithvael used every ounce of self-control when looking around. He was appalled by the sheer weight of numbers of the dark things; sixty or more, in all their grotesque, reeking forms. He wondered that they could believe they had duped him.

The veteran elf watched as Gilead and his party took their hearty appetites to the rotten food. Fithvael smiled at his friend, but all the food on his plate found its way under the table and onto the floor. He couldn't even bear to sully his clothes by secreting it in his pockets.

Then the speeches began. Gilead stood to toast his friends and his new home with joyous words. Fithvael looked up into his friend's eyes, and by the light of a thousand candles he saw what Gilead saw. He saw the beauty of the sumptuously decorated room and the glory of the feast before them. As Gilead's eyes moved across the room Fithvael saw, reflected there, a large party of elf warriors and then the serenity of a lovely elf woman, as his friend's eyes came to rest on Niobe.

In that moment Fithvael had his plan. He only prayed that it was not too late.

As Gilead resumed his seat, his old friend leaned towards him.

'Gilead, my true friend, it is time now for my toast,' he said softly. 'Promise me only this: look into my eyes and see what I see, see what is reflected there. Be by my side now.'

Gilead looked at him curiously.

'Promise me!'

With that, Fithvael got to his feet and cast his eyes around the room. He spoke slowly of his love for his friend, but concentrated his eyes, first on the decorations, then on the food, then on the Chaos band and finally on the monster that was Niobe.

Gilead looked into his friend's eyes.

Looked…

…*looked*…

As Fithvael came to the end of his speech, he turned to Gilead. The smile had entirely left the other elf's face.

'Now stand with me, friend, and let us raise our swords and salute each other.'

Gilead rose, drew a deep breath and raised his sword to his old friend. Emotions were swirling behind his fixed visage. Rage, disappointment, guilt, horror. But rage was the greatest.

The creatures around them, the filthy, decaying remnants of the noble line of Elios, perverted and corrupted by the baleful influence of the very barrow they had chosen to guard, raised their goblets in mock salute, and the two true elves began their attack.

Fithvael ran through three of his nearest neighbours before any of the fiends had even armed themselves. Gilead, already shadowfast, whirling and slicing in several places at once, had reduced a dozen dark things to a heap of spurting, disgorging corpses.

Then the battle began in earnest as the degenerate court of Talthos Elios fought back.

Fithvael used their weight of numbers against them. Battling on two fronts, he managed to slip out of the fight and turn on a third assailant, as the first two killed each other in their frenzy.

Gilead threw a table over, tipping its contents into the laps of the beasts. They struggled to rise, but Gilead was too fast, attacking them as they lay on their backs in the debris, or were trapped by the heavy dishes that rained down on them. The once-elf things were not prepared for attack and those who wore no weapons, fought with their hands, losing their limbs to Gilead's long sword.

Gilead was standing atop the great tables, swinging his great blade and thrusting his dagger into any and all chaos flesh he could find. He fought his way nearer the doorway, taking down half a dozen barrow-spawn with his flailing weapons. The elf-echoes tore at each other in their rage to reach him.

Fithvael ploughed on, slower, but just as efficient. Following the swing of his long sword with a lunge from his dagger, he tore the throat out of one barrow-thing, the eyes out of the next. Here he severed a leg, bursting a great artery and filling his nostrils with the stink of the oozing ichor. He had both strength and purpose and he used them to good effect.

He could not see Gilead, but he could see his work as more foul things fell near to him, their mortal wounds releasing more of the putrid reek of Chaos.

With each blow, each death, the room grew darker, filthier, older and more decayed. The piles of rotten food quickly became puddles of black liquid and then disappeared. The bodies of the foe wept their gory contents, decayed quickly to ugly skeletal forms and then to grey dust.

The elves fought on as the remnants of the foul horde weakened and succumbed. Soon, Gilead and Fithvael stood together at one end of what had been the great elf hall, then a terrifying Chaos gathering. Now it was a ruin.

'Our work is done here,' said Fithvael, sheathing his dagger and leaning on his sword.

Gilead bowed his head. The two looked at each other, then once more at the room, before turning to leave.

As he turned, Gilead saw movement. His sword and dagger were drawn and he spun back into the room, swinging his sword in a wide arc as he spun high off his feet. As he landed he plunged his dagger into the monster that had risen up in front of him.

Fithvael turned as he heard a loud thump. It was Gadrol's head hitting the floor. The lord of Elios's body followed its decapitated head, taking down with it the body of the wraith that had been Niobe. The hilt of Gilead's dagger could be seen sticking straight out from the second barrow-thing's ichor-pulsing throat.

Fithvael stared down at the last two bodies, Gadrol and Niobe twitched in their final death throws. Then they, too, began to decay before the elves' eyes.

'I'm sorry, Gilead,' said Fithvael. He could think of nothing else to say.

'Niobe...' his companion said softly.

'It was not her... she is still lost, taken by Lord Ire. These fiends played upon your dreams, your hopes.'

Gilead looked across at the veteran elf, then down at himself. He was suddenly deathly tired. He had not been washed, nor his bruises tended. He was shabby and dishevelled and the bruises he had received on the battlefield had not yet faded. He raised his hand to his face and was startled to feel the soft stubble that had grown there.

'Time was corrupted too, I'm still bruised and dirty. I dreamed it all, didn't I? How did they do this to me?' There was an odd mix of bitterness and sharp sadness in his eyes. 'I'm in your debt for... waking me.'

OUTSIDE, THE EVENING was slate grey along the pass. Crows rasped from the steep scarps. Two comrades moved out from nightmare into encroaching night.

Their torches lit the walls of the tower with flickering shapes. Fire began to twist and flurry around the desecrated tower. The Tower of Talthos Elios burned, its nobility and its curse sooting away into the night.

'Now the barrow,' said Gilead, ferocity burning in his tired eyes.

Fithvael followed him. There was work to be done.

VI
Gilead's Swords

*War tends to limit the length
of friendships.*

MY EYES MAY be old and clouded, but still I see doubt in your face. As if all I have told you this long winter night was nothing more than a tale-spinner's fancy. Well, if you ask me, it is the curse of some souls to be born at the wrong time.

Consider this: had Gilead Lothain come to this world a thousand years earlier, in a better age, most like his life and deeds would have been dutifully recorded and celebrated in the chronicles of his fair people, and earned him fame as a hero even you would have heard of.

But he did not. When he first drew sharp breath at the midwife's slap, in the cold midnight of a bitter winter, his noble and ancient race was already waning. Their civilisation, which once had held the whole world itself as its domain, had become nothing but a shadow on the fringes of life. The elves were beings of the edge places, relics of a brighter time. Their blood was running slower and cooling, their traces vanishing from the land, supplanted by the coarse young tribe of man. The legacy of Ulthuan had been eroded by history, worn away by fate. Even the great elven chronicles were, by then, patchy and incomplete, those that were still maintained.

So Gilead Lothain, last lord of Tor Anrok, was never a celebrated hero. He never became the subject of popular
story-songs, or verse cycles declaimed by courtly poets. His
deeds were never bound in buckskin to take pride of place in
a palace library. His name has never become proverbial, never
alluded to in the great poems and sagas of our day. It is his
curse to be nothing more than a story. A fireside tale told by
old folk to the young. A memory, or the memory of a memory. All that the world has of him now is myth – at worst,
ill-remembered nonsense; at best, half-truths swollen by
imaginative retellings. The rest is blank, a ghostly trace, like a
faint handprint in dust. A life imperfectly and fleetingly
glimpsed every now and then in the dim forests of rumour.

Except here, at this hearth. There is truth here, what truth I
know. A few fragments of his long, sad life that you can trust
to be truer than myths. I have told you most of them.

The last is Maltane, or more properly the Battle of Maltane,
also called the Tale of the Thirteen Swords. Or Twelve, or
Fourteen, depending on which account you follow. Whatever.

So, if the steward brings me more wine, and my lamp's wick
and failing voice last, we'll have that one, and it shall
assuredly be my last. The land is full of myths, but few are
truer or more worthy than this.

Winter had thawed to spring, and spring had ripened to
summer. Gilead and Fithvael, riding as shadows at the edges
of the estate of man, had roamed ever southwards, aimlessly,
since the murderous deceit of Talthos Elios. Now summer
itself, plump and golden on the bow, was about to turn and
wither and fall beneath the frosty touch of autumn.

What triumphs and defeats they had braved and shared
since the horror of Talthos Elios, it is not possible to say. But
there, at harvest time, chance, that most fickle and petty of all
divine blessings, led their wanderings to Vinsbrugge, during
their festival.

The harvest had been good and the grain towers, beehive-
shaped giants of white stone grouped at the lip of the town,
were full. The winding streets of Vinsbrugge were decked with
corn garlands, linen streamers and crop-gods woven from
golden straw. The priests of Sigmar had arranged processions
and services in the town basilica, and the guild masters had
paid for black powder rockets and flares to light up the night.

There was to be a week of thanksgiving, an excuse for revelry and disorder. A merry time to mark the turn of a hard year.

The hostelries and inns of Vinsbrugge were packed with strangers. Many were grain merchants, arriving early for the annual produce markets. Others were travellers and wanderers drawn in by the exuberance of the festival.

Two were not of mankind.

The rockets fizzing and flashing in the late summer evening and the sound of singing had drawn them to Vinsbrugge from a lonely road to the south-west. Fithvael had remarked that the sounds reminded him of victory feasts at Tor Anrok, lifetimes ago. If Gilead agreed, it was not clear. But he did not resist as his old comrade turned their path towards the happy lights of the small town.

They had found lodging, stables for their steeds, and anonymity in the bustling crowds, just two more hooded travellers in saddle-soiled robes. They ate in roast-houses along the main square, drank the night away in taverns at the north end and slept the days out. Fithvael's aching, tired limbs began to ease for the first time in months. Years, he did not doubt.

He hoped, indeed he silently prayed to the smoky, fading gods of Ulthuan, that simply mixing in these hospitable, joyous surroundings would thaw the misery and fatigue in his old friend.

Gilead said little, and Fithvael knew the scars of Talthos Elios were deep in his soul, forming calluses over the ravages of an already unkind life. Fithvael heard him murmur Niobe's name in his sleep more than once, through the hemp-cloth drape that partitioned their rented bedchamber.

Yet Gilead did seem to mellow. He watched the nightly fireworks with alert eyes, and laughed sometimes at the capering harvest fools in the street processions. They were white-faced fools in shirts of woven corn: some on stilts, some tumbling, some chasing into the crowds and beating laughing womenfolk with fertility staves.

Fithvael was simply glad to see a tinge of colour in Gilead's face, some meat back on his wasted limbs, a light in his eyes. It would do for now.

ON THE FIFTH night of the Festival, they found themselves in a crowded inn on Purse Lane, sharing a flask of wine at a corner table. A conjuror had come in off the street and was entertaining the crowd at the bar with sleight of hand. There was laughter and much amazement.

Fithvael was asking Gilead if he had thought where they might go once they were done with Vinsbrugge and the festival. He realised the warrior wasn't listening.

'What is it?' the veteran said.

Gilead looked down at his cup. 'We're being watched.'

'Where?' Fithvael also covered his gaze, pouring more wine for them both, but his eyes darted.

'At the bar, the far end. Ho! Not so obvious or he'll know we've seen him. Drinking alone, clad in a black cloak.'

Fithvael adjusted his boot, taking in the figure as he did so. Tall, slender, with his dark cloak swathed around him and its cowl drawn up to hide the face. The unmistakable shape of a longsword bulged under the folds of the cape.

'I agree. He is indeed observing us.'

'I seem to know the set of him,' Gilead murmured. He shook his head. 'Drink up and we shall go. I'm in no mood for trouble.'

They drained their cups and got up, pushing through the crowds to the door.

Purse Lane was cool and dark. Romping music issued from a nearby drinking parlour and most of the passers-by were laughing and loose on their feet.

They headed down to the north end, near the grain towers, where the air smelled of husks and was heavy with chaff.

'He's following,' Gilead whispered. Fithvael knew it without looking.

At an unspoken signal, they parted company, leaving the cobbled street in opposite directions. Fithvael slid into an alleyway, skirting round a whipmaker's shop to turn back on himself. He drew his sword.

Gilead melted into the shadows, sliding his own sword from its scabbard without a sound. Its weight felt good in his palm. It had been a while, he realised.

The hooded figure passed them. Fithvael stepped back into the street behind it, ready to–

They were gone.

The veteran swordmaster felt suddenly exposed and ridiculous, in the middle of the lane, sword drawn.

'You weren't really thinking of using that on me?' a mel-lifluous voice breathed in his ear.

Fithvael turned, flash-fast, and brought the point of his blade up to the throat of the hooded figure that stood behind him. Calmly, the figure hooked something over the end of the blade, something that slid down the keen length and stopped at the hilt. A necklace, silver, tied on a leather thong. It was the herald mark of Tor Anrok.

Fithvael gasped. The figure laughed softly and threw back his hood.

'Fithvael te tuin Anrok. I knew you from your gait in an instant. It has been such a very long time.'

'By Ulthuan! Nithrom?'

'One and the same,' said the smiling elf warrior in the black cloak. His long, fair hair was tied back, and under the cloak he wore form-fitting armour of dark green leather. He was still smiling as he whipped around and brought up his long silver blade to block Gilead's longsword. Sparks sprang from the chime of metal.

'Gilead! Put up your blade! It is Nithrom! Nithrom, you hear me? Don't you know him?' Fithvael flung himself for-ward to get between them, but Gilead pushed him aside with his free hand.

'Something that has his shape, perhaps,' the slender elf growled. 'Something that uses an old face as a mask to deceive us.'

Gilead spun around, circling his long, blue-steel sword in a blur, but again the black-cloaked figure blocked him.

'Ever the cautious one, son of Lothain. That is good. In these friendless days especially.'

Gilead and the stranger shadow-danced around each other. Gilead flexed his grip on the hilt of his longsword.

'Even the voice... you play him well. But the Nithrom I knew is long dead.'

'Am I?' chuckled the other. 'How did I die? I am curious to know.'

'You left...' Gilead corrected himself: 'He left Tor Anrok twenty-five winters past. Never seen again. No word, no mes-sage, no trace of his passing.'

'There is a large world outside the tower, Gilead, son of Lothain. To be lost in it does not make you dead. Given that you and old Fithvael are here in this gutter-town, skulking like wanted bandits, I would have thought you would have learned that by now.'

Gilead threw himself at the stranger. Their blades clashed six times in quick succession. Every impact was a parry of Gilead's strokes. The stranger made no effort to press an attack.

'Gilead!' Fithvael hissed at his old comrade. 'I love you as a brother, but you are acting like a fool! This is Nithrom, I would swear it! You were but a youth when he left! I knew him well, hunted in the chase with him, sparred with him, fought alongside him now and then.'

'And taught me all I know of woodcraft and bowmanship,' said Nithrom. 'You were the backbone of the warriors, Fithvael te tuin. What sorry turn of fate finds you following this hot-blood to the ends of the world?'

Fithvael sighed. He sometimes wondered that himself. He said, 'I don't follow... we travel together, as comrades.' It sounded like he was trying to convince himself.

'And how fares Tor Anrok? Your brave brother, Galeth? My old sire, hallowed be his wisdom, Lord Lothain?'

There was a silence broken only by the drunken singing from an inn in the next lane. The crescent harvest moon menaced the hot, dark sky like a goblin's curved blade. The smile on Nithrom's face faded.

'Gilead?'

'My father is dead. My brother is dead. Tor Anrok is but a heap of stones in a weed-choked glade.' Gilead lowered his sword. 'As you would have known, if you had ever come back.'

Fithvael could not see Nithrom's face because he suddenly looked down and the street shadows filled it. There was a dull clang as the silver sword fell from Nithrom's hand. It made Fithvael jump. A warrior such as Nithrom only dropped his sword when death stole him. Otherwise it was brandished or sheathed.

Nithrom walked away from them both, his head bowed. Fithvael stepped forward, picked up the silver blade gently and glanced round at the glowering Gilead with angry eyes.

'Will you put up your sword now, fool?' he snarled.

Gilead slowly sheathed his long blue-steel blade in its

leather scabbard. His lost brother's sword whispered softly as it slid inside, like silk against silk.

At the corner of Purse Lane, where it joined the main market street, there was a crumbling pile of worn and fractured millstones discarded by the granaries. They found Nithrom sitting on them, gazing at the moon. Fithvael sat down next to him. Gilead hung back, alone, watching.

'All gone?' whispered Nithrom at last.

'All gone.'

'All of it? All perished?'

Fithvael nodded.

'It is the way of this world that we will all fade and be forgotten,' said Nithrom. 'Our time is passed. I... I always hoped, trusted, that Tor Anrok would stand the menace of time. Away, abroad, following the path Fate dealt me, I cherished the notion that the tower still stood, as I had always known it. Waiting for me even if I never returned.'

Fithvael saw how lined and worn Nithrom's lean face had become. Weariness and care had etched their marks on his once-handsome features. They were about the same age, Fithvael perhaps a few seasons older. Nithrom was of noble blood, the son of Lothain's great uncle. He had been born into the warrior tradition, raised as a woodsman, and had eventually chosen the ranger's path to the outer world, to quest and journey alone.

Fithvael was of lower blood, the eldest of six sons born to the tower court's master-at-arms. But they had been friends, growing up together in the dark staircases and draughty halls of Tor Anrok. A soldier's boy and the son of a noble. Bound to his service in his lord's troop, Fithvael had been destined to stay and serve at Tor Anrok for life, and deeply missed his privileged friend when he left. Missed him and, at the time, envied his freedom. Now he had tasted that freedom himself, following Gilead, and he did not like it much. There was nothing left to envy. He had left Tor Anrok as a dutiful member of Gilead's war-band, and now he was the only one left. And seeing the age in Nithrom's face, he recognised his own. He felt spent, worn out. Regardless of the long-lived nature of his ancient race, Fithvael felt old.

He handed the graceful silver sword back to Nithrom, hilt first. Nithrom took it and set it across his knees.

'When I sighted you and the lord's son in the tavern, I felt joy. It seemed this day would be the happiest of many. But now I find it is the saddest.'

'What are you doing here?' Gilead stood beside them now.

'Mourning,' Nithrom replied, without looking up.

Gilead sat down on the millstones next to Nithrom.

'No... here. In this human nest, mixing with them.'

'The same as you.'

'We have no purpose. No reason to be here. No cause, no drive, no...' Fithvael's voice trailed away.

'Then not like you,' Nithrom said. 'I have a cause. I am here to purchase supplies, collect resources. To collect a few more good swords, if I can.'

He looked round at Fithvael, a smile – sad still, but a smile never the less – forming on his mouth. 'Perhaps the gods brought me here, and you too. Perhaps it is right that our paths cross, no matter the pain that meeting brings.'

'Why?' Gilead asked from the other side of the veteran elf warrior. 'What cause is it that holds you?'

AT DAWN, NITHROM led them down to a livery next door to the Temple of Sigmar. The ostler was just opening the shutters and unlocking the bolts. Early sunlight shafted into the livery barn.

There were three wagons lined up inside, fully packed. Sacks of grain, bolts of white linen, bundles of freshly fletched arrows and a three dozen unstrung longbows, a box of spearheads, two boxes of iron tacks, twenty flasks of lamp oil and twenty more of rubbing alcohol, a drum of pitch, a sack of padlocks, three coils of hemp-rope, five newly struck swords and thirty brand-new daggers, jars of salted figs and olives in oil, ropes of seasoned sausage, sheets of jerk-beef and dried fish, three cases of wine, two kegs of ale... More besides. Boxes, sacks, bundles.

'You're planning a small war?' joked Fithvael, taking in the amount and nature of the supplies.

'That is precisely what he is doing,' Gilead said sourly.

Nithrom looked round at them both and nodded to Fithvael sadly.

'A small war...' he murmured.

Gilead glanced across at Fithvael. His eyes were hooded and dark.

'We are departing now. Farewell, Nithrom.'

'Gilead–' Fithvael began.

'Now, friend Fithvael. Your old sparring companion has run mad and we are not staying to be drawn into his lunacy.'

'Do me one favour, son of Lothain,' Nithrom said. 'Stay until the others get here. Then make up your mind.'

'Others?'

'They are to meet me here. They will be along. Do me that kindness, at least.'

Gilead flapped his scarlet cloak with a curse and sat down on a straw bale.

IT WAS EARLY still, with the mounting sun barely peering through fidgeting clouds, as the first of them arrived. The day was going to be warm, but there was a dawn chill yet in the marrow of the town, and beads of dew winked on every outdoor surface.

A human lad appeared in the livery doorway, framed by the light. He was short and slender, almost delicate, with soft white skin not thus far troubled by a barber's blade. He wore a dark green surcoat and black leggings under a set of oily grey plate mail that had clearly belonged to a father or uncle with a much larger frame. And the broadsword in its sling on his back seemed to weigh him down. His hair was short, fingercut and blond. Fithvael thought him noble looking, for a human. He was reminded of poor Lyonen, the gods rest his soul. There was a fragile grace to him, more reminiscent of an elf than a crude, clumsy human. His eyes were wide and the colour of buffed copper.

'Erill,' Nithrom greeted him, gladly.

'I'm early,' the youth said. His voice was musical, sweet and unbroken, though he tried for gruffness. 'No one's here.' He seemed to deliberately ignore Fithvael and the brooding Gilead.

'I am here,' said Nithrom with a smile and an open-armed gesture that took in the barn. 'Welcome. I'm happy to see you,'

Master Erill seemed pleased by that, and entered the place, sitting down on a mounting block near the wagons, dropping his heavy sword and bulging pack as he did so.

'This is Erill,' Nithrom said plainly. Fithvael exchanged courteous nods with the shy youth. Gilead made no move at all.

A quarter-hour passed, and then a voice spoke from the back of the barn.

'A good turn out, I see.'

They all looked round. Erill got up in a hurry, and Fithvael also rose at the sight of the newcomer Nithrom crossed to greet.

He had come in through the back shutter of the barn, as if he did not trust the thoroughfares of the town, even at this early hour. A lean human, with great power in his long limbs, dressed in tightly bound leather armour and a hauberk of studded hide. His hair was the colour of sun-bleached barley, and he carried his sword, shield and helmet on his back.

'Vintze!' Nithrom said. 'Ever the stealthy one.'

They shook hands. The newcomer cast his hard blue gaze around the stable, eyeing Gilead and Fithvael. He seemed to ignore the lad.

'Who's this?' he asked. There was a twang of the Reik about his accent.

'Companions of mine,' Nithrom replied briefly.

'Elves,' Vintze said, as if he was sniffing a scent from the air. 'Figures. Still don't trust them… no offence, lord.'

Nithrom grinned. 'None taken. I still do not trust thieves. So that makes us even.'

Vintze put down his pack. 'No one else here yet? Madoc? The Norseman? That Bretonnian fool?'

'They will come.'

'Still sleeping off a hard night in the taverns, I'll wager,' Erill said, trying to sound masculine and cynical in the world-weary way that humans found so appealing.

Vintze continued to ignore him. The Reiklander walked over and flopped down in a pile of sacking. 'Wake me when we're ready to go.'

Another thirty minutes passed, and shadows flickered in the growing sunlight outside the stable door. Two riders reined up and dismounted. They entered the barn; short, burly men from the provinces of the Empire, dressed in heavy plate the colour of brass with tabards of black and white. On their shields was the red bull of Ostland. When they raised their visors, in unison, Fithvael saw near-identical, square-cut faces.

'Dolph, Brom. Welcome.'

The Ostlanders greeted Nithrom with nods, and set about bringing their horses into the shade and refilling their water-skins. They moved in the strange, mirrored way only twin brothers could manage. Fithvael saw that for the first time, Gilead seemed vaguely attentive. He watched the twins, as if remembering.

The Carroburger appeared a few minutes later. Tall and dark-haired, with a cropped goatee and a cruel face, he simply strode into the barn and threw his basket helm and huge two-handed sword into the back of one of the wagons along with his leather pack. He wore the slashed and puffed sleeves and leggings – dark red in colour – of a Carroburg man-at-arms, and his black breastplate was polished like a mirror.

'Master Cloden,' Nithrom nodded.

The Carroburg greatsword nodded back and went to sit on his own in the corner of the barn. By now, the twin warriors from Ostland were playing at cards with Erill. Vintze was apparently sleeping. Gilead still sat like a statue near the doorway.

'When are you going to explain the–' Fithvael began.

'When I am ready,' Nithrom answered.

A trumpet sounded outside the livery, a fanfare more noisy than tuneful. Everyone stirred and even Vintze seemed to wake up.

The Bretonnian knight, mounted on his huge white charger, seemed to fill the doorway, his chrome armour glinting in the sun and his helmet's great feather-plume a livid red. By his side, a sullen, balding squire on a palfrey rasped the fanfare again through a sadly buckled cornet.

'His most magnificent and lauded self, the victorious warrior Le Claux! Welcome him, you fine people...' The squire's declaration tailed off wearily.

Le Claux, huge in his gleaming armour, seemed to have trouble dismounting, and the squire had to slide off his squat mount quickly to assist. The knight clanked into the barn as if nothing untoward had happened and grasped Nithrom's extended hand eagerly. He raised his visor, cursed as the heavy thing snapped shut again, and raised it once more. Fithvael saw a handsome, well-boned face that looked tired and bloated.

'My dear Nithrom! I stand ready to ride with you to the mouth of hell and back, for glory's sake! For this, I propose a hearty toast!'

Le Claux produced a wineskin from his harness and squirted a serious measure into his open mouth. They he strode across to the gathering of the others, and offered the skin around. Vintze, sitting up on the sacking, was the only one who accepted it.

The squire stepped forward and whispered to Nithrom. 'Don't even begin to ask how I got him here this early. And for everyone's sake, don't give him anything sharp.'

'The Lady will honour your duty, Gaude,' smiled Nithrom.

Gaude, the squire, suggested something fruity the Lady might do instead and turned away.

'Who, by all that's sacred, are these miserable nobodies?' Gilead asked Fithvael darkly.

A Kislevite warrior-woman called Bruda was next to arrive. She slammed in through the stable doors, dressed in a knee-length chain shirt and high boots, her mane of red hair flowing behind her. She was as tall as any of the men present, and nearly as broad and muscled. Her curved sabre bounced against her hip in its sheath. Fithvael knew that humans had generally a larger build than elves, but he had never seen a female of this stature. She seemed huge, like a goddess walking the land. She stank of sweat and almost knocked Erill flat with a slap to his shoulders. Le Claux offered her the wineskin and she drained it with a rumbling laugh and a hefty belch. Then she set about testing the give of the new bows by bending them against her instep by hand. Biceps like grapefruit swelled as she twisted the sprung wood down. One snapped.

'Not wery good, Nithrom!' she bawled, her voice clouded by her thick, northern accent. 'Wery poor! I think we have trouble if we use these, yes.'

'They'll do, Bruda,' Nithrom said calmly. 'And I know you'll only carve your own from the local wood when we get there.'

'Here he comes!' interrupted Vintze.

A big, black-bearded monster stumbled in through the stable doors. He was the most massive human Fithvael had ever seen, dressed in a dirty bearskin and blue-black disc-mail and lugging his weapons and full-face helm behind him. An old, deep blade-wound dented the left cheek of his rugged face, half hidden by his beard. At last Bruda wasn't the largest in the company. The newcomer was clearly intoxicated and belched freely, leaning on the terrified Erill for support. He clamped his tarnished helmet with its fierce, snarling mouth over his face and barked 'Let's get on with it, shall us?'

He was a Norseman. His axe was huge and he dropped it several times. His name was Hargen Hardradasson, but he preferred Harg.

Madoc, the last of them, rode up just before midday. Blond-haired and powerful, he wore the wolf-pelt of Ulric over his armour. An old warhammer was looped in the thongs on one side of his saddle.

Madoc made no apologies for keeping them waiting. He simply greeted them in the clipped, surly accent of Middenheim. There was something cynical in his bearing, Fithvael thought, more cynical even than the sneering Vintze or the disdainful Cloden.

As the party assembled and made ready to leave, hitching pack animals to the forks of the wagons, Nithrom crossed to Gilead.

'Do you see now?'

'I have waited as you asked. I see who has arrived.'

'And?'

' If you intend to fight a war, even a small war, with them, you're going to lose.'

'That is well said. Why do you think I asked you to stay? Why do you think I need you?'

THE PARTY LEFT Vinsbrugge in the first hour of the afternoon, as the bells of the old temple chimed a single peal. The air was hot and flat and bright, and the sky was cornflower blue and without blemish.

Nine riders on horses, three wagons drawn by packhorse teams, with spare steeds running from the backs of the carts. The lad Erill, the squire Gaude and the beast-like Norseman Harg drove the wagons. The streets weren't busy, and they made their way to the south bridge without provoking much attention from the townsfolk.

Fithvael was the last to leave. He lingered for a moment in the doorway of the livery.

'I am going to go with them,' he said. 'I want to go.'

'You will die and we shall never find Niobe nor our people,' growled Gilead. He stood in the shade of the emptied barn, a dim form like a ghost.

'Maybe. But I would rather die with a purpose than ride on towards the empty doom we're heading for. Nithrom *needs* us.'

Gilead scowled. 'That's not what Nithrom needs...'

Fithvael turned away. He knew the tone, the black mood it signalled. He had weathered those moods once too often.

'Then you should suit yourself, Gilead.'

'I will.'

Fithvael pulled himself into the saddle, and cast a final look back. 'Come with us.'

Silence answered him.

'Then fare well, Gilead Lothain.'

The veteran elf turned his steed's head and cantered away after the others.

NITHROM, ASTRIDE A lean, black horse, was riding at the tail of the party, waiting for Fithvael to catch up.

'I am sorry,' said Fithvael.

'Don't be, Fithvael te tuin. You cannot set his destiny for him. Gilead has his own path to tread.'

They fell into pace alongside one another. Up ahead, Le Claux was trying to get the others singing a round. When no one took up the offer, he sang it himself anyway, attempting to do all the overlapping parts with one voice. Bruda and Harg barracked him loudly and some of the others laughed.

'Yet I feel guilty, Nithrom. It is almost as if I were abandoning him. After all we have been through together.'

'That is understandable. But he cannot set your destiny for you either. He is a stubborn soul, and melancholy. You've given him the best years of your life, Fithvael. But you haven't changed him. Perhaps it is best now you go your own way.'

They were thumping over the boards of the south bridge now. Scintillating damselflies purred among the nodding bulrushes below the rail.

'Maybe...' Nithrom ventured. 'Maybe you are also feeling sad because you know he's right.'

'What?' Fithvael seemed startled.

'He sees this as a fool's errand, that I'm leading this company into a battle it cannot win. Maybe you know he is right, hating the fact that your loyalty to our old friendship is making you leave him to ride to your doom.'

Fithvael frowned. 'I... I don't think so.' A long pause. 'Are we really riding to our deaths?'

Nithrom laughed. 'I don't think so... or I wouldn't be doing so. But many might think the odds are against us.'

Fithvael shook his head. 'I'm with you in this, Nithrom te tuin. It feels like the right thing to do.'

Nithrom nodded and smiled. 'Maybe I was just testing you,' he said.

Fithvael chuckled. He took a final look back down the trackway, past the wooden bridge, into the outskirts of the mill town.

He did not see what he was longing with all his heart to see: a lone rider coming after them.

ONCE THE COMPANY had assembled at the livery, Nithrom had briefly outlined the nature of the venture, though the matter was already known to most of the recruits. They were to ride south and offer protection for a small settlement called Maltane, which every year was raided by Tilean mercenary companies heading home after the fighting season. Most years, Maltane had bought the raiders off with produce, supplies and gold. But this year the harvest had been poor and the town coffers were low. They had nothing to pay off the Tilean dog-soldiers with.

So they had decided to use the little gold they had to hire mercenaries to defend the settlement. Nithrom, selling his sword thereabouts, had undertaken the venture, and travelled north to recruit willing swordsmen. The company and its meagre supplies were the best he could do.

'Barely a dozen warriors against a mercenary company?' Gilead had murmured after hearing Nithrom out. He said nothing more, but shook his head sadly.

'Have you no courage, wood-thing?' Vintze had asked curtly, rising from his sacking bed.

'As much as you, I am sure. However, I clearly have more brains.'

For a dreadful moment, Fithvael had thought a fight might ensue. But Vintze had simply flopped back onto his sacks, muttering, 'We don't need him, Nithrom.'

Others – Harg and the Kislevite goddess – had also simply nodded. They all seemed too weary to Fithvael, as if they would only draw their blades and their anger out if there were money in it.

Le Claux, however, had swaggered to his feet, his armour clanking. 'Braggart! Wretch!' he declaimed at the disinterested Gilead. 'Take back the insult you have laid upon this fair company, or I will smite thee!'

Everyone, even Fithvael, had been unable to resist laughing at the Bretonnian's courtly-phrased challenge. Le Claux faltered at their laughter.

'Sit down and shut up,' Gaude had said cruelly and Le Claux had sat back down with a metallic clatter.

But there was animosity still. Fithvael had seen it then. The dark Middenheimer, Madoc, and the Carroburger had both gazed at Gilead with undisguised contempt. Clearly neither wanted to make a fight out of it either – their mercenary nature was as world-fatigued as the others – but Gilead's insult had rankled.

Now they were on the track, rising up through harvested fields of golden corn stalks and dry earth. A sheath of deep, green woods awaited them at the top of the slope. White butterflies flickered around them, and across the wildflowers in the hedge-ditches.

'How big is this place, this Maltane?' Fithvael asked.

'Small – a millhouse, a tavern, a temple, fifty families. Three hundred people at most.'

'Defended?'

'They have an outer ditch around the general settlement, and an inner fenced mound upon which the temple stands.'

'Is there a well in the temple enclosure?'

Nithrom shrugged. 'I never had cause to ask.'

Fithvael's unease deepened. If it came to a siege, in the inner fence... without water? 'What size is the dog-soldier band?'

'It varies. Last year, it was two hundred.'

Two hundred... against twelve, if you counted Gaude.

'You can go back any time you like,' Nithrom told him lightly, seeing his expression.

* * *

THEY ENTERED THE fringes of the woods. Spruce, laburnum, elm, beech, years old and rich in leaf. Birds called through the sunlight patches under the soothing green canopy. They sighted deer several times, timid and fleeting in the glades off the track.

Bruda pulled out a curved bow and dropped one with swift, experienced grace. They would eat that night, at least.

The track spiralled down through the woods for six leagues. They passed gurgling streams that lapped over mossy stone beds under the bent limbs of twisted elms. Twice they passed groups of ancient standing stones, bearded with lichen, forgotten in the old woodland. Some of the stones had marks cut in them, intaglio carvings almost weathered smooth by years of rain and frost – spirals, sunbursts, stars, goddesses.

Fithvael saw how Nithrom nodded to each stone reverently as they went by. Madoc did too, though presumably for somewhat different reasons.

They reached a wider stream in late afternoon as the shadows began to lie long. Wood pigeons and cuckoos warbled and called in the quiet woodlands. They watered the horses at a shingled ford in the stream. The water was clear like fluid glass and the stones were all polished smooth; dark and shiny under the flow, pale and dry out of it.

Flies buzzed around the drinking horses. The company dismounted and flexed their limbs.

Several of the company were refilling waterskins. Vintze and Cloden both withdrew and lay down on the lush grass by the stream. Harg dunked his huge, scarred head into the water and shook silver pellets of spray from his beard and hair like a dog as he rose.

Le Claux wandered off into the woods. Dolph and Brom, the twin warriors, sat and played dice. Bruda began to gut the deer she had brought down.

Fithvael wandered over to the nervous boy Erill. 'I'll take a turn at driving the wagon, if you like.'

The youth seemed surprised at the offer, surprised that any of the company should even talk to him.

'Thank you. I'd like to ride for a while.'

Fithvael nodded and tethered his horse to the wagon's backboard as Erill loosed his own, undernourished steed.

'A change of drivers!' Nithrom called, seeing this. 'Who else will take a turn?'

Brom and Dolph both volunteered, trading places with Harg and Gaude.

Fithvael climbed up onto the driving seat and untied the pack-reins.

'Do we go on?' he said to Nithrom.

'Wait,' the old ranger said mysteriously, watching the trees around them.

Fithvael sat back and waited, dropping the reins into his lap.

Twenty minutes passed. The company began to collect themselves and return to their mounts. Even Le Claux reappeared from the woods, looking somewhat bewildered, knots of foliage tagged into his armour joints.

Suddenly, Vintze swung around, his sword drawn in a blur. Fithvael started. How could a human react so fast? What had he seen? Bruda and Madoc were also armed suddenly, watching the same part of the tree line.

Am I getting so old, Fithvael wondered, *so old I miss the signs?* Now he could hear movement in the undergrowth, sounds that at least three of the company had heard before him.

'Put up your blades,' Nithrom instructed, his voice commanding but calm, and walked towards the source of the quiet movements.

For a moment, for one wonderful moment, Fithvael thought Gilead had rejoined them.

But the elf warrior, who emerged from the trees leading his beautiful, steel-armoured stallion, was not the son of Tor Anrok. He was an unforgettable figure in polished armour of silvered ithilmar, his plume red and proud, a noble elf, as if stepped out of a myth.

'Well met, Caerdrath Eldirhrar tuin Elondith,' Nithrom said in the high elven tongue.

'Well met indeed, Nithrom te tuin Anrok. I am most pleased you waited for me.' The new elf's voice was musical and soft.

Nithrom looked around at the assembled company and continued speaking in the humans' own language. 'Our thirteenth sword, Caerdrath. He felt it best to meet us out here. Human towns are not for him.'

Most of the company looked on in amazement. Fithvael knew why. It was rare for him to set eyes on a true son of Ulthuan, let alone for this motley rabble.

'Then he's riding to the wrong place,' Vintze sneered suddenly.

Caerdrath looked over towards the lean human swordsman. His eyes, shielded behind their helmet slits, were fire-bright.

'I would not choose to do so ordinarily, rank man. But I owe Nithrom an old debt, and so I am here with him.'

'Elves!' spat Vintze and turned away.

They mounted up and moved on then, crossing the ford and crawling away into the woods beyond. Caerdrath rode alongside Fithvael's wagon for a moment.

'Brother,' Caerdrath said with a tilt of his head.

'I am called Fithvael, also of Tor Anrok. It is good to meet with you this day.'

Caerdrath nodded and spurred his fine steed forward, away down the track.

THE SUMMER NIGHT came down late and slow, and swifts shot like darts against the darkening sky, between the silhouettes of trees. The band made camp in a hollow near a forest pool. Bruda's buck was spit-roasting by the time the stars came out.

Nithrom set a watch rotation, but left out Le Claux, who had been drinking from a wineskin since dusk and was now snoring by the fire. Fithvael fell into a light but easy slumber, his patched, travel-worn cloak pulled around him.

Brom woke him with a shake deep into the night, to take his turn at the watch. It was cool now, and the fire was guttering low. Fithvael rose, stretched out his limbs, took a swig of water from his flask and made a circle of the sleeping camp, silent in the undergrowth. Hunting owls hooted in the dark woods around. The dish of the night sky above was so clear and so full of stars it looked like beaten silver.

Fithvael flexed his aching limbs. The night air was still and without breeze or any sound except the owls, the whisper of nocturnal insects and the crack of the fire. Moths fluttered around the flames like wind-billowed snowflakes.

The veteran warrior noticed that Caerdrath was absent. Somehow that did not trouble him. He had not expected the noble elf to share their camp.

Fithvael knew he was meant to take this watch with the Carroburger, Cloden, and now he saw the human, lurking in the spinney above the hollow. He found a path up to him, through the knee-deep ferns.

Cloden glanced around as he heard the elf approach, a sharp gesture that relaxed when he made out Fithvael's face. The man had unlaced his polished black breastplate and puff-sleeved jerkin, and his greatsword was stuck tip-down in the soil to his left like a small tree. Despite the sharpness of his eyes, Fithvael could see little of Cloden's face; just the suggestion of pale skin between the darkness of hair and goatee. Cloden's eyes were lightless, uninviting hollows.

Fithvael paused next to him and exchanged a nod. Cloden offered a flask of apple schnapps from Nuln, and a sip of the liquor, crude though it was by elven standards, warmed Fithvael's belly.

'Anything?'

Cloden shook his head. 'I doubt we'll meet much out here.'

A short, stuttering cry rose behind them from the camp and they both snapped around. Le Claux called out again in his sleep, wriggled uncomfortably, then slumbered once more.

'He worries me,' Cloden said shortly as they both relaxed.

'Do you mean his drinking?'

'Not so much his drinking, as why he drinks.'

They were silent for a long while.

'I did not expect you to join us,' Cloden said at length. 'Not when your comrade snubbed us so hard. I thought you would depart with him.'

Fithvael looked up into the brilliant zodiac of the sky as if he might read some augury there. 'I thought so too,' he answered, realising it for the first time.

'Why did not you? I thought you were bound and close by tradition, you... your kind.'

It was as if he couldn't say the word.

'We are. Master Gilead and I, bound together for so many years, so many troubles. Have you never had a comrade like that?'

'Never. Never had time for it. War tends to limit the length of friendships.'

'That is true enough. War... and time.'

Cloden nodded. 'So why? Why did you leave him back at Vinsbrugge and take this path? After all those years and troubles?'

'Because of those years and troubles, I think,' Fithvael mused. 'There comes an hour in any life that you need to make an account. To wonder which path to the grave is the best for you. I believe I had journeyed with Gilead far enough. It was an empty road. Nithrom's path has a purpose at least. Besides, I am indebted to Nithrom.'

The Carroburger laughed, coarse and hard. 'Is there anyone of this company who isn't? Isn't that, in truth, why we all ride to our deaths with him?'

'You think that is what waits for us at Maltane?'

'Like enough,' Cloden said. The dark twang of his accent made his sour words more bitter. 'And if not death, not glory either.'

Fithvael was about to reply when Cloden stiffened and plucked his sword out of the loam. It shone in the starlight like ice. He was stooped low, like a stalking wolf.

Fithvael had no need to ask why. He had heard it too: a low, haunting sound that drifted up from the woods beyond the hollow. Not a sound at all, in truth. Just a tremor in the air, a ghostly sigh that trembled the edge of hearing.

Fithvael drew his own blade and they hurried down the far side of the rise, running low, shadowing the trees. Fithvael was utterly silent, and several times Cloden, for all that he moved skilfully and quietly for a human, had to look askance to check the elf was still with him.

The sound came again, and hung on the still night air. It was as subtle and thin as the sound of thawing frost. And just as cold. It came from the watering pool.

The pair moved downwards, through the black trees. There was a scent in the air Fithvael could not place, and a deepening chill.

Ahead of them, through the deep grey silhouettes of the trees, the oval of the pool glowed like a silver mirror, bright with starlight. A white caul of mist hung around the water's sides and drifted like a phantom through the trees. Cloden scrambled round behind an oak's broad trunk to get a better view and Fithvael slid in beside him. He sensed the human was about to exclaim, and deftly clamped his hand across Cloden's opening mouth.

Below them, the noble elf, Caerdrath, stood in the pool, thigh deep, clad only in white luminae robe. The starlight seemed to lend his slender form a phosphorescence. Silver glittered as he raised his ancient blade from the water and held it aloft. Chains of bright water danced off its length and down his arm.

Cloden pulled at Fithvael, trying to break free and advance forward, but Fithvael tightened his grip and drew the Reiklander back, away from the pool.

When they were a good distance back, Fithvael let the human free.

'Why did you stop me?' Cloden hissed.

'Because we should not trespass. Caerdrath is baptising his blade for war, as was done in the old times. It would not be right for us to intrude.'

Cloden seemed dissatisfied with this answer, but made no move to go back. 'Should you not do the same?' he asked with a sneer.

'I find that Caerdrath's ways are as... unfamiliar to me as they are to you.'

Cloden turned and took a last look down the rise to the ghostly pool. Once more, the odd note fluttered the air.

Cloden spat into the ferns and made his way back up the rise to his watch.

Fithvael followed him after a moment or two. He knew he would never forget what he had seen. A sliver of the distant past, of the old ways, of the traditions and lore that he and his western kin had long since forgotten. It made him feel honoured and humble, all at once. And it made him feel older and more worn than he had ever felt before.

DAWN WAS EARLY, and as pale and hard as steel. They woke to mists and ribbons of birdsong. As the sun climbed and steamed the mist away, they were moving again, with Erill, Gaude and Harg driving the teams as before. Le Claux rode silently, lolling clumsily in his saddle as if nursing a black depression or a sore head, or both. Several times he fell behind the main group. At a bend in the track, half an hour after they had set out, Caerdrath rejoined them, armoured again, gleaming and fresh in a way that made them all feel dirty and dishevelled.

They rode up through water meadows and onto higher plains where old vine terraces, weed-blooming pastures and untended lemon groves were returning to the riot of nature. Skylarks, high and invisible, sang above them in the pale blue sky.

The track skirted a small clutch of crofts on the hillslope where a dirty, half-naked child and twenty moon-eyed goats watched their passage past with silent mystification. An hour later, they followed the track in a loop around a ruined broch that had once defended this impoverished scarpland. Defended whom from what, though, none could say.

As they passed the lonely ruin, with its tumble of travertine stones and tufts of weed, Caerdrath rode along past Fithvael. He nodded to the older elf.

'I offer you my thanks,' he said in a low, harmonious voice.

Fithvael shrugged. 'For what, lord?'

'For respecting my ritual.'

Fithvael was about to reply, but Caerdrath had spurred on again towards the head of the column.

The land was getting ever higher now, dry and sparse, with thickets of gorse and thorn, and straggled stands of elms. The sun was still high and hot, but the sky was so pale that the blue was more a grey and stacks of flimsy clouds marched along the horizon. Buzzards and red kites turned and wheeled in the wild air and sometimes dropped like stones into the steep valleys. They saw occasional hares racing in the gorse, but all were too distant for the eager Bruda to take a shot, and had long fled by the time their party came to where they had been.

The track had become a road now, unmetalled but still a worn, wide, marching road cut by generations of migrating soldiers heading north for the fighting season and south again each winter. The bones of horses and mules could sometimes be seen in the scrub of the track. Twice, a lonely grave was marked by a cairn of white stones or a rusting helmet hung on a snapped spear shaft.

This was the hinterland of the great and powerful Empire, the crossing place where one territory ended and blurred into others: other kingdoms; scattered border principalities; loose, casual territories. Here, life was hard and meagre and maintained by ceaseless, thankless toil. They passed olive groves partitioned by dry stone walls, and several terraces of thin but decent vines, neatly maintained. Stringy cattle and lean goats grazed the slopes above the road, but the riders saw no herdsmen.

By late afternoon, the sun was slipped down into the western banks of cloud, as pink and raw as a sleepless eye. The light fell long and low, and their shadows were stretched out beside them. They climbed a last, steep line of flinty hills for another hour, then came out on a broad place where the road curled back on itself to descend again. Below was a wide valley bearded by woods. At its heart, three miles hence, was a mound, fenced and ditched, with a clutch of stone and wood structures nested at its summit. Bare tracks led into the place from the north, east and west, the northern one being the trail end of the road they followed.

Nithrom halted the party. 'Maltane,' he said plainly, with a vague gesture.

There was murmuring, none of it complimentary. All of the warriors, even Le Claux, stared down to get the measure of the place. Some dismounted. Some shielded their eyes with their hands. Vintze produced a small spyglass and studied the view.

Fithvael took the time to get the lay. At the top of the mound, a good sized building of stone, well roofed, most likely the temple, adjoined a second, larger structure that was undoubtedly the main hall. They commanded a good position, and had a timber enclosure around them, inside a deep ditch cut into the hill's crown. A wooden bridge span crossed the ditch and linked the main enclosure to the clustering homes and outbuildings built ramshackle down the outer slopes. Around them, at the base of the mound, an embankment and another, shallower ditch.

Beyond Maltane, the woods were thick and rose to southern hills with jagged crests. To the west and east, more woodland, following the bowl of the valley. In their direction, rough hills swept down towards the outer ditch. It was obvious their northern approach provided the most expansive clear ground before the town. Anyone approaching from the other compass points would be masked until they were but a furlong from the outer ditch.

Fithvael could see no sign of life in the town. No movement, no figures, not even a stray dog or wandering goat.

''Tis dead,' muttered Harg.

'More than dead,' Vintze said, closing up his spyglass. 'Not even a hint of smoke. The day's ending. There should be cook-fires burning.'

'They're nervous, hiding,' said Nithrom. 'They have every reason to.'

'Did they see us coming?' Erill asked, speaking out loud to the group for the first time since Vinsbrugge.

'No,' said Madoc with utter certainty. 'We would have known of it.'

Nithrom nodded and Fithvael knew Madoc was right. With the likes of Nithrom, Caerdrath and Vintze in the party, no spy could have evaded their notice, certainly not some simple herdsman or vine-farmer.

'Let us presume the worst... that we are too late.' Nithrom turned in his saddle to face them all. 'We shall encircle before we go in. I'll lead the teams down. Fithvael... if you would ride with Cloden and Madoc around to the eastern road and enter that way. Vintze, take Brom and Dolph and sweep to the west. Caerdrath, a full circuit to the south. You can move faster than most and quicker alone. The rest should come with me.'

Most seemed content with this. Bruda readied her bow. Harg eased his war-axe from its loop and set it on the cart bench next to him. Most of the rest eased their blades in their scabbards to make sure they were free. Caerdrath simply nodded and turned his steed west.

'I should go with the outriders!' Le Claux exclaimed, however, pulling out his sword. There was something like indignation in his Bretonnian accent. 'I demand this honour! Am I not a noble champion of the Lady, sworn to uphold good? Am I—'

'Oh shut up!' Gaude spat. 'Do as you're ordered and stop making a fuss!'

'You fiend!' Le Claux exploded and spurred forward. His eyes shone with anger. Fithvael had seen how the lowly squire seemed quite happy to mock and rile his sire, but now he had gone too far. Close to sundown, before a new day's wineskin could be unstopped, Le Claux was as sober as he was ever going to be. His mailed fist caught the flinching Gaude across the cheek and spun him out of the cart.

'You won't speak to me like that, you offal-hound! You dung-eater! You won't disrespect me so!' Le Claux was snarling, his heavy steed stamping the track dangerously close to the dazed Gaude.

Nithrom rode in smartly and yanked Le Claux and his horse away hard by the reins. Erill and Brom dragged the bloodied Gaude back out of harm's way.

'Le Claux! Le Claux!' Nithrom growled. 'Calm yourself. I need you with me now! Why do you think I did not send you on an outer circuit? I'm driving these wagons down into the heart of what may be an enemy stronghold! I want a noble knight right at my side when I do that!'

Sullen but calmer, Le Claux pulled away and turned his horse down the track, leaving them behind.

'Will you be all right?' Nithrom asked the squire, who was climbing back into his cart. His nose was leaking a thin line of blood and there was a gash across his cheek.

'He gets like this. I should know better.'

Nithrom nodded sadly and then called them to order. Caerdrath was already on his way. Vintze rode off with the twin warriors in tow, also heading west. The wagons and their support trundled off at a lick down the main track, chasing after Le Claux. Fithvael, with Cloden and Madoc at his side, swung east and galloped on, following the lip of the valley bowl.

NONE OF THEM spoke as they rode east, crossing down into the wooded slopes. The spread of woodland soon became too thick for them to see Maltane any more. They took their horses down banks with practised ease, slithering sideways, jerking crabwise down through tracts of gorse, fern and nettle. Cloden checked his position with the sun, half blocked by the canopy. But Fithvael already knew where they were; another mile south and west, and they would meet the eastern track.

Fithvael saw Madoc hold up a warning hand and reined in. He could hear a stream rushing nearby – and the unguarded voices of men.

The trio walked their horses forward in line through the glades, quiet as gliding phantoms. More voices, louder; some coarse laughter.

There were seven soldiers, watering at the side of the brook in the next clearing. All large men, travel soiled, splashing water on their dusty faces or drinking from their helmets. Their steeds, hard-ridden and sweating, drank along the edge of the bank. The men wore light polished plate over grey chain mail, and their long-backed bowl helmets had ragged plumes of blue and white cloth. Tilean dog-soldiers, outriders, scouts by the look of them.

There was no time for conference. As one, Fithvael, Cloden and Madoc surged forward out of the trees and came down on them from the rear. Cloden's greatsword was low against his thigh like a lance. Madoc's warhammer was whirring in a deadly arc. Fithvael drew his slender elven sword and swung it up ready.

Taken unawares, the Tileans had barely turned before Cloden was amongst them. One fell back into the stream with a shriek, his throat torn out, and another dropped and rolled down the back, clutching his shoulder. The Tilean horses started and ran in all directions.

Cloden overshot and crashed into the stream, turning his steed amid plumes of spray to engage another Tilean who waded in and rushed him with a broadsword. Madoc smashed into the water too, chasing down two enemies who ran for their lives towards the weapons and equipment they had left scattered on the far bank. The glade was alive with shouts and curses.

Fithvael reached another Tilean just as the man pulled himself into the saddle of his agitated horse. The Tilean swung his steed around, pulled out his sword and swept a scything blow at the veteran elf. Fithvael ducked low under it and took the human off his mount with a backhanded swing.

Three Tileans dead, now four as Cloden butchered the man with the broadsword mid-stream. Madoc ran down his pair, hammering one sideways into the rushing water and letting his horse's churning hooves trample the other. The seventh, dropping his helmet, ran at Fithvael with a pike. The strike missed, but Fithvael and his horse went over as they evaded, hooves slipping out on the mossy bank. Both horse and elf sprang up unhurt, but Fithvael had no time to remount, and dodged another pike-lunge that came at his belly. He grabbed the passing shaft of the weapon with his free hand and cut it in two with his sword. The Tilean threw the broken wood aside and drew his own sword, slamming it round and down at Fithvael.

Their blades clashed. The Tilean was no mean swordsman. He parried well and managed to wrong-foot Fithvael with his next pass. The Tilean's blade cut a nick from Fithvael's shoulder guard.

Fithvael braced, darted left and then feinted in with a blow that looked like a slice but turned into a thrust. He impaled the Tilean through the gut and lifted him off his feet. Fithvael ripped the blade clear and the Tilean collapsed without a sound.

Stern-faced, Fithvael looked round at the others. Cloden had reached the far bank and dismounted to search through the mercenaries' packs and bags. Madoc sat astride his horse in the middle of the rushing stream, Tilean blood blackening the fast-moving foam around his horse's shins, and glancing back at Fithvael. There was a triumphant look in his eyes, the first real life or passion Fithvael had seen there. For all his sour, cynical bearing, it seemed like this burst of combat had revitalised something in the Middenheim wolf. Madoc grinned at Fithvael and raised his hammer in a brutal, victorious gesture.

A blue-fletched arrow hit him square in the throat, knocking him clean out of the saddle and into the water. His horse bolted, thrashing spray. Madoc's heavy armoured form rocked in the current, half-submerged, but did not rise.

Fithvael heard Cloden cry out as he darted for cover. The air was hissing around them. More arrows rained down. Some hit tree trunks or soil on Cloden's side of the stream. Others shattered or rebounded from the stream's stones or plopped out of sight into the flow. More thunked into the mossy ground around Fithvael, wretchedly close, driving down into the wet ground. At least three embedded themselves into the Tilean corpses littering the banks.

Fithvael ducked into the undergrowth, but not quite fast enough. A blue-trimmed arrow pinned the end of his cape to the ground and the garment yanked him back. He tore it off, breaking his cloak's brooch-clasp, and threw himself behind a tree. By then, his cloak was staked out on the wet grass by four more arrows. Another one smacked into the tree that sheltered him.

The archers rode into view, thrashing through the thickets on light chargers that leapt the fern cover in bold, clear bounds. There were nine of them, more Tilean outriders armoured much like the septet they had slain on the stream bank. All rode expertly, the reins between their teeth, their powerful composite bows raised to fire and fire again. Holsters of blue-feathered arrows slapped at their hips.

They loosed more arrows. Their skill with their bows was notable. Though they rode full pelt and without hands to guide their steeds, they managed a murderous rate of fire. Cloden had scrambled into cover over on the far side of the stream and darts whickered into the underbrush around him.

Now, and only now, was a chance, as the Tileans dropped their bows around their pommels to retake the reins and pull up their mounts before the stream. Three drew swords and galloped on through the water towards Cloden; the others circled around at Fithvael.

A singular whistle had brought the elf's trusted horse to him, traces trailing. Fithvael snatched his half-wound crossbow from his saddle, slapped his horse on and levered the bowstring back fully. There was a Tilean almost on him, but he did not let haste muddy his skill. He nocked a short quarrel, raised his weapon and put the bolt smack between the Tilean's eyes, spinning him out of the saddle.

There was no time to reload. Fithvael flung the crossbow aside and redrew his sword, hastening round behind a clump of willow that shielded him from the next nearest Tilean. He came out round the other side of the sinuous tree, and lanced his sword up through the neck of another mercenary who was charging round to block him. The man fell, shrieking, but Fithvael's sword was lodged tight in him and tore from the elf's hand.

Something heavy caught him across the shoulders from behind and slammed him into the bole of a larch. His vision swam and he could feel hot liquid dribbling down his back under his armour. He moved, slow and unsteady, barely in time to miss a sword stroke that clove into the bark. Then a sword hilt punched him in the side of the head and he went down.

Blood rushed in his ears, like he was underwater. He could hear curt Tilean voices shouting and cursing around him, the stamp of hooves.

A scream.

A cry, in a voice he knew as well as he knew his own.

Blinking, Fithvael looked up.

Blue-steel keening in the close woodland air, Gilead of Tor Anrok exploded into the Tilean horsemen from behind, his white hair and scarlet cloak lifting in the air behind him. Gilead's horse was foaming at the mouth, and its eyes were wild and bright, but not half so wild and bright as the eyes of his old friend. It was times like this that he was afraid of Gilead's warrior soul. The fear almost eclipsed his joy at seeing Gilead here, now.

Gilead severed the torso of the Tilean nearest him and the man's hips and legs rode away on his crazed steed. The son of Lothain churned forward to meet another two, severing the arms of one at the elbows and decapitating the other. The headless corpse dropped out of its saddle and was dragged by one stirruped foot. The other, blood jetting from his jerking stumps, disappeared into the woods as his horse bolted, his screams echoing through the trees for minutes afterwards.

On the far bank, the trio who had chased down Cloden turned and spurred back to the new fight with furious yells and brandished swords.

As they turned, Cloden exploded up from cover and took one off his horse with a massive sweep of his huge, two-handed sword.

Gilead blocked a sword-swing from the remaining Tilean on his side of the stream, broke the blade against his own, and cut down through the man's gold-armoured collarbone. Then he turned to meet the charge of the last pair who were powering up out of the streambed at full gallop, cascading spray.

Gilead became a blur, shadowfast. Two riderless horses passed by on either side of his steed and disappeared into the woods. Two dismembered bodies crashed to the ground beside him in sprays of blood.

The elf sat back in his saddle, his smoking sword low at his side. He looked across at Fithvael.

'So you changed your mind?' Fithvael said archly.

'Just in time, so it would seem,' Gilead replied.

Fithvael shook his head at the retort and splashed out into

the stream to reach Madoc. Coming from the far side, Cloden reached the Middenheimer at about the same time.

Madoc was alive, but the arrow was buried deep in his thickly muscled neck. Blood stained the rapid water around him. Madoc blinked up at them and tried to speak but nothing clearer than a gurgle issued from his lips.

'That's bad...' Cloden muttered, and looked as if he was about to put Madoc out of his misery, much as a man would a lame horse.

'Help me get him up. Now!' Fithvael commanded, his voice brooking no disagreement.

Cloden shrugged, sheathed his great sword across his back and helped Fithvael lift the saturated dead weight of the wolf. They dragged the lolling Middenheimer back to the bank where Gilead sat waiting on his stamping, wild-eyed steed.

Bodies littered the bank and the moss was soaked with blood. With a grunt, Cloden lowered Madoc onto his back and Fithvael whistled for his horse once more. He had herbs and dressings in his saddlebags, curative miracles beyond human knowledge.

'I thought you said you were done with him,' Cloden remarked, indicating the silent, waiting figure of Gilead with a jerk of his head.

'I did,' Fithvael answered quietly. 'But I don't think he is yet done with me.'

NITHROM'S COMPANY were assembled in the main public yard of Maltane, a scrubby area an acre square surrounded by dwellings that lay directly before the main slope of the inner mound. Dusk was falling.

Nithrom rode from the waiting group in concern as he saw Fithvael's party come in through the eastern gate of the town, the elf and Cloden riding slowly and supporting Madoc on his horse between then. Gilead rode in behind, some way back.

'By the gods! What happened?'

'Tileans, dog-soldiers,' scowled Cloden. 'We came upon a clutch and laid them low, but then more came down from the woods. A lot more. Bowmen.'

Nithrom leaned in to scrutinise Madoc's wound with distressed eyes. Madoc, weak but conscious, tried to brush him away.

'That needs attention, and quickly.'

Madoc made a gurgling grunt that was trying to be words.

'You have dressed it,' Nithrom said to Fithvael, who nodded.

'As best as I could. I can do a better job if we can get him to a cot and get a fire going. He is not co-operative.'

'Madoc was always robust.'

'He's got an arrow through his throat. He's sucking breath and he has lost too much blood, and the dart-head is buried in the bone of his neck! I do not care how robust he thinks he is, he will be dead by the time dawn comes, unless we can get that cruel shard out and staunch the flow.' Fithvael seemed far angrier than he had any right to be.

'Fithvael's right,' murmured Cloden. 'Get a dirty piece of iron like that wedged in your flesh, even a mild wound, and the iron'll brew up poison in your blood.'

'We will see to it,' Nithrom said sternly, 'and Madoc won't resist.' He said this last part whilst shooting a warning look at the swaying, sweating Madoc.

Then Nithrom looked beyond them and saw Gilead approaching slowly down from the east gate.

'Gilead te tuin Lothain...' he whispered. 'So you came after all.'

'He... turned the tide, when we were overrun,' Cloden said grudgingly. 'They had us cold, me and the elf.'

Nithrom rode over to Gilead and they regarded each other for a moment.

'Will you stay?'

'Perhaps. For a while at least.'

Nithrom nodded and turned his horse away, riding back to the main group and raising his voice so all could hear. 'Vintze found nothing to the west, and Caerdrath reports the southern edges are also clear of any trace. Only now, to the east, do we have a sign of them.'

'Scouts,' Fithvael suggested, drawing near. 'They had ridden hard, so they were probably outriders probing ahead of the main unit.'

'Usual Tilean company tactics,' said Brom, 'a vanguard pack of fast archers reconnoitring the land.'

'The main force would be but a day behind,' finished Dolph in what seemed the same voice, their words overlapping.

'Did any you met survive? Any ride back to carry a warning?' Harg asked.

'None,' Gilead replied simply, and all understood the truth of it.

'That is really no better,' Vintze said then, wiping a palm across his stubbled chin. 'When the vanguard don't return, they'll be just as well warned.'

'Wery bad…' growled Bruda, scanning the fading light on the northern slopes with hunting glances.

'So where is everyone?' Cloden asked, saying the words for them all, gesturing around the deserted town.

THEY RODE TOGETHER up the steep mound above the main settlement and reached the timber bridge that crossed the deep inner ditch. It was a deep, well-dug fortification, and the low evening sunlight did not penetrate its murky depths. The bridge itself was solid and firm, and built so that a horse team could pull it down from the inner courtyard in the event of a siege. But it was old, and the harness hooks were weed-choked and rusty.

Beyond it, the timber fence was firm and secure, and sat like a crown around the cranium of the hill. Iron braziers on the wall top were cold and dead. The gate itself, a single section of hardwood planks, was sealed tight.

Nithrom looked across at Gaude, who shrugged and pulled out his battered cornet. He blew a loose association of notes, some in the same key. To Fithvael it seemed a sadly appropriate fanfare for their band.

Silence followed.

'Again?' Gaude suggested, gesturing with his cornet and wetting his lips.

Nithrom shook his head and signalled instead to Vintze. Without question, the lean, leather-suited Reiklander slipped off his mount and crossed the bridge to the gate. His long, pale hair and the silver hilt of his sword caught the last of the sunlight as he climbed up the gate, as nimble as a squirrel.

Astride the top, he reached inside with dagger and cut something. Fithvael heard a heavy counterweight trundle to the ground. The gate began to swing inwards and, still astride it, Vintze kicked out at the gatepost, accelerating the motion.

He rode the gate as it swung wide and then jumped down, sword in hand.

Nithrom lead the other riders in across the bridge, indicating with a deft gesture for Caerdrath to remain outside on watch. The noble elf turned his steed and sat motionless in the dying light, gazing north.

As they moved in past him, Fithvael saw how Gilead cast Caerdrath a lingering, questioning look. Quite the last being Gilead had expected to find in this ragged human band, Fithvael was sure.

Inside the fortification, it was like black night already. Long bars of golden sunlight raked in through the open gate, but the high fence blocked everything else out. Above them, in a sky as dark blue as the trim of an Elector's cloak, freckles of early stars began to shine.

The main hall rose before them, dark, low-gabled and massive, with smaller outbuildings adjoining it. Behind it sat the narrower shoulders and thin tower of the temple. The party dismounted onto the soft, black marl of the mound's top and, weapons ready, approached the front portico of the hall. Gaude stayed back, watching over the huddled, cloak-wrapped form of Madoc.

Leading them, Nithrom stepped up under the mighty oak lintel. He hammered on the carved doors. 'Ho, within!' he called, in the tongue of the Empire.

Vintze gestured sidelong to the outbuildings with the point of his sword. 'Livestock in there, lots of it, close-packed and agitated.'

Fithvael had already detected the pungent animal smells, the scrabbling shuffle of hooves. 'And in there,' he said, 'I smell humans.'

Cloden and Vintze both shot him hard glances, but Nithrom grinned. 'He has it right.'

Nithrom put his shoulder to the doors, pressing his strength against the bas-relief, weathered image of some insubstantial human god. They did not budge, not even when Brom and Dolph added their weight.

'Barred,' Dolph said.

'From within,' finished Brom.

Nithrom waved up Harg, who hefted his great axe in his hairy paws. Again, Nithrom struck the doors and called out.

'Ho, within! If you won't answer, we are coming inside! Know that we are friends, come to aid you – and stand back!'

He moved aside and Harg, a bestial black shape in the thickening gloom, swung back his gigantic axe. Bruda knelt behind him on the steps, just clear of his back swing, her bow raised ready.

With one single blow, the disfigured Norseman stove the doors inwards. A trio spearhead of Nithrom, Cloden and Vintze led the way inside, with the others in tow.

The hall was high, wide and gloomy, ranged with benches and trestles, piles of sacks, barrels, full skins and other commonplace items. There was a stone-edged fire-pit at the far end, under a horn-shaped chimney flue. The crossbeams of the high roof were hung with salting meat, game and bunches of drying herbs. They scented the still, close air heavily.

A megaron, thought Fithvael, in the old style... a mead-hall, a communal one-room palace, as befits an old, traditional community like this. Rushes covered the creaking boards of the floor.

At the fire-pit end, thirty yards from them, ten men cowered in a tight group, facing them. By their clothes and stature they were farmers, two as young as teenagers, one as old as old men get, the other seven in stalwart middle years. But their faces – they were the faces of cornered killers, ready to fight to the very death, eyes glittering with fear and venom. Several held hoes, threshing flails or pitchforks. Two had corn sickles, one a vintner's pruning knife. The leader had an old, rusty sword.

'Begone!' he cried hoarsely.

'And leave you to the Tilean dogs? I think not.' Nithrom's voice was calm. The elf ranger stepped forward, sheathing his blade.

'In the name of mercy, get you gone!' the sword-wielder called again as the group huddled back against the fire-pit wall.

'Don't you know me? It is I, Nithrom! I swore to bring you defenders, and so I have. Where is Gwyll, your headman?'

'Dead!' spat the leader. 'Dead seven dawns now!'

'How so?' Nithrom asked, genuine surprise in his gentle voice.

'You said you would return, but weeks passed! Then the first of them came, a pack of those dogs, foraging ahead of their army! Gwyll and twenty of the menfolk took arms to drive them off. Four of our kinsfolk were left dead in the outer ditch! We never saw Gwyll or the others again!'

'Merciful gods... and you have hidden in here since then?'

'What choice had we? Seven nights and days, waiting for them to return and slaughter the rest of us!'

'Put up your weapons, men of Maltane. We are here now.'

'You bring an army, elf-who-promises-so-much?' the old man asked with a sneer.

'Those that you see, and three others besides.'

The leader threw his old sword onto the planking with a clatter and sat down on a bench. The cluster of others broke up, lowering their weapons, grumbling.

'Then we are all surely dead,' said the leader heavily.

'What's your name, friend?' asked Le Claux.

'Drunn.'

'Then, Drunn, you are not dead until we declare it to be so.'

'Is that a joke?' asked the wizened old man who had sneered before.

'Enough, Master Swale. Don't goad them.'

'No, I am not to be shushed, Drunn!' The old man strode forward, facing Le Claux, who smiled with slight bewilderment at the hunched, white-haired old man and his rusty flail. 'Where were you a week ago? How can you come here now, promising salvation, when there's but a baker's count of you and an army approaches? Eh? What can you do that twenty of our best could not?'

'We are warriors, old fool,' said Le Claux, his amused smile cooling. 'We know a sight more about the art of battle than a bunch of farmers.'

'Is that right, brave sir knight?' returned old man Swale, his rheumy eyes fierce. The knight took an involuntary step back. 'Oh yes, no doubt you know the delights of war, the glory, the comradeship, the songs, the gold you earn! But I'd wager we of the soil know more about real war! To see our beloved sons killed or mutilated, our daughters raped, our vines torched, our livestock swept away for camp feasts! We know what it feels like to toil a whole year to see it gone in a week, we know how hard it is to till burned soil, or worse, to dig it to make a grave! Don't talk to me about war, knight! You play at it, we live with the consequences!'

With an angry bark, Le Claux thrust his mailed hand out and pushed the scolding old man away. Swale staggered and fell, smashing over a trestle.

'Leave us! Go outside!' Nithrom told the Bretonnian, his voice as cold and hard as steel.

'But I–'

'Now!'

'I'll not be shamed by some–'

'So you would shame us all so we can share it? Get out!'

Le Claux turned and thumped heavily out of the megaron, his ornate spurs jingling against his greaves.

Erill crouched and helped the old man to his feet.

'My apologies,' Nithrom said to them all, his manner respectful. 'For that outburst… and for not being here a week back. It took too long to gather this band. But between them, they are more than thirteen swords. Heroes all, one way or another, from the ends of the land, from triumphs too numerous to count. We're here now, and by my oath, we will stand firm for you. We will protect Maltane.'

'From Maura and his dogs?' asked another of the farmers, his voice weary with disbelief. 'For that, you don't need to bring us a band of warriors, you need to bring us a damned miracle.'

'Then you should think of us as just that, my friend,' Vintze said with a twinkle in his eye. 'A bloody, dusty, mad-eyed bunch of miracles.' Behind him, Harg chuckled. Fithvael felt himself smile too.

'Where are the others?' asked Cloden.

'Others?' Drunn replied, looking away.

'The rest of the town,' said Dolph.

'The folk of Maltane,' Brom echoed.

'Gone,' Drunn shrugged darkly.

'Run, fled, long departed,' added Swale, pouring himself a cup of wine from a skin hung on the post-end near him.

The elves in the party exchanged glances. Ever so gently, Gilead thumped his foot down on the wooden floorboards twice. The sound it made was deep and hollow.

With a wide grin, Bruda pulled back her bow and shot an arrow into the boards between her feet.

The last six inches protruded from the floor, vibrating. There was a muffled series of human squeals and shrieks from beneath them.

Harg swept back the rushes on the floor with the flat of his axe blade and found the trap door in a moment. Fithvael stepped in beside him and, with Cloden's help, pulled it up and open. Below them, in the darkness, dozens of white, terrified faces looked up. A stench of human misery rose from the cavity.

Nithrom looked over at Drunn. 'How many?' he asked sharply.

Drunn sighed. 'More than two hundred. Mostly women and children.'

'Get a ladder! Get them out of there!' Nithrom ordered, face drawn.

It took coaxing to get them up. Eventually, for reasons that perplexed Fithvael, only he and the formidable Kislevite woman had any success in bringing them out, and only then when Drunn, Swale and the other men of Maltane pleaded reassurance. The floor of the megaron hall lay flush with the flattened crown of the mound, but a deep and massive scarcement had been dug underneath. The townsfolk had hidden there, in the stinking dark, for upwards of a week, huddled between the great earthenware vats of drinking water. As the last of them came up, tearful women with deathly pale, grizzling babes in their arms, Fithvael took a flaming torch and descended the ladder. The scarcement was a large as the hall above, deep and damp, with a floor of oozing marl and walls dressed with travertine blocks.

The stink of human excrement was intolerable. Fithvael found two miserable bodies: an old woman and a girl, crumpled in the furthest corner. He could not tell if it had been fear, hunger or suffocation had done for them. He did not want to know.

He heard a movement behind him and turned to find Gilead standing behind him in the torchlight. Gilead was rapping his knuckles against the bulky water jars.

'Two-thirds gone,' he said quietly.

'There is time to refill them from the streams or the well.'

'No well up here in the inner place.'

'I noticed.'

'Not a good sign if it comes to a siege.'

'I noticed that too.'

Gilead sighed and scratched behind his ear. 'Why did you come here, Fithvael?'

Fithvael cleared his throat. 'Because of Nithrom. Because someone had to. I see that more clearly now I am here. Someone had to.'

He paused. 'And why did you come?'

'Because you did. Because you are usually correct. Because... I did not know what else to do.'

Fithvael smiled, his white teeth glinting in the torchlight. 'Gilead te tuin... you will be the death of me.'

'I've always fancied it would be the other way round... Fithvael of the lost causes.'

'Lost causes?'

'Starting with me.'

'Oh.'

'But if it makes you any happier, I promise I will be the death of you,' Gilead said and clambered back up the ladder.

IN THE HALL, as lamps and fires were lit and food and wine shared out, there was hubbub. The place was suddenly crowded, much smaller and hotter as bodies mingled. The folk of Maltane, mostly women and children as Drunn had pointed out, huddled and grouped, some weeping, some singing, some asleep on their feet. The stench of their inhuman confinement rose from their bodies and blocked out the sweetness of the hanging herbs.

Gilead and Fithvael joined Nithrom, Harg and Bruda at a table where a flask of wine and pottery beakers had been set out. A passing girl slid a platter of husked corn, oil and dried goat-meat onto the tabletop.

'There is water below,' said Fithvael as he sat. 'But it needs refreshing and refilling.'

'So noted,' said Nithrom, taking a swig of wine.

'So... when was you going to tell us about Maura?' Harg asked.

'Aye, old friend, when?' added Bruda. 'When battle commenced? Or before that?'

'Does it matter who we face, my lady of Kislev?' Nithrom smiled, eyes guarded. 'The wars we've seen together, I'm surprised you concern yourself with the enemy's name.'

'When it is Bloody Maura, perhaps.'

Overhearing their talk, Cloden sat down with them, a beaker in his hand. 'Maura's Murderers? Great gods, Nithrom, I'm with the she-bear on this! You should have told us! I thought those were his damnable colours on those men we danced with in the woods. White for bone, blue for blood.'

'Blue?' asked Fithvael.

Harg grinned across at him, the smile ruffling the line of his beard and zagging the dreadful scar. 'Maura fancies his-self a noble prince of Tilea. He's naught of the sort, of course! I'm more a bastard king of the north than he is nobility!'

Nithrom looked over at them both. 'There's more truth in that remark than you'd first know, Fithvael te tuin. Isn't that so, King Hargen son of Hardrad?'

'Bah!' scoffed the hulking Norseman, filling his cup. 'No more of such talk!' He sipped down a big gulp of wine and stared across the table at Fithvael earnestly. 'Maura thinks his-self a prince, and delights in killing to achieve that rank. Hence blue for blood. Noble blood. Understand?'

'Transparently,' Fithvael said.

'And so Maura is the one we face here. Maura and his ver-min band. You should have told us, Nithrom.' Cloden's voice was grim.

'Cloden's not been so right since that day at Altdorf field. Then he was wery right.'

'Don't remind me, Bruda. That was another day... and we won, did we not?'

'Just, da.' Bruda smiled.

'He is just a mercenary, a human mercenary, with a band of dogs,' said Gilead abruptly. 'Sell-swords are all dangerous. Why should we be troubled? An armed company returning south after the war season is still an armed company.'

'You've been hiding in the woods for too long, friend,' Cloden said, without malice. 'Maura and his murders are sell-swords, yes, but more than that. Maura takes things... personally.'

'Meaning?'

'Imagine: you're a company of war-dogs. You take coin and assault a town. You fail. You say, "I did my best, goodbye, I'll not waste more trying"... yes?'

'Of–'

'Not Maura. Not "Bitter-End" Maura. Damn that he can't pay his men, damn that it takes three months when it should have taken a week. Victory is all he wants. Victory is all he will accept.' Cloden looked down into his drink. 'A skirmish won't drive him off. He plays to win, and he'll keep sending his men on until he has that victory.'

'But that would break morale...' Fithvael began.

Harg smiled, sadly. 'Not the Murderers. Maura has that, that charm – what do you call it again, Nithrom?'

'Charisma.'

'They're with him all the way. To hell and beyond. He draws to himself the best and the meanest and the most insane. That ogre sergeant of his–'

'Klork,' growled Bruda.

'Aye! The tales I've heard of him. And the leaders of his dog pack: Hroncic and Fuentes! Animals! Bastards! Death-dealers!'

The group was silent for a moment as the sounds of the busy hall washed about them.

'They were good, I will say that,' said Fithvael eventually. 'Those we met in the woods. Just scouts, but they fought like... daemons. Good swordsmen, good horsemen. And their archers, if they were but a taste, I have a dread of what is to come.'

The huddle looked around to see Gaude leading Madoc in. Fithvael stood up, urging the Maltaners to find a cot and heat up some clean water. He still wasn't sure what he could do, but that arrow had to come out. Attended by Gaude and a gaggle of townsfolk, the elf set to work.

Le Claux returned, but paused in the doorway. He glared across at Nithrom.

'Le Claux?' the elf said patiently.

'Caerdrath summons you. There are lights on the northern trail.'

IT WAS TRULY night now and a loose wind from the southwest scudded rafts of grey cloud against the moons. Leaving Fithvael and Gaude inside to tend Madoc, Nithrom's ragged band emerged from the main hall and crossed to the open gate of the inner mound. Caerdrath, still attentive astride his patient mount, was like a gleaming statue in the half-light

beyond the bridge. He heard them approach without looking
round and pointed off into the gloom.

On the northern path, the road that the carts had followed
that very afternoon to enter Maltane, a string of torches jig-
gled slowly down. Twenty or more.

'More scouts?' suggested Erill.

Cloden frowned. 'Too many. This could be the front end of
the main company.'

'Or an expeditionary force coming to learn the fate of the
scouts,' Gilead suggested.

'Aye... and we don't know what numbers lurk just beyond
that rise,' added Harg.

Nithrom swung into his saddle. 'We will go to meet them.
Make your peace with whatever gods you observe and come
on. This may be done sooner than we expect. Master Erill: stay
here, watch the gate. Make ready to close it fast if we return in
a hurry, and get the townsfolk to prepare torches. Lots of
them. Light the tops of the inner fence with as much light as
you can.'

Erill nodded and hurried back in through the gate.

Nithrom looked from side to side and regarded the warriors
drawn up on horses beside him. 'Vintze, Harg, Gilead... with
me to meet them. The rest of you keep out of sight and
behind the outer ditch. Come when I call. If it all goes bad,
withdraw to the inner mound and close the gate. If my vanguard falls, Cloden has the lead.'

Le Claux started to say something but thought better of it.

Along the line of riders, final preparations were made.
Vintze put on his helm and slid his left arm into the loops
of his small shield. Harg rested his war-axe across the chin
of his saddle as he donned his snarling, full-face helmet.
Dolph and Brom buckled on their helms and loaded their
long, bulky handguns with synchronised movements, resting the primed pieces across the specially raised rests of their
saddle mounts. As one, they closed their brass visors. Bruda
placed a fur-trimmed, spiked bowl-helmet on her head,
gathering her red hair beneath it, and tested her bow.
Cloden adjusted his basket helm and slid on kidskin gloves
before drawing his greatsword. Le Claux made a blessing to
the Lady and settled a lance across his looped shield.
Caerdrath, already prepared, raised up a slender javelin, one

of six nested in his steed's saddle-sling, and propped the butt against his right hip.

Gilead, like Nithrom, was bareheaded and carried a long, leaf-pattern elven shield. The rangers of Tor Anrok drew their longswords, Nithrom's silver, Gilead's blue-steel.

The ten riders spurred away together down the mound into the lower part of Maltane. At the main yard, most pulled away to left and right, disappearing into the rambles of huts and dwellings on either side, leaving Nithrom, Vintze, Harg and Gilead riding in a tight pack down to the northern gate.

The torchlights were gathering and milling just outside the outer ditch as they came down. The gathered firelights revealed a troop of more than fifty Tileans, all on horseback, all bearing the blue and white badge.

Some called out and pointed as the four riders appeared on the far side of the outer ditch, emerging from the darkness of the apparently dead town. Nithrom's group reined up just short of the crude ditch bridge.

The Tileans' leader, a thickset man with an eye patch and a long blue cloak, rode forward with six of his men in flank, until they were facing Nithrom's group across the bridge. Gilead took the man in: heavy and muscled, his armour more ornate than his common soldiers. He had no shield, but wore a short sword on each hip. His expression was haughty, triumphant and vain.

'Greetings to you!' the mercenary called out, his coarse voice shredding the soft vowels of the Tilean tongue.

'And to you,' Nithrom replied in perfect Tilean.

'We are but a few journeying veterans, looking for a place to rest.'

Nithrom nodded. 'More than a few, perhaps.'

The commander looked around at the gathered men behind him, as if surprised to find them there. He laughed. 'Aha, yes! My merry band! They wouldn't harm a horse tick, so please you. There's no need for those drawn blades.'

'Is there not?' Nithrom's voice was cool. Gilead was struggling to translate as the exchange continued. Suddenly, he did not need to.

'What is this place, that I am greeted by two noble sons of Ulthuan, a Norse bearshirt and an Imperial swordsman?' the commander asked in perfect low elfish.

If Nithrom was surprised, he did not show it at all. Maura's band travelled the world, Gilead told himself; they have surely mixed with many peoples and places. Just because they were killers did not mean they had to be stupid.

'A peaceful place,' replied Nithrom, switching language himself. 'One that has no desire or ability to harbour a full company of men-at-arms. There are streams in the woods where you may refresh yourselves and fine glades where you can camp. On the morrow, you can get on your way, and we can all be happy there was no… unpleasantness.'

'Unpleasantness?' the man laughed, and a couple of his men cackled with him. 'Who said anything about unpleasantness? Come, Ulthuare te tuin, my gentle friend… all we seek is a roaring fire pit, a sound roof, and hay for our tired steeds. Maybe we could also purchase some game and some ale.'

'I must off you my apologies, for I must be failing to make myself understood,' Nithrom said flintily. 'Perhaps your fine command of my language is not so sharp after all. There is no place in this town for you.'

There was a long silence. Gilead flexed his grip on the pommel of his sword, waiting. The commander bent and spat dust-spittle into the mud, and then sat back on his steed, gazing absently up at the night sky as he adjusted the fit of his gauntlets. His men waited. The crickets clicked.

'Who,' he began at length, as if patiently trying to deal with a small child, 'who do I have the… pleasure of addressing?'

'I am Nithrom, of Tor Anrok. And you?'

The eye-patched man grinned. 'I am called Fuentes, master-at-arms, colonel. These are my boys and they have ridden long and hard this day. You see, Nithrom of Tor Anrok, I believe you have it about right: we have indeed misunderstood each other. We are peaceful men, the war season is over, we are just going home. All we ask is hospitality.'

'And that, I'm afraid, is the only thing we can't offer you.'

'You know,' said Fuentes, turning in his saddle to address his men in Tilean, 'if that kind of protest had been presented to me by poor, starving farmfolk, I might have seasoned my bearing with respect and humility. But when it comes from a quartet of armed warriors… well, I start to have my doubts. From the likes of these…' and he gestured round at Nithrom and his companions, 'well, it smacks of unfriendliness.'

'Master Fuentes,' Nithrom said in clear, precisely enunciated Tilean, 'we both know that if humble farmers had met you at this gate and denied you access, you would have slaughtered them without a second thought. Perhaps the presence of myself and my comrades will make you think again. You will not cross that ditch unharmed.'

Fuentes shrugged, as if it were nothing. He turned his horse around and moved back through his waiting men in the torchlight.

'We are beaten,' they heard him say to his men, 'fully and soundly by these overwhelming numbers. Let's away.'

Gilead stiffened. He heard Harg curse beside him softly and Vintze hiss the words 'Here it comes…'

His back to them still, Fuentes dropped his hand sharply, and the first dozen dog-soldiers ploughed their horses forward onto the rough bridge, pulling swords.

'Meet them!' Nithrom bawled.

The four defenders powered forward, smashing into the head of the assaulting phalanx as it was bottled by the bridge so only three could ride aside each other.

Nithrom ran the first Tilean through with his silver blade as Harg reaped his way into the thick of them, roaring like a wounded bear and swinging his axe around. Two riders, one missing a head, tumbled left off the bridge into the ditch.

Gilead charged in, deflecting a sword thrust with his shield as he bent low and then ripping the Tilean off his horse with a slice that cut him from belly to chin. Gilead's blue-steel blade had severed the breastplate; the flapping sections of metal fell away with the body.

Vintze was beside him, slamming a Tilean rider off his horse with a sideways blow of his shield, and plunging his broadsword through the eyeslits of the Tilean behind his first victim.

Inside ten seconds, the boards of the ditch bridge were sodden with blood and strewn with the dead and dying. Horses that had fallen into the ditch shrieked and whinnied like banshees. On the far side of the defence, Fuentes turned, his face now shining with rage, and drew two hooked short swords, one in each hand, guiding his horse with his knees.

'On them! On them! Take them!' he screamed.

The main force of the Tileans, forty or more, poured in at the bridge.

'We can take them!' barked Vintze, ducking a sword sweep and slashing out as he fought to control his bucking steed.

'Aye! We can hold this bridge!' Harg added, his axe-blade spraying Tilean blood as it swung.

But already some of the lithe Tilean chargers, under the skilled hands of their sell-sword masters, were leaping the ditch itself and thrashing up the inner slope.

'Break!' Nithrom cried. 'Now! Break and fall away!'

Harg and Vintze, both reluctant, tore away, digging their heels into their horses' flanks, heading back into the compound. Nithrom had to yell a second time before Gilead seemed to hear him.

Then the four of them were galloping back from the ditch into the outskirts of the town, with the main force of Tileans raging after them.

The quartet raced in between the first of the huts, heading towards the public yard and the mound. The first two Tileans on their heels went down hard, horses cartwheeling and crushing their spilled riders as arrows took them in quick succession.

Bruda appeared on the roof of the first hut, drawing her bow with her powerful arms. A third rider went down, a fourth. She whooped.

Several more mercenaries had gone inside past her, and were now cornering in the inner yard. There was a flash and a roar, and one was slammed off his mount. His immediate companion started, tried to turn his horse and died as a lead ball exploded his steed's head, passed through it and punched through his own chest.

Reloading their handguns, Dolph and Brom ran their horses forward. They fired again, and two more steeds buckled and crashed over. Then they were in the thick of the charge. The twins from Ostmark stowed their deadly but slow handguns and laid in with maces. They broke heads, their brass armour flashing in the flickering firelight.

Cloden had dismounted. A greatsword worked better on foot. He came round one of the miserable huts and laid his massive blade into the next few speeding Tileans. His first strike cut completely through man and leaping horse alike.

Nithrom, Harg, Vintze and Gilead turned back to meet the incursion, having lured them into the killing embrace of the lower town.

Le Claux came charging out of the dark and lifted a Tilean off his horse on the end of his lance. He laughed out loud, triumphant.

Like a terrible ghost from distant times, the noble figure of Caerdrath also emerged from cover and charged in, his stallion racing. Each of his six javelins found their mark, and then he drew his sword. He became a steely blur, scything the Tilean cavalry down like corn.

In the thick of the ferocious fighting, Gilead slashed and whipped his sword around, severing limbs and heads, smashing shields and breaking weapons. For the first time in a long while, he felt he had found his place. In a company of proud warriors, however ragged the band, fighting for a cause.

He was still hacking when the Tileans melted back in retreat, destroyed and driven out. Gilead saw Fuentes riding with no more than half a dozen men towards the ditch bridge. Nithrom's warriors had killed almost forty of the Tileans.

Bruda whooped again and Vintze joined her in a cheer, riding around the body-littered street. Gilead lowered his sword and tried to contain the rage inside him.

Above them all, the fence of the inner mound shone with the lights of a hundred torches, suggesting a garrison of massive strength. Erill had done his work.

The first attack had been repulsed.

THE VICTORS, IN exuberant mood, returned to the inner mound and the gate was shut and barred behind them. Dolph and Brom, ever grounded and practical, had suggested their immediate course of action should be to secure and bolster the defences of the lower ditch, for it seemed certain the Tileans would return sooner rather than later.

Nithrom thought this good council, but did not take it. Such work by night would be thankless and hard, and difficult to co-ordinate. He wanted to give his warriors time to rest and enjoy their victory. For tonight, they would simply lock themselves in the inner mound. If Maura's men returned, then it would be bad luck but they would at least be fortified.

Besides, Le Claux was already calling for a wine skin, his face glowing with excitement and pride, and Harg, Vintze and Bruda would not need much convincing to join him.

Wine was brought to them, along with hot food that Erill had ordered to be prepared. Minor wounds and scrapes were dressed and bound as the warriors grouped in the inner hall to celebrate. The telling scale of their victory had also raised the spirits of the Maltane townsfolk too. As the middle night passed, a veritable feast was underway with much singing, drinking and general good spirits.

Nithrom watched over it all from the door of the hall, a cup of ale in his hand. He saw Harg and Bruda joking and singing their way through a rowdy, suicidal drinking game, surrounded by a circle of laughing townsfolk. Cloden and the twins from Ostmark were running an all-comers arm-wrestling contest near the fire-pit. Vintze had the utterly undivided attention of several village girls. Le Claux held court, retelling the action like an epic poem for a giddy group of villagers, his metaphors and symbols enhanced by each draft of wine. Even Gaude and Erill were relaxed, flagons in hand.

It would do them good, Nithrom thought. Good for morale. He took a sip of his ale. He would watch the wall till dawn.

Fithvael was suddenly by his side, wiping bloody hands on a rag.

'Madoc will live, for now,' said the veteran. 'The barb is out. He is sleeping.'

Nithrom raised his cup. 'To you, worker of wonders. Your hands are as bloody as ours. You've seen a life or death fight of your own this night.'

Fithvael nodded. 'I don't think Madoc will ever speak again,' he murmured. 'His larynx was torn away.'

Nithrom sighed. 'A tragedy. The tales he can tell, from his time with the Templars.'

'Madoc was a Wolf Templar? A White Wolf?'

'Of great renown. Leader of their Gold Company, doughty in battle. Did you not note his wolf pelt and his warhammer?'

'But not now?'

Nithrom smiled. 'He... acted in a way that brought dishonour to his regiment and was cast from the temple. He's been a sell-sword ever since.'

'What did he do?' Fithvael asked.

'He refused to kill me.' Nithrom sipped again, his mind clearly on distant memories. 'The most courageous thing, to throw away his career to help a friend, especially one of another race. I will tell you the tale some time, Fithvael te tuin. Just know this: though he was cast out in dishonour, I have never known a man more honourable. To his friends. To what really matters.'

Nithrom turned towards the door.

'Where are you going?'

'Someone must stand watch, and I have asked more than enough of this brave band tonight.'

'I will stand it with you, friend, if I may,' said Fithvael. 'We can watch the town and talk of old times.'

GILEAD LOTHAIN SAT alone, oblivious to the merrymaking, gazing into the flames of the fire-pit at the rear of the hall. He became aware of a figure beside him and looked up. It was Caerdrath. The elf carried a goblet of wine in each hand and offered one out to Gilead. The last son of Tor Anrok accepted it with a nod and Caerdrath took that as an unspoken invitation to sit down next to him. The elf had removed his helm but his long hair was still braided up on his scalp. The scintillating sculpture of his armour was flecked with Tilean blood.

'I am called Caerdrath Eldirhrar, tuin Elondith, grandson of Dundanid Flamebrand, of the line of Tyrmalthir and the clans of High Saphery and the Marble Hills.'

'Gilead te tuin Lothain, of Tor Anrok.'

They drank to each other.

'We are alone here,' Caerdrath said, though it was clear he meant symbolically, as the place was crazy with noise and bodies. 'Old world, old blood. Your companion, Fithvael, he mixes better with the human breed, and Nithrom is so worldly, he is neither man nor elf anymore.'

'Do you despise him for that?' Gilead asked.

'Not one scrap. Nithrom is the truest friend I know. He has made a place for himself in this ugly world. Why else would I ride with him?'

'But what finds you here, Caerdrath Eldirhrar, tuin Elondith?' Gilead savoured the chance to use the ancient high tongue, with all its formal modes of address. It was like old music, half remembered.

Caerdrath did not answer directly. 'Nithrom tells me that you and Fithvael are the last of your house. That you have ventured out into this bitter world to find traces of our vanishing people.'

'That is so.'

'Then we are kindred in that also. I too came to the human world to uncover the past. The old realms, the lost cities, most of them now buried beneath the foundations of new human settlements, it seems. I wanted to find traces of the world we had lost. We are alike.'

The notion shocked Gilead. Since, well, forever, it seemed – since Galeth died, at least – he had been driven to seek out the forlorn scraps of the old race. He had also felt himself to be a diluted being, just an echo of elfhood, tarnished by the dull human world. But here was an old one, so much more glorious than himself, an example of the very wonder he had been seeking... who professed exactly the same drive. It was a sobering revelation. So long he had been trying to regain his heritage, and here came a pure, unalloyed part of that provenance, equally lost and equally unfulfilled.

As if sensing the thoughts, Caerdrath said, 'Our age has passed, Gilead te tuin Lothain. Our stars have set. The day fast approaches when we must step aside for brute mankind forever.'

'I have a favour to ask of you,' Gilead said.

'I will grant it, if it in my power.'

'When this is done, this little war, I would see the peaks of Ulthuan before I die. Show me the best way, the routes I should take.'

'I will do better than that, Gilead te Anrok. I have been out in this wearying world too long myself. When we are done here, I will journey with you back to Ulthuan and we will feast together at my father's table in the Marble Hills.'

GILEAD WOKE LONG after dawn. The hall was cool and full of the after-scent of smoke and cooking. A few of the townsfolk were asleep upon the rush flooring and Le Claux was slumbering in a corner.

Pulling off his leather jerkin and his undershirt, Gilead strode out of the hall into the cold daylight. The sky above was bright and grey, with a threat of rain, and the gate of the inner fence was open. Womenfolk were washing pans and platters in a water trough and he crossed to them, naked to the waist, and dunked his head and shoulders. The women huddled coyly as he shook out his mane of white hair.

He nodded a courteous, flirting thanks to them and walked off towards the gate, his jerkin and shirt folded under his right arm.

From the gate, he looked down across Maltane, ugly and stark in the glare of a new day. Smoke rose from the ditch at the north end, black and rancid as the wind carried it back. He could see figures at work in the town below, most of them townsfolk.

Pulling on his shirt, he wandered down the mound into the common ways of Maltane.

Nithrom had roused those he could early and set them to work. Dolph and Brom who, with their artifice guns and tactical minds seemed to Gilead to have almost mechanical souls, had begun to command the defence work. Nithrom clearly valued them for their strategic, engineering bent. Gilead saw townsfolk working in teams to widen the outer ditch, and others who used their spoil to fill sacking to raise an inner bulwark. In the public yard, Bruda was training some of the young men of Maltane – and at least three of the strongest young women – to pull bows. As her pupils flexed, released and missed the straw-stuffed targets yet again, she grinned at Gilead as he passed.

Gilead saw Gaude entertaining a flock of the children, and Erill supervising villagers as they erected tar-soaked bales of straw at the street corners. Down by the outer ditch, Dolph and Brom, both stripped to the waist and sheened with sweat, were overseeing the digging work.

He also saw Fithvael, sat amongst a group of diligently working farmers and crossed to him. The elf was showing them how to fashion arrows, and some were so advanced in this work they were binding the heads with pitch-wetted rags.

'Fithvael,' he greeted his oldest friend.

His companion looked up. He smiled broadly. In truth, he doubted he had ever seen Gilead so happy and carefree.

'The work abounds,' Fithvael said by way of greeting. 'Harg has got a team out in the wood felling timber to shore up the outer dyke. That Kislevite woman is raising a new army of archers.'

'I saw her.'

'Vintze and Caerdrath have ridden out to spy for a sign of our enemies.'

'I had better find myself some gainful work as well, it seems,' Gilead said, and walked on towards the outer ditch.

Nithrom and Cloden, rags tied around their faces, were watching the fire in the ditch pit. Mule-teams guided by similarly masked villagers were dragging the last of the Tilean carcasses, horses and men, to the ditch. The pyre of the enemies they had slain the night before belched black, fatty smoke. A pair of scrawny buzzards circled high overhead.

Nithrom saw Gilead approaching. He left Cloden in charge of the work with a brief word, and jumped down from the ditch head, pulling off his rag-mask.

'What can I do?' Gilead asked him.

Nithrom shrugged. 'Can you cut timber?'

Gilead shrugged back. 'If I have to.'

'Well, you can sharpen blades, at least. From the way your own sword cuts, I can tell you know how a whetstone works.'

'Bring me the blades. I will sharpen with pleasure. I feel almost useless amid all this toiling.'

'Ah, they've done well since dawn,' Nithrom commented, glancing around. 'We've strengthened the inner ditch and raised more obstacles that cavalry won't like. A few other tricks besides. When Harg comes back with the timber, we'll raise a solid bulwark inside the dyke.'

Gilead pointed up along the main avenue that led to the public yard and the mound. 'We should get some barrels or stable planks, and make a few points of cover along there, to the left, you see? The bulwark may slow their horsemen, but a few good nests for bowmen would break the line of the street and stop their vanguard getting up any speed if they make it in.'

Nithrom shrugged and nodded. 'Well said. I will get the elder, Swale, on it. He's a devil with the strength of a giant. Maybe you can show him what you mean.'

'Of course.'

'And I did as you suggested... the water jars in the scarcement of the hall are refreshed and full again.'

'You would have thought of that without my help.'

Nithrom grinned. He took Gilead's hands in a tight clasp. 'By the old gods, it's good to have you here, Gilead te tuin! The spirit of Tor Anrok will keep this place safe!'

Mule-pulled carts laden with freshly cut timber were approaching from the woods. Astride the first, bare-chested, Harg waved his great axe to salute the town.

AN HOUR PASSED in helping to unload Harg's expertly felled timbers and lift them into place, then another teaching old Swale and four of his grandsons to build angled cover in the main street. Passing by, Dolph noticed the defences and nodded in admiration.

Then midday came, and found Gilead up in the cool shadows of the inner mound fence again, sharpening blades. He had acquired a block of spruce as a rest, and a crowd of children as an audience. They oohed and aahed as he unwrapped his whetstones from their oilcloth bag.

The weapons had been brought to him: Fithvael's sword, Nithrom's long blade, Harg's battered axe, Bruda's sabre, Le Claux's broadsword; all of them, and the spare weapons besides.

He set to work, wearing out nicks and gouges, finishing edges, testing sharpness with a few strands of his own long hair, and explaining each piece of work and weapon to his retinue.

'This is a longsword, from an elven smithy. It belongs to Nithrom, the tall elf warrior in the dark green armour.'

'With the kindly face?'

'Him indeed.'

'He's your master.'

'He is my friend.'

'What's an elf?'

'You are looking at one.'

Laughter. Some whispers.

'No, we do not steal away new-borns in the dead of night. You humans have so many wrong ideas about my kind.'

'What's a human?'

Laughter, some playful punching.

'See here, how I make the stone strokes long and unbroken. A little oil… and now the edge comes sharp. See?'

'I could do that!' this from a tall lad at the front.

'Then you may come here and do it. No, let it slope against your leg. That's it. Again, no… against the way of the metal. Like this.'

'Am I doing it?'

'Yes you are. Well done. Now both sides, mark, and both edges of both sides. That is good.'

'It looks easy!' A girl at his shoulder.

'Come around here and try it. Now this is the scimitar of the red-haired Kislev woman.'

'She's beautiful,' said the older boy already at work, More laughter and some jibes.

'She is, and so is her sword.' To the girl now, her hands trembling with the whetstone. 'Long clean strokes now. Careful, do not cut yourself on the edge. And there's only one edge to this blade, so you'll be done in half the time.'

'Why's there only one edge?' piped a small boy in the huddle.

'It's a weapon design for slashing, rather than stabbing or slicing. You work it so!'

Some gasps, some backing off.

'It is very different from this blade. This is my sword. My brother's, in fact. He gave it to me. Taller than you, eh? This is meant both for slashing and thrusting. Ha! And ha!'

More excited yelps.

'Come on now, take a stone in your hand and come here… that's right, some oil… no, not too much… now, along the blade to the tip. Good.'

A little industry around him, small faces concentrating and determined. Gilead smiled.

'Now, the Norseman's great axe! Who's brave enough to whet that?'

A forest of grubby hands.

'You… come on. Here's the trick, rub the stone both ways. Keep the haft wedged against the ground. Yes, good. Back and forth.'

'And now, this is a greatsword, forged in Carroburg! Have you ever seen a sword so big? It'll take two of you at least. You… and you, lad, with the freckles. In you come…'

THE AFTERNOON WAS waning, and all the blades were polished sharp. Gilead was at work on the last – Le Claux's trusty broadsword – with the last of the children grouped around him. Most had wandered away at intervals as more interesting things happened in the town below. A woman had brought him a plate of stew and some ale, but it sat untouched and the food had gone cold.

Thunder rumbled in the cold, windy distance. The summer storm that had been threatening all day was about to break. A first few spots of rain pattered down.

Gilead felt… something. He rose, Le Claux's ornate sword ready before him.

He went to the gate, some of the children scampering after him.

Below, away on the flank of the northern hills, were the shapes of two riders, galloping down to Maltane as fast as they could, kicking dust: Vintze and Caerdrath.

'Get inside. Hurry,' Gilead instructed the children.

Maura was coming.

RAIN WAS HAMMERING down by the time the Murderers appeared in full force. They lined the top of the northern scarp, blue and white banners flopping in the downpour. From his position on a flat roof in the lower town, Fithvael sighed. Nithrom had estimated two hundred, and the night before they had sent forty to their doom. But there was no mistaking the size of the force ranged up there: three hundred, at the very least.

The batter of drums rolled down the valley slope into Maltane, blurred by the rain. The Tilean infantry were beating the march. As Fithvael watched, more drew into view: horse teams, further squadrons of infantry, six-horse limbers that dragged great cannon.

Fithvael looked away, across the rise of rooftops, and saw Nithrom already mounted upon his steed, waiting in the public yard. Le Claux and Caerdrath were with him. Nithrom saw the veteran elf's glance and signed for patience.

Yes, I shall wait, Fithvael thought, though doom itself comes to overlap me.

There was no parley this time. Fuentes had taken word back to his chieftain, and so sealed Maltane's destruction. Fithvael, craning his eyes against the rain and the dying light, could see a brute of a man on a great horse, trotting the length of the

escarpment, looking down and issuing orders to the rows of
cavalry and foot soldiers that stood around him. The man's
silver helmet was plumed with blue and white feathers. That
had to be Maura himself.

Fithvael gauged distance and crosswind and knew he had
no chance of hitting the Tilean leader, even with his best bowshot. On a roof across the street, he saw Bruda doing much
the same. They caught sight of each other and both shook
their heads.

What will he do, this Maura? wondered Fithvael. *Lay us to
siege? Pound us with cannon? Assault all out with foot and horse?*

Personally, he prayed it would be the latter. He hoped this
Tilean dog-lord would be characteristic of his kind, keen for a
swift and arrogantly crushing defeat achieved by force of
manpower. That they would greet. But a siege? Such a tactic
would kill them, and an artillery barrage would flatten
Maltane and leave nothing left standing to be looted.

Though from what he'd heard of Maura, such a punishment
would be signature. Fithvael was sure, after the defeat and
humiliation of his advance guard, that Maura wanted nothing
from Maltane except its death rattle.

A horn sounded. The clear note rang around the bowl of the
valley.

Fithvael picked up the human-made composite bow next to
him. It had been a while since he'd wielded one of these, and
it was crudely constructed compared to what he was used to,
but his trusty crossbow's rate of fire was too slow for what was
coming.

A wave of Tilean cavalry broke down the funnel of the hill
towards them, fifty abreast. Their thunder was louder than the
storm rumbling across the sky.

MALTANE HAD NO cavalry force to meet a tide that great, and so,
under Nithrom's terse instructions, it did not begin to try.
Instead the defenders waited, tensed, as the horse army
charged down on them – crossing the low scrub, crossing the
slake of marshes that skirted the town, charging up the low
rise towards the outer ditch and the bridge.

Which only seemed to still be there...

The weight of the first eight outriders on the ditch bridge
brought it down in a tumult. Harg's expertise with a wood axe

had severed the beams just to the point of cracking. The bridge falling out from under them, horses and riders, moving at full pelt, cartwheeled and tumbled into the ditch. Those immediately behind were slammed into the gulch by the weight of the charge.

The cavalry broke, moving aside in both directions. But behind them, down the slope, came the infantry, a pouring horde.

Some horsemen tried to jump the ditch, but it was deeper than Fuentes had known it, and the bulwark on the far side was piled up and lined with out-facing stakes. More horsemen foundered in the ditch, some leaping up and calling for the footmen to help them pull their struggling horses free. Others tried the leap and were disembowelled on the timber points.

The first of the infantry were now at the ditch, many clambering over and up the other side. Now Fithvael, Bruda and Erill, along with the half-dozen Maltane folk who had shown any bowmanship, began their work, picking off as many of the troops who crawled over the bulwark as they could.

Fithvael cursed as he saw infantry teams on the far side of the ditch dragging timber boards with them and heaving them out across the mire. They were just out of his bowshot.

A few infantry climbed over the bulwark. Fithvael and Erill picked them off with clean shots. The lad was good with a bow, Fithvael noticed. That plate armour and elderly sword was all for show.

Now the first straggles of infantry were over the ditch, more than the archers could manage. Further bowmen, under Cloden's direction, villagers all, began firing down the main street into the press.

The Tileans had managed to get three boards across the ditch, and that was enough for the milling cavalry. They romped over the vibrating boards, kicking infantry aside as they spilled up into the town, lances and swords glittering.

The first dozen fell on the lethal tripwires that Vintze had fixed across the street. Charging steed limbs snapped as they tripped and went over. Others leapt on, the wires now broken, dodging the sprawling bodies of their comrades and their horses, galloping up the streets.

Now more wires, pulled suddenly taut at head-height by waiting villagers, snapped into place. Tileans cracked back out of their saddles, several virtually decapitated. The horses ran on.

Others assayed the main street towards the public yard, peppered by arrows. Several fell. A quartet of riders made it as far as the town pump, where gunpowder charges buried under a dusting of soil by Dolph and Brom erupted and killed them.

The heat was out of the cavalry now. They fell back, many not even daring to cross the ditch. In their stead, the mass of infantry rolled in, clawing over the bulwarks and the makeshift bridge faster than Fithvael and the bow teams could match.

The infantry seethed up the main street

Fithvael saw Nithrom's signal but he already knew what to do. He lit a pitch arrow and shot it into a tarred straw bundle on the edge of the street. Bruda and the other archers did the same. In a few moments, the main street was a fire-lined inferno that gave the Tilean soldiers little room to move. Gunshots rolled down the street as Dolph and Brom began firing.

But there would still come a point, Fithvael knew in his heart, when all their tricks and skills would be overwhelmed by sheer numbers.

Then Fithvael saw Nithrom, Le Claux and Caerdrath charge into the head of the infantry spread from the main yard, cutting them back. On their heels, on foot, Dolph and Brom, maces swinging.

Cloden, Gilead, Harg and Vintze sprang, also on foot, out of houses further down the street to meet the influx side-on and press them against the horsemen. They had taken the battle to close quarters.

Fithvael realised he had no arrows left. Raising his sword in one hand and his wound crossbow in the other, he leapt down off the roof and charged into the melee.

THE ELF VETERAN emptied his crossbow into the belly of the first Tilean he met, then laid about himself with his sword. It was thick and close in the muddy, wood-walled street, lit by the burning tar-bundles. He glimpsed Bruda nearby, slashing with her scimitar and baying like a she-wolf.

He saw Erill. The youth had come down from the roofs too, his sword in hand, and almost at once had become surrounded. He had killed one Tilean with a lucky thrust, but others were stabbing at him. The lad fell.

Fithvael blundered that way through the press, hacking left and right. Erill was down, blood leaking from a shoulder wound, his aged armour broken and pitted.

Fithvael cut right, removing a head, and then left to open a belly. In the space that he had made, he scooped Erill up and tossed him his short sword.

The lad managed to catch it. It was a pearl-inlaid blade, two feet in length, made by the master craftsmen of Tor Anrok. He stared at it for a heartbeat, flexing it in his hand.

'Don't admire it! Use it!' Fithvael shouted.

Erill swung left, wondering at the lightness of the elven blade, and severed the weapon arm of a Tilean almost on him. The youth laughed with sudden glee, and set into the mob.

Fithvael struggled to join him and set his back to the youth. Murderers, in great numbers, massed around them. They fought like devils, man-boy and elf-sire thrown together by the gods of war.

A figure erupted in through the press around them, swinging his sword and destroying the foe.

The newcomer said nothing, because he could not. It was Madoc. His trusty warhammer lost in the flood of the stream when he fell, he had resorted to the unfamiliar weight of a broadsword, which now he spun and chopped almost as deftly as a great hammer of Ulric.

Side by side, though the hot blood of their enemies covered them, Fithvael, Erill and Madoc held the street.

GORE DROOLED OFF Gilead's longsword. He had lost sight of Vintze and Cloden, but that hacking and splintering nearby could only be the work of Harg and his axe. The elf cut into the press once more, blue-steel spinning, and slit through wrists and windpipes. There was a pack ahead, Tileans mobbing over a victim in the firelight. He sliced them down.

The white warsteed was dead, its eyes staring. Le Claux was trampled in the dust nearby, his armour torn and shattered, two lance heads and a sword thrust through his torso. The knight looked up at Gilead with misty eyes.

'Have we won?' he asked.

Gilead paused. 'Of course, warrior. Thanks to you.'

'I thought as much,' Le Claux mumbled, blood gurgling in his throat. 'I'm thirsty. Have you a drink at all?'

Gilead swung aside and cut down a Tilean who loomed out of the fire-dark.

Then he knelt by Le Claux's side and pulled out the last of the flasks of elven wine that he had taken from Tor Anrok and carried with him ever since. It was almost empty. The Bretonnian finished the remains.

'Ah…' smiled Le Claux. 'Quite the best I–'

The Bretonnian continued to smile up at him, but Gilead knew Le Claux was dead.

He turned, severing a marauding Tilean from armpit to armpit with his voracious sword before the mercenary could strike him down as the man had intended, and leapt back into the battle.

BLOOD, MEAT, SINEW, flesh, steel, bronze, iron, fire. The currencies of war were played out and exchanged until dawn.

As the sun rose, the Tileans fell back to the north scarp. They left seventy cavalry and a hundred and twenty infantry on the plains before and the streets inside Maltane.

The defenders, many injured, all weary to the point of sleep, had lost Le Claux, and old Swale, and nineteen of the other villagers: four women, three boys, twelve men, all of them fighters.

Yet, by any standards, they had won another extraordinary victory. Maltane had become the Tilean's curse. But it had also become a place of fatigue, of spurting wounds, of broken weapons.

Nithrom called his troops and the villagers back into the inner mound. They had done all they could. They had waged an immortal defence. If Maura now continued, they would have nothing left in them but the pride of denying him the first time. They had nothing left to give.

As dawn rose, true to his nature, the unforgiving Maura began his second assault.

IT WAS A distant sound at first, like a stick being snapped, then a splash of mud. Fithvael and Vintze were outside the megaron's portico, binding the wounds of the villagers, when they heard it.

Vintze cursed.

Again it came, a sighing cough-crack, far away, then a wet thud below down the slope.

Fithvael grabbed up his crossbow and ran to the wall. He was in time to see two of the nine great cannon on the distant northern scarp puff white smoke. A second later, that cracking sound. Fifty yards below the inner ditch, plumes of wet mud vomited upwards.

'Has he not the range?' asked Fithvael.

Brom was on the wall decking next to him, using Vintze's scope to spot.

'No, he's just getting his aim.'

The man leapt down, tossing the scope back to the Reiklander. 'Get them inside! The villagers all! Get them inside and down into the scarcement!'

Motion seized the throng. Clutching bewildered children to their skirts, the womenfolk hustled them into the main hall. The surviving menfolk of Maltane, some thirty in number, picked up their makeshift weapons and shields. Amongst them were at least a dozen boys who looked too young for combat, and twenty women who refused to hide. Nithrom's warriors, meanwhile, were assembling on the wall.

The first cannon shell hit home, punching through the tower of the old temple behind the inner hall. There was a growl of punctured stone and part of the tiled roof fell in.

A second later, and another shot hit the outer wall, cracking the boards and making the ground shake. One of the Maltane men was thrown off his sight-deck and fell into the mud below.

They have the range now, gods help us, Fithvael thought.

He turned. The gate exploded in, crushing the water butt in a powerfully outflung sheet of stone and water, and killing several goats. The smashed gateway looked so open and vulnerable.

Two more shots screamed in, one tearing through the roof of the inner hall, the other slicing low through the top rails of the wall. Part of the decking collapsed, spilling two more Maltaners. One clambered up. The other, just a boy, lay still in the marl, his left side sheared away.

Gilead and Nithrom ran to the open gate and looked down.

Skirmish lines of Tilean horse were cantering in across the outer ditch and through the lower town. Behind them were infantry files, bearing pikes, halberds and bows.

More shells whistled down, over-shooting the mound and falling in the lower ditch behind.

'We cannot fight this!' Gilead cursed.

'No, we can't.' Nithrom gazed out again and then turned to the defenders. 'Inside! Into the scarcement. They will have to stop shelling before their foot troops get up here. We can ride it out. I ask for two to stand with me, to give the call.'

All the defenders volunteered. Nithrom paused a moment, then made his choices. 'Bruda, Dolph. The rest of you below. Gilead will lead you out when the time comes.'

Even the Maltaners hesitated at this. Nithrom had always given the second command to Cloden. Gilead himself was surprised. If not Cloden, then Caerdrath, surely, before him.

'Do as he says!' Cloden roared, dismissing the slight. 'Get below!'

The defenders scrambled inside and down the ladders into the scarcement. More cannonballs hissed down, smashing the megaron roof and the chancery of the temple. Some struck the wood fence, shattering sections of it.

Nithrom, Dolph and Bruda struggled into cover.

IN THE TIGHT, cloying air of the scarcement, Cloden called for calm. The earth around them shook with the impacts outside, and dust and mud dribbled in between the beams. The Maltane villagers were terrified, and with good reason.

Harg rose, a hefty shaggy bulk in their midst. He opened his arms. 'I've known worse'n this, friends! Much worse! Let's lift our spirits and sing a song!'

He started to sing a phlegmy Norse battle hymn, singing slow so they could learn the words and the return, clapping his meaty hands in time to the song and to the impacts above.

Seeing his efforts, most of Nithrom's band made the effort to join in – Cloden, teaching the children how to clap in time; Vintze, over-enunciating the gristly Norse words; Erill, whispering the words and conducting the womenfolk.

Brom sang too, but Fithvael saw how he kept glancing up at every missile hit. He should be with his brother, the elf thought.

Gilead saw the gunner's nervousness too, and winced. He knew all too well the pain of separation from a twin. He paced through the huddled mass, clapping his hands in time, encouraging them all.

Madoc sat at the back of the chamber, near the steps, his broadsword across his knees, clapping time, mouthing the verse.

Fithvael stepped over to Gaude, who was hunched over the cloak-wrapped corpse of his lord.

'What are you doing?' he asked delicately over the song and the impacts.

Gaude looked round. He had taken Le Claux's sword from his dead hands. 'What I should have been doing.'

Fithvael hunched near to him. 'You're no fighter...' He let the implications hang between them.

'Not now, perhaps.' Gaude cleared his throat, as if nervous. 'I was once... Sir Gaude. I was a champion of the blessed Lady. At Alesker's Field, I lost my nerve and my honour. Since then, I have followed this poor, drunken fool as his squire. Poor Le Claux – he was never made to be a knight.'

'He did us proud.'

'Maybe. The Lady rest him, he never had the spirit.'

'And you do?'

Gaude rose, drawing the beautiful, knightly sword from its scabbard.

'I did. I think it has become time I found it again.'

Fithvael was almost shocked by the squire's raw bravery. He half-expected angelic choirs to begin singing. When they did, he had to shake himself.

But it was Caerdrath. He had brought out an elven lyre, and was strumming and singing along with Harg's rough chant. The Norseman blinked and looked around, but found a smile in Caerdrath's eyes and continued. It was the oddest, most plaintive sound ever heard on the surface of that world. A for-lorn high elf of Saphery, with the purest golden music in his voice, singing along with a sour, brutal northman's epic.

They sang it together, in a harmony that none present would ever forget, and now, drowning out the deathly pounding of the enemy's cannon for a few moments, every voice in the scarcement joined in.

* * *

THE REPETITIVE THUD of the impacts, always intermingled with the crunch of breaking stonework, the crack of sundering wood and the smash of falling tiles, fell suddenly silent.

They had been holed in the scarcement for two hours. In the gloomy cellar, all fell silent and turned their faces up to look at the roof. Gilead, Vintze and Cloden lifted their blades. Caerdrath wrapped his lyre and put on his helmet. Brom moved to the foot of the ladder, his mace in his hand.

They heard a voice, from far outside. What it said, they could not know. But Gilead, Fithvael and Caerdrath knew at once that it was Nithrom who had called.

'Now!' cried Gilead, pushing up the ladder after Brom, who was already monkeying up to the hatch.

The fighters followed – Cloden, Caerdrath, Harg, Vintze, Fithvael, Madoc, young Erill – and Gaude on their heels, still dressed as a squire but bearing the broadsword and shield of his dead master.

After them, came the warriors of Maltane, the men, women and youths who were able and prepared to fight, farm implements and rusty weapons in their grips.

Gilead and Brom climbed up through the hatch and hurried down the dust-choked hall of the megaron in advance of the others. From without came shouting, the sound of sporadic combat. They barely noticed that the great hall's roof was broken open to the sky and that they ran over shattered tiles and slumped beams.

Outside, the inner fence was a vestige of its former self. The entire north-facing wall and the gate was a splintered ruin. In truth, the entire inner mound had taken a heavy beating, but the north wall had seen the worst of it. Smoke plumed around and livestock loosed from the stables by a series of cannonball strikes ran wild.

Nithrom, Bruda and Dolph filled the gap, ranged side by side, hacking at the Tilean foot troops who even now were forcing entry up the ditch. Nithrom had taken the inner bridge down, but sheer weight of numbers welled up and into the inner compound.

Gilead was with Nithrom in an instant, his sword slicing and slashing a deadly pattern. A moment later, Dolph was joined by Brom and Vintze, and Cloden dove in to support Bruda. Like sword-wielding daemons, they hacked and slashed and thrust and threw the baying Murderers back on themselves.

'Alarm! To the left!' Erill screamed as he and the rest flooded out of the inner hall.

More Tilean mercenaries were pushing in through a splinter in the curtain of timber to their left, where a cannonball had staved in the fence.

Erill rushed to it, Fithvael and Gaude at his heels. The trio laid into the first intruders. Fithvael saw how the lad handled the elven shortsword well, like he was born to its grip. But he lacked skill and experience. His wild, untrained strokes left him open to the dog packs raging in through the fence break, and his wounds did not help him any either. A thrusting halberd mashed into the side of his face, and Erill fell.

Fithvael was surrounded by a thicket of Tileans, swinging his sword savagely. 'Gaude! Get the boy clear!' he yelled.

But Gaude was occupied too. He had cast Le Claux's shield aside and engaged the foe, his borrowed broadsword glinting. It was the most extraordinary display of swordsmanship Fithvael had ever seen from a human. Whether driven by grief or a need for vengeance, Gaude parried, ducked and swung like a master, his sword moving like fluid metal.

Harg and Madoc slammed into the melee from behind, and as Madoc laid in with his own sword, Harg dragged the bloody form of Erill clear. Other Maltaners ran in, joining the fight at the wall's breach.

SWOOPING IN AND out of consciousness, Erill came round to find himself lying clear of the fight by the steps of the ruined hall. He pulled himself up, then passed out in a savage explosion of pain, and then came round and pulled himself up again. The left part of his face was numb and cold, and he knew by the blood on his collar and front that he had a dreadful wound. He couldn't see out of his left eye at all, but he dared not touch it with his fingers, lest he not like what he found.

But through his right eye... by the gods, what legends were being forged.

At the main gate breach, Nithrom, mighty elf ranger, towered over a pile of corpses, his blade slicing back and forth, misting the air with blood. To his left, Cloden, slicing the

greatsword of Carroburg into the armoured heads of the
scrambling foe... the twins of Ostmark, Dolph and Brom,
reunited in combat, maces smashing... Vintze and Bruda,
Reiksword and Kislev sabre, laughing as they faced the endless
tide of blue and white liveried soldiers, bathed in blood...
Gilead, a daemonic blur, raging his longsword into the foe...

At the gap in the fence to the left, the grizzled elf Fithvael,
side by side with Madoc and Harg, slicing and chopping in
bloody abandon. Harg's great axe circled and spun as it did its
work, Fithvael's sword stabbed and thrust, and Madoc – well,
he seemed to use his weapon as if it were a warhammer, spinning and flexing and turning it down at each stroke, trying to
use his boundless mastery of the hammer to good effect with
a sword.

And Gaude, was that truly him? Almost lost in a thicket of
Tileans, revealing a skill with a blade that a humble squire
could and should not possess.

Drunn and the impromptu warriors of Maltane were in the
thick of the carnage too, jabbing and slicing, pummelling and
stabbing. Erill saw several fall beneath the experienced skill of
the Tilean dogs, but none died without honour.

He rolled sideways and saw Caerdrath. The elf had seen
another hole in the timber fence and had raced across to close
it. Four Maltane villagers went with him, spurred on by his
cries.

What came through the breach was not a man. Not an elf.
Not something Erill ever wanted to see again.

The ogre was three times the size of the largest and most
crudely put-together human. He was dressed in rags, tattered
blue and white, and he swung a flint-bladed adze in each of
his huge fists. Tileans squirmed in through the ragged breach
around him, urging him on.

'Klork! Klork! Klork!' they howled to goad him.

The ogre killed the first two Maltane warriors that reached
him with a single slice of one blade. The beast bellowed, spittle flying from his broken teeth as his sinewy neck turned his
misshapen mouth to the sky.

Caerdrath was there in three paces, a golden blur. His sword
prismed light it flew so fast. One of the massive stone adzes
fell to the marl, still gripped in the ogre's clawed hand. Black
blood fountained in all directions.

The ogre – Klork – howled, and smashed at the elf in return.

Caerdrath dodged the mankiller adze, and as he dived ahead, raked his blade down the flank of the monster.

Klork turned slowly, striking as he went, his remaining adze blade dinting the side of Caerdrath's beautiful silvery armour.

The elf fell, rolled and came up facing the ogre square on. Erill stiffened as he saw the high elf spit crimson blood down his fine breastplate.

Ignoring the pain that lanced through him, Erill clambered to his feet, and found his sword. Giddy, he ran towards the fight, towards the ogre. A Tilean charged him and somehow he side-stepped, slicing the Tilean's head clean off in a single move he did not even think about.

Klork was chopping at the darting Caerdrath, but Erill saw how the elf was slower than before. Blood wept through the cracks in his ithilmar plate mail.

Erill threw himself forward, his sword held ahead of him. The superb elven blade smashed into the ogre's back and the point came out through the huge beast's throat.

Klork vomited blood and fell, crashing down into the ditch like a felled tree.

Erill swayed. He saw Caerdrath smiling across at him. Then four Tilean pikes ripped the wounded elf apart, spitting him from every angle.

Erill dove upon the Tileans, yelling, his sword, stained with ogre blood, flying. He was vaguely aware of Madoc and Cloden reaching him, driving into the breach.

Then the pain of his head wound became too much and the world span about him. Rushing sounds, ghosts in the air, the dying sigh of an elf, darkness.

FOR THREE HOURS straight, until noon had passed, they held the inner mound of Maltane against the hordes that swarmed up from below. Only foot troops could reach the top of the mound, for the ditch and steepness of the slope made cavalry access impossible. Many Tilean riders dismounted and joined the infantry push. The mercenaries harried the space that had once been the gate, and clambered in through punctures made by cannon shells in the stockade. Some even tried to scale the fence. The climbers and the clamberers could bring nothing with them longer than a sword, but at the fallen gate, lines of long pikes and halberds thrust in at the defenders.

Yet at least, as Nithrom had predicted, the shelling had stopped once the Tilean foot had moved into range.

Twice the Murderers broke clear into the inner yard and defeat seemed to be about to overtake fragile Maltane. On the first occasion, at the main gate soon after Klork and Caerdrath had fallen, Cloden, Vintze and Gaude waged a maniacal counter-push from the left side of the shattered entrance, cutting off the harried group of Tileans already inside and closing the breach, driving further attackers back with flailing swords that were so wet with blood they glowed dull red. At their backs, Harg and the twin gunners from Ostmark engaged and destroyed those who had got into the compound in a brutal melee played out on the marl in front of the megaron's portico.

On the second occasion, just short of midday, a new force of Tileans none had seen skirted round the inner mound on the outside of the timber fence, and brought a section of it down with axes. This was round to the west, almost behind the temple, a direction not yet assaulted. The din of the raging combat covered the sounds of their axe-strokes, but a small boy, one of those who had helped Gilead sharpen the blades, saw the incursion from a window of the temple where he was hiding. His wails alerted his mother and an old woman, who darted out through the inner hall and screamed the news to the defenders' line.

Three Maltaners managed to break off and were first to hurry round the mound yard and meet the attack. One was a ploughman called Galvin, tall, with shoulders like a barn roof's tie beam. The other two were a herdsman and a weaver.

There were eight Tilean dog-soldiers already inside the fence by then, and dozens more pushing through the hole behind them. They were all shieldless, and most just had axes and shortswords, all they dared bring on the treacherous circuit of the outer fence. But two had crossbows.

The herdsman dropped, a quarrel through his neck, before the trio had even got within sword-reach. The other crossbowman buried his dart in the meat of Galvin's left thigh, but the doughty warrior did not slow. He killed both bowmen as they tried to reload, with savage blows of his halberd. It was a Tilean weapon he had taken from a corpse earlier in the battle, and he laughed at the justice. Then he and the sword-wielding weaver were in the thick of them.

Two Tileans brought the weaver down with axe-blows, their seasoned experience bettering his fevered eagerness. Then they were all on Galvin, and more came in the breach besides. By then, Gilead had freed himself from the main fight at the gate mouth, and he ran to the second front by the most direct route: through the shattered megaron hall, leaping out through a broken window at the west end where it met the crumbling wall of the temple. On his way through the hall, he managed to scoop up his black longbow and quiver from the equipment stacks they had carried in on their arrival.

Gilead stood, braced, on the low, tiled roof of a midden overlooking the influx, and began to loose red-fletched arrows into the enemy force. Each draw of his bow sent a long, ash-wood arrow juddering into a Tilean body. He cut down six, enough for the wounded Galvin to barge and hack his way clear of the press of Murderers.

More arrows flew in. Bruda was kneeling on the roof lip of the hall itself, shooting down with her double-curved Kislev bow. Together, the two hawk-eyed archers slaughtered the milling Tileans. There was nowhere to run, no cover from the deadly hail, except back out through the fence. As the last few scratched and clawed their way out, leaving twelve dead or dying on the churned earth, Bruda and Gilead sent more shots into their backs too.

Once they were out of sight, Gilead dropped his bow and leapt down, drawing his gold-hilted sword. He raced to the breach and, with Galvin's help, dragged a haycart in to cover it. Once she was sure no more Tileans would appear, Bruda also lowered her bow and vaulted down to help. The trio wrestled the cart into place, and then used a mattock to stake it firm with broken timbers from the wall. Better repairs would have to wait.

Galvin sat down suddenly, weak from blood loss. Apart from the quarrel wound, he had been gashed and sliced in a dozen places. He was splashed with gore from head to toe, but by no means was all of it his.

'What can I do?' he wheezed to the elf and the Kislevite.

'Watch here,' Bruda told him.

'They may try again. Stay here, rest and watch the breach,' Gilead agreed.

'But I can't just...' Galvin began. He was swaying eccentrically, but the rolling roar of the main fight was too loud to ignore. 'I must fight, for Sigmar's sake! My village—!'

'Then recover our arrows as you watch. We will need them later.'

Bruda quickly showed the ploughman how to use a short knife to cut out the arrows without breaking them.

GILEAD AND BRUDA returned to the fight, barely in time to lay in beside Nithrom and Madoc, who were being driven back by Tilean swordsmen.

'Where's Caerdrath?' Gilead bellowed over the ring of steel and the hoarse yells of pain.

Nithrom glanced at him. Gilead did not know how the other elf had fallen, he realised.

Below, a horn sounded down the valley and drums rolled. The Tileans were signalled to fall back. Even the strongest assault can only maintain its impetus for so long without advantage – and all their advantages had been denied.

Maura's Murderers broke off and fell back down the mound, many running in retreat, for they knew the embittered defenders would not let them leave unhindered. True enough, Bruda and Fithvael, and Dolph with a borrowed bow, fired on them as they ran, dropping half a dozen and wounding more. The inner ditch and the northern slope of the mound were littered with the southern raiders' dead.

The defenders sagged almost as one, overcome with exhaustion. Most of the villagers who had fought fell, weeping or gasping for breath. Women, children and the elderly came gingerly out of the inner hall and the temple to tend those they could help.

Madoc found Erill and carried the lad into the hall. Erill was unconscious and the left part of his face was a bloody ruin.

Fithvael found Gilead standing silently over the mangled body of Caerdrath. Fithvael could feel the pain and anguish throbbing inside his old friend at the sight. It quite eclipsed even the pain Fithvael himself felt at the loss.

'Gilead! Gilead!' The voice rose above the moaning and the weeping, and the distant drums. But Gilead did not turn until Fithvael touched his arm. He swung around sharply, a tall, pale murderous figure in gore-flecked black mail, his eyes as blood-dark as his scarlet shoulder guards and cloak.

It was Gaude yelling. He was on the other side of the inner compound, by the shattered gate. Gilead strode over to him through the press of exhausted and injured townsfolk. Fithvael hurried a pace behind him.

As they approached him, Gaude said nothing more. He turned and looked at the trampled, blood-soaked ground – where Nithrom's body lay.

Vintze knelt down beside the wrecked figure, cradling the elf's head. Nithrom looked as if he was asleep. A broken Tilean sword blade jutted out from between the ribs of his studded leather armour.

Now Fithvael felt a pang much deeper than he had at Caerdrath's loss. Tears stung his eyes, hot and harsh. He looked around, and found they were all there: Cloden, Madoc, Harg, Bruda, the twins. Their eyes were all dimmed with grief. Bruda turned her face to the sky and began to whimper a Kislev prayer-hymn. Cloden spat on the ground, averted his eyes and shook his head sadly. Harg came forward and knelt with Vintze, meek and gentle as a child. Madoc was silent, like a statue. The twins, in unison, made the benediction sign of Sigmar.

'How?' Fithvael asked.

'In the last moments,' Gaude answered, quiet. 'After the horn sounded, as they fell back. One of the last of them to run, the lieutenant, Fuentes, as I saw it.'

'Fuentes!' Gilead hissed the name.

The villagers were also grouping around now, in a silent, disbelieving mass. Fithvael knew this was the worst possible outcome. For all they had done, for the incredible resistance they had put up to defeat the savage enemy, this tore the heart out of them all. Nithrom was their leader, their head. None had countenanced the possibility that he could ever fall, not his warrior band of friends and old comrades, not the villagers who had believed every last one of his rousing words. And not the two elves of Tor Anrok, last of their line, who saw him as a final link to their heritage.

Their morale had died with Nithrom.

The east wind rose and the already dark sky began to weep heavy rain. Down in the valley, the Tilean drums sounded again, and the returning mercenary troops began to reform in skirmish lines around the outer ditch. There were more than ten score still: cavalry, foot, archers, not to mention the gunnery teams on the north scarp.

'We should reinforce the defences,' Dolph said.

'Rebuild what we can before they return,' Brom finished.

'To hell with that!' Vintze snarled, laying down Nithrom's head gently and getting to his feet. 'It is over. We are done. Let's get out, retreat before they can come upon us again. Grab what we can and break through the back of the mound's fence. We can be down in the woods by night.'

'All of us?' Gaude asked bitterly. 'Women and children? The old, the infirm, the wounded?'

'We did what we could!' Vintze cried, turning away. 'We did more than anyone thought we would!' With this, he cast a lingering, contemptuous look in Gilead's direction. 'But it is over now.'

'We leave them?' Gaude pressed.

Vintze shrugged. 'They can come. Whatever they like.'

'And be hunted down in yon woods by the Tilean dogs?' asked Harg. 'Thou knows Maura won't just let us run, Vintze. He'll come a hunting after'n.'

'Without food, provisions, weary as we all are?' Cloden finished the picture. 'And them, supplied, eager for blood? Some of us might get away, the more able-bodied, perhaps. Those that can ride, or fight if they have to. Those who have made a career out of slipping away like a thief.'

Vintze took a step towards the Carroburger and then turned aside. 'Damn you, Cloden!'

'We stay. We fight. We finish this,' Cloden said adamantly. 'We–' He stopped himself short and turned to Gilead. 'Forgive me, lord. I was forgetting my place. Nithrom named you his successor. I… am too used to being his second.'

Fithvael tensed. For a long moment he thought Gilead might not reply. The son of Lothain was an arrogant bastard at the best of times, but now, surrounded by the human chattel he despised, with Nithrom and Caerdrath dead… now would not be a good time to act true to nature, to damn and curse all, to despair and let the black moods overtake him as they had done all his life. But Gilead chose the moment to surprise his companion.

'I am not offended, Cloden. Perhaps it is best if you carry on in the role you know.'

Cloden shook his head. 'Nithrom named you. He did that for a reason. I owe Nithrom te tuin my life three times over in combat and as many times again in word, because I listened to him. Nithrom named you and that's good enough for me.'

Gaude and Madoc both nodded. The twins did too.

'Da,' said Bruda.

'Twas his will thee should lead,' Harg agreed.

Gilead looked at Fithvael.

'Do you have to ask, old friend?' his old friend said.

Then Gilead's eyes turned to Vintze. 'And you?'

Vintze paused, then turned and grinned with a shrug. There was sadness in his face, but the grin was genuine, a scoundrel's look, bright as a clean flame.

'If all these idiots agree,' he smiled.

Gilead turned and looked down the slope through the gateway. Maura's regiment was drawing up behind the ditch. Gilead could see campfires. They would not be coming again until they'd had rest and food, but the cannonballs might.

'Carry the dead in state and place them in the hall,' said Gilead. 'Then everyone into the scarcement. Their guns will speak again before the day is out. You, and you three–' he picked out some of the older children who had worked the blades with him. 'Stand watch up here. Come to us if they fire their guns. I don't want you out here then. But cry out if they move in again.'

Eager, the children ran to the gate.

'What about the defences?' Dolph and Brom asked in one voice.

'There is no point in relying upon them any more. The dogs will break down whatever we build with their cannon. We need a better plan.'

THE SCARCEMENT WAS as dingy and foul as they remembered it. Now there were wounded down here too, whimpering and stinking the air with open wounds. Water and food was shared out, though the supplies were getting low. Fithvael did what he could for Erill. The lad was conscious again, his face wrapped in dressings.

'A fine scar you will have,' chuckled Fithvael as he wound the bandages off and applied herbal dressings to the wounds.

'Caerdrath is dead. I saw it,' the lad whispered.

'I know.'

'The women told me Nithrom fell too.'

'It breaks my heart to say... but yes. He fell, and gave his life. Valiant to the end.'

'Make me fit. Make me well enough to stand with you.'

'You've got a bad wound, boy, and the eye, well, it–'

Erill sat up smartly. 'I don't care. Make me fit enough to stand with you at the last. I need to do that. If I fall dead a moment after the last of us is conquered or the last of them flee, I don't care a damn. I need to fight now, for my father's sake.'

Fithvael paused. He realised that he had never understood why Erill was with them. The others, all old comrades of Nithrom, who'd fought and warred and drunk beside him, and all of whom owed him a battle debt or a blood-pledge. But this one? Fithvael had always assumed Erill was here because he was trying to make a career as a pay-sword and Nithrom had given him a chance.

'What? What do you mean?'

'Nithrom... was my father.'

Fithvael set down his herbs. Such a thing was not totally unheard of, in the tales, but still...

One of elf kind and a human female? It could explain the boy's fragile looks and his graceful strength. In fact, now Fithvael saw it, he fancied he saw something new in the boy's ancestry. And yet, was it truly possible for the races to mingle so?

'How?'

'I was raised in a village near Altdorf. My mother, always told me my father had died in an Empire war, drafted to the east. But when she died of the fever in my sixteenth summer, Nithrom came. He told me the truth. He provided for me.'

Fithvael sighed. He thought of Nithrom, out in the crude human world, building friendships, fighting wars, finding solace for his loneliness amongst the brief human kind. Nithrom had cast aside the old ways more surely and more completely than Fithvael and Gilead had ever managed. He had become part of what the humans innocently called the Old World, not some phantom watcher on the outskirts. He had lived his life, and raised this human boy to be a son to be proud of, however against the old ways it was.

Fithvael felt the deepest and most starkly hollow pain of his life. It took him moments to speak again. He busied himself in redressing the wound, and turned away from the sprawled boy on the cot, returning a moment later with Nithrom's longsword.

'Use it well, Erill te tuin,' he said as he pressed it into the boy's hands. Whether or not the lad's tale was true or a mere fiction was irrelevant here, with all of them so close to losing everything.

'I already have yours,' whispered Erill, pointing to the short-sword Fithvael had lent him. 'It felt right in my hands.'

'So it should. And your... your father's blade will feel righter. You will live, Erill. If you can stand, stand. If you can fight, fight. I will not stop you. You are owed it.'

'So, ARE WE sitting here and waiting for them to come?' asked Bruda, sharpening her sword with a whetstone. Thanks to Galvin, her quiver – and Gilead's too – was almost full again. Now the wounded ploughman was being tended in the back of the scarcement.

'No,' said Gilead. 'Answer me this...' He looked to them all, the remaining pay-swords sat or stood around him in the cellar. 'How did they hurt us most?'

'With thern blasted blades, damn you!' Harg spat.

'No, worst of all,' the elf replied patiently. 'What made us almost give up?'

Madoc made a sign. He tried to speak first, but his mouth clacked wordlessly. Remembering, he drew in the air with his index finger. The elven rune that was Nithrom's initial.

'Just so. They took our leader. For a while then, we were lost, on the point of defeat.'

'Speaking of points,' Vintze said coldly, 'I'm sure you have one.'

'I can see where he's going,' Gaude said.

'And I,' said Cloden.

'Maura!' said the twins together.

'Maura the Murderer. Just so.' Gilead smiled. It was not a comforting expression to see.

'These filth have been driven at us time and again, and paid the price. Would they come on if there were no Great Murderer at their backs with a whip? If Maura were dead, what would they do? Attack? I don't think so. They would give up and run.'

'So,' said Vintze getting up and sipping from a wineskin, 'your plan is to kill Maura and destroy them at the head. Fine. Let's go. Oh… just one more thing: *how the hell do we do that?*'

Gilead called the headman, Drunn, over to them. 'How old is this place?' he asked the drawn village elder.

'Older than my memory or my family, lord,' the man said.

'The hall, the temple?'

'Have been here years, generations, the town grew up around its skirts. My father's father said that in his father's mother's time, or was it is his great uncle's d–'

'It does not matter right at this moment.'

'No, I'm sure it don't. Anyway, this was once a noble's manor, up here on the mound. Before it was a village, my folk said. The temple, that's from then. The great hall's newer, of course. The Big Winter Fire when my grand-grandfather was a youth razed it and they built another. Looks like we'll have to do the same again, if we have the chance.'

'And this cellar?'

'Oh, that's a relic from the old hall.'

'And this?' Gilead slid behind one of the big water vats and lifted a loose flag. There was a dark, oozing hole beneath it.

'I never knew that was there!' said Drunn, a startled look written upon his pale face.

'How did you know?' asked Fithvael.

'I noticed it that first time we came down here. I was looking for it. Humans who build fortresses never leave themselves without a back door out.'

'Wery impressive,' murmured Bruda.

'But how do you know that?' Fithvael pressed.

Gilead paused. 'Nithrom told me.' He coughed and continued. 'Here is what we should do now: we climb down there, follow it out, we can come out of this mound without the Murderers knowing. That is how we get to Maura.'

'But where does this thing go?' asked Dolph.

'Where does it come out?' added Brom.

Gilead shrugged. 'I do not know that. Away in the woods beyond the village, if this follows the usual way of things. My suggestion, if you are in agreement, is that we get someone who is used to slipping out of things to find out.'

Everyone turned to look at Vintze. He blinked and stood up, reaching for a lamp. 'Oh, it'd be my absolute pleasure,' he said dryly.

He lit the lamp and crossed to the hole without further protest. Gilead held his arms as he lowered himself into it.

Before he broke his grip, Gilead fixed the flax-haired Reikland thief with his eyes.

'You do not want to dream about what will happen if you do not return.'

'I know. Trust me, elf.' He winked broadly. 'Nithrom always did.'

JUST AFTER THE fourth hour of the afternoon, the Tileans resumed their cannonade. The children Gilead had set on watch felt the first impacts rather than saw them. Then spouts of liquid mud shot up from the silt-slope of the mound and they ran inside, yelling at the tops of their frightened voices.

The rain had not let up all afternoon. Now it was torrential and sheeting under the gusts of a blustering north wind. The sky was prematurely grey and opalescent. It seemed the rain showers were but the heralds of a worse storm to come.

Wet through and shivering, the children tumbled down into the deep scarcement, all screeching at once, but their noise needed no interpreter. All had felt the quaking of the mound.

Vintze had still not returned.

Gilead sent Dolph and Brom slinking above to assess the shelling and to discern what they could of the enemy tactics. The storm was darkening the sky to night-pitch and distant lightning was licking the mountains far to the north. The Ostmarkers reported movement in the enemy camp, plainly some form of preparation, but nothing was yet moving their way except cannon-fire. That was, unless the Tileans were using some art of concealment or shrouding sorcery that even their sharp eyes could not make out.

Gilead had just sheathed his sword and slung it between his shoulder blades, about to climb down into the hole below the scarcement, when Vintze returned.

The Reiklander was utterly covered in black mud and slime so only the whites of his eyes showed. Many Maltaners drew back and gasped to see him heaving himself up out of the floor, almost an undead thing covered in mulch from the grave.

He did not speak until he had rinsed his mouth with wine, spat out several gobbets of mud and then drunk properly. He wiped his mouth with his sleeve, revealing it white and stark against his dirt.

'Two full miles, turning west,' he reported, gasping. Fithvael could see he was tired and out of breath. 'Then it rises and turns north and comes out in the woods by the shoulder of the scarp, about half a mile west of Maura's camp by my reckoning, above and behind it.'

'And not easy going,' remarked Gilead.

Vintze spat again.

'But it will serve,' Bruda said, eager.

'Who goes?' asked Cloden.

'We all do,' Gilead replied. 'To take Maura in his camp will take all of us… at least.'

'But what if he attacks in the meantime, while we're underground?' Cloden countered.

'Two then, to hold the gate and keep them busy as we move around.'

'Who?'

Gilead faltered for a heartbeat.

'I remember,' Vintze said, 'Nithrom used to draw lots.'

'Then that is what we do,' Gilead said.

They pulled straws from the clasped hands of Drunn. Brom and Gaude plucked out the short ones.

'Then those two it shall be,' said Gilead.

'Those three.'

They looked around and found Erill standing behind them, Nithrom's fine elven sword in his hand. He looked pale and weak, and his lost eye and face was bandaged, but there was a measure of courage in his youthful voice.

'I'll be no good to you down there, but I'll gladly stand here with Gaude and Brom.'

'So be it,' Gilead said, his eyes proud. 'Now, let us about our purpose.'

BELOW, IT WAS far worse than Vintze had described. A ragged chimney of mouldering stone dropped down into the heart of the mound, wet with mud and other, less wholesome slime. They passed into blackness almost at once, feeling their way down. The chimney itself was treacherous, and all quickly realised the extent of Vintze's nimble skills. Hand and footholds had to be made blind in the disintegrating stone. After Cloden slipped and nearly fell, Gilead instructed them to take the chute one at a time and call up once they had reached the bottom. He did not want anyone falling and taking another two or three with him. As it was, if anyone fell and broke bones, he doubted they could be hauled back up out of the narrow shaft. Any such person would doubtless die trapped down there, blocking the passage for them all

At the bottom, it was lower and narrower still, just a tunnel bored through wet, black sediment. They had to crawl, single file, pushing their weapons and equipment ahead of them. It was humid and airless, and stank of mould and decay. They crawled on, breathless, through the endless dark. Every now and then, there came a distant rumble. None could tell if it was the storm outside, the shelling overhead, or the slumbering growl of great serpents lying far below the earth.

Fithvael cursed each bone-numbing inch of the crawl. He lost all sense of time and position, possibly for the first time in his long adulthood. The depth, the confinement, the blackness, all overwhelmed his natural abilities to judge distance and place. His mouth and hair were full of clammy soil, and he was filthy all over. This was no place for an elf.

He had made his long shield into a sled for his weapons and pack, and dragged it behind him by a long strap tied to his waistband. Every few minutes the shield would snag and stop him and he would have to reach around or kick back to free it. He had no contact with the others. Harg was ahead of him, too far ahead to be seen; Bruda, he believed, was behind. He could hear only scrambling and distant dull curses. Occasionally, a low call would float back down the tight tunnel, from Vintze or Gilead far ahead, but he could not make out any words.

He almost clawed his way into Harg from behind. The Norseman was stationary and moaning.

'Harg? What is it?'

'Who's there?' Fithvael had forgotten how poorly humans saw in darkness.

'It is Fithvael.'

'Have care! Canst thou turn?'

'Turn? Around? No! The tunnel's too tight!' A cold sliver of panic shivered in his heart.

Harg cursed. 'I'm stuck fast.'

Fithvael felt his flesh crawl. He felt the walls close in. If the Norseman was stuck, then there was no going forward... or back. The thought made his head swim.

He peered around the bulk of the big man's legs. The already narrow tunnel was narrower still here, and the roof belled low. He thought of lighting a lamp to see better, but remembered how quickly the flame would use up their scant air. Use up their air... Fithvael tried to bury the fear that clawed at him.

He dug at the mud around Harg and then pushed against him, hoping that the narrowness was temporary. If it wasn't, he was wedging Harg more securely into his grave. The northerner did not seem to move at all. They both clawed at the mud. Fithvael could hear Bruda approaching behind now, panting hard as she made her way.

'What is problem?' she called.

'Harg is jammed tight,' Fithvael cried back, pushing again at the dead weight of the big man. Damn them all that none of them had thought of this! Harg, the biggest and broadest of them, was not made to slip easily where a lean thief like Vintze could go.

'Push him!' Bruda exhorted.

'I'm trying!' grunted Fithvael.

'Let me past! I will push him!'

'There is no room!' spat Fithvael, clearing his mouth of slime. He rolled over onto his left side, braced his legs against the tunnel walls and heaved again with greater leverage.

''Tis no good!' Harg moaned, a note of panic fluttering in the edges of his deep, bass voice.

It would be, by the gods, Fithvael screamed inwardly. He pushed again with all his strength.

The resistance weakened abruptly and Harg slithered away from him with a cry. Fithvael sprawled nose-down in the slime of the floor and heavy gobbets of mud and chunks of stone tumbled out of the roof.

'Harg?'

'I can move... by't blessed worldtree! I can move!' The tunnel had widened again beyond the slump, and Fithvael could hear Harg slithering on.

'Let's go!' he called back to Bruda. As he resumed his relentless pace, Fithvael realised suddenly just how fast his heart was hammering.

FAR ABOVE, IT was approaching the eighth hour of the evening, and the storm gripped the night around Maltane. At every few beats, the sky flashed incandescent with white fire and booming thunder rattled the trees, the tiles, the walls and the ground. Sheet rain had been falling continuously for several hours.

Wrapped in sodden cloaks, Gaude, Brom and Erill cowered by the gate of the inner mound, gazing down through the deluge at the Tilean lines. The shelling had ground to a stop about an hour and half before, and there was no sign of anything in the storm below except the few pot-fires the mercenaries had lit under lean-tos and awnings out of the rain.

'At least they've stopped with the cannons,' muttered Gaude.

Brom nodded. He was sitting on an upturned bucket devouring a bowl of stew that he was keeping out of the rain with a fold of cloak spread like a fisherbird's wing. 'They can't set matches or powder in this. But then, neither can I.' He gestured forlornly to his handgun, shrouded in oilskin, leaning under the lip of the wall.

Erill was watching with the lightning. Every flash revealed the landscape clearly for a second, stark and blue-white. Staring into the flashes made him blink, and hurt his good eye, but each blink recaptured the fleeting image in negative, burned into his mind. The pain in his wounds ached and throbbed intolerably.

'They've been a long time,' said Brom, putting down his bowl. 'Twice the time it took Vintze to scout, and he went there and back.'

'They'll get there,' Gaude murmured.

Another flash and a roar. Even the heavy rain seemed to wince.

'Movement!' Erill barked. They leaped up to join him.

'Where?'

'Inside the outer ditch, in the town dwellings,' Erill said, pointing.

'Just your imagination... '

'Wait for another flash.'

'But–'

'Wait!' The lad's voice was certain.

Lightning shivered across the sky again.

'There!'

'I saw nothing,' complained Gaude.

Brom shook his head.

But Erill knew what he had seen. Dark dots, shiny black in the wetness, glinting in the storm-light below them. And in that latest flash, he realised that some were as close as the foot of the mound.

'Send to the hall. Get the others out here!'

'You're jumping at shadows,' Gaude said patiently, and flinched as another hammerblow of light and noise exploded above them.

'He's not,' Brom said suddenly, drawing his bow.

'What?'

'I saw them too that time. Erill, go and get any of the townsfolk capable of fighting.'

Erill ran off through the storm towards the hall, wading up to his shins in the standing water inside the fence.

Gaude had his sword drawn by now and was looking where Brom pointed. He made some sense of the dark shapes and blotches in the rain. Things that he had taken to be fences and drain-ditches, or hillocks of grass, were moving: scores of armed men working their way up to the mound silently.

'By the Lady!' he breathed, and there was real fear in his voice.

Erill returned with Galvin, Drunn and some twenty-five remaining fighters or would-be fighters; the very last few.

Brom assembled those with bows along the northern fence and around the gate, where the sword, pike and scythe carriers formed a phalanx with Gaude behind the wall of shields they had stuck in the gate-mouth. Water streamed off fists and noses, helmet-plates, weapons. All were motionless and resolute.

There came a hissing, pattering sound as if the rainfall had increased in heaviness once more. But it was a blizzard of blue-fletched arrows slicing up the hill. They thudded into shields, fence posts and soil. The farmer beside Erill fell with an arrow through his throat and another in his hip. The man had never even spoken.

Now dark shapes were running up the mound, dark shapes they could see even without the aid of the lightning. Drawn weapons glinted.

'Stand ready, stand ready…' Gaude cautioned.

Another blizzard of arrows. As they buried their metal heads in the fence, they seemed to make louder cracks. Erill smelt the incongruous scent of smoke.

More arrows came, describing orange arcs in the sky. Pitched arrows set alight, the slick tar burning despite the rain. They hissed and fizzled against the wet logs of the fence, but some caught where the tar spread. Erill knew that now the storm was on their side. Because if the rain let up, Maltane would begin to burn.

COUGHING AND RETCHING slime, Dolph crawled up out of the stone-built opening in the northern slope woods. He was the last to emerge. The opening was overgrown with gorse and bramble, but Gilead and Vintze had cut the worst of it aside to make the way easier.

The last part of the long crawl had been the hardest, negotiating a rising tunnel almost as steep as the one they had descended from the floor of the scarcement, but without the benefit of old stone for toeholds. And they were all pushing or dragging equipment and now were weary beyond measure.

There were no stars to take the time from, and above the rustling trees, the storm was pounding. But Fithvael reckoned it had taken them four or five hours to make the journey. They all stood around, leaning or slumped against tree trunks, breathing hard. Madoc turned his face to the sky and let the pelting rain wash the slime off his features. Harg took a deep drink of wine from the skin in his pack. It seemed as if the last thing any of them was ready for was an armed raid.

Gilead gave them a few moments to stretch out their limbs and check their packs. With rainwater running down his face and arms, he set his red cloak around him, adjusted the sit of his quiver and bow, and slipped his arm in through the thongs of his long, undecorated shield. Everything set, he drew his sword.

He strode over to Vintze, who sat with his back to an elm, his face in his hands. Though better equipped for the journey than any of them, he was exhausted by having made it three times in the space of eight hours.

'Vintze?'

'Ready when you are,' the Reiklander sighed without looking up.

Gilead turned to the others. Bruda was on her feet again, her sword drawn and her small round shield secure on her arm. Harg had his axe ready. Madoc was tightening the leather thongs wrapping his broadsword's grip, and nodded to Gilead. Cloden had stripped the coverings off his greatsword and was testing the edge. Dolph had his shield and his mace, not to mention a bulky shoulderpack that he had dragged from the mound with his handgun in it.

Fithvael set his crossbow, his sword sheathed, his shield cinched across his back now.

'We shall do this,' he said to Gilead. 'We have already come so far.'

Gilead nodded. Fithvael saw a darkness in his look, a darkness that he hadn't seen so intensely since the long lost days when they had quested after Galeth's killer.

It was a look of vengeance. Immediately, Fithvael realised what had driven Gilead this far, what had fired his admirable command of the company. Revenge… for Caerdrath, for Nithrom, for the hope they had symbolised…

And, Fithvael was sure, sheer bloody-minded rage for the pains and agonies of a lifetime. With great sadness and clarity, Fithvael realised Gilead expected nothing out of this venture except the chance to slake his vengeance, to flirt once more with death. He did not need victory. He did not need to save Maltane. He did not even need to live long enough to see the dawn.

He just wanted to send Maura, the architect of all of this, and his lieutenant Fuentes, the scum who had slain Nithrom, screaming on their way to hell.

Fithvael felt ice form in his heart. He had joined Nithrom to find a purpose, and had been overjoyed when Gilead joined them. But it had done nothing except destroy Nithrom and waken in Gilead that dreadful, melancholic urge which had already wasted most of his life.

They were moving off to clash with a murdering maniac, led by a commander who was not a great deal saner, and whose decisions would be clouded by the worst emotions.

THE MOTLEY BAND scurried down the scarp in cover of the swishing trees and the rain, closing on the hindquarters of Maura's camp. The storm did not let up.

As they paused in cover, they saw darts of fire flying up at the distant inner mound, and in the flashes of the storm, saw dark shapes milling on the slopes. One part of the fence was ablaze in patches.

Nearer at hand, just below them and the end of the trees and brambles, lay the Tilean camp: a huddle of tents and larger canopies, lit from within by lamps and small fires. To the west were pens of horse and mules, the pack teams of the gun limbers and pack-wagons, and the steeds of the cavalry. All of Maura's men were moving on foot in the new attack, it seemed.

To the east of the camp, nearest to them, the Tilean cannon were ranged on the slopes, gunner teams huddled under small awnings, smoking and drinking. A few figures wandered about in the main tent camp, and drums beat.

With a silent gesture, Gilead waved his line forward.

They came into the camp from the back. Bruda, Vintze and Gilead, swords sheathed, fell on the gun teams from behind with daggers and silenced them. In twos and threes, the men were left dead without knowing what had befallen them.

Dolph halted them then and, with Harg's help, manhandled several of the squat tubs of black powder from the gun stacks into a pile. Dolph hauled an oilskin over them, and used his flints to spark up a slow-burning fuse string.

Gilead seemed impatient, but he waited until the work was done. Then they were moving again, in amongst the tents.

Madoc cut a slit down a tent's back with his sword and stepped in, surprising two Tilean officers who were playing dice. He killed them both before they could cry out.

Bruda ducked under a guy-wire and waited until a sentry came level with her before sweeping out and slicing him down with a sure stroke of her sabre.

Harg caught another sentry with his meaty paws and broke his neck.

Gilead slipped towards one of the larger tents and burst inside, his sword ready.

It was empty. Gilead re-emerged and looked around, searching for another likely target.

Fithvael, just down the aisle between tents from his old friend, saw the Tilean sentry loom behind Gilead. The man started to cry out an alarm that was cut short by Fithvael's crossbow. But the hasty shot had only winged the man. He went down, shrieking with pain.

Gilead turned and slew him, then snapped an angry look in Fithvael's direction. By then, the camp had already come to life, and blue and white-clad mercenaries were emerging into the rain from all around, weapons in their hands.

The fight began in earnest.

AT THE MOUND, the defenders could only keep the Tileans at bay for so long. Apart from extinguishing most of the flaming arrows, the rain was helping them by turning the mound's slopes into mudslides that caused many of the advancing infantry to fall and slither back. Under Brom's command, the archers of Maltane quickly learned how to pick off an advancing Murderer near the top of the slope so he would fall back and knock some of his comrades down with him in the dire conditions.

But it was not enough. The Tilean bowmen at the mound's foot maintained their rain of missiles, and by force of sheer numbers, the Murderers were reaching the gate, charging in at Gaude, Erill and the Maltane defenders with swords and pikes.

A ferocious melee erupted in the gate mouth. Erill realised how truly disadvantaged he was by the loss of his injured eye. He had trouble gauging space and size quickly, and the atrocious light and weather made it all the harder. He was surrounded by a dizzying, screaming, stabbing, whirling mayhem.

Brom leaped down from the wall, throwing aside his bow now he was out of arrows, and laid into the thick of the attackers with his mace. He smashed his way in next to Galvin, sending Tilean dogs flying, and they drove in at the press, mace and halberd raking and swinging.

Gaude swung his ex-master's sword with the same formidable skill as he had shown before. His armour and clothes were tattered and bloody. With one hand he pulled up a young Maltaner who had been knocked down in the surging mass, hacking with his sword at the same time. He couldn't see Erill anymore. Was the lad down? Before he could look around, another two Tileans were at him with blades.

In a sudden pause in the melee, Gaude realised the rain had eased. Combustive thunderflashes still lit the fight, but the wind was up and the billowing clouds above were spent.

Fanned by the wind, the stockade walls began to burn as another hail of lit arrows thunked into them.

BRUDA, CLODEN AND Fithvael were locked in a hand-to-hand fight in one of the narrow rows between tents. Tileans milled all about them, snarling and yelling. The Carroburg greatsword whispered as it swung and two men in cavalry armour were sent flying backwards, bringing a tent awning down on a pot-fire. Flames licked up out of the collapsed material. More tents fluttered and fell, some dragged down under falling bodies. Fithvael ground forward over swathes of loose canvas, trading sword blows with a trio of brutish mercenaries. His long shield was on his arm now, and the Tileans were gouging ribbons of wood out of it.

Bruda felled a gunner who came at her with a horselance, and then moved in beside Fithvael, spinning one of his assailants away, dead. Fithvael slew another with a jab of his sword, but more rushed in to fill the Tilean's place.

Flailing left and right, Dolph broke skulls with his mace. He was cornered by a row of latrine dugouts, cracking out at anything that came near with his heavy weapon-head.

Vintze and Madoc stood together by the horse pens, blades dancing. Vintze was putting his small shield to good use as an offensive weapon, driving off as many with his shield blows as he did with his sword. The broadsword in Madoc's hands spun and whirled like a hammer, making orbits and circuits in the air, cutting through armour and flesh and sending helmets flying.

With a savage cry, Gilead ripped his way out from a tent that was starting to slump over him, leaving three Tileans dead under its flopping shroud. Through the confused tumult, he suddenly caught sight of Fuentes, Maura's lieutenant, wading in with a hooked shortsword in each hand. Gilead cried the dog's name and hurled himself at him.

Fuentes heard the shout and wheeled his thickly muscled frame around with an answering snarl. His slabby face was sheened with sweat and his good eye was so hooded and dark it matched his eye patch, making his face a death's head in the storm-light. Roused from slumber or a drinking bout in the tents, he had not had time to pull on his rich blue cloak, but his ornate golden cuirass and shoulder guards were in place, gleaming with raindrops like extra jewels.

They slammed at each other like rutting stags, splitting the press aside to reach sword-length. Gilead slashed a dog-soldier carrying a billhook in two as he cut a path to Nithrom's killer. Fuentes showed equal contempt for his own, slaying two more of his own mercenaries who were foolish enough to get in his way, with scissoring blows of his hooked swords. He had taken the first defeat personally, and no doubt had suffered Maura's anger for the failure. Now nothing would stay the blood-rage that drove him after the ones who had bested him. Nithrom had already paid. Now this other inhuman dog was in sight, and Fuentes knew him from the meeting at the outer ditch.

They clashed hard, Gilead blocking one shortsword with his own blade as the other raked a gouge down his long elven shield. Fuentes wheeled and set in again, swinging his paired swords in independent arcs. For all his bulk, he was as swift as a cat, and the twin blades made it impossible to address him in any conventional way. It was like fighting two expert swordsmen simultaneously.

Gilead leapt one scything sword as if he were a salmon, and blocked the other with a downswing of his sword in mid-leap, while turning his upper body and swinging the long shield around like a blade. The tip caught Fuentes below the chin and sent him reeling and choking.

Gilead had seen how well Vintze used his shield as a proactive weapon, but then Vintze's shield was a small, weighted buckler. It took a being of unnatural strength – or of unhinged mind – to swing a long, leaf-pattern shield the same way.

Fuentes rallied and came back at him, chopping down with his right sword as his left dug inwards in a low thrust. That left blade sliced through the edge of Gilead's shield and cut a wound through the ithilmar mail-shirt above his left hip. The last son of Lothain drove in with his shield and slammed the face into Fuentes's chest, before following through with his sword in a side-thrust that Fuentes barely parried.

They broke, circling, for a second. The hooked shortswords spun in interlocking windmill patterns under Fuentes's deft touch. Then the big Tilean lunged in again. His right short-sword buried itself through Gilead's shield, wedged fast, and slashed Gilead's shield-arm. His left ripped through the mail of Gilead's right shoulder, and bit flesh there too.

Gilead wrenched his shield aside, tearing the wedged blade out of Fuentes's grip. The other sword swept in, but Gilead made it rebound from his blue-steel long-sword, angling it vertically. Then he tore downwards with his blade, and cut Fuentes diagonally across the face and down to the chest.

Blood spurted out and Fuentes stumbled back with a howl. He clamped his hands to his face, screaming and cursing in rage and despair as he realised that Gilead had taken his sur-viving eye. Blind, drenched in blood that pumped out from his savage wound, he slashed and cut frantically at the air around him with his remaining sword.

With a cruel smile on his gaunt elven face that Fithvael knew he would never forget, Gilead side-stepped and placed himself so that Fuentes's next blind lunge carried him onto the elf-blade. Three feet of blue steel jutted from Fuentes's back. Blood gushed out over the gold dragon hilt and over Gilead's hand.

'For Nithrom, you bastard dog!' Gilead spat into the dying man's face in clipped Tilean.

FITHVAEL WITNESSED THE brief, explosive clash from twenty paces away, as he and Bruda battled the scrum of Tileans around them. Bruda yelled out in joy to see Fuentes fall and another, Harg or Vintze, lost in the thick of it, also bellowed.

Meanwhile, Cloden was surrounded by spearmen and halberdiers. He chopped and hacked, urging the greatsword round in circles, breaking hafts and lances, splintering each weapon that jabbed at him. But a pike-tip got through intact, long enough to punch through the Carroburger's left shoulder. Blood gouted and Cloden stumbled to his knees, dragging the pike down with him. He lost his grip on his greatsword and tried with both hands to tear at the lance transfixing him.

Madoc cut his way through to the man, slaughtering the halberdiers who were rushing in to finish the fallen man of Carroburg. Madoc's mouth was wide open in a battle yell that made no sound. The fire of Ulric, the White Wolf, was in his limbs, and his broadsword demolished them. Four Tilean dogs broke and ran in terror. Others, braver, closed in on the silent Wolf guarding the bowed Cloden. There was a loud report, and the first of them fell, his skull shattered. Dolph threw aside his handgun and ran to Madoc's side, mace swinging. Together, they fought off the waves of Tileans, dragging Cloden back towards the horse pens.

Harsh cries came from nearby and another tent frame collapsed. Two battling figures ripped their way out of the flopping canvas, swords clashing and stroking and biting. It was Vintze. He had found Maura the Murderer – or the Murderer had found him – and the pair were now locked in a combat to the death.

MALTANE WAS BURNING. The wooden walls blazed brighter than the intermittent flaring of the storm above. The night was bathed in a hot, flickering flame-light.

Overwhelmed, the defenders had fallen back into the compound, into the ruins of the inner hall, and were making their last stand there against the driving hordes that flooded in through the burning gates.

Just before they had broken from the wall, Gaude had issued commands to those about him who could hear. He sent Brom and three of the remaining Maltaners back into the scarcement with orders to lead any who could still move out through the tunnel into the woods. He knew full well this would leave dozens too sick, hurt, old or young in the scarcement hole, but to save any would be a victory. The rest he would defend to the end of his life.

With him stood Erill, Galvin, two youths called Malkin and Froll, three older farmers named Guilan, Kelfer and Hennum, a drover called Bundsman and an old goatherd that everyone knew as Old Perse. Drunn had wanted to stay, but Gaude had despatched to help Brom evacuate the cellar.

The last ten men used the hulk of the hall against the foe, cutting them down in ones and twos as they pressed in through the open doorways and shattered windows.

Erill kept the main door with Nithrom's silver blade. He had marvelled at the weight and balance of the short sword Fithvael had loaned him, but it was as nothing compared to this longsword. In his hands, it seemed to adjust for his faulty depth of field and inexperience, twisting and writhing like a living thing as it ate into the attackers. Erill knew such blades had individual names. He wished Nithrom had told him the name of this one. He prayed Fithvael or Gilead might know. And he hoped he would live long enough to learn it from them.

Tilean dog-soldiers dropped down into the hall through a rent in the roof, some tumbling, spraying loose tiles with them. They had climbed up to find a way in and brought a section of the damaged roof down with them. Galvin and Bundsman killed the first few with Guilan's help, but more jumped in, deliberately now, and the first to find his bearings lopped Hennum's head from his shoulders with a mighty blow.

Gaude rallied and chopped the Tilean beast in half, bearing down on the next and the next after that. Malkin lost a leg at the knee and fell screaming before another strike of a mercenary's axe silenced him.

More pushed in through a window on the left side, overrunning Old Perse, who fell under their kicking, trampling boots. They did not even bother to finish him. He was left, broken and moaning, under the shattered window frame.

Three Tilean pikemen burst in from the south end, and pinned Froll, twitching like a puppet, to one of the hall's roof posts. Gaude broke to meet them, leaving Bundsman and Galvin to stem the flow from the roof. He saw Guilan lying dead on the soaked boards in a pool of his own blood. He hadn't even seen the man fall.

The whole place was lit by the flickering blaze outside, darting shadows and skirmishing black shapes moving through the ruddy smoke-haze.

Kelfer screamed as a sword took off both his hands. The scream turned to a gurgle as the blade switched back and cut through his neck.

The sword's owner threw Kelfer aside. Gaude recognised him in an instant. It was Hroncic, the other trusted lieutenant of Maura the Murderer. Hroncic was a huge, swarthy man from the south of Tilea, with a wispy beard and bad teeth. The wizened ears of past victims dangled on a thong around his olive neck, bumping on his chest-guard as he moved. He carried a long, curved blade from Araby and a crescent-shaped buckler. His ornate leggings were dressed in gold braid tassels.

Gaude turned on him, cursing foully in Bretonnian. Gaude's blade, the sword that had belonged to Le Claux, was an old one, and had been witness to several crusades into the burning south where it had despatched many of the godless who carried just such curved swords. It felt to Gaude as if it smelled an old foe.

Bretonnian crusader's steel rang against Araby blade and sparks flew in the half-light. Hroncic seemed to giggle in delight as he fought back against the other's frenzied attack. Gaude battled him down the length of the hall in a whirling blur of blades.

At the hall door, Bundsman fell to three simultaneous swordstrokes, and Galvin collapsed as a pike-end smacked into his head. Erill realised Galvin was still alive, just dazed, and stood over him, keeping the foe at bay with Nithrom's sword. He lost count of the wounds he had inflicted. The floor of the hall was littered with bodies and awash with blood.

Hroncic parried Gaude's sword and spun around, coming up hard. Gaude stiffened and froze. Hroncic giggled. The entire length of his sabre had stabbed through Gaude's neck and the only thing keeping the brave ex-squire on his feet was the blade on which his body hung.

Gaude's eyes were wide. Cackling, Hroncic tugged the blade out again.

Gaude should have fallen then. His face was white but the rest of him, front and back, was bathed in gore from the dreadful wound. But the Bretonnian had one last ounce of vengeance-inspired energy in him. Dead by any standards, he swung his beloved sword one last time as he fell. The blow almost decapitated Hroncic. It did not. The brute flinched back in shock and the tip of the blade cut open one cheek.

Pawing at his torn face, Hroncic stepped over Gaude's corpse, dark eyes fixed on Erill. He wasn't giggling now. He spat blood copiously and, slurring from the wound in his cheek, ordered his men back.

The Tilean dog-soldiers fell away from Erill. The youth looked round and saw that Bundsman was curled in a corner with a lance through his chest.

He was the last, Erill realised. A one-eyed lad, the very least of the company that had ridden out to save Maltane, facing a bloodied bastard who had just defeated their best.

Smoke welled into the ruined hall. The flames were now eating at the hall itself. The Tileans pounded their hands together and chanted Hroncic's name. The gore-smeared killer stepped forward.

Erill spat and raised the glorious elven blade.

THE DUEL BETWEEN Vintze the thief and Maura the Murderer lasted perhaps ninety seconds, and in that time, hundreds of blows were traded, faster than most eyes could follow.

Vintze, six feet tall and as hard and fast as a whip's cord, had his basket-hilted Reikland straightsword in one hand, and a foot long poignard held blade up in the other, under his buckler guard.

Maura was a monstrous man, nearly seven feet tall, dressed in heavy golden Tilean plate mail of intricate ornament. His head was covered by a silver hound's-skull helmet, topped with a blue and white plume, visor down so that none could see his face. None of Gilead's company ever would. But they could hear the bellowing Tilean oaths that the beast spat as he circled in towards Vintze with his jewelled broadsword clamped in one gauntlet and a cavalryman's axe in the other.

They were a blur, Reiklander and Tilean, swirling and circling and exchanging two, three blows each second. Broadsword and axe rained and jabbed at straightsword and buckler. Sparks flew. Maura's axe dug a chunk out of Vintze's thigh. In return, the thief's poignard punched a hole through Maura's shoulder.

From the speed of their blows, they sounded like mad tinkers working metal in a forge to fend off some curse.

The appearance of Maura himself had driven the Tileans back and allowed the remnants of the company to close. Gilead, Bruda, Harg and Fithvael hacked through the mob to reach the duel, and Dolph and Madoc stood over Cloden, watching in awe.

Thunder rolled above them. None saw the way Maltane's inner fastness blazed on the top of the mound.

Sword against axe, sword against buckler, sword against sword, axe against buckler, poignard to thigh, axe to buckler, sword against sword... shrieking down the length in a fizzle of sparks. Tilean broadsword into Reikland shoulder.

Reikland buckler into grilled Tilean helmet.

Reikland straightsword against Tilean shoulder plate.

Tilean broadsword into Reikland buckler again, and again.

Reikland straightsword clean through Tilean helmet plume.

A fluttering mass of blue and white feather-plume.

Tilean axe into Reikland swordarm.

A great spray of blood.

Reikland straightsword bouncing off the mud from nerveless fingers.

Tilean broadsword glancing off desperate Reikland buckler. The sliding sword blade caught between the blade and bulky tines of the Reikland poignard.

A twist of a Reikland wrist.

Fragments of broken Tilean broadsword shattering in every direction.

Tilean axe-head hard into Reikland chest.

Ninety seconds, barely as many heartbeats.

Vintze fell.

The company, even Gilead hacking through the foe, paused in dismay. Maura boomed a victory call from his hound's-skull helmet.

A second later, a far louder boom shook them all.

Dolph's set charges blew, lighting the sky with a flare brighter and more brilliant than the worst of the lightning. The powder threw a forty-yard chunk of earth into the air and set off a landslide of wet mud that rolled down over the Tilean camp. Dozens of Tileans were buried. Many more were maimed by splinters and flying rocks. An entire gun carriage with a two-ton cannon flew through the air and crushed down onto the Murderer's files as they fled and fell. The horse pens were smashed open and panicked steeds stampeded in all directions. Everyone else was thrown flat.

Eyes swimming, ears dull, they struggled up. The main force of the Tileans in the camp were fleeing, those that were still able. Upwards of forty Murderers lay broken, wailing or dismembered in the torn mud.

Bruda thought she was first back on her feet. When a blade cut across her back and felled her into the mud, she realised she wasn't. Then she passed out.

Madoc saw Bruda fall, and saw Maura standing over her, his golden armour blackened by soot, a massive blade in his hands, about to finish her.

Madoc sprang in, blocking the downward blow. The broadsword shattered.

Calmly, Maura looked around for a fresh weapon and found Cloden's greatsword lying in the mud. Effortlessly, he swung the massive blade of Carroburg. The Murderer smashed Madoc away, reopening his throat wound.

Dolph's mace crashed into the Murderer's side, denting the golden armour. It was like striking a boulder with a twig.

Maura roared and turned about, transfixing Dolph through the torso on the length of the greatsword. He lifted the Ostmarker clean off the ground. Then he shook him off the blade, like a cat suddenly bored of the dead vermin it had been playing with.

Dolph's armoured corpse slammed into Fithvael as he ran forward in horror, and the weight dropped him like a cannonball. Fithvael felt something in his left leg snap as he went down under the heavy, metal-shrouded mass.

Maura turned to meet Harg, who raged at him like an angered bear. Hargen Hardradasson, lord of the faraway fjords and ice lands, was berserk, frothing at the mouth, channelling his battle-madness into each swing of his axe.

He was a terror to behold, but Maura met that terror and smashed open the old face wound almost precisely along the jagged line that had been there for twenty summers. Harg fell, trying to hold his face together, yowling like a wounded wolf in a trap.

Maura hefted Cloden's smoking blade above Harg's bowed head and muttered something in Tilean.

The blow never fell.

Shadowfast, Gilead was there in an eye-blink, his blade, his dead brother's blue-steel blade, ripping into Maura.

Maura reeled and fell back, deep gouges across his ornate chest plate, some of which oozed blood. By the time he managed to throw a swing of his own, Gilead had slashed the Murderer's chest plate clean away with his blade.

The two of them, swords scything, battled across the camp clearing. The whirling greatsword nicked Gilead's precious sword again and again, and ripped away the elf's long shield.

Dragging himself clear of poor, dead Dolph, wincing as the broken bone-ends ground at every move, Fithvael watched them battle. Part of him was proud of Gilead, part of him deathly afraid. He wanted to see this as titans clashing, as was written in the myths, but all he could think of were monsters assailing each other. He saw Maura rip open Gilead's shoulder, saw Gilead thrust his longsword clean through Maura's thigh.

They were both washed with blood. Maura was driving Gilead back into the edges of the woods, where the land fell away sheer to the valley floor. Sword against sword, return, pass, parry, clash, steel of Tor Anrok against Carroburg power.

Then they were lost from view in the brambles and the trees. It was treacherous in the sheer woods. Cliffs of mud, loosened by the storm, poured cascades of dark water down into the clearings below. Plunge pools had formed in the dark crevices of the escarpment.

Neither would break. Maura, a powerhouse, swung the greatsword two-handed with all the deftness its master Cloden had ever shown. Gilead sliced and chopped, parried and stabbed, instinctively recalling every move and pass he had been taught.

By his father; by Fithvael te tuin, master-at-arms; by dead Nithrom, so many years ago.

Maura hit Gilead in the face, ripping open a wound that would leave a scar for the rest of his life. Blinking aside the blood, Gilead threw himself at Maura. The pair lost their footing and went over the edge of a mud cliff, falling through a cascade of rain-flood into a basin below.

They hit the water in a spray, churning round to find each other. Maura was weighed down by his armour and his massive weapon, but still he came up first.

They were chest-deep in the water. Maura hacked at Gilead, but his greatsword's blade struck only the water.

Gilead pushed himself at Maura and the two of them fell again, down the next flash-flood cliff, through another cascade, into another churning pool.

Gilead surfaced first, but Maura had struck below the water. The greatsword stuck into Gilead through the left hip. The water swirling around them went darker still.

Maura surfaced, snorting and hacking inside his hound's-skull helm. He twisted the blade under the water.

Gilead screamed. And in his rage sliced the helmeted head clean off with the blue-steel blade forged in Tor Anrok so long ago, Galeth's blade.

Maura's head bobbed away in the current, washing over on another cascade, still encased and unseen in its helmet.

Gilead, the greatsword still through him, sank to his knees in the bloodstained water, and began to drown.

So, THERE IT IS, just as I promised you. The tale of the Battle of Maltane, in all particulars. A better, more rousing, bloodier tale of heroism you'll never hear at my fireside.

What's that you say? Ah, but there's always one! Why can't you be content? Must I really tie up all the loose ends?

Very well. No, he did not drown. Bruda found him. She was weak from her wounds, but she had seen the battlers slide over the edge. She found Gilead and dragged him out of the pool and blew life back into his lungs with her own mouth.

The greatsword? They never found it. As he sank, Gilead must have pulled it out. It is rusting, even now, in a glade pool west of Maltane, I am sure. Cloden had to travel back to his homeland to get another and that, as I understand, was an adventure in itself.

Well, yes, of course Cloden lived. His shoulder was never quite the same, of course, but he went on to greater things. Had a warrior band of his own, so I am told. Never lost his touch with the greatsword, to the end of his days.

Harg? Well, he had the same scar as before, just fresher. I
have no idea what eventually happened to him, but every
winter I get sent another bearskin and a flask of foul Norse
mead. I like to think he's probably a king again somewhere,
somewhere frozen and uninviting.

And Vintze, it took him a while to mend, and the winters
still make his chest ache. He rode with Cloden, so I heard. I
saw him ten years or so back, in Vinsbrugge. He had a snowy
beard by then, and further scars. We had a drink to the old
times. But he's probably dead now.

Bruda? Like I said, she lived. She spent the winter in
Maltane, healing up, then was gone by spring. I don't know
how many years after that she survived. I always liked her
tremendously, though. Well, yes, I am old, and thank you for
mentioning it! But believe me, I can still recall how handsome a woman is!

Madoc? It took a long time with him. Bad wound. But you
know he survived. The legends of the Silent Wolf are commonplace in this neck of the woods and beyond. Yes, that is
him. The very one.

What more do you want? Oh yes, Brom and Drunn led the
evacuees down the tunnel and out into the woods. Fifty villagers they saved that way. Drunn stayed on as headman, as
you know, elected year after year after year for his bravery. Yes,
I miss him too.

Master Brom, he was never the same after his twin was
gone. He and Gilead had so much alike in that, but I don't
think they ever spoke about it. Elves, heh? Too close. Brom...
heh... I sometimes think about him and wonder where he
ended up. Alone, truly alone, wherever it was.

Ah, what's that? Be patient. I was saving that part. Pour me
another cup. Good.

Of course, the Tileans broke when Maura died. They never
found his head, did I mention that? And actually, they broke
long before that. Right after Dolph's explosion. The heart was
out of them by then. They came at Maltane with a warhost
maybe four hundred strong and left fully three-quarters on
the fields and the slopes around the town. That's quite a
thing, don't you think?

I'm getting tired and my cup is half-empty. What more do
you want?

Oh, of course, of course.

When the Tileans had fled, the company went up to the inner mound, which was all ablaze by then. But they got the wounded and the infirm out of the scarcement all the same. Add those to the evacuees, and you'll see that Nithrom's band saved seventy-seven folk from Maltane. Not that there was a lot of Maltane left by then. It took us years to rebuild.

Oh, hush now. Very well, since you persist, they found young Erill in the courtyard, where Galvin had carried… him. Only the two of them had survived. No one knows what happened exactly, but they found the beast Hroncic's head in the temple, lying on Sigmar's altar.

The survivors burned Le Claux, Caerdrath, Nithrom, Gaude and Dolph on a great pyre, with full honours and much mourning. It was only fit.

The last I saw of the two elves was when they rode away one misty spring morning. They had wintered here to heal and left in the spring, just after Bruda. Both of them still limped when they walked.

No, I don't know where they were going. I don't think they knew either. I doubt Master Fithvael was going to stay with Gilead much longer. His companion had become so surly and withdrawn that winter.

Who am I to say? Maybe they're still travelling this sorry world together even now.

I liked Fithvael. He had a soul. His lord, well, I'm not too sure. I would doubt he'll ever find what he's looking for, but I know that losing the scent here, with Caerdrath's death, was one of the worst things that ever happened to him. The dark cloud that lived over him glowered over all of us that winter, and though I feel churlish to say it, it was almost a relief when that elven lord departed.

I think of them from time to time. I do wonder whatever happened to them. I suppose they just faded away and were forgotten. Like all myths, and, Sigmar help me, the land is full of them!

Me? I've been content to stay here in Maltane all these seasons, until now I am old and bent. Yes, my eye still hurts me, usually in winter when the wind bites and cuts into this old patch.

It often pleases me that I was part of a myth, given that this land is so full of them. I miss my father, though... if father he truly was to me. Certainly, I believe that to be so. And I never did learn what this glorious sword of his is called.

ABOUT THE AUTHORS

Dan Abnett lives and works in Maidstone, Kent, in England. Best known for his comic work, he has written everything from Rupert the Bear to Batman in the last ten years, and is currently scripting Legion of Superheroes and Superman for DC Comics, and Sinister Dexter and Durham Red for 2000 AD. His work for the Black Library includes the popular strips Darkblade and Titan, and a trio of novels featuring the celebrated Imperial Guard unit known as Gaunt's Ghosts. There is, it seems, no stopping him.

Nik Vincent was born one Christmas Eve in a tiny seaside village. Some years later, she adjourned to Scotland to live beside a loch and study English. She has written professionally for three years, mostly for pre-school children and would probably have continued to do so had she not attended GW's infamous annual Games Day, which heralded the end of cuddly characters and the beginning of some serious shooty death-kill. Nik lives and writes in a haunted garret in Kent.

Coming soon from Dan Abnett
and the Black Library...

XENOS

Book 1 of the Eisenhorn trilogy

TWO DAYS LATER, aboard the *Essene* at anchor beyond the treacherous reaches of system KCX-1288, we made our rendezvous with the imperial taskforce outbound from Gudrun.

We'd made good our escape from the world of the plateau in less than two hours. As Aemos had predicted, the place seemed to unravel around us, as if that apparently timeless realm of the sea, the beach and the uplands had been nothing but an ingenious construct, a space engineered by the saruthi to accommodate the meeting with their human 'guests'. As we rode the gun-cutter back to the waiting *Essene*, the hazy radiance had begun to dim and atmospheric pressure dropped. We were beset by turbulence, and natural gravity began to reassert its influence. The impossible cavity had begun to decompose. By the time that Maxilla was running the *Essene* down the dark corridor of arches as fast as he dared, the inner space where we had confronted the aliens was nothing but a dark maelstrom of ammonia and arsenical vapours. Our chronometers and horologiums had begun to run properly again.

We left the fractured planet behind, braving flares and gravity storms as we made a dash for the outer system. Forty minutes after leaving that place, rear-aligned sensors could find no trace of the 'wound', as if it had collapsed, or had never been there to begin with.

How the saruthi came and went I had no idea, and Aemos was little help. We had seen no sign of other vessels or other points of egress from the planet's crust.

'Do they live within the planet?' I asked Aemos as we stood at an observation platform, looking back at the retreating star through glare-dimmed ports.

'I fancy not. Their technologies are beyond my ken, but I feel that they might have arrived on the plateau through those archways from another world, into a place they had built for the meeting.'

Such a concept defied my imaginings. Aemos was suggesting interstellar teleportation.

Outside the system, there had been little trace of the heretical fleet. As far as Maxilla was able to tell from drive and warp wakes, the three ships, no doubt bearing Locke and Dazzo, had rejoined their attentive flotilla and moved away almost at once into the immaterium.

Other warp indicators informed us that the taskforce was approaching, no more than two days away. We dropped grav-anchor, saw to our wounds, and waited.

THIRTY WEEKS BEFORE, as we departed Damask, I had sent my request for assistance to Gudrun via Lowink astropathically. I had outlined as much of the situation as possible, providing what detail and conjecture I could, and had hoped the Lord Militant would send a military expedition to support me. I did not demand, as the likes of Commodus Voke were wont to do. I was sure the urgency and importance of my communiqué would speak for itself.

ELEVEN SHIPS LOOMED out of the empyrean before us in battle formation: six Imperial frigates running out in the vanguard, fighter wings riding out ahead of them in formation. Behind this spearhead of warships came the battleships *Vulpecula* and *Saint Scythus*, each three times the size of the frigates, each a bristling ogre of a vessel. To the rear was an ominous trio of cruisers, black ships of the imperial Inquisition. This was no military expedition. This was an inquisitorial taskforce.

We exchanged hails, identified ourselves and were escorted into the fleet pack by an honour guard of thunderhawks. Shuttles transferred our wounded, including the still unconscious Fischig and the prisoner Malahite, to medical facilities aboard the *Saint Scythus*. An hour later, at the request of Admiral Spatian, I also crossed by shuttle to the battleship. They were awaiting my report.

MY LEFT ARM bound and tightly slung in a surgical brace, I wore a suit of black and my button-sleeved leather coat, my rosette pinned at my throat. Aemos, in sober green robes, accompanied me.

In the echoing vault of the *Saint Scythus*'s docking bay, Procurator Olm Madorthene and a detail of navy stormtroopers waited to greet us. Madorthene wore the impressive white dress uniform in which I had first seen him, and the men's blue armour was rich with gold braid and ceremonial decoration.

Madorthene greeted me with a salute and we strode as a group towards the elevators that would carry us up into the command levels of the ship.

'How goes the uprising?' I asked.

'Well enough, inquisitor. We understand the Lord Militant has declared the Helican schism over and quashed, though pacification wars are still raging across Thracian.'

'Losses?'

'Considerable. Mainly to the population and materials of the world affected, though some fleet and guard units have taken a beating. Lord Glaw's treason has cost the Imperium dear.'

'Lord Glaw's treason has cost him his life. His body rots on a nameless world in the system behind us.'

He nodded. 'Your master will be pleased.'

'My master?'

LORD INQUISITOR PHLEBAS Alessandro Rorken sat in a marble throne at the far end of a chapel-like audience hall two decks beneath the main bridge of the *Saint Scythus*. I had met him twice before, and felt no more confident now for those experiences. He wore simple robes of crimson over black clothing and gloves, and no other decoration except for a gold signet ring of office on one knuckle. The austere simplicity of his garb seemed to accentuate his authority. His noble skull was shaved except for a forked goatee. His eyes, deep set and wise, glittered with intelligence.

Around him was his entourage. Ten inquisitorial novices of interrogator rank or below, upholding banners, sacred flamer weapons, caskets of scrolls and slates, gleaming tools of torture on red satin cushions, or open hymnals. Flanking them, four bodyguards in red cloaks with double-handed broadswords held stiffly upright before their faces. Their armour was ornate, and the full visors had been fashioned and painted into the likenesses of four apostolic saints: Olios, Jerido, Manezzer and Kadmon. The masks were flat-eyed and expressionless and almost naive, lifted exactly from representations on illuminated manuscripts of old. A huddle of dark-robed savants waited nearby, and a dozen cherub servitors in the form of podgy three-year-olds with golden locks and the spiteful faces of gargoyles circled around, scolding and mocking, on grav-assisted golden wings.

'Approach, Eisenhorn,' Lord Rorken said, his soft voice carrying down the chamber effortlessly. 'Approach all.'

At his words, other figures emerged from anterooms along the sides of the hall, and took their seats to either hand. One was Admiral Spatian, an ancient, skeletal giant in white dress uniform, attended by several of his senior staff. The others were inquisitors. Titus Endor, in his maroon coat, alone save for a hunched female savant. He cast me an encouraging nod as I passed by. Commodus Voke, wizened and shuffling, helped onto his seat by a tall man in black. The man's head was bald and hairless apart from a few sickly clumps. His scalp, neck and face were livid with scar-tissue from injuries and surgery. It was Heldane. His encounter with the carnodon had not improved his looks. Like Endor, Voke nodded to me, but there was no friendship in it.

Next to him, Inquisitor Schongard, stocky and squat, the black metal mask obscuring everything but his raddled eyes. He took his seat and was flanked by two lean, supple females, members of some death-cult by the look of them, both nearly naked save for extensive body art, barbed hoods and harnesses strung with blades.

Opposite Schongard sat Konrad Molitor, an ultra-radical member of the ordos I had little love or respect for. Molitor was a fit, athletic man dressed head to toe in a tight weave-armour bodyglove of yellow and black check with a polished silver cuirass strapped around his torso. His black hair was close-trimmed and tonsured, and he affected the air of a warrior monk from the First Crusade. Behind him stood three robed and hooded acolytes, one carrying Molitor's ornate power-sword, another a silver chalice and paten, and the third a reliquary box and a smoking censer. Molitor's pupils were bright yellow and his gaze never wavered from me.

Last to take his seat, at Lord Rorken's right hand, was a giant in black power armour, a Space Marine of the Deathwatch chapter, the dedicated unit of the Ordo Xenos. The Deathwatch was one of the Chambers Militant, Marine chapters founded exclusively for the Inquisition, obscure and secret even by the standards of the blessed Adeptus Astartes. At my approach, the warrior removed his helmet and set it on his armoured knee, revealing a slab-jawed, pale face and cropped grey hair. His thin mouth was curled in a frown.

Servitors brought a seat for me, and I took my place facing the Lord Inquisitor. Aemos stood at my side, silent for once.

'We have read your preliminary report, Brother Eisenhorn. Quite a tale it is. Of great *moment*.' Lord Rorken savoured the last word. 'You pursued Glaw's heretic fleet to this Emperor-for-saken outer world, certain that they planned to trade with a xenos breed. That trade, you stated, was for an item whose very nature would threaten the safety and sanctity of our society.'

'I reported correctly, lord.'

'We have known you always to be earnest and truthful, brother. We did not doubt your words. After all, are we not here in... unusual force?'

He gestured around and there was some laughter, most of it forced, most of it from Voke and Molitor.

'And what was this item?'

'The aliens possessed a single copy of a profane and forbidden work we know as the Necroteuch.'

The reaction was immediate. Voices rose all around, in surprise, alarm or disbelief. I heard Voke, Molitor and Schongard all call-ing out questions and scorn. The assembled retainers, novices and acolytes around us whispered or gabbled furiously. The cherubs wailed and fluttered into hiding behind Lord Rorken's throne. Rorken himself studied me dubiously. I saw that even the grim Space Marine looked questioningly at the Lord Inquisitor.

Lord Rorken raised his hand and the hubbub died away.

'Is that confirmed, Brother Eisenhorn?'

'Lord, it is. I saw it with my own eyes and felt its evil. It was the Necroteuch. As far as I have learned, the xenos breed – known as the saruthi – came upon a lost copy thousands of years ago, and through recently established lines of communication with the Glaw cabal, agreed to exchange it for certain artefacts of their own culture.'

'Preposterous!' spat Commodus Voke. 'The Necroteuch is a myth, and a wretched one at that! These twisted alien filth have fabricated this as a lure for the gullible heretics!'

I looked over at Voke and repeated, 'I saw it with my own eyes and felt its evil. It was the Necroteuch.'

Admiral Spatian looked up at Lord Rorken. 'This thing, this book – is it so valuable that these heretics would throw the entire sub-sector into schism to cover their attempts to retrieve it?'

'It is priceless!' cut in Molitor from across the chamber. 'Beyond worth! If the legends of it are even fractionally true, it contains lore surpassing our understanding! They would not think twice of burning worlds to get it, or of sacrificing their entire resources to acquire the power it would bring them.'

'It has always been plain,' Endor said softly, 'that the stakes in this matter have been astonishingly high. Though I am shocked by Brother Gregor's news, I am not surprised. Only an icon as potent as the Necroteuch could have set this bloodshed in motion.'

'But the Necroteuch! Such a thing!' hissed Schongard.

'Were they successful, Inquisitor Eisenhorn?' the Space Marine asked suddenly, staring directly at me.

'No, brother-captain, they were not. The effort was desperate and close run, but my force was able to spoil their contact with the xenos saruthi. The aliens were driven off, and most of the heretics' advance guard, including Lord Glaw and a blasphemous child of the Emperor allied to his cause, were slain.'

'I read of this Mandragore in your report,' said the Marine. 'His presence was fundamental in the decision for my unit to accompany this force.'

'The Emperor's Children, Terra damn their souls, clearly wanted the book for themselves. They had sent Mandragore to assist Glaw in its recovery. That beings such as they took it seriously confirms the truth of my story, I believe.'

The noble Marine nodded. 'And Mandragore is dead, you say?'

'I killed him myself.'

The Deathwatch warrior sat back slightly, his brows rising gently in surprise.

'Some heretics escaped your purge?' Schongard asked.

'Two key conspirators, brother. The trader Gorgone Locke, who I believe was instrumental in forging the original contact between the saruthi and Glaw's cabal. And an ecclesiarch named Dazzo, who I would see as the spiritual force behind their enterprise. They fled from the fight, rejoined the waiting elements of their fleet, and left this system.'

'Destination?' asked Spatian.

'It is still being plotted, admiral.'

'And how many ships? That bastard traitor Estrum ran with fifteen.'

'He lost at least two frigates in that star system. A non-standard merchant ship that I believe belongs to Locke is with them.'

'Have they taken to their heels and run defeated, or have they some further agenda?' Lord Rorken asked.

'I have further research to make before I can answer that, lord.'

Spatian stood and looked towards the Lord Inquisitor. 'Even if they're running, we can't permit them to escape. They must be hounded down and annihilated. Permission to retask the battle-pack and prepare to pursue.'

'Permission granted, admiral.'

Then Molitor spoke up. 'No one has asked the most important question of our *heroic* Brother Eisenhorn,' he said, stressing the word 'heroic' in a way that did not flatter. 'What happened to the Necroteuch?'

I turned to face him. 'I did what any of us would have done, Brother Molitor. *I burned it.*'

UPROAR FOLLOWED. Molitor was on his feet, accusing me of nothing short of heresy at the top of his reedy voice. Schongard raised his own serpentine tones in support of the accusations, while Endor and Voke shouted them down. The retinues howled and bickered across the floor. Both the Deathwatch captain and I remained seated and silent.

Lord Rorken rose. 'Enough!' He turned to the glowering Molitor. 'State your objection, Brother Molitor, quickly and simply.'

Molitor nodded, and licked his lips, his yellow eyes darting around the room. 'Eisenhorn must suffer our sternest censure for this act of vandalism! The Necroteuch may be a foul and proscribed work, but we are the Inquisition, lord. By what right did he simply destroy it? Such a thing should have been sequestered and brought before our most learned savants for study! To obliterate it out of hand robs us of knowledge, of wisdom, of secrets unimaginable! The contents of the Necroteuch might have given us insight into the archenemy of mankind, incalculable insight! How might it have strengthened us and armed us for the ceaseless fight? Eisenhorn has disgraced the very heart of our sacred Inquisition!'

'Brother Schongard?'

'My lord, I agree. It was a desperate and rash action by Eisenhorn. Carefully handled, the Necroteuch would have provided us with all measure of advantageous knowledge. Its arcane secrets would have been weapons against the foe. I may applaud his rigorous efforts in thwarting Glaw and his conspirators, but this erasure of occult lore earns only my opprobrium.'

'Brother Voke? What s–' Lord Rorken began, but I cut him off.

'Is this a court, my lord? Am I on trial?'

'No, brother, you are not. But the magnitude of your actions must be analysed and considered. Brother Voke?'

Voke rose. 'Eisenhorn was right. The Necroteuch was an abomination. It would have been heresy to permit its continued existence!'

'Brother Endor?'

Titus did not rise. He turned in his seat and looked down the hall at Konrad Molitor. 'Gregor Eisenhorn has my full support. From your moaning, Molitor, I wonder what kind of man I am listening to. A radical, certainly. An inquisitor? I have my doubts.'

Molitor leapt up again, raging. 'You knave! You whoreson bastard knave! How dare you?'

'Very easily,' replied Endor, leaning back and folding his arms. 'And you, Schongard, you are no better. Shame on you!

What secrets did you both think we could learn, except perhaps how to pollute our minds and boil away our sanity? The Necroteuch has been forbidden since before our foundation. We need not know what's in it to accept that prohibition! All we need is the precious knowledge that it should be destroyed, unread, on sight. Tell me, do you need to actually contract Uhlren's Pox yourself to know that it is fatal?'

Lord Rorken smiled at this. He glanced at the Space Marine. 'Brother-Captain Cynewolf?'

The captain made a modest shrug. 'I command kill teams charged with the extermination of aliens, mutants and heretics, lord. The ethics of scholarship and book-learning I leave to the savants. For whatever it's worth, though, I would have burned it without a second thought.'

There was a long silence. Sometimes I was almost glad no one could tell when I was smiling.

Lord Rorken sat back. 'The objections of my brothers are noted. I myself commend Eisenhorn. Given the extremity of his situation, he made the best decision.'

'Thank you, Lord Inquisitor.'

'Let us retire now and consider this matter. I want to hear proposals for our next course of action in four hours.'

'WHAT NOW?' TITUS Endor asked as we sat in his private suite aboard the *Saint Scythus*. A female servitor brought us glasses of vintage amasec, matured in nalwood casks.

'The remnants must be purged,' I said. 'Dazzo and the rest of the heretic fleet. They may have been cheated of their prize, and they may be running now. Perhaps they'll run for years. But they have the resources of a battlegroup at their disposal, and the will to use it. I will recommend we hunt them down and finish this sorry matter once and for all.'

Aemos entered the chamber, made a respectful nod to Endor, and handed me a data-slate.

'The admiral's astronavigators have finished plotting the course of the heretic fleet. It matches the estimations Maxilla has just sent me.'

I scanned the data. 'Do you have a chart, Titus?'

He nodded and engaged the functions of a glass-topped cogitator unit. The surface glowed, and he entered the reference codes from the slate.

'So... they're not running back into imperial space. No surprise. Nor out to the lawless distances of the Halo Stars.'

'Their course takes them here: 56-Izar. Ten weeks away.'

'In saruthi territory.'

'In the heart of saruthi territory.'

LORD INQUISITOR RORKEN nodded gravely. 'As you say, brother, this business may be less finished than we thought.'

'They cannot hope to count the saruthi as allies, or believe they would give them safe haven. The entente between Glaw's forces and the xenos breed was fragile and tenuous to say the least, and what peace existed between them was ruined by the violence. Dazzo must have some other reason to head there.'

Lord Rorken paced the floor of his state chamber, brooding, toying with the signet ring of office on his gloved finger. His flock of cherubs roosted uneasily along the backs of armchairs and couches around the room. Twitching their gargoyle heads from one side to another, they watched me keenly as I stood waiting for a reply. 'My imagination runs wild, Eisenhorn,' he said at last.

'I intend to question the archaeoxenologist, Malahite, directly. I am sure he can furnish us with additional intelligence. Just as I am sure he lacks the capacity to resist displayed by his aristo master Urisal.'

Rorken stopped pacing and clapped his gloved hands together with a decisive smack. Startled, the cherubs flew up into the air and began mobbing around the high ceiling. 'Course will be laid for 56-Izar at once,' said Lord Rorken, ignoring their lisping squawk. 'Bring me your findings without delay.'

NAVAL SECURITY HAD imprisoned Girolamo Malahite in the secure wing of the battleship's medicae facility. The injury I had given him had been treated, but no effort had been made to equip him with a prosthetic limb. I was looking forward to opening his secrets.

I passed through the coldly lit infirmary, and checked on Fischig. He was still unconscious, though a physician told me his condition was stable. The chastener lay on a plastic-tented cot, wired into wheezing life-supporting pumps and gurgling circulators, his damaged form masked by dressings, anointing charms and metal bone-clamps.

From the infirmary, I passed down an unheated main companionway, showed my identification to the duty guards, and entered the forbidding secure wing. I was at a second checkpoint, at the entrance to the gloomy cell block itself, when I heard screaming ringing from a cell beyond.

I pushed past the guards and, with them at my heels, reached the greasy iron shutters of the cell.

'Open it!' I barked, and one of the guards fumbled with his ring of electronic keys. 'Quickly, man!'

The cell shutter whirred open and locked into its open setting. Konrad Molitor and his three hooded acolytes turned to face me, outraged at the interruption. Their surgically gloved hands were wet with pink froth.

Behind them, Girolamo Malahite lay whimpering on a horizontal metal cage strung on chains from the ceiling. He was naked, and almost every centimetre of skin had been peeled from his flesh.

'FETCH SURGEONS AND physicians. And summon Lord Rorken. Now!' I told the cell guards. 'Would you care to explain what you are doing here?' I said to Molitor.

He would, I think, have preferred not to answer me, and his trio of retainers looked set to grapple with me and hurl me from the cell.

But the muzzle of my autopistol was pressed flat against Konrad Molitor's perspiring brow and none of them dared move.

'I am conducting an interview with the prisoner...' he began. 'Malahite is my prisoner.'

'He is in the custody of the Inquisition, Brother Eisenhorn–'

'He is *my prisoner*, Molitor! Inquisitorial protocol permits me the right to question him first!'

Molitor tried to back away, but I kept the pressure of the gun firm against his cranium. There was no mistaking the fury in his eyes at this treatment, but he contained it, realising provocation was the last thing I needed.

'I, I was concerned for your health, brother,' he began, trying to mollify, 'the injuries you have suffered, your fatigue. Malahite had to be interrogated with all speed, and thought I would ease your burden by commencing the–'

'Commencing? You've all but *killed* him! I don't believe your excuse for a moment, Molitor. If you'd truly intended to help me, you would have asked permission. You wanted his secrets for yourself.'

'A damn lie!' he spat.

I cocked the pistol with my thumb. In the confines of the iron cell, the click was loud and threatening. 'Indeed? Then share what you have learned so far.'

He hesitated. 'He proved resilient. We have learned little from him.'

Boots clattered down the cell bay outside and the guards returned with two green-robed Fleet apothecary-surgeons and a quartet of medical orderlies.

'Throne of Terra!' one of the surgeons cried, seeing the ruined man on the rack.

'Do what you can, doctor. Stabilise him.'

The physicians hurried to work, calling for tools, apparatus and cold dressings. Malahite whimpered again.

'Threatening an Imperial inquisitor with deadly force is a capital crime,' said one of the hooded acolytes, edging forward.

'Lord Rorken will be displeased,' said another.

'Put away your weapon and our master will co-operate,' the third added.

'Tell your sycophants to be silent,' I told Molitor.

'Please, Inquisitor Eisenhorn,' the third acolyte spoke again, his soft voice issuing from the shadows of his cowl. 'This is an unfortunate mistake. We will make reparations. Put away your weapon.'

The voice was strangely confident, and in speaking for Molitor, displayed surprising authority. But no more than Aemos or Midas would have done for me should the situation have been reversed.

'Take your assistants and get out, Molitor. We will continue this once I have spoken with Lord Rorken.'

The four of them left swiftly, and I holstered my weapon.

The chief physician came over to me, shaking his head. 'This man is dead, sir.'

AT LORD RORKEN'S request, the warship's senior ecclesiarch provided a great chapel amidships for our use. I think the shipboard curia was impressed by the Lord Inquisitor's fury.

We had little time to repair the damage done by the incident, even though the medicae had placed Malahite's lamentable corpse in a stasis field.

Lord Rorken wanted to conduct the matter himself, but realised he was duty bound to offer me the opportunity first. To have denied me would have compounded Molitor's insult, even if Rorken was Lord Inquisitor.

I told Rorken I welcomed the task, adding that my working knowledge of the entire case made me the best candidate.

WE ASSEMBLED IN the chapel. It was a long hall of fluted columns and mosaic flooring. Stained glass windows depicting the triumphs of the Emperor were backlit by the empyrean vortex outside the ship. The chamber rumbled with the through-deck vibration of the *Saint Scythus*'s churning drive.

The facing ranks of pews and the raised stalls to either side were filling with Inquisitorial staff and ecclesiarchs. All my 'brothers' were in attendance, even Molitor, who I knew would not be able to stay away.

I walked with Lowink down the length of the nave to the raised plinth where Malahite lay in stasis. Astropaths, nearly thirty of them, drawn from the ship's complement and the inquisitorial delegation, had assembled behind it. Hooded, misshapen, some borne along on wheeled mechanical frames or carried on litters by dour servitors, they hissed and murmured among themselves. Lowink went to brief them. He seemed to relish this moment of superiority over astropaths who normally outranked him. Lowink had not the power to manage this rite alone; his resources were enough for only the simplest psychometric audits. But his knowledge of my abilities and practises made him vital in orchestrating their efforts.

I looked at Malahite, flayed and pathetic in the shimmering envelope of stasis. Grotesquely, he reminded me of the God Emperor himself, resting for eternity in the great stasis field of the golden throne, preserved until the end of time from the death Horus had tried to bestow upon him.

Lowink nodded to me. The astropathic choir was ready.

I looked around and found Endor's face in the congregation. He had placed himself near Molitor and had promised to watch the bastard closely for me. Schongard sat near the back, disassociating himself from his fellow radical's transgression.

I saw Brother-Captain Cynewolf and two of his awe-inspiring fellow Space Marines take their place behind the altar screen. All of them were in full armour and carried drawn bolters. They weren't here for the show. They were here as a safeguard.

'Proceed, brother,' Lord Rorken said from his raised seat.

The choir began to nurse the folds of the warp apart with their swelling adoration. Psychic cold swept through the vault, and some in the congregation moaned, either in fear or with involuntary empathic vibration.

Commodus Voke, helped from his seat by the baleful Heldane, shuffled forward to join me. As a concession to Lord Rorken for allowing me this honour, I had agreed that the veteran inquisitor could partake of the auto-seance at my side. The risk was great, after all. Two minds were better than one, and in truth, it would be good to have the old reptile's mental power at close hand.

'Lower the stasis field,' I said. The moaning of the astropaths grew louder. As the translucent field died away, Voke and I reached out ungloved hands and touched the oozing, skinless face.

THE VEIL OF the warp drew back. I looked as if down a pillar of smoke, ghost white, which rushed up around me. In my ears, the harrowing screams of infinity and the billion billion souls castaway therein...

Thought begets heresy. Heresy begets retribution. XENOS, the first book of the Eisnehorn trilogy coming soon from Dan Abnett and the Black Library.

More Warhammer mayhem from the Black Library

HAMMERS OF ULRIC

A Warhammer novel by Dan Abnett, Nik Vincent & James Wallis

ARIC RODE FORWARD across the corpse-strewn ground and helped Gruber to his feet. The older warrior was speckled with blood, but alive.

'See to von Glick and watch the standard. Give me your horse,' Gruber said to Aric.

Aric dismounted and returned to the banner of Vess as Gruber galloped back into the brutal fray.

Von Glick lay next to the standard, which was still stuck upright in the bloody earth. The lifeless bodies of almost a dozen beastmen lay around him.

'L-let me see…' von Glick breathed. Aric knelt beside him and raised his head. 'So, Anspach's bold plan worked…' breathed the veteran warrior. 'He's pleased… I'll wager.'

Aric started to laugh, then stopped. The old man was dead.

IN THE SAVAGE world of Warhammer, dark powers gather around the ancient mountain-top city of Middenheim, the City of the White Wolf. Only the noble Templar Knights of Ulric and a few unlikely allies stand to defend her against the insidious servants of Death.

More Dan Abnett from the Black Library

FIRST & ONLY
A Gaunt's Ghosts novel
by Dan Abnett

'THE TANITH ARE strong fighters, general, so I have heard.' The scar tissue of his cheek pinched and twitched slightly, as it often did when he was tense. 'Gaunt is said to be a resourceful leader.'

'You know him?' The general looked up, questioningly.

'I know *of* him, sir. In the main by reputation.'

GAUNT GOT TO his feet, wet with blood and Chaos pus. His Ghosts were moving up the ramp to secure the position. Above them, at the top of the elevator shaft, were over a million Shriven, secure in their bunker batteries. Gaunt's expeditionary force was inside, right at the heart of the enemy stronghold. Commissar Ibram Gaunt smiled.

IT IS THE nightmare future of Warhammer 40,000, and mankind teeters on the brink of extinction. The galaxy-spanning Imperium is riven with dangers, and in the Chaos-infested Sabbat system, Imperial Commissar Gaunt must lead his men through as much in-fighting amongst rival regiments as against the forces of Chaos. FIRST AND ONLY is an epic saga of planetary conquest, grand ambition, treachery and honour.

More Dan Abnett from the Black Library

GHOSTMAKER
A Gaunt's Ghosts novel
by Dan Abnett

THEY WERE A good two hours into the dark, black-trunked forests, tracks churning the filthy ooze and the roar of their engines resonating from the sickly canopy of leaves above, when Colonel Ortiz saw death.

It wore red, and stood in the trees to the right of the track, in plain sight, unmoving, watching his column of Basilisks as they passed along the trackway. It was the lack of movement that chilled Ortiz.

Almost twice a man's height, frighteningly broad, armour the colour of rusty blood, crested by recurve brass antlers. The face was a graven death's head. Daemon. Chaos Warrior. *World Eater!*

IN THE NIGHTMARE *future of Warhammer 40,000, mankind teeters on the brink of extinction. The Imperial Guard are humanity's first line of defence against the remorseless assaults of the enemy. For the men of the Tanith First-and-Only and their fearless commander, Commissar Ibram Gaunt, it is a war in which they must be prepared to lay down, not just their bodies, but their very souls.*

More Dan Abnett from the Black Library

NECROPOLIS
A Gaunt's Ghosts novel
by Dan Abnett

GAUNT WAS SHAKING, and breathing hard. He'd lost his cap somewhere, his jacket was torn and he was splattered with blood. Something flickered behind him and he wheeled, his blade flashing as it made contact. A tall, black figure lurched backwards. It was thin but powerful, and much taller than him, dressed in glossy black armour and a hooded cape. The visage under the hood was feral and non-human, like the snarling skull of a great wolfhound with the skin scraped off. It clutched a sabre-bladed power sword in its gloved hands. The cold blue energies of his own powersword clashed against the sparking, blood red fires of the Darkwatcher's weapon.

ON THE SHATTERED world of Verghast, Gaunt and his Ghosts find themselves embroiled within an ancient and deadly civil war as a mighty hive-city is besieged by an unrelenting foe. When treachery from within brings the city's defences crashing down, rivalry and corruption threaten to bring the Tanith Ghosts to the brink of defeat. Imperial Commissar Ibram Gaunt must find new allies and new Ghosts if he is to save Vervunhive from the deadliest threat of all – the dread legions of Chaos.

More Warhammer mayhem from the Black Library

THE WINE OF DREAMS

A Warhammer novel by Brian Craig

THE SWORD FLEW from Reinmar's hand and he just had time to think, as he was taken off his feet, that when he landed – flat on his back – he would be wide open to attack by a plunging dagger or flashing teeth. As the beastman leapt, Sigurd's arm lashed out in a great horizontal arc, the palm of his hand held flat. As it impacted with the beastman's neck Reinmar heard the snap that broke the creature's spine.

As soon as that, it was over. But it was not a victory. Now there was no possible room for doubt that there were monsters abroad in the hills.

DEEP WITHIN the shadowy foothills of the Grey Mountains, a dark and deadly plot is uncovered by an innocent young merchant. A mysterious stranger leads young Reinmar Weiland to stumble upon the secrets of a sinister underworld hidden beneath the very feet of the unsuspecting Empire – and learn of a legendary elixir, the mysterious and forbidden Wine of Dreams.

INFERNO! is the indispensable guide to the worlds of Warhammer and Warhammer 40,000 and the cornerstone of the Black Library. Every issue is crammed full of action packed stories, comic strips and artwork from a growing network of awesome writers and artists including:

- William King
- Brian Craig
- Gav Thorpe
- Dan Abnett
- Barrington J. Bayley
- Gordon Rennie

and many more

Presented every two months, Inferno! magazine brings the Warhammer worlds to life in ways you never thought possible.

LET BATTLE COMMENCE!

NOW YOU can fight your way through the savage lands of the Empire and beyond with WARHAMMER, Games Workshop's game of fantasy battles. In a world of conflict, mighty armies clash to decide the fate of war–torn realms. In Warhammer, you and your opponents are the fearless commanders of these armies. The fate of your kingdoms rests on your shoulders as you control regiments of miniature soldiers, to do battle with terrifying monsters and fearless heroes.

To find out more about Warhammer, along with Games Workshop's whole range of exciting fantasy and science fiction games and miniatures, just call our specialist Trolls on the following numbers:

IN THE UK: 0115-91 40 000

IN THE US: 1-800-GAME

or look us up online at:

www.games-workshop.com